I0593633

Raphael Ledos de Beaufort, Whitelaw Reid

Memoirs of the Prince de Talleyrand

Vol. I

Raphael Ledos de Beaufort, Whitelaw Reid

Memoirs of the Prince de Talleyrand
Vol. I

ISBN/EAN: 9783337166595

Printed in Europe, USA, Canada, Australia, Japan

Cover: Foto ©Raphael Reischuk / pixelio.de

More available books at **www.hansebooks.com**

l'abbé de perigord./

PRINCE TALLEYRAND AS ABBE, FROM AN ORIGINAL PASTEL, IN THE POSSESSION
OF MONSIEUR MOREAU-CHASLONS, THE WELL-KNOWN AMATEUR.

MEMOIRS

OF THE

PRINCE DE TALLEYRAND

EDITED, WITH A PREFACE AND NOTES, BY

THE DUC DE BROGLIE

Of the French Academy

TRANSLATED BY

RAPHAËL LEDOS DE BEAUFORT, F.R. Hist. S.

WITH AN INTRODUCTION BY

THE HONOURABLE WHITELAW REID

American Minister in Paris

VOLUME I

WITH AN AUTOGRAPH LETTER AND PORTRAITS

GRIFFITH FARRAN OKEDEN AND WELSH
NEWBERY HOUSE, CHARING CROSS ROAD, LONDON
AND SYDNEY
1891

? Rights of Translation and Reproduction are R

PREFACE.

THE Prince de Talleyrand died on the 17th of May 1838.

On the 10th of January 1834, he had made a will relative to the division of his fortune among his heirs, and to the various bequests he left as remembrances to his relatives, friends or servants.

Two years after, on October 1, 1836, he added to his will the following declaration, of a very different nature :—

"This is to be read to my relatives, to my heirs and to my private friends, as a sequel to my will.—In the first place, I declare that I die in the Catholic, Apostolic and Roman Faith.

"I do not wish to speak here of the share I had in the various decisions and measures taken by the Constituent Assembly, or of my first journeys to England or to America.

"This portion of my life will be found in the *Memoirs*, which shall be published some day. But I feel it a duty to furnish my family, and the persons who displayed friendship, or simply kindness towards me, with some explanations concerning the responsibility I had in the events which happened in France after my return from America.

"I had resigned the bishopric of Autun, and my resignation had been accepted by the Pope, by whom I have since been secularized. The instrument of my secularization is annexed to my will. I considered myself free, and my situation required that I should find my way. I did so alone, for I did not wish my future to be linked to any political party, for they none of them tallied with my views. I carefully considered the matter and decided on serving France for her sake alone, in whatever situation she might be placed : some good was to be done in each. Therefore, I do not blame myself for having served all the political parties which ruled France, from the Directory to the government existing at the time of my writing this. After the horrors of the Revolution, all that was calculated to lead, one way or the other, to order and security was useful ; and, at that time, sensible men could wish for nothing more.

"To restore monarchical institutions was a matter of impossibility in the state in which France then was. To do so, intermediate forms of government—several of them—were needed. One could not expect even the shadow of royalty in the Directory ; the spirit of the Convention must predominate there, and so it did, in reality, though in a milder form : but, by reason of this spirit, that government was not to last long. It paved the way for the Consulate, which already contained the principle of royalty, though as yet in disguise. Some good was to be done there ; that form of government possessed a remote, it is true, but real resemblance to monarchy.

"The imperial rule which followed was more like an autocracy than a regular monarchy. This is true, but at the time when Bonaparte put the crown on his head, war with England was raging again ; other wars were imminent ; the spirit of faction was rampant, and the safety of the country might have been jeopardized if its ruler had confined himself to the exercise of the sole prerogatives of a simple king. I therefore served the Emperor Napoleon, as I had done the Consul Bonaparte : I served him with loyalty, so long as I could believe him exclusively devoted to France. But, as soon as I saw him enter on the revolutionary path which led him to ruin, I left the cabinet, and for that he never forgave me.

"In 1814, the Bourbons, with whom, since 1791, I had had no relations, were recalled. They were so, for the only reason that their reign was deemed more favourable than any other to the rest so much needed by France and by Europe. I have related, in my *Memoirs*, the chief part I played in that great event, and the rather bold steps I took in those memorable days. The recall of the princes of the House of Bourbon was not the acknowledgment of pre-existing rights. If they so construed it, it was neither on my advice, nor with my assent ; for here is my opinion on the matter.

"Monarchs are such only by virtue of public instruments which constitute them the heads of civil society. These instruments are, it is true, irrevocable for each monarch and for his posterity so long as the reigning monarch keeps within the limits of his own province ; but if he attempts to go beyond it, he loses all right to a title which his own acts either have belied or would soon belie. Such being my opinion, I have never found it necessary to disclaim it in order to accept the functions which I have discharged under various governments.

"As I now, in my eighty-second year, call to mind the numerous events of my political life, which has itself been long, and weigh them, on the eve of entering into eternity, I find as the result:—

"That of all the governments I have served, there is

not one to which I have not given more than I have
received.

"That I have never abandoned any, till it had, first of all,
abandoned itself.

" That I have never considered the interests of any party, my
own, or those of my friends, before the *true* interests of France,
which besides are never, in my opinion, contrary to the *true*
interests of Europe.

" This judgment, for which I am alone responsible, will, I hope,
be confirmed by all impartial minds ; and should this justice be
refused me. when I am no longer living, the conviction of its
truth will yet serve to brighten my last days....

" My wish—and I consign it here, giving it the same force as
my will—my wish, I say, is that the writings that I leave
behind me, be published only when thirty years, dating from
the day of my death, shall have elapsed, in order that those of
whom I have had to speak, being no longer alive, may, none of
them, have to suffer from what the truth may have compelled
me to say to their disadvantage, for I have never written with
the intention of hurting any one, whoever he might be.   Thus,
even thirty years after my death, my *Memoirs* are only to appear
if those of my heirs to whom I leave them, judge that they can
be published without inconvenience to any one.

" I also enjoin the trustee of my papers to neglect no precaution that may be necessary, or at least calculated to prevent, or
defeat any furtive attempts that may be made against them.

" Further, as in the times in which we live, we are inundated
with spurious memoirs, forged some by starvelings, or covetous
characters, others by cowardly and unprincipled scoundrels,
who, in order to exercise their party spite without risk to them-

selves, dare to brand as far as lies in their power, the memory of the great dead, under whose name they spread the grossest lies and most absurd calumnies,—I expressly charge the trustees of my manuscripts to publicly, peremptorily and without delay, disclaim, as I hereby now disclaim, any writing whatever which may chance to be published under my name before the expiration of the thirty years above specified.

"VALENÇAY, *October* 1, 1836.

"(*Signed*) PRINCE DE TALLEYRAND."

This important paper has, as may be seen, two very different aims in view.

The first is to make a profession of principle, which M. de Talleyrand only submits to the judgment of his conscience and of posterity, and which therefore necessitates no comment.

Then follow prescriptions relative to the keeping and publication of his papers.

It is for these latter only, and for the measures which had to be taken accordingly, that the editors of these *Memoirs* have to account.

These prescriptions were repeated and completed in a codicil joined to the will and instrument of 1836, dated March 17, 1838, and couched in the following terms :—

" I, the undersigned, hereby declare that the Duchesse de Dino, as my universal legatee, has alone the right of collecting all my papers and writings *without exception*, in order to do with them what I have enjoined her, and what she already knows ; and I forbid her to divulge in any way the contents of the papers that I shall leave, save after the expiration of thirty years after my decease; nevertheless, M. de Bacourt, the king's minister at Baden, to whom I give and bequeath a diamond of fifty thousand francs in value, which I beg him to accept as a token of my esteem and friendship for him, will be so good, in default of the Duchesse de Dino, and in that case only that she departs this life before myself, as to take charge of all my unpublished papers that I have left in England."

The Duchesse de Dino, who was soon afterwards called upon to assume the title of Duchesse de Talleyrand and Sagan, died on September 29, 1862, six years before the date fixed by M. de Talleyrand for the publication of his papers by his heirs.

The Duchesse de Talleyrand had none the less taken full and entire possession of all the papers of her uncle, as shown in her will, made September 19, 1862, at Sagan, and which bears, in paragraph 17, the following injunction :—

"The papers of my late uncle, the Prince de Talleyrand, which have been handed over to me in accordance with the instructions contained in his will, are to be found, for the most part, in the keeping of M. Adolphe de Bacourt ; some of them with the necessary instructions relative to them, are to be found amongst the property disposed of in my will. By this present writing, I order that, after my decease, this part of the papers as well be remitted to M. de Bacourt, who will receive them under the same conditions fixed by my late uncle, as I myself received them."

M. de Bacourt, who died April 28, 1865, did not long survive the Duchesse de Talleyrand ; but even during the lifetime of the Duchesse he had, as we have just seen, been associated with her in the keeping of the papers and their classification, with which the illustrious statesman had charged her. He had been instructed by her to collect all the papers that had been left her, those that had been left in England, just as well as those that might yet be found in France.

Left in sole possession of this mass of papers for three years, M. de Bacourt applied himself with indefatigable zeal to the task of revising them and preparing the publication of the *Memoirs*, which formed a principal part of them. With this intention, he had arranged numerous notes, complementary or explanatory, bearing on the most important points in the life of the prince, and on those over which the greatest amount of controversy had raged. Finally, he had neglected no means of enlarging the precious trust confided to him, by the acquisition of a number of unpublished documents emanating either from M. de Talleyrand himself, or addressed to him by various people, or which were likely to throw some fresh interest on his life.

It was assuredly with the design, that this work, to which he had given himself with an almost religious devotion, should be continued after his death in the same spirit in which he had treated it himself, that he thought fit to introduce into his will a number of injunctions, of which the text must be literally reproduced.

"On account of the arrangements made in the two wills that I have just quoted (those namely of the Prince and of the Duchesse de Talleyrand), I find myself compelled to provide for the consequence that might ensue, if I died before accomplishing the duty which has been laid upon me with respect to the papers left by the Prince de Talleyrand, which are all in my possession.

"I thought the best plan was to choose, according to the custom adopted in England, so called *Trustees*, or persons of trust, who in case of my death, would be charged: 1st, To take my place as guardians of the said papers; 2nd, to provide for the time fixed by me for the publication of those of these papers which are destined to be published. I have therefore appointed for this purpose M. Châtelain, ex-notary, living in Paris, No 17, Rue d'Anjou-Saint-Honoré, and M. Paul Andral, a barrister in practice at the imperial courts at Paris, dwelling in that city, No 101, Rue Saint-Lazare, who have both willingly accepted the mission I thus entrust them with. I require and command that these two gentlemen be informed immediately after my death of the place where these papers are deposited, and told that they are there at their disposal; and that means of taking possession of them, together with all necessary measures of security for so doing be afforded them. . . . I impose, as a special injunction, on MM. Châtelain and Andral, that no publication taken from these papers be made, in any case whatever, before the year eighteen hundred and eighty-eight thus adding a term of twenty years to that of thirty fixed by the Prince de Talleyrand."

M. de Bacourt adding, as we have just seen, a fresh prorogation of twenty years to that of the thirty fixed by M. de Talleyrand, made use of a power reserved by the prince himself to his heirs. Those who, in their turn, received the legacy of M. de Bacourt had no right to exempt themselves from this restriction.

Before the expiration of this prorogation, one of them, M. Châtelain, had ceased to live, and had to be replaced by his son ; and when the fixed term had elapsed, his partner, M. Andral, was already attacked by the disease which, in the following year snatched him away from his sorrowing friends.

It was then only at the beginning of the current year that I was informed of the honour that my ever lamented friend had paid me, by handing on to me the accomplishment of the task which the last will and testament of M. de Bacourt had imposed on him, and which his illness hindered him from carrying out. Nothing had prepared me for it, and no communication on his part had led me even to suspect it. I had understood and shared the impatience which the public had long shown for becoming acquainted with a work of high value, and one which was a legitimate object for curiosity. But however great may have been the wish of M. Châtelain and my own in this respect, it was yet necessary to take time, in order to neglect no care demanded by the publication of a work of such importance.

It will have been noticed how careful both the Duchesse de Talleyrand and M. de Bacourt were to state that they were in possession of all the papers of the prince *without exception*, and that nothing could either have been taken from or escaped them. The fear of seeing, throughout the long years of silence that had been imposed upon them, the name of M. de Talleyrand at the head of fictitious memoirs, and apocryphal documents which would have misrepresented him (as but too often happens in the case of celebrated men), had evidently deeply affected them. It is against all abuse and forgery of this kind that they firmly protested beforehand, remaining faithful in this to the thought that had dictated to M. de Talleyrand himself

the injunction he gave his heirs in the instrument of 1836, to
preserve his memory from all *stealthy* publication.

This precaution, very natural in itself, was moreover
especially justified by the knowledge of a very serious fact,
and one of which the consequences had even before the death
of M. de Talleyrand caused an anxiety to himself and his family
that may easily be understood.

A secretary who had enjoyed his confidence throughout the
years in which, either as minister or ambassador, he had been
charged with the gravest interests of the State, had been dismissed
after twenty years of this intimate service for sufficiently serious
reasons ; and although the precaution of demanding from him to
deliver up any pieces that might be in his hands was by no
means neglected, it was not long before it was found that not
only had this restitution been far from complete, but that the
secretary thus dismissed, boasted of having kept back more
than one important document, which he threatened to make
use of, without the permission of his old patron, and with
the express purpose of doing him harm.

What made the conduct of this faithless agent as dangerous
as reprehensible was, that during these years of familiar intercourse with M. de Talleyrand, he had learnt to counterfeit his
handwriting, in such a manner as to deceive those who ought to
be best acquainted with it, and it was soon found that he had
turned this paltry talent to advantage by circulating as having
emanated from M. de Talleyrand, writings, forged or falsified, of
such a character as to cause unpleasantness in his relations
with his family and friends, and to accredit the most infamous
accusations against him.

Chance allowed M. de Bacourt to get genuine and undeniable

proofs of this fraud ; these he put into a special drawer amongst his papers where they are still. With respect to the original letters of M. de Talleyrand, he has produced facsimiles, found among the papers of the copyist, so closely resembling the originals that they could not be distinguished from them, were it not that certain sentences, manifestly introduced with evil intent, betray the imposture.

It is thus not difficult to conceive the anxiety which the executors of the will of M. de Talleyrand must have experienced when, three days after his death, May 20, 1838, the English paper, the *Times*, published the following :—

"With regard to the political *Memoirs* of M. de Talleyrand, it is well known that they were only to see the light thirty years after his death, but his secretary, M. Perrey, being possessed of a large portion of the manuscript, it is believed that the intentions of the deceased will not be realised, except at the cost of a great pecuniary sacrifice. Amongst the papers that M. Perrey is known to possess, are satirical portraits of more than a hundred of our contemporaries."

Let us add that the *Times* named as among these con-temporaries all the personal friends of M. de Talleyrand and his family.

It is true that eight days later, on May 28, M. Perrey himself (the *Times* being the paper that had mentioned his name in the matter) in a letter addressed to it, denied the allegation, and said that he was ready to bring an action before the courts against " whomsoever should venture to use his name in order to give some appearance of authenticity to these so-called writings of M. de Talleyrand." But what weight did this disclaimer carry, a disclaimer which could not be dispensed with, without allowing the shadow of criminal dishonesty to rest upon one's self, and what foundation was there for the allegation of the *Times* ? Had M. Perrey attempted this process of reproduction, amplifying and altering, at which he was known to be an adept, on some stolen fragments of the *Memoirs*, or on some notes prepared for their publication ? If he had attempted anything of this kind, what guarantee was there that he had destroyed all trace of it, and was there no risk of its being introduced to the public through some intermediary, to whom he might have given it gratis or for a money consideration ?

No precaution whatever was thought superfluous by the Duchesse de Talleyrand and M. de Bacourt ; and, in order to render all challenge or confusion impossible, M. de Bacourt undertook to transcribe with his own hand the text of the *Memoirs*, as he had received it from M. de Talleyrand, with the complementary notes and documents.

This copy is mentioned in the inventory of the papers of M. de Bacourt, subjoined to his will in the following terms :—

"Four volumes, bound in leather, which form the only complete and authentic copy of Prince Talleyrand's *Memoirs*, done by M. de Bacourt from the original manuscripts, dictated documents, and copies whose purpose M. de Talleyrand had indicated to him."

Furthermore the first of these four volumes bears on its last page the following declaration :—

" I, the undersigned, testamentary executrix of my late uncle, Charles-Maurice, Prince de Talleyrand, declare and certify that the present folio volume, containing five hundred and one hand-written pages, comprises the only original, complete, and faithful copy of the first five parts of his *Memoirs*, and of a fragment on the Duc de Choiseul left by the Prince de Talleyrand-Périgord.

" SAGAN, *May* 20, 1858.

" DOROTHÉE DE COURLANDE,
" DUCHESSE DE TALLEYRAND ET DE SAGAN."

A declaration, similar in all respects and bearing the same signature, closes the second volume.

At the end of the third, it is M. de Bacourt, sole survivor, who thus expresses himself :—

" I, the undersigned, testamentary executor of the late Prince Charles-Maurice de Talleyrand-Périgord, and of the Duchesse de Talleyrand and Sagan, Princesse de Courlande, declare and certify that the present folio volume of five hundred and six manuscript pages comprises the sole original, complete, and authentic copy of the eighth, ninth, and tenth parts of the *Memoirs* left by Prince Charles-Maurice de Talleyrand-Périgord.

" AD. DE BACOURT.
" BADEN, *January* 20, 1863."

No declaration is found at the end of the fourth volume, for the reason that the last part of this volume was to have been completed by subjoined extracts, whose complete transcription was not accomplished when death overtook M. de Bacourt.

It is from the text prepared for press by the very people whom M. de Talleyrand had charged with doing so, and according to the instructions that they held of him, that the present publication is made. Neither suppression, nor even toning down, have in any degree been allowed. Only some of the notes prepared by M. de Bacourt have been omitted, owing to their having, by this time, lost their interest. On the other hand, other notes, a considerable number of them, have been added, containing either biographical information concerning persons mentioned in the *Memoirs*, or explanation of facts reported in them, of which the reader of to-day might not have retained a sufficiently clear recollection.

With regard to the writing relative to the ministry of the Duc de Choiseul, mentioned in the declaration of the Duchesse de Talleyrand, M. de Bacourt thought that it ought to appear at the head of the first part of the *Memoirs*, although it would not naturally find a place there, having been composed at a later date. But it has been found more convenient to place this detached document at the end of the last volume, where some other writings of M. de Talleyrand that have been either unpublished hitherto, or forgotten, but which may still be read with interest, will also be relegated.

II.

The twelve parts of which the *Memoirs* are composed will be found to be very far from forming a complete and consecutive whole. They can be divided into two distinct portions. The first extends from M. de Talleyrand's birth to 1815, being the close of his ministry under Louis XVIII. There are clear indications to show that this portion of the *Memoirs* was drawn up during the Restoration. The second commences after the revolution of 1830, with the embassy of M. de

Talleyrand to London, and contains the account of this mission. It was probably written during the retirement which followed his resignation given in 1834.

A break of fourteen years, as well as the brevity with which the narrative passes over certain portions of the political career of M. de Talleyrand (among others, the part he played in the Constituent Assembly), witness sufficiently that his intention was by no means to present a complete picture of his whole life in his *Memoirs.* He himself, in a note put at the head of the first part, warns the reader that *Memoirs* is an improper expression, and only employed from want of a better one. That which will least be found in them as a matter of fact is that which is generally most sought after in memoirs, viz., revelations of incidents but little known in the life of the writer, or his personal impressions on events that he himself witnessed. Apart from a few pages devoted to his childhood and youth, the narrative of M. de Talleyrand is more than reserved as to his private life; and that of those whom he has known finds still less place there. His criticisms of the society amid which he lived are full of penetration and good taste; but the reader who expects to find anecdotes, indiscretions, or confidences among them, and who would not object to the spice of a little scandal, will be completely deceived. The tone of the narrative, uniformly earnest, never lends itself to disclosures of this nature.

M. de Talleyrand also seems to have not the slightest intention of replying, by way of explanation or apology, to the various charges that have been brought against him. Save the share that some writers have ascribed to him in the outrage that put an end to the days of the Duc d'Enghien, and which he indignantly disclaims in a special note, he preserves a silence which

does not merely appear to be that of disdain : it is rather a sort
of resolution taken to occupy the attention of his readers with
nothing that concerns himself alone, but to reserve all their
attention for the great political and national interests, whose
fate he held, on several occasions, in his own hands, and for
which France and posterity have the right to demand account.

If such has been his object (and everything leads to this
conviction), if he has really thought neither of satire, pleading,
nor confession of any kind, but merely of showing that the
fortune of France had not lost by being entrusted to his care,
he could scarcely have found a better way of clearing his
memory from the accusations, which, having never been spared
him in his lifetime, were not likely to be spared him in the
grave. There have been errors and mistakes in the private life
of M. de Talleyrand which no one has a right to justify, since
some of those he himself, of his own free will, solemnly re-
tracted on the point of death. His part in home politics, during
the various phases of the Revolution in which he mixed, will
always give rise to different judgments ; and as he belonged
to none of the parties into which France was at that time
divided, there is no one but believes himself justified in
severely criticising some of his actions. But when he had to
defend, whether as ambassador or minister, the greatness and
independence of his country in the face of the foreigner (foe,
rival, or ally,) it would be difficult to question, and it will be
found that he has not exaggerated, the importance of the
service he has rendered.

To do him full justice in this respect, one must not stay
at the recital he gives of the action he was enabled to take as
minister of the Directory or of the First Empire. He himself

passes fairly quickly over these first phases of his ministerial career, and however great be the events which follow each other at that time, if he often draws a picture of them with the art of a consummate historian, it is rather as a witness, than as an actor in them that he speaks. He leaves his reader to understand that, whatever high office, he, at that time, held, his power was in reality but nominal. He only carried out decisions that he had, as often as not, first combated. Being unable either to make himself understood by the incapable upstarts of the Revolution, or listened to by an imperious master who only asked counsel of his genius or of his passions, all his ingenuity was employed, after giving advice which was not followed, in repairing the faults which he would never have committed. It is at the Congress of Vienna, after the Restoration, at the embassy at London, after 1830, that, invested with the full confidence of the sovereigns whom he represented, he showed himself free to act as he would.

In these two circumstances, the most brilliant of his long career, and which naturally hold the foremost place in the volumes now submitted to the reader, Talleyrand gave diplomacy a place such as it perhaps had never before enjoyed, and imparted to the person of an ambassador an importance almost without precedent in history. As a general rule, the most renowned ambassadors have only been the fortunate interpreters of a thought that was not their own, and the clever executors of designs handed to them by those above them in office. What would Father Joseph have been without Richelieu? Their credit, besides, depends less on their own merits, than on the use they know how to make of the fear or the confidence which the governments that they represent inspire. What would the great negotiators of the peace of Westphalia, or of that of the Pyrenees have been, without the victories of Condé and Turenne? No support of this kind came to Talleyrand on the two occasions on which all the interests of our country were entrusted to him. In the one as in the other, he had to rely upon himself alone.

At Vienna, he presented himself before four victorious powers, closely united, and still under arms ; he spoke in the name of a monarchy restored after twenty-five years of trouble, on a tottering basis, in a country still covered with foreign troops, whose decimated army was not even loyal. Before the congress had finished its work, the sad mishap of the Hundred Days reduced him to the almost ridiculous position of ambassador of an exiled prince. At London, he was the agent of a still budding power, proceeding from a revolution, held for this reason in contempt by all the monarchies of Europe, and threatened every moment (at least, it was so believed), with destruction by the very popular force that had called it into being. There were days when the voice of the ambassador, bringing assurances of peace to the conferences, was drowned by echoes from Paris bearing shouts of war, and the rumbling of rebellion.

It cannot however be called into question (and if there did exist any doubts in this respect, the reading of the *Memoirs* would at once dispel them) that M. de Talleyrand never ceased a single day, either at London or Vienna, to be the soul of the congresses and conferences, and the true inspirer of the resolutions of assembled Europe, of which, when all is summed up, and the difficulties of the circumstances allowed for, France has in no way suffered. It is easier to state than to define the sovereign art, which enabled him to supply, by means of his cleverness and intellect alone, that support which, at every moment, failed him from without. In public as in private life, the ascendency which one man knows how to exercise over all those who in any way have dealings with him, is a natural gift for which no species of supremacy will ever adequately account. The unexpected successes which he obtained, are, however, to be explained in a great measure, as may be seen from the *Memoirs*, by the rare accuracy of glance which enabled him to perceive at once, and before all trial, the resources which could yet be drawn from a situation which any other man would have considered hopeless.

Thus, in 1814, on entering the European senate, devoid of all means for making himself feared, he discerned at once, that even on the morrow of a victory, material force is not every-thing, and that the course of events which appeared to be most unfavourable to him, had yet put at his service a moral force, which, cleverly managed, could take the place of weapons of a different character, which he lacked. This moral force, superior even to the force which the allied courts against us owed to the number of their soldiers, he sought and found in the principle loudly proclaimed of monarchical legitimacy. The text of the instructions he took to the Congress and which he gave to himself—being at once minister and ambas-sador—will be read; it is a general scheme for the restoration of legitimate monarchy over the whole surface of Europe, and as a natural consequence the restitution to all sovereigns of whatever lands their forefathers possessed. The project is systematically applied, article by article, state by state, without reserve, without restriction, without embarrassment; I might almost say, without false pride, without Talleyrand ever sus-

pecting, for a moment, that this monarchical faith will cause
some surprise in the mouth of a former minister of the Republic
and of the Empire.

To those who would have expressed this surprise to him,
I feel convinced that he would have been ready to reply with
his habitual *sang-froid*, that this contradiction on his part was
only one more homage rendered to necessity by experience.
But the truth is that, after twenty years of strife, which,
saturating the soil of Europe with blood, had mutilated,
lacerated, cut up all territories in a thousand different ways,
an extreme weariness, and a profound disgust of conquests
and revolutions had taken possession of the public mind. The
rapid succession of the republics instituted by the Directory,
and of the kingdoms created by imperial whim, the speedy
passage of these phantasms, that sprung up one day, only to
vanish on the next, had fatigued as much as dazzled the gaze
of peoples. Subjects and princes alike demanded rest, the one as
wearied with passing from hand to hand, and master to master,
as the others with being, by turn, crowned and dethroned,
according to the chance of the day. Some principle of public
law was demanded on all hands, which by regulating the
orderly transmission of power, should strengthen the basis
of all states, tottering from the effect of so many shocks. It
was the credit of Talleyrand to understand the imperious
character of this general sentiment, and the influence which
the representative of Louis XVIII. could draw from it. The
French monarchy restored within its former limits, deprived
only of those annexations which had been acquired by but
transient success, seemed the first and noblest application of
the principle of reparation. In making of Louis XVIII. an

interpreter of the common wish and a living protest against the barbarity of a *régime* of usurpation and violence, he assigned to him at once an original and paramount position among his royal peers. Restored by the acts of a war in which he had not concurred, the King of France was under obligations to, and protected by, those who had reopened to him the gates of his country. Re-established by virtue of a right which did not depend on force, he became once more their equal, and considering the antiquity of his race, in a certain measure, even their superior. That which the fear of his arms could not effect, respect for a principle obtained for him, and by restraining the ambition of Napoleon's conquerors, hindered them from imitating his example and appropriating, as he had done, at their own caprice and desire, territories occupied by their armies.

It has been said, I know, that there were here considerations stamped with a chivalrous loyalty, whose somewhat stilted expression could scarcely have been sincere, or even quite serious on the part of Talleyrand. We are given to understand that, instead of thus following up, from Dresden to Naples, and in fact over all Europe, the restoration of legitimate sovereigns, he could with less trouble, have obtained more solid and substantial advantages. For example, if he had allowed Russia and Prussia to extend as they chose in the north at the expense of their neighbours, it would have been possible (it is thought) to have driven back the German frontier from our own, thus preventing conflicts in the future, and giving us a better place in the new European equilibrium. This judgment, which claims to be essentially useful and practical, has seemed always to me to depend upon a narrow and superficial acquaintance with

facts. I doubt whether it could be maintained in face of the
account of M. de Talleyrand's first appearance at the Congress of
Vienna. There is nothing more dramatic than the account of this
first interview, in which the great powers still allied, declared
to him with a haughty coldness, that, even after peace was
concluded, they intended to maintain themselves in a close and
impenetrable bond, meaning to form a smaller assembly within
the great one, in which the fate of Europe would have been
decided with closed doors, and whose resolutions France would
have had no other alternative but to submit to. Had Talleyrand
done nothing else except break this *cordon sanitaire*, by showing
himself to be animated with a monarchical sentiment, even more
exaggerated than that of those who suspected him ; had this
unexpected manœuvre had no other result than to cause one of
his interlocutors to say, with a surprise which but ill-concealed
his deception : " In truth, Talleyrand speaks to us like a minister
of Louis XIV. !" those who care for our national dignity, even
in the past, ought yet to be grateful to him for it. But it was,
at bottom, a very different question from one of mere dignity or
even honour. It was (as the event but too soon proved) the
very existence of France and its unity which were continually
at stake. For by what other title after all than that of his
hereditary right, had Louis XVIII. got complete restoration of
the territory of his forefathers ? Besides, to allow elsewhere the
principle of heredity to be violated at the expense of the weak,
without a protest, after having benefited by it one's self, would
have been an inconsistency, nay, even a species of moral ingratitude which would soon have borne fruit, and the perpetrator of it
would soon have had occasion to repent. Ten months had not
yet elapsed, when France having met with fresh disasters, saw her

fate once more placed at the mercy of her conquerors, in days of inexpressible anguish. One map was already drawn, which took away some of her dearest provinces. Louis XVIII. had once more to proclaim the inviolable nature of his heritage. But how could he have raised his voice and gained a hearing, if he had himself connived by complying through the complacency of his ambassador at Vienna, in other robberies, as little justifiable as those with which he was threatened? Suppose, for example, that, from motives of self-interest, Talleyrand, instead of defending the patrimony of our old and faithful friend, the King of Saxony, had given it up as a prey to the King of Prussia who coveted it, who could, after Waterloo, have stayed these same appetites whose insatiable greed was already only too well known, from extending beyond the Rhine, as far as the Meuse and the Vosges? In reality, the position of defender of legitimate rights assumed by Talleyrand, was never better justified than on the day when the shadow of the material power of the sovereign whom he represented had vanished, and there only remained to him this moral power, ideal in appearance, but whose force, the least fanciful man that ever lived well appreciated on that day.

Fifteen years pass: fifteen years' break in the active life of Talleyrand, fifteen years' silence in the *Memoirs*. Then he re-emerges, coming to London to demand admission to the councils of Europe, for a new power, created on the morrow of a revolution, whose first act had been to interrupt the regular course of the royal succession. The transition is sudden, it must be admitted, and this change of *rôle* as of language takes the reader by surprise. On second thoughts, however, it is seen that, in spite of the difference and even often of the contradiction of words, the man has not changed ; that the end he pursues is the same, and that he displays the same art, and the same talents, whose application alone differs. At Vienna, it was a question of dissolving a coalition, which, maintaining itself in full peace condemned us for ever to powerlessness by isolation. At London, it was necessary to hinder the same coalition from re-forming for a new war ; the danger was not less pressing and everything led to the opinion that it would be more difficult to overcome ; for nothing had changed in the external condition of Europe since 1815 ; the same sentiments apparently animated the same cabinets, presided over by the same men : the same generals were ready to take command of the same armies, and the rumour of a revolution in France was more than sufficient to re-awaken the scarcely-lulled hostilities. By the most singular chance, it was the conqueror of Waterloo himself who presided over the council of the ministers of England. It seems that he had only one word to pronounce, one order to give, to set in motion all that mass of men whom he had led to victory.

And yet all is not the same, for, during these fifteen years "this large slice of mortal life," as Tacitus says, time has done its work, and underneath the apparently unchanged surface, a great change has taken place in the heart of public opinion, and nowhere more profoundly than in that land of Britain, where M. de Talleyrand, a refugee and proscribed, has already passed a part of his youth. That old England which he knew at that time, the England of Pitt and Castlereagh, the England which had been the soul of the European coalition, which had breathed into it the inspiration of its hate, and paid for it with its cash ; that England whose aristocratic pride and moral instincts Burke had excited against the revolutionary excesses, that England was no longer recognizable. A breath of democratic reforms had crossed the Channel and penetrated even the Gothic vaults of Westminster, and when the rising of July 1830 broke out at Paris, no voice was raised to curse the new revolution. On the contrary, England remembered complacently that she had herself had her revolution, and passed the crown from one branch to another of the reigning family. The new French monarchy was formed after the model of the English monarchy of 1688, and gave signs of remaining faithful to it; this resemblance pleased British pride, which was flattered that any one should copy her example. M. de Talleyrand had no sooner set foot upon English ground, than he was warned of this change by every current of political atmosphere that surrounded him, and divined at once new means of action that a new situation had given him. His plan was made; to the coalition of the monarchies of the Continent which were frightened by all revolutions, he opposed the alliance of two liberal monarchies, both founded on national will; and, in the speech he addressed to the King of England, the first time he was received in solemn audience, he did not hesitate to offer to the heir of the House of Brunswick the friendship of the King of the French in the name of a community of principles, and of a common origin.

From this moment his course was safe. The accession of a liberal ministry, whose coming into office he had foreseen, only served to remove all obstacles. He took a lever that he knew how to use. The threatening coalition was crushed in the bud, as soon as England retired from it. The English alliance even became the pivot of a long negotiation, which was to end in substituting on our frontiers, an amicable neutrality

for a very inconvenient neighbour, by creating, at Brussels, one
more kingdom which, like that of France, was the result of
the national choice.

Here we are, and we must acknowledge it, far from Vienna,
and the absolute principle of legitimacy. It could of course
no longer be appealed to, at least with the same authority. It
is the respect due to the national will that has replaced it.
There are certainly many objections to make to that suppleness of mind which permitted political principles to be
considered not as ultimate truths compelling assent, but as
instruments of a practical utility, which could be made use of
according to the convenience of their application. Do we not,
however, see in that the almost inevitable result of frequent
revolutions? Talleyrand, assuredly, is not the only man of that
generation of 1789, who, having entered life with noble illusions,
after several unsuccessful attempts, followed by as many disappointments, conceived a contempt for theory, and acquired a
stock of political scepticism. Allowing full weight to this
reservation, it is difficult not to be sensible of the suppleness
and richness of that mind which, proceeding from most dis-
similar cases, from entirely opposite sources, could draw to the
service of the same cause an inexhaustible variety of arguments
and resources : and it is only fair to acknowledge, besides the
flexibility of his form, the perseverance of his patriotism, and
that he never lost sight of the fact that, whatever might be the
internal condition of France, whether she be preparing revolutions or restorations, it was still France, and that she had a right
to be served with equal care for her present security and future
greatness.

Finally, we should still fall short of doing full justice, if, by

VOL. I.

J'apprends dans l'instant que les Prussiens ont mis e-d terponts de
Sena, ce que vraisemblablement ils veulent le faire sauter certainont
même, le D. d'Orantea dit au G.al Maison qu'il empêchera par tous
les moyens qui sont en son pouvoir, mais vous savez bien qu'il ya
a venir, faites toute ce qui est en votre pouvoir, soit par vous-même
soit par le Duc, fait par Lord Castlereagh &.ᵃ Quant à moi, j'ai
le faut, je me porterai sur le pont, on me fera sauter, si l'on veut.
J'ai été fort content des deux Lords pour ta contribution.

Samedi à 10 heures   Louis.

A mon Cousin le Pce de Talleyrand.

AUTOGRAPH LETTER OF KING LOUIS XVIII. TO PRINCE
TALLEYRAND, THE TRANSLATION OF WHICH IS
GIVEN IN THE FOOTNOTE ON THE OPPOSITE
PAGE.

the side of the personal share taken by Talleyrand in the happy results of the negotiations he conducted, the honour of which accrues to him, we failed to attribute an honour as great, or almost so, to the firm and intelligent support rendered him by the two sovereigns whom he served. The *Memoirs* have the merit of acknowledging this share, and of rendering to both representatives of the House of France the exalted position which is their due.

The letters of Louis XVIII. that have been already published will not be read without emotion, letters which compel admiration for the nobleness of the language which is only equalled by the sublimity of the sentiments it expresses, and the unmistakable royal tone that pervades them. Certain papers, not yet published, will but serve to confirm and increase this impression.[1] In the negotiation relative to the creation of the kingdom of Belgium, the correspondence of Louis Philippe, presents a character, different indeed, but which does him no less honour. They are the counsels of perfected experience, of a restless vigilance, noting the most minute details, and giving the preference consistently, to every public interest, as against

[1] There will be found, worthy of special note, in the third volume of the *Memoirs*, a letter from King Louis XVIII. which is of such keen interest that I feel that I ought to give it at once. It is addressed to M. de Talleyrand in 1815, at the time of the second occupation of Paris by the allies, on receipt of the news that the Prussians were proposing to destroy the "Bridge of Jena," whose name aroused painful memories. The following is the tenor of it :—

"I have just been informed that the Prussians have undermined the bridge of Jena, and that they will probably blow it up to-night. The Duc d'Otrante carries instructions to General Maison to prevent this by every means in his power. But, as you know, he has none at all. So do all you possibly can, by means of the Duke (of Wellington) and Lord Castlereagh. As to myself, I will, if necessary, go to the bridge in person ; they may then blow me up, if they like.

"LOUIS.

"*Saturday*, 10 A.M."

This document, signed by the king himself, is to be found in the papers of M. de Talleyrand, who took the more care to preserve it that this generous trait of Louis XVIII., already mentioned, though it is in the writings of the time, has often been questioned.

those of dynasty, or family, while, on critical occasions, his decision is always manly and sensible. Both of them, in a word, have been the faithful guardians of the powerful French unity created by their ancestors, and which they have had the good fortune to leave intact to their successors, whose blunders and follies have since compromised it. If the lamentable mutilation that this unity has undergone were irreparable, history would say that it perished on the day on which the race that founded it left the throne.

INTRODUCTION.

THE appearance of these memoirs has been long awaited with much curiosity and some alarm. Their author was believed to possess more dangerous secrets of high importance than any other man of his time; and whether or not he had friends to reward it was known that he had many enemies to punish. When it was found that he had forbidden the publication of his manuscripts until thirty years after his death, the belief in their compromising and dangerous character was confirmed; and when, after the lapse of the required time, they were still withheld, they began to be looked upon as a species of historical dynamite, only to be exploded after everybody in danger had been removed from the field of human activity. But if this anticipation were disappointed—if it were found that the old diplomatist had been thinking, as was his wont, of himself rather even than of his enemies, and if his memoirs should not teem with scandalous revelations concerning great personages, it was still thought certain that they would undertake to vindicate what had been portrayed by French writers and statesmen as well nigh the most scandalous career of the two centuries to which it belonged; and such a vindication, whether successful or not, would necessarily shed a flood of light on some of the greatest transactions and some of the most extraordinary men of modern times.

Whatever effect the memoirs may now have, the place of their author in history has not hitherto been materially changed in the fifty-two years that have elapsed since his death. No revelations affecting French annals, from the days preceding the

Revolution of '89 down to the reign of the Citizen King, have diminished Talleyrand's share in events or modified the accepted estimates of his work and character. His career was—and it remains—unparalleled in modern Europe, for length and variety of distinguished service. Beginning with Louis XVI., from whom he received his first appointment, and from whom he went, later, with a letter to the King of England, he served in all eight known masters, not to reckon a great number of others who were, at one time or another, said to have him secretly in their pay. He was President of the Constituent Assembly which organized the French Revolution. He was sent to London on a secret mission with a passport from Danton. He was Minister of Foreign Affairs under the Directory, under the Consulate, under the Empire, under Louis XVIII., and under Louis-Philippe. In diplomatic skill and success contemporary public opinion held him the first man of his period ; that is to say, for half a century the first man in Europe. As to real influence on affairs, it is doubtful if any minister since can be said to have exerted more, with the exceptions only of Bismarck and Cavour. Even they did not cover so wide a range or deal with such a bewildering variety of negotiations, extending over so great a time and furthering the views of so many masters.

Sir Henry Bulwer has a phrase that, in a way, measures him. " He was the most important man in the Constituent Assembly after Mirabeau ; and the most important man in the Empire after Napoleon." But to gauge fairly his extraordinary public life, it must be remembered that he held place and gained in power for forty years after Mirabeau's death ; and that having been one of the leading men of France before Napoleon was heard of, he remained a minister and an ambassador of France long after Napoleon had eaten out his heart at St. Helena.

Yet in spite of this amazing career, his countrymen have not been generally disposed to speak well of him. Napoleon said of him, and to him, that he was a silk stocking filled with filth. Carnot said, " He brings with him all the vices of the old *régime*, without having been able to acquire any of the virtues of the new one. He has no fixed principles ; he changes them as he does his linen, and takes them according to the wind of the day —a philosopher, when philosophy is the mode ; a republican now, because that is necessary in order to become anything. To-morrow he will declare for an absolute monarchy, if he can make anything out of it. I don't want him at any price." Mirabeau called him "this vile, base trickster," and again wrote, "It is dirt and money that he wants. For money he has sold his honour and his friend. For money he would sell his soul—and he would be right, for he would be trading muck for gold." The very member of the Assembly who secured his recall from exile, Chénier, wrote of him, " This letter of the Abbé Maurice proves to me that after having been Anarchist and Orleanist, and not having been Robespierrist only because Robespierre wouldn't have him, he has now become a partisan of the Directory. This limp-foot, without respect for his bishopric, is like a sponge, which sucks up every liquid into which it is dropped, but, unlike the sponge, he never gives anything back. Here he is, recalled from exile yesterday, and proposing proscriptions for to-morrow. If the Directory wants blood, look out for your head ;—Maurice will not refuse it."

Modern French writers, while of course less passionate, have been apt to agree in admitting his extraordinary venality, his treachery to his chiefs, and his lack of veracity. Lamartine admired him, but Louis Blanc was as severe as the bitterest of his contemporaries. Chateaubriand wrote of him, "When Monsieur Talleyrand is not conspiring, he is making corrupt bargains."[1] Guizot said he was a man of the court and of diplomacy,—not of government ; that he was indifferent to means and almost indifferent to the end, provided he found in it a personal success. And, to quote but one opinion not coming from his countrymen, Gouverneur Morris said of him, " This man appears to me polished, cold, tricky, ambitious and bad."

Few men, indeed, spoke well of him. Towards the close of his life, when he was ambassador in London, an attack was made upon him in the House of Lords by the Marquis of London-derry. The Duke of Wellington offered a spirited defence. He had held official relations with M. de Talleyrand in most critical

[1] " Quand Monsieur Talleyrand ne conspire pas, il trafique."

periods. Never had he encountered a man more vigorous and
skilful in protecting the interests of his own country, or one
more upright and honourable in his attitude towards other
countries. Talleyrand was found the next day reading the report
of this debate with tears in his eyes ; and he said to his visitor,
" I am all the more grateful to the Duke, since he is the one
statesman in the world who has ever spoken well of me."

Later, while the diplomatist, now a very old man, was still
in office, in the reign of Louis-Philippe, Alexandre Sallé published
in Paris a volume undertaking to give an "impartial history of
Talleyrand's political life." It bore upon its title-page as a
motto, a verse by Barthélemy, which may be roughly rendered
thus : " The incarnate lie, the living perjury, Prince de Bénévent ;
impenitent Judas, anointed with the sacred oil, he opens his
career by betraying God himself. Alike at the altar and at the
Court, the double apostate treats the State as he treated the
Church." The introduction to this same work concludes with
the story that Louis XVIII. when asked to express his opinion
about his famous Foreign Minister, replied by quoting some
lines of Corneille regarding Richelieu, of which this is the
substance: " He has done me too much good that I should
speak ill of him, and too much harm that I should speak well of
him." [1]

The evil in a public man's life is apt to attract wider attention
than the good, and certainly his countrymen have made no
exception to this rule in Talleyrand's favour. Taking his career
from their records, what an extraordinary portrait is presented !
Here are a few of the lines in it :—

A profligate priest, who owed his start in life to an ill-
flavoured joke about the immorality of Paris, made in the
drawing-room of Madame du Barry, the king's favourite.

A bishop who was forced into the public journals to explain
that the money he had recently made in gambling was not won
in gambling houses, but in clubs ; and that it was not so much
as reported—being only 30,000 francs, instead of six or seven
hundred thousand.

---

[1] " Il m'a fait trop de bien pour en dire du mal,
    Il m'a fait trop de mal pour en dire du bien."

A confidential friend of Mirabeau, yet accused of poisoning him.

A minister, and for years the intimate of Napoleon, yet suspected of a plot to assassinate him.

A great statesman whose enormous and continuous receipt of bribes from the beginning to the end of his long career is unquestioned.

A trusted Minister of Foreign Affairs, who, while in office under the Directory, thwarted their measures and plotted for the *coup d'état* of Napoleon ; who, while in office under Napoleon, conspired with the Emperors of Russia and Austria to defeat his plans, and plotted for the return of the Bourbons ; who, while in office under Louis XVIII. schemed for his overthrow, and for the accession of Louis Philippe.

The Constituent Assembly forbade his return to France. Pitt expelled him from England. Washington refused to receive him in America. The Pope excommunicated him.

And yet he lived to be summoned back to France and appointed Minister of Foreign Affairs for the revolutionary government ; lived to return to England as ambassador from France, with the prestige of the most distinguished living diplomatist, to meet with a reception which could scarcely have been more respectful if he had been a crowned head ; lived to give notice to the American Ministers Plenipotentiary in Paris that they must buy peace or leave the country ; lived to have the Pope's excommunication withdrawn, and died in the odour of sanctity, with his king at his bedside, and the blessings of the Cardinal of Paris.

Many of the lineaments in this strange portrait drawn by the French historians are not to be much changed. There is little chance to erase the licentiousness, the treachery, the deceit, the monstrous venality. In recalling them, however, it must always be remembered that he can be only fairly judged by the standard of his time, which was lax to a degree we can hardly comprehend, especially with reference to the first of these vices and the last. When the American Commissioners resented Talleyrand's demand for a bribe of 250,000 dollars for himself, and a bigger one called a loan, for the Directory, his representa-

tive said naively, " Don't you know that everything is bought in
Paris ? Do you dream that you can get on with this Government without paying your way ? "

It must be further remembered, and to his honour, that while
he may be said to have betrayed her rulers, he never betrayed
France. On the contrary, when he was secretly thwarting his
masters, he was often helping his country. On notable occasions he rendered her service of incomparable value, and almost
saved her from destruction as a first-class European power.

It was a touching eulogy pronounced on him at his death in
varying phrases by both Thiers and Mignet, that he had always
shown an aversion to persecutions and violence, and that he had
never done harm to anybody. In the main this praise is
deserved. " But," exclaims St. Beuve, in protest, "there are
three points in his life which raise terrible doubts—the death of
Mirabeau, the affair of the Duc d'Enghien, the affair of Mem-
breuil." This last was the plot for the assassination of Napoleon.

Talleyrand was perfectly aware of the shocking charges
against himself in connection with the death of Mirabeau, but
he makes no reference whatever to them in the portion of his
memoirs treating of that period. The fact that they were
believed at the time only shows the estimate then placed on him
by some of his contemporaries. On the other hand, it must be
said that many things make the story improbable, and that the
so-called evidence is circumstantial and trivial. Napoleon,
repeatedly, in conversation and in writing, charged the murder
of the Duc d'Enghien to him. Talleyrand devotes one chapter
to repelling the accusation, and fixing the responsibility for the
crime on Napoleon himself. As to the plot to have Napoleon
assassinated, even Talleyrand's enemies must admit that, while
some circumstances were certainly suspicious, the proof of his
complicity is fragmentary and not convincing.

No portrait of the man can be just which does not relieve by
many light touches the sombre colours in which he has generally
been depicted. He had the uniform courtesy and dignity of the
old *régime.* He was the most accomplished of courtiers ; the
most correct of masters of ceremonies. He spoke well, and he
wrote better—his few appearances at the Academy being really

events. In the brilliant *salons* of the Court circles before the Revolution, he was a social lion. Women always liked and helped him. His witty sayings were the talk of Paris. In prosperity he was not arrogant; in times of trouble he bore himself with unruffled dignity and composure. When Napoleon denounced him in the presence of others, for treachery and venality, he merely said, as he went down the staircase, " What a pity that so great a man should have been so badly brought up." At another time, when Napoleon, then First Consul, asked him how he had become so rich (he was said to be already worth thirty millions of francs), he replied, " Nothing could be more simple, General; I bought Rentes the day before the 18th Brumaire (the day on which Napoleon seized power), and I sold them the day after." He had taken office under Louis XVIII., and was representing France at the Congress of Vienna, when Napoleon suddenly came back from Elba. He merely discovered that his liver was a little out of order, and he must go to Carlsbad. " The first duty of a diplomat," he observed, " after a Congress, is to take care of his liver." A few months later, after Waterloo, there were fresh symptoms of trouble with the same organ, while Louis XVIII. regarded him askance ; but the moment he was reappointed Minister of Foreign Affairs all was well.

The evil Talleyrand did was chiefly to individuals. The good he did was to France. His public action in the Constituent Assembly was most important, and in the main most judicious. The French writers of that period, and even down to the day of his death, habitually ascribed sinister motives to every act, and professed to find his hidden hand in many excesses of the Revolutionary party. But he can only be fairly judged now by what he is known to have done ; and by that standard there is no Frenchman who might not be proud of his record in the Constituent Assembly. He was the pioneer in the establish- ment of the metric system. He opposed the issue of the *assignats*, and accurately foretold their end. He presented an elaborate and well-considered plan for the reform of the finances, and the establishment of a sinking fund. He urged the suppression of lotteries. He presented in a comprehensive report and bill, a judicious system of national education, including a plan for the

secularization of the schools. He favoured the policy of peace
and alliance with England. Bishop as he still was, he presented
the measure for selling the property of the clergy, and thus
secured for the almost bankrupt treasury of Louis XVI. two
milliards of francs. He carried the measure for abolishing the
oppressive tithes of the clergy. In effect this representative of
the old nobility of France showed himself among the earliest to
recognize the inevitable changes, and loyally endeavoured to
introduce reforms which would enable the monarchy to adapt
itself to them without too violent a wrench. As time went on,
he became convinced of the incapacity of the king to meet the
crisis. Thenceforward he went with the tide, but strove rather
to moderate and restrain it. The address to the people of France
which the Assembly chose him to prepare, breathed throughout
a spirit of genuine and almost republican devotion to the rights
of man as we now understand them.

In other and widely differing occasions his influence was
exerted to promote peace, and to discourage wars of mere ambition. He faithfully warned Napoleon against his Spanish
policy, and fell into disgrace for a time through efforts to thwart
it. With that Spanish policy, the downfall of Napoleon began.
At Erfurt he protested against the schemes of wanton attack
upon Austria, and even maintained private relations, and had
nightly interviews with the Czar Alexander to keep him from
being led into them by Napoleon's importunities. At another
stage in Napoleon's extraordinary aggressions he protested, " I
do not want to be the torment of Europe." He lost his place
in the cabinet of Louis XVIII. because that king would not
tolerate his plans for an alliance with England. Later on, he
went to England as the ambassador of Louis-Philippe, and
there negotiated the treaty of 1834, which secured his country
many years of peace and prosperity. He rendered useful service at the peace of Amiens. At the Congress of Vienna his
efforts were directed to an English rather than to a Russian
alliance ; and for this Thiers and others have criticized him, but
the memoirs make an end of that criticism. In the negotiations
before and after the " Hundred Days " Talleyrand is now seen to
have rendered his country one of the greatest services, perhaps

the greatest service, of his life. He may be said perhaps to have saved her from dismemberment, and certainly to have preserved her great place in Europe.

Two other acts of Talleyrand's in widely different fields, may here be cited, out of many which this generation should not allow to be forgotten.

He proposed under the Consulate a practical system of Civil Service for the Department of Foreign Affairs. He was only permitted to introduce it in part, but his remarkable memorandum on the subject can be read with profit to this day.

He defended the liberty of the press under Louis XVIII. against the tendency of the king and the court. Twice, in the Chamber of Peers, in successive years, he faced the reaction on this subject, and exposed the fatal path on which the court party wished to enter.

"Let us take for granted," he once said, "that what has been held good and useful by all the enlightened men of a country, without variation, during a succession of years of various governments, is a necessity of the time. Such, gentlemen, is the liberty of the press. . . I do not say that governments ought to hasten to recognize these new necessities. But when they have been recognized, to take back what was given, or—which comes to the same thing—to suspend it indefinitely, that is a rashness which I, more than any one else, hope may not bring a sad repentance to those who have conceived the convenient but pitiful thought. You must never compromise the good faith of a government. In our days it is not easy to deceive for a long time. There is some one who has more sense than Voltaire, more sense than Bonaparte, more than any Director, more than any Minister, past, present, or to come. That is everybody. To undertake or even to persist in a controversy, where all the world is interested against you, is a fault ; and to-day all political faults are dangerous." Students of current American politics are accustomed to the phrase, "Everybody is wiser than anybody." It may interest some of them to note that Talleyrand said so, before the American politicians.

The memoirs have been expected to clear up some of the dark charges against him, and to do much towards clarifying our views of that extraordinary epoch. They are sure to leave

a better impression as to the work of Talleyrand himself. One
of his most merciless critics, St. Beuve, writing in 1867, as to
the anticipations then felt concerning the present publication,
judiciously says : " I am persuaded that everything to be found
in the letters and other writings of Talleyrand will give one a
more favourable idea of him.   People of genius like his never
put the worst of their thoughts or of their lives on paper."
What we now find that he did put on paper proves to be, and
was intended by its author to be, as the French say, a "serious
book,"—meaning thereby that whatever its variety of subjects or
interest in treatment, it is written throughout with a constant
view to a serious purpose.   Whoever comes to it for the entertainment which a man with such a well-grounded reputation for
wit and repartee might easily have furnished—for anecdotes,
amusing reminiscences of court incidents, and in general, for the
table-talk of the ruling classes during the momentous periods of
which it treats, will be disappointed.   Whoever seeks details
even of the author's own life will be disappointed.   The memoirs
are obviously meant to be the elaborate vindication of a great
career ; not an autobiography, nor a lively account of the author's
times, not a collection of scandalous anecdotes, nor even a series
of malicious revelations of state secrets to the hurt of old enemies.
Incidentally, some state secrets may be revealed ; as a means of
vindication some of the highest reputations are mercilessly
assailed, and certainly some of the most important occurrences
in the history of modern Europe are set in a new light.   But the
one controlling aim of Prince Talleyrand was to elucidate and
vindicate his own large part in the events of his time.

He does it with a certain haughty dignity.   He apologizes
for nothing.   He conceives that he gave to every government he
served as much as he received from it, and he goes far towards
adducing the proof.   He narrates without passion, and reasons
generally on the high plane of the real interests of his country,
and the real interests of Europe, which he declares were not
antagonistic.

He has been well served by those to whom he committed his
memoirs.   They have been able to secure the admirable execution of his wishes, even after they have followed him to the grave.
The author himself could not fail to be content with the admir-

able editing which it finally fell to the Duc de Broglie to give to his work; and the eminent abilities of that French statesman have never accomplished more skilfully a more difficult task than in his prefatory analysis and appreciation of Talleyrand's career. The memoirs are written in a pure and admirable French style, the charm of which defies translation; but in M. de Beaufort the publishers have found a translator whose previous rendering of the memoirs of the late Duc de Broglie, and of Prince Jerome's *Napoleon and his Detractors*, gave every guarantee of accuracy, while his scholarship and familiarity with the subject lend value to the notes he has added.

The great periods in Talleyrand's career were the Constituent Assembly; the first years of his co-operation with Napoleon; the later years when he resisted but was still able to influence Napoleon's aggressions; the Congress of Vienna and the last mission to England. On the first of these, for reasons hereafter suggested, the memoirs give less new information than was to be expected. Their account of the resistance to Napoleon enhances the estimate of Talleyrand's work at that epoch; and in their story of the transactions at Vienna we see for the first time in an adequate light, the great diplomatist at the height of his powers, and winning his worthiest triumphs. He went to Vienna the representative of a prostrate nation, and of a throne propped up by the bayonets of the army that had conquered it. He found the victors apportioning the spoil without reference to him, and without even admitting him to their conferences. He had neither physical power nor moral prestige behind him; no great army, no established institutions; hardly even a country; and the very instructions he bore he had written himself. He stood alone against Europe. And yet in a few months, by sheer force of intellect and skill, he had divided the allies, had secured the territorial integrity of his country, had negotiated most useful alliances, had greatly strengthened the French throne, had done something towards preventing the wanton partition of other nationalities, and had put France again in her leading position in Europe.

The popular idea was (in accordance with the hint which he himself threw out), that he forbade the publication of his manuscripts for so long a period after his death because they compromised too many reputations. It is quite as probable that his sense of the generally hostile judgment of his contemporaries and particularly of his countrymen, was so keen that he wished to make his final appeal on behalf of his own reputation to another generation.

On this theory of the purpose with which they were written, these memoirs have an interest from the points on which they are silent, as well as from those they elucidate. What he could not defend, or what he despised too much to care to defend, he ignores.

On the subject of his early and constant receipt of bribes, there is a profound silence. Yet his venality was so notorious and so monstrous that Napoleon denounced him for it again and again; details had repeatedly appeared in specific cases, and statements had been published during his lifetime, undertaking to show the various items and sources for his receipts of some thirty millions of francs, acquired in a few years of official life before the proclamation of the Empire.[1] It was a

---

[1] In the life of Talleyrand by Louis Bastide, published in 1838, a few months only after Talleyrand's death, the following table is given of his receipts for three years :

	Francs.
From Portugal	1,200,000
From Austria for the secret articles in the Convention of Campo Formio in 1797	1,000,000
From Prussia, for having advised it of these articles, and prevented their execution	1,000,000
From the Elector of Bavaria	500,000
From the King of Naples, as the price of recognizing his neutrality	500,000
From the Pope	150,000
From the King of Sardinia	300,000
From the Grand Duke of Tuscany in order that the French troops should respect his territory	500,000
From the Cis-Alpine Republic, in order to obtain a new agreement	1,000,000
From the Batavian Republic, for the same object	1,200,000
During the first six months of the Congress of Rastadt . . .	1,800,000
For his share in the prizes made by French privateers on neutral vessels	2,000,000
From the Prince de la Paix	1,000,000
From the Grand Vizier	500,000
From the Hanseatic cities	500,000
Net profits from speculations in French and foreign funds during the negotiations of Lord Malmesbury at Lille .	1,500.000

14,650,000

To which should be added the enormous profits which he realized by his operations on the Stock Exchange on the 18th Brumaire. The author adds that all these details had

subject on which there was nothing to be said, and the sagacious diplomat knew when to say nothing.

But aside from Napoleon's charges, oral and written, as well as from those of French politicians and journals which he perhaps thought he could afford to ignore, there was one arraignment against him for blackmail, so direct, detailed, and authoritative, that he might have been expected to offer either an explanation, a denial, or a counter-attack. This was the case set forth by the three American Commissioners and Ministers Plenipotentiary, Messrs. Charles C. Pinckney, John Marshall, and Elbridge Gerry, in a series of official despatches to the Secretary of State of the United States, transmitted to Congress in special messages by John Adams, then the President. In effect, Talleyrand, as Minister of Foreign Affairs under the Directory, refused the commissioners official recognition unless he could be assured that they would give him personally a "gratification" of two hundred and fifty thousand dollars, and make a loan to the Directory of thirty-two millions of Dutch florins. He kept them dancing attendance for months, and long declined to take up their business at all, the demand for the money being meantime often repeated. Mr. Bellamy of Hamburg and Mr. Hautval, with one or two others whose names have been preserved in the State department at Washington, but never disclosed, acted at first as intermediaries.[1] They presented the demands, orally and in writing, and persistently argued the necessity for compliance. They bore messages from Talleyrand, arranged for meetings with him, and some of them accompanied the commissioners to these meetings. Talleyrand himself repeated the demand for the loan, exactly as they had presented it, and urged it with the same arguments. He even put it in writing, permitted one of the commissioners to read it, and then withdrew and burnt the manuscript. He did not personally demand the "gratification" of a quarter of a million dollars, but merely said, in reply to Mr. Elbridge Gerry's remark that these seemed much the same financial views Mr. Bellamy had been urging, "that

been published in various works, and that M. Talleyrand had never dared to refute or correct these figures.

[1] *Treaties and Conventions between the United States and other Powers, with Notes on the Negotiations.* Government edition, p. 998.

the information Mr. Bellamy had given him was just, and might always be relied on."[1] Mr. Bellamy was the one who had been most pertinacious and explicit about the "gratification," and he was present at this conversation. The American commissioners, through months of solicitation, sturdily refused the demands, and diplomatic relations between the two countries were finally broken off. The President, in communicating the last of the correspondence to Congress, said, "I will never send another minister to France without assurances that he will be received, respected, and honoured as the representative of a great, free, powerful, and independent nation."[2] The documents leave no moral doubt of the story; they were printed in the volumes comprising the President's official communications to Congress, and had been before the world for a quarter of a century when these memoirs were completed. The absence of a line of reference to them is as interesting in its way as anything Prince Talleyrand could have said on the subject.

He spent many months in the United States soon after the establishment of their independence, in which France had aided, and while a revolution, stimulated in part by the American example, was in progress in his own land ; but he found, in his recollections of his American visit, almost nothing suggested by either event, and nothing concerning the great man then Chief Magistrate of the country which gave him hospitality. His lack of sympathy with republicanism, whether in the United States or in France, explains the one ; and General Washington's refusal to receive him explains the other. Lord Lansdowne had given him a warm letter of introduction to Washington, setting forth that Talleyrand was really in exile because, although a bishop, he had desired to promote the general freedom of worship, and eulogizing him for having sacrificed his ambition in the Church to his devotion to principle. Washington possibly had his own views as to the extent to which Talleyrand's exile was due to his high religious principles. Hamilton's influence, always great—was joined to Lord Lansdowne's eulogy ; but both were unavailing. The refusal to receive the French exile, however, was quietly put upon political grounds.

[1] *American State Papers*, 1798–1803, vol. iv. p. 25.   [2] *Ibid.* p. 137.

To men of this time it seems that no part of Talleyrand's life was more creditable or useful than that spent in the Constituent Assembly. But this scion of the old nobility of France had never changed his real political views. He was always a monarchist—in the Assembly, under the Directory, under Napoleon. He wished to assist Louis XVI., until he became convinced that the constitutional feebleness and obstinacy of that monarch were beyond help. "The ministers," he says, "did not know that arbitrary power has no right to punish with moderation those who resist it, and that by its very nature it is required either to ignore or to crush its enemies." When he found that the king would not attempt in season to act upon such principles, Talleyrand abandoned the monarchy, and took care of himself. But while he went with the Republican current, he was never republican. He found, therefore, little satisfaction in his honourable and brilliant record in the Constituent Assembly, and his account of it, in view of its real importance, is meagre.

So he touches very lightly his extraordinary relations to the Church. But he takes pains to make it clear that he was forced into the priesthood, and that he never felt any real calling for his sacred vocation. He is equally careful to show that in critical emergencies he had been able to do Rome service, and that the feelings of the Pope towards him were friendly.

The scandals of his private life as priest and bishop receive only sufficient allusion to indicate his contempt for the subject. Thus his relations to the Countess Flahaut were known, and a letter to her had been published, in which, describing his exercise of his sacred functions at the great ceremony of the National Oath, in the Champ de Mars, he first hints at his own lack of religious faith, and then says : " I hope you feel to what divinity I yesterday addressed my prayers and my oath of fidelity. You alone are the Supreme Being whom I adore, and always will adore." The husband of the Countess afterwards lost his head on the guillotine ; and the widow in exile at Hamburg, was about to contract another marriage, as Talleyrand, returning from his exile, came to the same place. When she heard of his purpose she requested him not to come, since she feared that his presence, coupled with the stories of their former relations, might embarrass her approaching marriage. The old man of eighty puts this in his memoirs as an amusing instance of feminine simplicity, and says that, of course, he paid no attention to the request. He goes on then to tell of meeting Madame de Genlis again, and of finding her unchanged—the same Madame de Genlis of whom in relation to the Duc d'Orléans he had taken occasion to say in his merciless portrait of that prince, " Madame de Genlis always surrendered early, to avoid scandal."

Talleyrand evidently cherished bitter memories of his ex- pulsion from England by Pitt, but he finds it well to pass the subject with the slightest possible mention. Nor does he refer at all to the strange letters he had previously sent his Govern- ment, reporting that England was practically on the verge of a revolution like that of France, analyzing the inadequate military resources at hand to meet it, and proposing a plan for a French invasion and capture of Ireland. Eight days, he said, were sufficient to land 60,000 men at twenty or thirty different points. As a matter of prudence, they might perhaps go in the character of *émigrés*, so as to avoid arousing the suspicions of the Govern- ment. " Once masters of the principal ports," he continued, " once with the English fleet in our power, we can easily bring from France such reinforcements as are needed ; and besides, as the march of our troops will have been preceded by a proclamation in the name of the sovereign people of France, addressed to the sovereign people of Great Britain and Ireland, as their faithful allies, no doubt this country will be thrown into a revolution more prompt and more happy than that of 1688. The elements for a republic are riper in England than they were in France four years ago, and it may take fewer weeks for England to accomplish this great and salutary change, than we spent years."[1]

With the gravest charge affecting his reputation as a pub- lic man, Talleyrand does deal at length, but after his own fashion. He makes not the slightest concealment of his efforts to thwart the plans of his masters. He narrates them often in detail, with entire simplicity and the utmost directness. But

[1] Letter of Talleyrand to Lebrun, dated October 10, 1792.

the narrative always tends to show that the course he pursued was in the interest of France, and that the rulers he thwarted either did not know that interest or wished to sacrifice it for their own. Thus, after telling how he had secretly laboured with the Czar Alexander, at the Erfurt Conference, to defeat Napoleon's plan for an alliance.against Austria, and had succeeded, he calmly says, "It is the last service I was able to render to Europe while Napoleon continued to reign, and that was, in my opinion, a service rendered also to him." There is nowhere a hint that in his mind private and surreptitious conferences with the sovereigns of other countries to defeat the plans of the sovereign whose representative and confidential adviser he was, had the slightest immoral quality.

But he takes care to show Napoleon in a light that must make the world rather rejoice at seeing such a man betrayed. The memoirs scarcely touch a critical point in the emperor's career without dealing him a stab. They make him paltry in the business of the divorce. They picture him as an ignorant blusterer in the affairs of the Concordat. They detail his cheap devices to gain the admiration of men of letters. They show with malicious precision how he laboriously copied out the draft of a treaty which Talleyrand had prepared for him, that the Czar, finding it in the emperor's handwriting, might think it was his own work. They preserve his letter, complaining that the heir to the Spanish throne wrote him as "My Cousin," and requiring the minister to instruct this prince of ancient royal lineage that the only word proper for him to use in addressing Napoleon was "Sire." They stoop even to such trifles as his fretting on the evening of Austerlitz, over some gossip of a fancied slight to him by the society of the Faubourg St. Germain. Everywhere they paint him as heartless, vain, vulgar, wanton in attack, ungenerous and pitiless to the defeated, untruthful, proud of his ability to deceive, wholly without principle and without gratitude. And they do this, not so much by ascribing to him these qualities, as by the careful and precise narration of incidents that exhibit them.

The inference which Prince Talleyrand expects his readers to draw from all this is plain. It was right, when in power, under such a man, to thwart him when it seemed needful in the interest of France. When this could no longer be done, it was right to prepare the way for a Bourbon successor—in the interest of France. When the restored Bourbons did not meet his views, it was right to plot for their displacement by the son of that Duc d'Orléans whom he had painted as a brainless and heartless monster—in the interest of France. In other cases the suggested defence is always the same ; wherever he deceived her rulers he did it all for the good of France.

No doubt the plea will have force, especially with his country-men. Moralists indeed will regard with surprise the claim that a minister, though holding on to his office, no longer owes personal loyalty to his sovereign, when in his judgment the sovereign is sacrificing the interests of his country to his own. They will ask whether, even in such great emergencies, the end can be admitted to justify the means. Whatever the answer, French-men, at any rate, and very possibly the world at large, will have a kindlier feeling for the veteran public servant who is able to show that, even at such cost, he did in great crises serve his country. The memoirs will not change the world's verdict on the profligate Abbé of Périgord and Bishop of Autun. They will not lighten the censure on the Foreign Minister who made merchandise of his treaties, and became a millionaire on bribes. They will not make the world think it honourable in him to have deceived or betrayed in turn almost every man under whom he held office. Nevertheless, they will heighten and broaden his fame. The old man was wise, as usual, in making his appeal to a later generation. He played a great part ; and as its proportions are here revealed, the space for him in the history of his times must be materially enlarged.

AUTOGRAPH LETTER OF PRINCE TALLEYRAND, PROBABLY WRITTEN JUST AFTER THE BATTLE OF EYLAU (FEBRUARY 7, 1807). IT BEARS NO SUBSCRIPTION, BUT IS DOUBTLESS ADDRESSED TO HIS BANKER OR TO HIS SOLICITOR. IT IS CURIOUS AS CONTAINING AN ALLUSION TO HIS WIFE, WHOM HE DOES NOT MENTION ANYWHERE IN THE "MEMOIRS."

I DO not know what title to give to this writing. It is not a literary work: it is full of repetitions. I can scarcely call it *My Memoirs*, for my life and relations will be found mentioned in it as seldom as I could help. To give this large work the title of: *My Opinion on the Affairs of my Time*, would be a term, perhaps justified, but also too decided to be at the head of the production of a man who has doubted as much as I have in my life. A philosophical title would be incomplete or exaggerated. I therefore begin without title, and without a dedication, for I recognize in the Duchesse de Dino alone the obligation of defending my memory.

CONTENTS.

PART III.

THE CONVENTION, THE DIRECTORY, THE CONSULATE, THE EARLY
YEARS OF THE EMPIRE.

1791—1808.

PART IV.

SPANISH AFFAIRS.

1807.

Napoleon at Finkenstein—His love of deceit—Situation of France at the close of the year 1807—Napoleon's designs on Spain—The pretext he chose to carry them out—Talleyrand endeavours to dissuade the emperor from wronging the old ally of France—Treaty of Fontainebleau—Napoleon's shameful breach of faith towards Charles IV. of Spain—Don Juan de Escoïquiz, Canon of Toledo, and the Prince of the Asturias—The intrigues of Godoy, Prince of the Peace—Don Escoïquiz' plan to thwart them—The French ambassador and Don Escoïquiz—Napoleon's *ruse*—Letter of the Prince of the Asturias to Napoleon—Letter of the

PART V.

THE ERFURT INTERVIEW.

1808.

l'abbé de perigord a l'honneur de faire
mille complimens de Monsieur de
vergennes, et il le supplie de lui
faire parvenir aujourd'huy avant six
heures du soir les reponses s'il s'en
pouvoit quelque en L'honneur de lui
accorder.

mercredy matin

AUTOGRAPH LETTER OF PRINCE TALLEYRAND TO M. DE VERGENNES, MINISTER OF FOREIGN AFFAIRS OF LOUIS XVI.[1]

[1] This letter, in which the writer solicits a reply to a memorandum handed by him to the French Foreign Secretary, was, in all likelihood, written at the time the young abbé was either *promoteur*, or *agent-général* of the clergy.—(*Translator.*)

MEMOIRS

OF THE

PRINCE DE TALLEYRAND.

PART I.

THE YEARS PRECEDING THE REVOLUTION.

1754—1791.

Talleyrand's birth—His parents—Early years—Is trained for the Church—Sent to Rheims—Coronation of Louis XVI.—Appointed Agent-general to the clergy—French society before the Revolution—Comte de Choiseul-Gouffier—American War of Independence—Relations between England and France—Turgot—de Vergennes—Calonne—Necker—The deficit—The Assembly of the Notables—The meeting of the States-General—Public opinion and the clergy—The French aristocracy on the eve of the Revolution—Talleyrand appointed deputy of the clergy to the States-General—Premonitory symptoms of the Revolution—The Comte d'Artois — The emigration of the nobles — The Constituent Assembly—Restriction of the royal prerogatives—Civil constitution of the clergy—Talleyrand consecrates the first constitutional bishops—Resigns the bishopric of Autun—Interview between Talleyrand and the Comte d'Artois—Baron de Vitrolles' letter to M. de Bacourt.

I WAS born in 1754[1] ; my parents had a very small fortune but held at court a position which, if properly taken advantage of, could secure for themselves and their children the highest offices.

[1] Charles-Maurice de Talleyrand, the author of these memoirs, was the son of Charles-Daniel de Talleyrand-Périgord (1734—1788), lieutenant-general and *menin* * to the Dauphin ; and the grandson of Daniel-Marie de Talleyrand, Comte de Grignols, brigadier-general of the king's armies. Alexandrine de Damas, daughter of Joseph de Damas, Marquis d'Antigny, was his mother. Marie-Elisabeth Chamillard, daughter of Michel Chamillard, Marquis de Cany, was his grandmother.

* The name given, under the old monarchy, to a nobleman attached to the person of the Dauphin. —(*Translator.*)

For a long time, the chief families of France, though not actually disdaining to hold offices attaching them to the person of the sovereign, displayed little anxiety to obtain them. They were satisfied with believing, or affecting to believe, themselves in the foremost rank in the nation. Thus the descendants of the old chief vassals of the Crown had less occasion to be personally known to the king than the descendants of some minor barons of the duchy of France, holding, for this reason, higher offices about the sovereign's person.

The pride which induced most families of high lineage to keep aloof from court, caused the king to view them with less favour.

In order to enhance the royal power, Cardinal Richelieu summoned the heads of chief families before the king. They settled at court, forewent their independence, and, by a more profound devotion, endeavoured to make up for the disadvantage of having come last.

The glory of Louis XIV. was one of the reasons why, under his reign and subsequently, all men's ideas were centred within the limits of the château of Versailles.

The Regency was, so to speak, an interregnum, undisturbed either by financial disasters or by the depravation of morals, the premonitory symptoms of which had been so severely checked at the close of the former reign.

Louis XV. was then enjoying universal respect, the first subjects of the Crown still considered obedience to the sovereign as glorious; they did not conceive any other power or lustre than those proceeding from the king's majesty.

The queen[1] was reverenced, but the very melancholy of her virtues did not prepossess people in her favour. She was wanting in those outward charms that caused the nation to be so proud of the fine features of Louis XV. Hence the mixed feeling of justice and indulgence which on one hand led people to pity the queen, and, on the other, induced them to excuse the inclination shown by the king towards Madame de Pompadour.[2]   M. de

[1] Maria Leczinska, Queen of France, daughter of Stanislas, King of Poland, and of Catherine Opalinska. She was born in 1703; in 1725 she became the wife of Louis XV., by whom she had two sons and eight daughters. She died in 1768.

[2] Jeanne-Antoinette Poisson, Marquise de Pompadour, born in Paris in 1721,

Penthièvre,[1] the *Maréchale* de Duras,[2] Madame de Luynes,[3] Madame de Marsan,[4] Madame de Périgord,[5] the Duchesse de Fleury,[6] M. de Sourches,[7] Madame de Villars,[8] M. de Tavannes,[9] Madame d'Estissac,[10] doubtless grieved at the fact, yet were afraid of disclosing by open reproach what was looked upon as one of those known family secrets, which nobody dares to deny, but hopes to palliate by hushing them up and behaving as though one were not aware of their existence. All the persons I have just mentioned would have considered that they were

died in 1764. She was the daughter of an army contractor, and when quite young married Lenormand d'Etioles, a *fermier-général.* In 1744, she left her husband to become the mistress of the king, who in the following year created her Marquise de Pompadour, with a yearly income of 200,000 livres (about £8,000). In 1756, she was appointed lady of the queen's household. Madame de Pompadour was as remarkable for her taste as for her beauty; she was long the queen of fashion. She preserved her influence until her death. The memoirs and letters published under her name in 1785 are apocryphal.—(*Translator.*)

[1] Louis de Bourbon, Duc de Penthièvre, born in 1725, was the son of the Comte de Toulouse, illegitimate son of Louis XIV. and of Madame de Montespan. He married Mademoiselle d'Este. The Prince of Lamballe was one of his sons; the Duc d'Orléans married one of his daughters. The Duc de Penthièvre was appointed grand-admiral in 1734, and lieutenant-general in 1744. In 1787, he was president of one of the committees of the *assemblée des notables* (a deliberative body whose members were chosen by the king, chiefly from the Third Estate [*Translator*]). He lived on his estates until his death, which occurred in 1793.

[2] Angélique de Bournonville, daughter of the Prince de Bournonville, Comte d'Heim, became in 1706 the wife of Jean-Baptiste de Durfort, Duc de Duras, Marshal of France. She was lady in waiting to *Mesdames* the daughters of Louis XV., and died in 1764.

[3] Marie Brûlart de la Borde, daughter of a chief judge in the *parlement* of Dijon, was the second wife of Philippe d'Albert, Duc de Luynes, whom she married in 1732. She was lady in waiting to the queen and died in 1763.

[4] Marie-Louise de Rohan-Soubise, a relation of the marshal of this name, was born in 1720. In 1736, she married Gaston de Lorraine, Comte de Marsan. She was governess to the *enfants de France* (the graceful name given to the royal children under the old *régime* [*Translator*]).

[5] Marguerite de Talleyrand, daughter of Louis de Talleyrand, Prince de Chalais, was the grand-aunt of the author. She was born in 1727, and married Gabriel de Talleyrand, Comte de Périgord, in 1743.

[6] Anne d'Auxy de Monceaux, born in 1721, married in 1736, André de Rosset, Duc de Fleury, a relation of the cardinal of this name. In 1739, she was appointed lady of the queen's household.

[7] Louis François du Bouchet, Comte de Sourches, Marquis de Tourzel, knight of Malta, grand provost of France, was born in 1744. In 1764, he married Louise de Croy d'Havré.

[8] Gabrielle de Noailles, daughter of the Marshal Duc de Noailles, was born in 1706. In 1721, she became the wife of Armand, Duc de Villars, son of the marshal of this name. She was successively lady of the queen's household and lady of the bedchamber, and died in 1771.

[9] Charles, Comte de Saulx-Tavannes, was born in 1713. In 1758, he was lieutenant-general and *Knight of Honour* (equerry) to the queen.

[10] Marie de la Rochefoucauld (known as Mademoiselle de la Roche-Guyon), was born in 1718. In 1737, she was married to Louis de la Rochefoucauld de Roye, Duc d'Estissac, grand master of the wardrobe.

forfeiting their honour by admitting too openly the failings of the king.

My relatives held various situations with the royal family. My grandmother was lady of the queen's household, and was treated with especial regard by the king ; she always resided at Versailles and kept no house in Paris.

She had five children. Like that of all persons connected with the court, their early tuition was rather neglected, or, at least, devoted to few important branches of knowledge. As to their subsequent education, it was to consist merely in imparting to them what was termed the usages of society. Their outward appearance was prepossessing.

My grandmother had noble, refined and reserved manners. Her piety won universal respect for her, and the fact of her numerous family caused the frequent steps she took towards securing and promoting the future of her children to be regarded as quite natural.

My father held the same views as his mother concerning the education befitting children whose parents enjoyed a position at court. Thus mine was rather left to take care of itself : not through any indifference towards me, but owing to the special disposition of the mind which leads some people to consider that the best plan is *to do or to be like everybody else.*

Too much care would have seemed pedantry ; affection too openly expressed would have been regarded as quite unusual and therefore ridiculous. Children, at that time, inherited their father's *name and coat of arms.* Parents considered they had done enough for their progeny by opening a career to them and securing for them advantageous posts ; by marrying them and increasing their allowance.

Paternal care had not yet come into fashion ; the fashion was indeed the very reverse, when I was a child ; thus my early years were cheerlessly spent in an outlying district of Paris. At the age of four, I was still there, when I accidentally fell from the top of a cupboard, and dislocated my foot. The woman to whose care I was entrusted only informed my family of this several months afterwards. The truth became known only when my parents sent for me to go to Périgord to visit Madame de Chalais,[1] my grandmother, who had expressed a wish to see me. Although Madame de Chalais was my great-grandmother, I always called her *grandma*, very likely, I think, because this name implied a closer relationship. The dislocation of my foot was already too old to be remedied ; even my other foot having had to bear alone the whole weight of my body, had grown weaker, and thus I remained lame for life.

This accident had a great influence on my after-life. It indeed led my parents to think I was unfit for a military career, or at least, that, in such, I should labour under great disadvantages ; they were thus induced to seek for me some other profession, which, in their eyes, would be best calculated to serve the interests of the *family*. For, in great families, the *family* was far more cared for than its members individually, especially than those young members who were still unknown. These considerations are rather painful to my mind . . . so I will not dwell further on them.

In the Bordeaux coach, I was entrusted to the care of a kindly woman named Mademoiselle Charlemagne, and after a journey, which lasted seventeen days, I reached Chalais.[2]

Madame de Chalais was a most refined and distinguished lady ; her mind, her language, the dignity of her manners, the sound of her voice, were most winning. She still retained what was termed the wit of the Mortemarts, being indeed a Mortemart by birth.

My appearance pleased her ; she acquainted me with feelings hitherto unknown to me. She was the first member of my family who displayed any affection towards me, and also the first who taught me the sweetness of filial love. God bless her for it ! . . . For I was really fondly attached to her ! To this day, her memory is dear to me. Many a time have I regretted her ! Many a time have I bitterly understood how priceless is the

[1] Marie-Françoise de Rochechouart, daughter of Louis de Rochechouart, Duc de Mortemart, married Michel Chamillart, Marquis de Cany, by whom she had a daughter —the author's grandmother. After the death of the marquis, Marie-Françoise, his widow, became the wife of Louis Charles de Talleyrand, Prince de Chalais, Spanish grandee, who died in 1757.

[2] Chalais, chief town of the *canton* (administrative district) of Charente, near Barbezieux.

sincere affection of some member of one's own family. Such
affection affords immense comfort through the trials and troubles
of life, when those who inspire it are near to us. When they
are away, it soothes both the heart and the mind, and enables
us calmly to collect our thoughts.

The time spent at Chalais left a deep impression on my mind.
The dispositions of children and their after-life inclinations
are often determined by the objects which first impressed their
eyes and minds.

In the provinces distant from the capital, a certain care paid
to dignity and position, ruled the relations existing between the
members of the old aristocracy still residing on their estates, and
the lesser nobility and the tenants on the said estates.   The
chief nobleman of a province would have considered it beneath
him not to have been kind and polite.   His more distinguished
neighbours would have considered it a want of self-respect
to fail in displaying towards the bearers of ancient names
that regard and respect, which, expressed, as it was, freely and
without emphasis, seemed but the homage of the heart.   As to
the peasantry, their lord only visited them to assist and address
to them some kind and comforting words, the influence of which
was felt in the neighbourhood, for the minor nobility endeavoured
to follow the example set them by the leading aristocracy of
their province.

The manners of the Périgord nobility resembled their old
castles ; they were imposing and firmly based ; the light of modern
refinement only came subdued.   People were moving slowly but
wisely towards a more enlightened stage of civilization.

The tyranny of petty lords no longer existed ; it had been
stamped out by the spirit of chivalry, by the gallant and
courteous feelings the latter gave rise to amongst Southern
nations, and chiefly by the growth of royal power based on the
emancipation of peoples.

Those whose career at court was over, were fond of retiring
to the provinces that had witnessed the greatness of their
families.   Once back on their estates, they there enjoyed the
affectionate and respectful consideration of all around them—a
consideration enhanced by the traditions of the province and the

recollection of the past might of their ancestors. This regard reflected a certain credit on the persons composing the *entourage* of the descendants of the families which were formerly the sole dispensers of lordly favours in the district. The Revolution itself failed to tarnish the lustre of, or to break the spell possessed by, these ancient seats of sovereign power. The castles of provincial lords are like those old deserted shrines from which the faithful have fled, but whose traditions still enforce respect.

Chalais Castle was one of the relics of those revered and dear old times. My grandmother there held, as it were, a court composed of several gentlemen of ancient families, very different from the vassals of the thirteenth century, but whose deference and refined manners were mingled with the loftiest feelings. M. de Benac, M. de Verteuil, M. d'Absac, M. de Gourville, M. de Chauveron, M. de Chamillard, delighted in accompanying her every Sunday to the parish mass, each of them discharging towards her duties dignified by exquisite politeness. A little chair close to my grandmother's *prie-dieu* was reserved for me.

On returning from mass, everybody met in a spacious hall in the castle called the *Apothicaireric*.[1] This room contained various large jars carefully disposed on shelves and kept with scrupulous cleanliness ; they were filled with ointments, the recipes of which had always been faithfully preserved at the castle. Every year they were prepared with the greatest care by the village surgeon and vicar. There were besides a few bottles of elixirs and syrups, as well as boxes containing other medicaments. In the cupboards was stored a considerable stock of lint and of very fine old linen bands of various widths.

All the sick persons who required assistance were assembled in the preceding room. We greeted them as we passed through. Mademoiselle Saunier, a chambermaid who had been longest in my grandmother's service, introduced them in turn. My grandmother was seated on a velvet armchair ; in front of her was placed an old black lacquered table. She wore a silk dress, trimmed with lace, with a riband collarette and sleeve-knots suited to the season. She also wore triple cuffs with large designs ; a tippet, a head-dress adorned with a butterfly, and a

[1] The surgery.

black mantilla tied under the chin.   Such was her Sunday attire, more elegant than that she wore on week-days.

The red velvet bag trimmed with gold lace, containing my grandmother's books of devotion, was carried by M. de Benac, who, on his great-grandmother's side, was distantly related to us.

My close relationship secured for me a seat next to the old lady.   Two sisters of mercy, having questioned each patient as to the nature of his disease or sore, mentioned the special ointment likely to heal or relieve him.   My grandmother pointed out where the remedy was kept ; one of the gentlemen who had waited on her at church fetched it, whilst another brought the drawer containing the linen : of this I took a piece, from which my grandmother herself cut the quantity required for bandages. Each patient then received some plants for his potion, some wine, the medicine prescribed, and always some other substantial relief, but that which most touched his heart, were the kind and considerate words from the good lady who endeavoured to alleviate his sufferings.

More learned and elaborate drugs, even if distributed as gratuitously by famous doctors, would have failed to attract as many poor people, and especially, to do them as much good. Carefulness, respect, faith, and gratitude, the chief means of cure for the lower classes, would have been absent.

Man is a compound of a body and soul, which latter rules the former.   Wounded men to whose sores the balm of consolation has been applied, patients to whom words of hope have been spoken, are on the high road to recovery ; their blood flows more freely, their humours get purified, their nerves are invigorated, sleep returns to them, and their bodies regain strength. Confidence is the most efficient of all remedies, and it is strongest when it proceeds from the solicitude of a lady of rank with whom all ideas of power and protection are connected.

I am perhaps dwelling too long on these details, but I am not writing a book, I am only noting my impressions.   The recollection of what I saw and heard during these early years of my life is extremely pleasant to my mind.   " Your name," I was daily told, " was always held in veneration in our province."—" Our family," people affectionately said to me, "was at all times serving some member of yours. . . . This piece of ground we received from your grandfather . . . he it was who built our church . . . my mother's cross is a gift from your grandmother . . . he who comes from a good stock cannot degenerate ! You will be kind too, will you not ? " . . . I am very likely indebted to these early years for the general spirit of my conduct in life. If I displayed affectionate and even tender feelings without too much familiarity ; if, in various circumstances, I showed pride without haughtiness ; if I love and respect old people, it is at Chalais, by the side of my grandmother, that I imbibed all the good feelings which surrounded my relatives in that district, and which they enjoyed with delight. For, there are feelings which increase from generation to generation. For a long time to come, people, whose fame or fortune are of recent origin will be unable to appreciate their sweetness.[1] The best of them are always too much inclined to act the part of protectors. Let the wife of Marshal Lefebvre[2] say to the head of some noble Alsatian family, devoid of resources and just returned from emigration : " What shall we do with your eldest son ? . . . In what regiment shall we place his brother ? . . . Have we got some living in view for the abbé ? . . . When shall we marry Henrietta ? . . . I know a convent where we ought to send the little girl . . ." Though wishing really to be kind, she will simply appear ridiculous. Inward feelings will cause him to decline her kindness, and the pride of poverty will even experience a certain satisfaction at such a refusal. But, I am quite forgetting that I am but eight years old ; and as yet incapable of foreseeing that present manners bear evident signs that these inherited feelings will gradually dwindle away.

I learned at Chalais all that could possibly be learned in the

---

[1] The article in the Charter * stating that the old and new titles are preserved has no more sense than the motion made by M. Mathieu de Montmorency to the Constituent Assembly, to abolish all titles. In our government, the political nobility resides wholly in the House of Peers ; and there, it is individual. Outside of it, some people bear names connected with some historical facts, but which confer no legal rights, and which it is impossible either to over- or underrate.—(*Prince Talleyrand.*)

[2] When but a private, Marshal Lefebvre, Duc de Dantzig, had married the laundress of his regiment.

* The Charter of liberties granted to France by Louis XVIII. on his return from Mittau.—(*Transl.*)

place, that is, to read, write and to a certain extent, to speak the *patois* of the province. My studies had been limited to this when I had to return to Paris. On taking leave of my grandmother I shed tears, and so did she, so great was her affection for me. As on coming down, so on returning, the Bordeaux coach was seventeen days on the way.

At eleven o'clock on the morning of the seventeenth day, I reached Paris. An old valet of my family was waiting for me at the station in the Rue d'Enfer, and took me direct to the Collège d'Harcourt,[1] where, at twelve o'clock, I was seated at dinner by the side of a charming boy of my age who shared, and still shares, all the cares, pleasures, and dreams of my life. This was M. de Choiseul, known ever since his marriage under the name of de Choiseul-Gouffier.[2] I had been painfully impressed by having been so hurriedly despatched to college without having been previously taken to my father and mother. I was then eight years old, and the eyes of my parents had not yet rested on me. I was told, and believed it, that all this hurried arrangement was due to some unforeseen and unavoidable circumstance : so I followed my path.

On arriving at college, I was led to the apartment of M. de la Suze,[3] a cousin of mine, and entrusted to the care of his own tutor.[4]

If I succeeded at all in my studies, that result cannot be ascribed either to the example of my cousin, or to the talents of my teacher.

[1] This college, which had been founded for the benefit of twenty-four poor students from Normandy, in 1280, by Raoul d'Harcourt, canon of the Paris clergy, was, at the time of the Revolution, the oldest educational establishment in Paris. It was turned into a prison during the Reign of Terror, and afterwards became the quarters of the *École normale.* It resumed its first character only in 1820, when it took the name of Lycée Saint-Louis, which it preserves to this day.

[2] The Comte Auguste de Choiseul-Beaupré, born in 1752, married Marie de Gouffier, whose name he added to his own. He was at first captain in the Cuirassiers, but gave way to his taste for travelling, and visited all the East. In 1784, he was appointed ambassador at Constantinople. In 1789, he retired to Russia, returned to France in 1802, was appointed peer of France, State Minister, and member of the Privy Council by Louis XVIII., and died in 1817.

[3] Son of Louis-Michel Chamillard, Comte de la Suze, who was born in 1709, and became in 1748 Grand Marshal of the King's Household, and lieutenant-general (1748). His mother having become a widow at an early age, married Daniel Marie, Prince de Talleyrand, and became the grandmother of the author of these memoirs. Young de la Suze, who is mentioned here, was therefore the cousin of Prince de Talleyrand.

[4] The Abbé Hardi.

Once a week, the Abbé Hardi called with me on my
parents, and we dined with them.   On rising from table,
I went back to college always hearing the same injunction :
"*Be a good boy, and give satisfaction to the Abbé.*"   I got
on pretty well ; my schoolfellows liked me and I cheerfully
submitted to my new position.   I had been living that life
for three years when I caught the small-pox ; the latter
being contagious, I had to leave college.   My family, having
been informed of my illness by my tutor, my parents sent me a
sedan-chair to take me to the Rue Saint-Jacques, to the house of
Madame Lerond, a nurse employed by M. Lehoc, the college
physician.   In these days, small-pox patients slept in beds
surrounded by double curtains ; the windows of their room were
made proof against draughts, a blazing fire was kept up in it,
and fever excited by means of suitable beverages.   In spite of
this murderous treatment, which killed many people, I got over
the disease, and was not even marked.

I was then twelve years old ; during the time of my con-
valescence the peculiarity of my position struck me.   My heart
was full at the little interest aroused by my illness, the fact of
my having been sent to college without having seen my parents,
and some other grievous recollections.   I felt myself isolated,
helpless and always shut up in myself : I do not complain of it, for
I believe that my early meditations developed and strengthened
my thinking powers.   My sad and cheerless childhood is the cause
of my having exercised these powers at an early age, and of
having accustomed myself to think more deeply, perhaps, than
I should have done, had my early life been filled with happiness and joy.   It may also be that these first trials of my
life taught me to bear misfortune and disappointment with
indifference, and to meet the latter with the resources which my
self-confidence showed me I possessed.

There is a sort of pleasant pride in these recollections of my
youth.

In after-life, it has struck me that my parents, having decided,
in consequence of what they regarded as the interest of the
family that I should be trained to a profession for which I
showed no aptitude, were afraid that they might fail to carry

out their object, if they saw me too often. That fear is a proof
of affection, for which I ought to feel indebted to them.

When M. de la Suze's education was finished, or, rather,
when he was sixteen years old, the Abbé Hardi, his tutor,
retired. For a few months, I was entrusted to the care of a
gentleman named Hullot, who soon after went mad. My new
tutor was M. Langlois, with whom I remained until I left college,
and who brought up my brothers afterwards. He was a perfect
gentleman, but versed in nothing but French history, and who
had devoted too much attention to the perusal of the *Court
Directory*. In books of that kind he had learned that the post
of *cape-bearer to princes* [1] conferred nobility, and that such a post
was given on the introduction of the Grand-Marshal. The
Grand-Marshal being my uncle,[2] we secured for M. Langlois the
post he was so eager to obtain. In 1790, my former tutor had his
court-dress made and emigrated, so that his letters of nobility
might bear a good date. He, however, was in too great a hurry
to enjoy his new privilege, and, having returned to France during
the revolutionary period, was sent to prison. So that now, having
a twofold fame, by emigration and imprisonment, he calmly
spends the rest of his life in the noble company of the Faubourg
Saint-Germain. From this, it may be judged that if I have,
since these days, given way to the temptation of playing a
part in public affairs, M. Langlois is in no wise responsible
for it.

I might have been a successful scholar: my natural bent
leads me to think so, and I notice that this opinion is almost uni-
versally shared by my schoolfellows. The little encouragement
given me, for fear lest I should become too clever a young man, is
the cause that the first years of my life were spent in a rather
dull and insignificant manner.

When the time of what is termed the *conclusion of studies*
arrived, the complete silence of my father as to my future, and
a few conversations held in my hearing, were the first intimation I had of the career intended for me.

In order to give me a high and even tempting idea of the
profession marked out for me, it was thought advisable to send

---

[1] *Porte-manteau chez les princes.*   [2] The Comte de la Suze.

me to Rheims, the chief archbishopric of France, to the titular of which one of my uncles was coadjutor.[1] As, for my family's sake, it was not becoming for me to alight from the coach at the archbishop's residence, my journey to Rheims was more comfortable than that to Chalais had been. A post-chaise called for me at the Collège d'Harcourt, and drove me to my destination in a couple of days.

My parents did not send for me before I left. I repeat this here, and hope never to think of it again. I am, perhaps, the only man of distinguished birth and belonging to a numerous and esteemed family, who did not, for one week in his life, enjoy the sweetness of being under his father's roof.

The disposition of my mind led me to consider my new abode as but an ill-disguised exile, notwithstanding all the precautions taken to render it attractive.

The opulence, the consideration, the very pleasures of the Archbishop of Rheims and of his coadjutor were to me indifferent. A life full of formalities was unbearable to me. At the age of fifteen, when all our impulses are still natural, we can scarcely conceive that circumspection, that is, the art of disclosing only a portion of one's actions, thoughts, feelings, and impressions, should be the foremost of all qualities. In my opinion, all the wealth and pomp of Cardinal de la Roche-Aymon,[2] did not deserve the complete sacrifice of my sincerity, which was asked from me.

All the care and attention paid me only tended to impress me deeply with the idea that, my lame foot rendering me incapable of serving in the army, I must necessarily enter holy orders, as no other career was open to a man of my name. . . . Yet what was to become of the lively imagination and wit with

[1] Alexandre de Talleyrand was born in 1736. He was successively coadjutor of the Archbishop of Rheims (1766), Archbishop *in partibus* of Trajanopolis, Archbishop-Duc of Rheims (1777), and deputy of the clergy to the States-General (1789). In 1801, he declined to resign, was called to Mittau by Louis XVIII., in 1803, and became Grand-Chaplain of France in 1808. Peer of France in 1814, Cardinal in 1817, and finally Archbishop of Paris, he died in 1821. He was the paternal uncle of the author.

[2] Charles-Antoine, Comte de la Roche-Aymon, was born in 1697. He was Vicar-General of Limoges and Bishop *in partibus* of Sarepta in 1725. Bishop of Tarbes, Archbishop of Toulouse in 1740, and of Narbonne in 1752, he became Grand-Chaplain of France in 1760, Archbishop-Duc of Rheims in 1762, Cardinal in 1771, and died in 1777.

which I was credited ?   The only plan then was to hold out to
me the attraction of public life, and to picture to me the advantages to be obtained from it.   They sought to avail themselves
of the characteristics I might happen to possess.

With this object, I was induced to read the *Memoirs* of
Cardinal de Retz, the life of Cardinal Richelieu, that of Cardinal
Ximenes, and that of Hincmard, a former Cardinal of Rheims.
. . . Whatever might be the path I entered upon, my parents
were disposed to agree to it, provided I crossed the threshold of
the Church.

The constant pressure brought to bear on me did not fix my
resolution, but rather unsettled it.   Youth is the time in life
when we are most honest.   I did not then understand what it
was to embrace one profession with the intention of following
another, to assume a part of constant self-denial in order the
better to succeed in an ambitious career ; to join the Church
in order to become Minister of Finances.   It required too great
a knowledge of the society which I was entering, and of the
times in which I was living, to regard this as a matter of course.

But, being alone, I was defenceless ; all the persons who
surrounded me spoke a conventional language, and carefully
concealed from me all means of avoiding the carrying out of the
plan my parents had formed respecting my future.

I spent a year at Rheims, at the expiration of which, seeing
that my fate could not be avoided, my wearied mind submitted :
I allowed myself to be taken to Saint-Sulpice College.[1]

More thoughtful than is usual at the age I was then, rebellious,
but powerless, indignant, without either daring to, or being justified in, displaying my indignation, there are few instances of a
lad of sixteen being as despondent and cheerless as I was on
entering that college.   I formed no intimacy.   I did everything
in cross-temper.   I had a grudge against my masters, my
parents, institutions generally, but chiefly against the sway of
social propriety to which I saw myself obliged to give way.

[1] Saint-Sulpice College was founded in 1542 by M. Jean-Jacques Oliier, curé of
the parish ; it was at first situated at Vaugirard.   It soon acquired considerable
importance, owing to the excellence of its tuition and to its strict ecclesiastical
discipline.   The present building was erected by M. Le Ragon de Bretonvilliers, curé
of Saint-Sulpice parish.   It contains a magnificent ceiling painted by Charles Le
Brun, the famous artist.—(*Translator.*)

I spent three years at Saint-Sulpice College, and hardly spoke at all during the whole time ; people thought I was supercilious and often reproached me with being so. This seemed to me so to point out how little they knew me, that I deigned no reply ; they then said that my arrogance was beyond all endurance. Good Heavens! I was neither arrogant nor proud : I was merely a harmless young man, extremely miserable and inwardly irritated. *People say*, I often thought to myself, *that I am fit for nothing.* . . . . Fit for nothing. . . . . After giving way to despondency, for a few moments, a strong and comforting feeling cheered me, and I discovered *that I was fit for something, even for good and noble deeds.* What forebodings, a thousand times dispelled, did not then cross my mind, always placing me under a spell which I was unable to explain !

The library of Saint-Sulpice College had been enriched by gifts from Cardinal de Fleury ; its works were numerous and carefully selected. I spent my days there reading the productions of great historians, the private lives of statesmen and moralists, and a few poets. I was particularly fond of books of travels. A new land, the dangers of a storm, the picture of a wreck, the description of a country bearing traces of great changes, sometimes of upheavals, all this had deep interest for me. Sometimes, when I considered these voyages to distant lands, these dreadful scenes described so vividly in the writings of modern explorers, it seemed to me that my lot was not so hopeless as I had thought. A good library affords true comfort to all the dispositions of the soul.

My third and really useful education dates from this time, it was self-taught in lonely silence ; as I was always face to face with the author whose work I was reading, and could only use my own judgment, it nearly always happened that, when my opinions differed from those of another, I thought mine the right one. My ideas thus remained personally my own : the books I read enlightened my mind, but never enslaved it. I do not pretend to say that in so acting I was right or wrong, I merely state what I was. Such lonely self-tuition must have some value. If injustice, whilst developing our faculties, has not embittered our hearts too much, we derive greater comfort from lofty thoughts and noble impulses, we feel stronger in confronting life's trials. A feeling of hope, vague and indescribable, like all youthful passions, excited my mind : I never allowed it to rest.

By the merest chance, I met a person who had some influence in modifying the disposition in which I then was. I recollect this meeting with pleasure, because I am most likely indebted to it for having been spared all the effects of melancholy brought to its most intense degree. I had reached the age of the mysterious revelations of the soul and of the passions, the moment in life when all our faculties break forth in super-abundant and full activity. I had several times noticed, in one of the lateral shrines of Saint-Sulpice church, a hand-some young lady whose simple and modest look pleased me extremely. At eighteen, this is an attraction for any young man who is not depraved : I attended the chief services more assiduously. One day, as she left the church, a severe shower set in which emboldened me to propose to her to see her home, provided she did not live too far. She agreed to share my umbrella. I accompanied her to Rue Férou, where she was lodging ; she allowed me to see her to her apartments ; and, quite naturally, like a very pure young lady, she proposed that I should come again. At first, I availed myself of her offer about twice a week, and afterwards more often. Her parents had sent her on the stage against her wish ; I was a clerical student against mine. This sway of interest in her case, and of ambition in mine, brought about mutual unreserved confidence between us. All the troubles of my life, all my fits of ill-humour, her own trials and disappointments, occupied all our conversations. I have since been told that she had not much sense : although I saw her almost daily for two years, I never noticed it.

Thanks to her, I became even in college more amiable, or at least better-tempered. My superiors cannot have failed to have had some suspicion of what had reconciled me to my position and even made me somewhat cheerful. But the Abbé Couturier [1] had taught them the art of being blind when necessary ; he had told

---

[1] The Abbé Couturier was born in 1688. He was a friend of Cardinal de Fleury, who appointed him Abbot of Chaumes, and afterwards head of Saint-Sulpice College. He died in 1770.

them never to find fault with a young student whom they regarded as destined to fill high posts, to become coadjutor to the archbishop of Rheims, perhaps a cardinal, perhaps even *Ministre de la feuille.*[1] How could any one tell?

I left college[2] some time before the coronation of the king.[3] My parents sent me to Rheims in order to attend this ceremony. The power of the clergy was then at its height; the bishop suffragan of Rheims was to officiate, in case the old age of Cardinal de la Roche-Aymon should, as it was feared, prevent him from attending this solemn ceremony. . . What a glorious time! . . .

A young king, scrupulously moral and uncommonly modest; ministers, well known for their ability and uprightness; a queen whose affableness, grace and kindness tempered the austere virtues of her consort; everybody filled with respect! the heart of every subject overflowing with affection for the young sovereigns! joy was everywhere! . . Never did such a bright spring precede such a stormy autumn, such a dismal winter.

My acquaintance with several women remarkable in different ways, and whose friendship never ceased to give a charm to my life, dates from the coronation of Louis XVI. These ladies were the Duchesse de Luynes,[4] the Duchesse de Fitz-James,[5] and the Vicomtesse de Laval.[6]

---

[1] Literally, Minister of the Roll (of benefices). The *feuille* was a book in which were inscribed all the vacant benefices in the gift of the Crown. This book was kept by a prelate, to whom, in fact, the power of nomination was delegated by the king. All the bishoprics or abbeys in the gift of the Crown were thus conferred by the *Ministre de la feuille.*

[2] It may be noticed that M. de Talleyrand does not mention here either the exact date of his ordination, or the circumstances attending this ceremony. The Comte de Choiseul-Gouffier, speaking on this subject, related that, having called on M. de Talleyrand on the evening preceding his ordination, he found him in a state of violent inward struggle, all in tears, and giving way to despair. M. de Choiseul then endeavoured to persuade his friend not to consummate the sacrifice; but the fear of his mother, of a tardy scandal, a certain false pride, held him back, and he exclaimed, " It is too late, there is no retreating now."—(*M. de Bacourt.*)

[3] 11th June, 1775.

[4] Elisabeth de Montmorency-Laval, daughter of the Marshal Duc de Montmorency Laval, married in 1768 Louis d'Albert, Duc de Luynes, who was Brigadier-General, Deputy to the States-General, and Senator under the Empire.

[5] Probably Marie de Thiard, daughter of Henry de Thiard, Comte de Bissy, who married in 1768 the Duc de Fitz-James, Brigadier-General.

[6] Catherine Tavernier de Boullongne, who, in 1765 married Mathieu de Montmorency-Laval, known under the name of Vicomte de Laval.

The assembly of the clergy[1] was about to sit, I was elected by the province of Rheims to be a member of this assembly.. I carefully watched how business was conducted in this important body. Ambition was there represented in various disguises. Religion, humanity, patriotism, philosophy, each of these had its so-called supporters ! Whenever the pecuniary interests of the clergy were threatened, all the members rose in defence of these interests, though they did not all resort to the same arguments. The most pious bishops expressed the fear that the proposed reforms would diminish the share of the poor ; those who belonged to the high aristocracy, were afraid of any innovation ; those whose ambition was an open secret, claimed that the clergy, being the most enlightened body of the kingdom, should be at the head of all government administrations, and, in order not to be a burden on the State, should find, in the wealth bequeathed them by our pious forefathers, the means of facing the expenses necessarily involved in the tenure of high State offices. Thus, in the management of their temporal affairs, the clergy of the eighteenth century made no concessions to the spirit of the times. When M. de Machault,[2] Minister of Finances, proposed to tax the property of the clergy like that of all other subjects, the whole clergy rose to oppose the motion, and declared that they would not submit to this measure. Property given to the Church, they said, belongs to God and is consecrated to Him. This consecration has the effect of imparting to such property a peculiar destination, and the ministers of religion are its sole dis-

[1] These assemblies or general meetings of the clergy dated from the sixteenth century. Since 1567, they were held every five years. Their object was to determine and portion out the amount of supplies (free gift) to be paid to the king. They also dealt with religious matters. They were divided into ordinary and extraordinary or plenary assemblies, which sat alternately. The session of the latter lasted six months, and comprised two deputies of the first order, and two of the second, for each ecclesiastical province ; the ordinary or minor assemblies only lasted three months, and were only composed of a single deputy of each order for each province.

[2] Jean-Baptiste de Machault, Comte d'Arnouville, was born in 1701, from an old family of magistrates. He became successively Counsellor of *parlement* * (1721), Comptroller-General (1745-1754), Keeper of the Seals (1750), and Secretary of State to the Marine Department. He was dismissed from all his posts in 1757, and lived in retirement until the Revolution. Having been arrested in 1794, he died in prison a few weeks later.

* The *parlements* were but courts of law established in the chief cities of old France. They had no political character : the *parlement* of Paris, however, assumed this character on several occasions, and refused to register certain royal edicts, which registration constituted its exclusive privilege, and gave the edicts the force of law.—(*Translator.*)

pensers and managers ; the immunity of Church property is a
principle of French public law.   The interference of conscience
in all these financial quarrels enabled the clergy to display, in
the discussion of this important matter, a degree of eloquence
which they alone possess.   M. de Montauset,[1] M. de Breteuil,[2]
and M. de Nicolaï,[3] having attracted attention by their brilliant
speeches, took up a prominent position in the assembly, and
enjoyed all the importance given them by M. de Machault's
resignation.

The government gave way on the subject of possession, but
mooted another point, which referred to the mode by which the
clergy had obtained possession of their property, and might lead
to the shaking of the very principle of possession. The question
was, to decide whether the clergy were subjected to fealty and
homage, to avowal and enumeration, in short, to feudal duties
towards the king.   It had been discussed several times since the
beginning of the seventeenth century, and, on every occasion, the
clergy had obtained a favourable decision ; but, as they could
not produce any documentary evidence in support of their claims,
they had been subjected to renewed attacks. In 1725, the clergy
having refused to admit the tax of the fiftieth, the government
enforced the execution of a previous declaration, according to
which the clergy's pretension that they were excused from discharging their feudal duties, was pronounced null and erroneous.
Since then, on various pretexts, the clergy had obtained at each
subsequent assembly, orders, which, without deciding the case,
suspended the application of the law of 1674.

Some difficulties and some delays in the engrossing of the
order of suspension[4] of 1775, induced the clergy to make fresh
efforts.   The works of Dom Bouquet[5] were consulted ; and, in

----

[1] No person of this name existed at that time.   The author probably means
M. de Montazet, born in 1713, chaplain to the king in 1742, Bishop of Autun in 1748,
Archbishop of Lyons in 1759, and who died in 1788.

[2] François-Victor le Tonnelier de Breteuil, born in 1724, Bishop of Montauban in
1762.

[3] There were at this time, two prelates belonging to the Nicolaï family : Louis-
Marie, born in 1729, Bishop of Cahors in 1777 ; Aimar-Claude, born in 1738, Bishop
of Béziers in 1771, who emigrated in 1792, and died in Florence in 1814.

[4] *Arrêt de surséance.*

[5] Dom Martin Bouquet, a learned Benedictine monk, born at Amiens (1685–1754).
Chief Librarian of the Abbey of Saint-Germain-des-Près.   He is the author of a work

numerous memoirs, of one of which, I believe, I am the author, the clergy set forth that seeing that they held their immunity from the munificence of the kings of France, their case was ruled by the general legislation of the kingdom, which protects equally the rights of all the orders[1] and the property of all citizens. Going further into the details of the case, they pretended that all the property they possessed previous to the year 1700, proceeded from tithes, allodium, or free gifts.[2] So that no feudal service being due for tithes, allodium, or free gifts, the conclusion was that all the property of the clergy should be free from feudal duties. I do not recollect how they got over the difficulty arising from spiritual peerages.[3] The Archbishops of Narbonne,[4] of Aix,[5] of Bordeaux,[6] and the Bishop of Nevers,[7] displayed great ability in the course of this great debate. But the explanations obtained from the Chamber of Accounts[8] in pursuance of an Order in Council, and furnished

entitled *Recueil des Historiens de la Gaule* ("Collection of the Historians of Gaul"). Another Bouquet, a renowned jurist and a nephew of the latter, died in 1781; he published various works on ecclesiastical law. There may have been some confusion between the two, and the works of the nephew may thus have been erroneously ascribed to his uncle.

[1] The nation, as is known, was divided into three orders : the clergy, the nobility, and the third estate.—(*Translator.*)

[2] *Franches aumônes* was the name given to free gifts made to churches or hospitals.—(*Translator.*)

[3] The spiritual or temporal peers of the kingdom owed fealty and homage to the king, and had to discharge all the feudal duties towards him.

[4] Arthur de Dillon, born in 1721, Bishop of Evreux (1753), Archbishop of Toulouse (1758), of Narbonne (1762), President of the States of Languedoc, and of the assembly of the clergy held in 1780.

[5] Jean-de-Dieu Raymond de Boisgelin, born at Rennes in 1732, Bishop of Lavaur (1765), Archbishop of Aix (1770), President of the States of Provence, deputy of the clergy to the States-General, President of the Constituent Assembly (1790). He emigrated, returned to France in 1802, was appointed Archbishop of Tours and Cardinal, and died in 1804.

[6] Ferdinand Mériadec, Prince de Rohan-Guéménée, born in 1738, Archbishop of Bordeaux (1769), and of Cambrai (1781). He emigrated in 1792, returned to France in 1802, and was appointed chaplain to the Empress Josephine.

[7] Jean Antoine Tinseau, born at Besançon (1697), Bishop of Nevers (1751).

[8] The *Chambre des Comptes* was a supreme court from whose decisions there was no appeal. It was instituted for the hearing and verification of the accounts of all officials entrusted with public money. It had also to take all necessary measures for the preservation of the Crown estates and property. Besides the Chamber of Accounts of Paris, there were similar courts in the chief towns of the kingdom. The Chamber of Accounts of Paris was founded by Philip the Fair. The Chamber of Paris verified and registered all the ordinances concerning estates, revenues, or expenditure of the Crown, the letters of nobility, the deeds of recognition or legitimization of natural children, the deeds relating to the sinking of debts, the deeds of appanage, &c. It received the oaths of allegiance and homage to the king from his vassals, and registered all Crown leases and generally all matters concerning the finances of the State.—(*Translator.*)

by M. de Saint-Genis,[1] were on the point of bringing about a decision exactly in opposition to the pretensions of the clergy, when the States-General dispersed everybody.

Some philosophical views shared, as already mentioned, by the most ambitious portion of the clergy, had induced several prominent bishops to solicit the carrying out of the Order in Council of 1766, according to which the king was to appoint a commission to deal with reforms to be introduced in a few regular religious orders.[2] A particular reform such as this, so much in keeping with the ideas of the time, must necessarily lead to a general attack upon these illustrious bodies. Having once dispersed all that learned staff, it became easier to approach the whole ecclesiastical edifice, which, being thus deprived of what constitutes its leading spirit and strength, could not long defend itself with the weapons afforded by the external ceremonies of religion alone.

M. de Brienne,[3] Archbishop of Toulouse, who sought support in the new ideas, was chairman of the Commission in 1776. The religious orders of Sainte-Croix and of Grandmont, the Camaldules, the Servites, the Celestines, had already been abolished. The order of Saint-Rufus had just shared a similar fate.[4] The commissioners, in the reports in which they proposed

[1] Nicolas de Saint-Genis, born in 1741, died in 1808 ; *Commissaire des guerres* (an officer in the Commissariat) (1762), auditor in the Court of Accounts (1769). He is the author of a valuable work on ecclesiastical law.

[2] The reform of religious orders was urged in 1765 by the assembly of the clergy itself. In consequence, the King's Council, in an order dated May 26, 1766, appointed a commission to examine the reforms which it was proper to apply to conventual life. This commission was composed of five prelates and five councillors of state ; it drew up the ordinance of March 24, 1768, which set forth—1st, that the age at which vows should be valid was henceforth to be twenty for men, and eighteen for women ; 2nd, that members of religious orders of either sex should be French ; 3rd, that no town should have more than two convents of the same order ; 4th, that each monastery should comprise at least fifteen monks or nuns.

[3] Etienne de Loménie, Comte de Brienne, born in 1727, Bishop of Condom (1760), Archbishop of Toulouse (1763), chairman of the Board of Finances (1787), Prime Minister, Archbishop of Sens (1788), Cardinal in December, 1788 ; he took the oath to the civil constitution (of the clergy), and gave up his dignity of cardinal. He was arrested in 1793, and died suddenly.

[4] The regular canons of *Sainte-Croix*, whose head convent was at Liège, only possessed in France twelve establishments numbering forty-seven members ; their congregation was abolished October 14, 1769.—The order of *Grandmont*, founded in 1124 by Saint-Stephen at Murat (Limousin), only numbered 108 members, occupying seven convents, in the eighteenth century. It was abolished by an edict of March 3, 1770, confirmed by a papal bull of August 6, 1772.—The *Camaldules*, whose order dated from the tenth century, comprised eight monasteries of monks (the most im-

these measures of destruction, and the royal orders which enjoined the closing of these convents, alluded with regret to the necessity of having recourse to such extreme steps ; but it was then wished to consider them as indispensable in order to strengthen the discipline of the Church, and to preserve from corruption those orders which it was hoped could still be allowed to exist.

I am far from thinking that the bishops who had drafted the project of that permanent commission, were aware of all the danger its adoption was to present for the clergy. They surely believed that they would be able to direct its application, and, if needed, even to suspend it. But the time had already come when people had ceased to be moderate in all questions relative to religious orders. Hardly a day passed without some work being published concerning the abusive practices of one order, the uselessness of another ; and I do not recollect that, during the twenty years that preceded the French Revolution, a single clever pen was raised in defence of religious orders. The historians no longer even dared to say that convents and monasteries, more than any other cause, imparted a peculiar character to the great European civilization and made it distinctly unlike any other. It has often occurred to me that the celibacy of priests powerfully contributed to preserve Europe from the spirit of caste; and it is but necessary to refer to history to see that this spirit tends generally to check the progress of civilization. M. de Bonald could find in this the text of a paper much in keeping with his own ideas.

The peculiarity of the period I am now reaching, was that everybody was anxious to be noted for talents or aptitudes foreign to his pursuit. The formation of the provincial assemblies [1] furnished the occasion of calling public attention to

portant of which was on Mont Valérien *) and twelve convents of nuns. It was the wealthiest order in France.—The order of *Servites* was founded at Florence in the thirteenth century by seven merchants. Their chief establishment was the convent of the Annunciade in Florence ; they had spread to France, where they were known under the name of *Blancs-Manteaux* † on account of their dress.—The order of Saint-Rufus dated from the sixth century. At the time of its abolition, it only possessed fifty-seven monasteries, numbering 200 monks. At their request, Pope Clement XIV. secularised them, and incorporated them in the military order of Saint-Lazarus (July, 1771).

[1] The provincial assemblies were collective administrations instituted under

* A well-known hill near Paris. The fort erected on it caused much trouble to the Germans in 1870-71.—(*Translator.*)   † Literally, "White-cloaks."

the persons elected to preside over them. M. Necker,[1] who was always afraid of being reproached for being a Calvinist, thought he could shield himself by appointing to the different posts of his department all bishops endowed with some talent ; thus it was that within a few years, all the provincial administrations were managed by the most distinguished bishop of each province. Is it not remarkable that a clergy, composed of men, some of whom were most pious, others specially good administrators, others, again, worldly, and, like the Archbishop of Narbonne, taking a certain pride in relinquishing for a while the grave and severe duties of their avocation to lead the life of a nobleman [2]—is it not remarkable, I say, that being composed of so many different elements, this clergy should, nevertheless, preserve the same spirit ? Yet, it is an undeniable fact, and more than substantiated by an incident which I could scarcely credit, had I not witnessed it personally. A few days after the opening of the States-General, I attended with the chief members of the clergy a conference held in Versailles at Cardinal de la Rochefoucauld's[3] ; there, M. Dulau,[4] Archbishop of Arles, earnestly proposed to seize *so*

Louis XVI. in the twenty-six *généralités d'élections* * of the kingdom. Turgot was the first to think of this institution ; it was however reserved to Necker to apply the idea. Those assemblies were formed of members of the three orders, the Third Estate sending twice the number of the other two. They held their session once in two years, and only sat for a month ; they were entrusted with the levying and distribution of taxes, and possessed besides, nearly all the attributes of the present General Councils in France. Half the members were appointed by the king, and these elected the other half.

[1] Jacques Necker belonged to a family of English origin, which emigrated to Germany in the sixteenth century. In 1724, his father took up his residence in Geneva, where he became professor of law. Jacques was born in 1732, came to Paris in 1750, and founded a banking concern there. He became Director of the Treasury in 1776, and afterwards General Director of Finances, with all the power of a Minister of State—a title which could not be conferred upon him for the twofold reason of his being a Protestant and a foreigner. He retired to private life in 1780, was exiled in 1787, resumed office in 1788, was exiled again on July 11, 1789, and called again to power by the Assembly ten days later. His popularity, however, did not last long : he resigned on September 18, 1790. He retired to Coppet, where he died in 1804.

[2] M. de Dillon, Archbishop of Narbonne, possessed an estate near Soissons, where he hunted large game six months in the year. *Haute-Fontaine* was the name of this estate. —(*Prince Talleyrand.*)

[3] Dominique de la Rochefoucauld, Comte de Saint Elpis, born in 1713, Archbishop of Albi (1747), of Rouen (1759), Cardinal (1778), Deputy of the Clergy to the States-General. He emigrated in 1792, and died in 1800.

[4] Jean-Marie Dulau, born near Périgueux in 1738 ; Archbishop of Arles in 1775,

* The financial jurisdictions of old France ; each of them was administered by an official named *intendant*. The *généralités* of the *pays d'états* were those where the province still enjoyed the privilege of fixing its own taxation. In the *pays d'élection*, the taxes were fixed by royal delegates called *élus.*—(*Translator.*)

favourable an occasion (these were his own expressions) to get the
nation to pay the debts of the clergy. This motion, like that of
M. de Thémines[1] when he advised the clergy to solicit the meeting
of the States-General, met with no opposition. The Archbishop
of Arles, in whose ability and wisdom everybody placed confidence, was appointed to second the motion of M. Dulau, and
press its adoption by the States-General, whenever he thought
the moment opportune. It required the lapse of many months and
all the ominous events that happened in the meantime, to enable
the good sense of M. de Boisgelin, Archbishop of Aix, to persuade
the clergy, not only to waive this absurd motion, but even to
make a considerable sacrifice in order to cover the famous deficit
which had been the pretext for all that was going on for a year ;
it was too late ; it is true, the pretext was forgotten ; besides there
was no longer any need of it, since the States-General had
become the National Assembly.

I notice that while speaking of the clergy, I do not observe
chronological order ; I am compelled to do so. A work on any
given subject, confined to studying the progress of events year
after year, must needs often be obscure and always devoid of
interest. I think it preferable for clearness of exposition to
mention at once that naturally belongs to the subject one is
dwelling upon. Besides, it has the invaluable advantage of being
much easier, and when people do not pretend to write a book,
they may be allowed to take it easy.

Cardinal de la Roche-Aymon, by appointing me promoter of
the assembly of 1775,[2] gave me the opportunity of attracting
notice, and from that moment, I was destined to become agent-
general of the clergy.[3]

deputy of the clergy to the States-General. Arrested after August 10, he was imprisoned at the "Carmes," * and fell a victim to the September massacres.
  [1] Alexandre de Lauzières de Thémines (1742–1829), chaplain to the king, Bishop
of Blois (1776). He emigrated in 1791, refused to resign his see in 1801, never
acknowledged the *Concordat*, and died in Brussels in 1829 without having ever
returned to France.
  [2] The duties of the *promoter* were to plead the defence of public interests. His
functions were equivalent to those of the public prosecutor in criminal courts. He
had to expose faulty ecclesiastics, and to see that the rights, liberties, and discipline
of the Church were not infringed.
  [3] There were two agents-general of the clergy. Their duties consisted in representing the interests of the clergy with the government, in all that related to the

  * The convent of a religious order of this name used as a prison during the Revolution.—(*Translator.*)

When the session of the assembly of 1775 was over, I entered the Sorbonne. I spent two years there, engaged with anything but theology, for pleasures occupy most of the time of a young graduate. Ambition also takes up a portion of one's time, and the memory of Cardinal Richelieu, whose fine mausoleum was in the Sorbonne church, was not unsuggestive in this respect. At that time, I only knew ambition in its noble acceptation, I was anxious to undertake all that in which I thought I could succeed. The five years of exasperation, silence and reading which, at Saint-Sulpice college, seemed so long and dismal to me, were not altogether lost. The trials of youth are profitable ; it is a good thing to have been steeped in the waters of the Styx, and, for many reasons, I am thankful to have undergone the trials of those days.

On leaving the Sorbonne, I found myself at last entirely free to do as I pleased.

I took up my residence at Bellechasse,[1] in a comfortable little house. My first care was to form a library, which became valuable eventually by the care with which the works composing it were selected, the rarity of the editions, and its choice and elegant bindings. I sought to make the acquaintance of the men most renowned for their past life, their works, their ambition, or the prospects held out to them by their birth, their friends or their talents. Being thus placed by my own action in the wide circle where so many brilliant and superior minds were shining in various ways, I enjoyed the proud pleasure of being indebted to myself alone for my position in life. I even had a very sweet moment when, having been appointed by His Majesty to the benefice of the abbey of Saint Denis at Rheims, the first income I derived from it enabled me to pay to the principal of Harcourt College a considerable portion of the fees still due for my education, and to recompense M. Langlois for the care he had taken of me in my youth.

revenue and expenditure of the Church, and the maintenance of her privileges. They were elected for five years by the *assemblées* of the clergy.

[1] The Hôtel Bellechasse was situated in the Faubourg St. Germain, Rue de Verneuil, near the Rue de Bellechasse. The Bellechasse inclosure has given its name to the convent of the Canonesses of the Holy Sepulchre, whose property it was ; it was situated near the Rue St. Dominique.—(*Translator.*)

Saint-Sulpice and the Sorbonne had separated me from M. de Choiseul-Gouffier. Of all the young men with whom I had been brought up, he was the first whom I sought to meet again. Since I had missed him, he had married, and had one or two children ; besides, he had made a dangerous and interesting journey which had brought him into notice in society, begun his reputation, and determined his choice of a career.

I shall so often have to speak of M. de Choiseul, in the course of these memoirs that I must indulge in the pleasure of acquainting my readers with him. Nature has endowed M. de Choiseul with imagination and talent ; he is cultivated ; he converses and speaks well ; his delivery is fluent and unaffected. If in his youth he had less admired the fine sentences of M. de Buffon,[1] he might have achieved a certain reputation as a writer. People say he gesticulates too much ; it is also my opinion ; it helps him when speaking ; and, like all speakers who make many gestures, he feels amused with what he says and repeats himself a little. His old age will be irksome to those who may have to nurse him, for the old age of persons who only possess mediocre talent is generally over-punctilious, and preserves merely the outward forms of urbanity. Wit alone can make old age amiable, because it gives an air of novelty to experience, and invests it almost with the charm of a discovery. M. de Choiseul is naturally noble-minded, kind, full of confidence and sincerity. He is affectionate, easily to get on with and forgetful. That is why he is a very good father and an excellent husband, although he seldom visits his wife or his children. He has friends, is fond of them, wishes them happy and would fain do them a good turn, but he gets on very well without seeing them. He devoted but a small part of his life to public affairs ; he found occupations which took up all his time. The exquisite taste and erudition which he displayed in Art rank him among the most useful and distinguished of amateurs.

M. de Choiseul is the man I have most loved. Although, in society, the names of M. de Choiseul, M. de Narbonne,[2] and

---

[1] The Comte Georges Louis Leclerc de Buffon, the famous French naturalist and writer.—(*Translator.*)

[2] The Comte Louis de Narbonne-Lara, born in 1755 at Colorno (Duchy of Parma)

Abbé de Périgord[1] were often associated, our intimacy with M. de Narbonne had less the character of friendship. M. de Narbonne possesses a kind of mind which aims only at effect, which is either brilliant or insignificant, which exhausts itself in a note or in a sally. He is uniformly polite ; his mirth often runs foul of good taste, and his character does not inspire the confidence required by intimate relations. His company is entertaining, but one seldom feels at ease with him. A sort of grace that, better than any one else, he knows how to give to his companionship, has gained him much success, chiefly among witty and somewhat vulgar men. He is less to the taste of men who appreciate what, in our youth, was termed good breeding. If any one spoke of the men who had supped on a certain day at the house of the Maréchale de Luxembourg,[2] and he had been there, the names of twenty persons would have been mentioned before his own ; at Julie's he would have been named first.

My room, where we gathered every morning, and where my friends shared my frugal meals, presented a singular medley : the Duc de Lauzun,[3] Panchaud,[4] Barthès,[5] Abbé Delille,[6] Mira-

---

of a very ancient family from Spain. Having come to France in 1760, he served in the artillery, after which he entered the Foreign Office. He was brigadier-general in 1791, Minister of War from December, 1791, to March, 1792. A writ of accusation being issued against him after August 10, he managed to escape, and resided abroad. In 1805, he was re-instated in his grade, and appointed Governor of Raab, and afterwards of Trieste ; minister to Bavaria, aide-de-camp to the emperor, ambassador at Vienna (1813). He died soon after at Torgau. M. de Narbonne married Mademoiselle de Montholon, by whom he had two daughters.

[1] It was under this name that M. de Talleyrand was known in his youth.

[2] Madeleine Angélique de Neufville-Villeroi, grand-daughter of the Marshal Duc de Villeroi, born in 1707, married at first to the Duc de Boufflers, who died in 1747. In 1750, she married the Marshal Duc de Luxembourg, and died in 1787.

[3] Armand de Gontaut, Comte de Biron, then Duc de Lauzun, born in 1747, entered the army, fought in Corsica, then in America ; deputy of the nobility of Quercy to the States-General, he joined the party of the Duc d'Orléans. General-in-Chief of the army of the Rhine in 1792, then of the army of Vendée, he was accused of treason, arrested, and guillotined in 1793.

[4] Panchaud was a Geneva banker established in Paris. He has published on the finances of his time an interesting work entitled, *Considerations on the Present State of the Credit of England and of France.* (Paris, 1781.) *

[5] Joseph Barthès (1734–1806). Physician and philosopher of great reputation.

[6] Abbé Delille, born at Aigues-Perse (Auvergne) (1738–1813), one of the most agreeable poets of the eighteenth century. He was a member of the Academy.

* " Réflexions sur l'état actuel du Crédit de l'Angleterre et de la France." (Paris, 1781.)

beau,[1] Chamfort,[2] Lauraguais,[3] Dupont de Nemours,[4] Rulhière,[5] Choiseul-Gouffier, Louis de Narbonne met there habitually and always with pleasure. We touched upon every subject and with the greatest liberty. It was the spirit and fashion of the time. These conversations were both pleasant and instructive, and besides, they held out some more or less remote prospect of gratifying our ambition. It was a delightful way of spending our mornings and I should enjoy doing so still.

The news of the day, political, commercial, administrative, and financial questions all in succession furnished topics of conversation. One of the matters with which the mind of the public was most engrossed at that time, was the commercial treaty just concluded between France and England.[6] The details of that great transaction were of special interest to educated men such as Panchaud, Dupont de Nemours and others. As for us ignorant ones, Lauzun, Barthès, Choiseul and myself, though anxious to learn, we confined ourselves to gener-

---

[1] Honoré-Gabriel Riquetti de Mirabeau, the grand orator of the Constituent Assembly (1749–1791), son of the Marquis de Mirabeau, the well-known economist and agriculturist.

[2] Sébastien Chamfort (1741–1794), born near Clermont-Ferrand. He wrote several tragedies and poems, which obtained for him the favour of the public. He was acquainted with the leading personages of the Revolution, and collaborated in the works of Sièyes and Mirabeau. A writ of accusation having been issued against him in 1794, he killed himself as they came to arrest him.

[3] Léon de Lauraguais, Duc de Brancas (1733–1824). He secluded himself all his life for the study of letters and scientific works. He was appointed a member of the Chamber of Peers in 1814.

[4] Pierre Dupont de Nemours (1739–1817), one of the most fervent adepts of the physiocratic school. He was a Councillor of State and Commissary-General of Commerce under Calonne ; deputy to the States-General. Imprisoned during the Reign of Terror, he was saved by the *coup d'état* of the 9th Thermidor. Member of the *Conseil des Cinq-cents.** He lived in retirement under the Empire, emigrated in 1815, and died in America.

[5] Claude Rulhière, born at Bondy, near Paris, in 1735, was aide-de-camp to Marshal de Richelieu. Later, M. de Breteuil took him to St. Petersburg as private secretary (1760). He witnessed the Revolution of 1762, and undertook to write an account of it. This work—*Les Révolutions de Russie*—had such a success that its author was commanded to write a history of Poland, intended for the instruction of the Dauphin. Member of the Academy in 1787, he died three years later.

[6] The Treaty of September 26, 1786, signed under the ministry of Vergennes, in accordance with Article 18th of the Treaty of Versailles of 1763. It raised numerous criticisms ; Vergennes was accused of having sacrificed our manufactures.

* The *Conseil des Cinq-cents* (Council of the Five Hundred), thus named because of its being composed of five hundred members, was instituted by the constitution of the year III. It had legislative powers. Its members were elected from among citizens of more than twenty-five years of age. The functions of the *Conseil des Cinq-cents* were similar to that of the House of Commons in England, or of the present Chamber of Deputies in France, with the difference that the upper chamber or *Conseil des Anciens* (Council of Elders) had the power to accept or reject, as they pleased, the decisions of the Council of the Five Hundred, and was thus omnipotent.—*(Translator.)*

alities.   I am anxious to record here what I recollect of these
discussions, because they belong to an order of ideas so different
from those I have heard people express since, that I think it
useful to state them. With this object I will give a rapid sketch of
the various events and negotiations which took several years to
bring about that great result.

The cabinets of Versailles and of London were convinced of
the reciprocal advantage which would accrue from the official
recognition and protection of commercial relations between the
two countries.   No previous period of history had ever offered so
favourable an occasion for a commercial treaty between England
and France.   Since the peace of 1763,[1] national antipathies
seemed to have died out, and immediately after the recognition
of the independence of America by England, frequent communication between France and Great Britain had destroyed, in great
measure, many repugnances.   Mutual inclination was becoming
evident ; the point now was how to make it lasting and mutually
advantageous to both nations.   The two governments named
plenipotentiaries to discuss this important question.

In England, they recollected that Lord Bolingbroke[2] after
concluding the treaty of Utrecht, had some intention of proposing
a commercial treaty with France.   This project, which he had
failed to carry out, had been one of the motives, or one of the
pretexts, for the persecution he had experienced on the part of
the Whigs.   The reasons alleged then against a commercial
treaty with France may have been plausible.   English customs
were still frightened at French luxury ; too close relations might
arouse the fears of English manufacturers with regard to the
competition of French goods in which the English had not
yet attained a standard of superiority.   The advantage that
the productions of French soil might take over those of
Portugal was also a course of apprehension.   The Treaty of

---

[1] The Treaty of Paris, which put an end to the War of Seven Years.
[2] Henry Paulet de Saint-Jean, Viscount Bolingbroke, born in 1672 at Battersea
(Surrey).   Member of the House of Commons (1700), Secretary of State (1704),
Minister of Foreign Affairs (1713) ; he was one of the signatories of the Peace of
Utrecht.   Exiled after the death of Queen Anne (1714), he took refuge in France,
returned to England in 1723, and was for ten years the most redoubtable adversary of
Walpole.   He died in 1750, without having been able to regain power.   He married
as second wife the Marquise de Villette, niece of Madame de Maintenon.

Methuen [1] was yet too recent to make it prudent to compromise its advantages by setting up a rivalry between the productions of France and Portugal. These arguments, which were not devoid of force, either no longer existed, or had lost their weight. England was in a state of commercial prosperity which was rendered incalculable by the invention of its machines and the immensity of its capital ; fashion took upon itself to destroy the objections resulting from the increase of luxury. The influence of the ministry and the interests of manufacturers met other objections victoriously, and the treaty was received in England with almost universal approbation.

Public opinion in France took an entirely different view or the treaty. The interests of her maritime population were, in this case, in direct opposition with those of the inhabitants of her manufacturing districts. The treaty was therefore received at first with some astonishment. Its first results were not favourable to us. The English, being better prepared than we were, derived large profits from it. The city of Bordeaux, the provinces of Guyenne, Aunis and Poitou, found indeed a few more outlets for their wines, their brandies and the other products of their soil ; but it was argued that, in the general evaluation, these local advantages could not compensate for the inconveniences of the consumption of twenty-five million inhabitants, anxious to purchase goods superior in quality, and which England could provide at a figure much lower than that of the French market.

Normandy, so skilful in the defence of her own interests, so important by her wealth and population, was the first to express her discontent. She published a long manifesto against the treaty. The cause she pleaded soon found supporters throughout the land ; all the old prejudices, all the former motives of hate and animosity re-appeared. The voice of the consumers was stifled, and the government soon incurred general blame for having signed the treaty.

---

[1] The Treaty of Methuen between England and Portugal, so-called after the name of the English ambassador, Lord Methuen, who negotiated it, was signed in 1703. It was a treaty of alliance and of commerce, by which England reserved to herself the monopoly of importation into Portugal. The latter submitted to this commercial vassalage up to the beginning of the nineteenth century.

And yet the spirit that inspired that great transaction was dictated by the best principles. M. de Vergennes [1] and M. de Calonne,[2] who were instrumental in its adoption, will each some day derive some credit from it. The object of the treaty was to put an end to the smuggling that was going on between the two countries, and to furnish the public treasury with a revenue founded on duties moderate enough to leave no margin for fraud. This advantage was evident and reciprocal for the two countries. If it increased for France the facility of gratifying the taste and fancy her wealthy people showed for English goods, it enabled England to enjoy more luxuries, for which she paid France, by a reduction of duty on the wines of Champagne and Bordeaux, a reduction which must increase their consumption in England.

The result of this reduction of duties both on the necessaries of life and on luxuries, must have been, for consumers, to balance more equitably the taxes levied on them, and to facilitate their payment ; as for the public treasury, the result of the treaty would have been to increase the revenue in proportion as the consumption was augmented.

It may also be mentioned that the spirit of the treaty provided that all classes of industries should be divided between the two nations, each being awarded the class of industry for which

[1] Charles Gravier, Comte de Vergennes, was the second son of a *Président à Mortier** of the *parlement* of Dijon. Born at Dijon in 1717, he entered the diplomatic service. In 1750 he was appointed minister, and sent in that capacity to the Elector of Trèves. About that time he was initiated into the secrets of the king, of whom he became one of the most devoted agents. Ambassador at Constantinople (1754) ; recalled by Choiseul in 1768, he lived in retirement until the fall of that minister, when he was (1771) sent as ambassador to Sweden. Louis XVI. appointed him Minister of Foreign Affairs (1774). He signed the Treaty of Versailles and the Treaties of Commerce with England and Russia. He became President of the Council of Finances (1783), and died in 1787.

[2] Charles Alexandre de Calonne was the son of a distinguished Artesian family ; he was born January 20, 1743, at Douai, where his father was first president of *parlement.* He was attorney-general to the *parlement* of Douai, intendant of Metz (1768), of Lille, where his reputation as a skilful administrator led to his being appointed comptroller-general by Louis XVI. After the meeting of the Assembly of the Notables, which he had suggested, he was dismissed from his post and exiled to Lorraine (1787). Thence he went to England, returned to France in 1789 in the hope of securing his election to the States-General. He however failed, went back to England, where he played an active part amongst the *émigrés*, and died in 1802.

* This was the official appellation of the chief-judge of the *Grand' Chambre* of the *parlements*, that is to say, the tribunal appointed to take cognizance of verbal appeals against the decisions of the "*presidiaux*" (minor judges), *bailliages*, and other inferior courts. They were so named from the shape of their caps, somewhat resembling a mortar (*mortier*).—(*Translator.*)

nature seemed to have fitted it best, and from which it was likely to derive most advantages.

This latter provision might, in the course of a few years, have brought about the triumph of the principle of free-trade, but prejudices decided otherwise. They have too deeply rooted a hold upon men, for it to be prudent to endeavour to destroy them too suddenly. I refused for a long time to acknowledge this sad truth, but seeing that the philosophers of the eighteenth century, with all the good and bad arguments they employed, did fail in that undertaking, I shall henceforth follow the example of the philosophers of the nineteenth century, who are indeed of a very different stamp from that of their predecessors, and allow it to trouble me no longer.

A public career being open to me, I, rather cleverly, took advantage of the position of agent-general of the clergy, which had been promised me, to extend my relations. Early in life, I made the acquaintance of M. de Maurepas,[1] M. Turgot,[2] M. de Malesherbes,[3]

---

[1] Jean Phelypeaux, Comte de Maurepas, and of Pontchartrain, was born in 1709. His father, his grandfather, his great-grandfather, and great-great-grandfather had been, like himself, Secretaries of State, so that from 1610 to 1749 the Phelypeaux family was represented in the councils of the king. As early as 1715, Maurepas obtained the reversion of the post of Secretary of State, which his father had resigned. The Marquis de la Vrillière was selected to discharge the duties of that office in the place of his relation, who soon became his son-in-law. In 1725, Maurepas took the direction of his department in hand, and was appointed Secretary of Paris and of Marine. He fell into disgrace in 1749, was exiled to Bourges, and afterwards to his estate of Pontchartrain, near Versailles. His father-in-law had replaced him. He took office again under Louis XVI., who appointed him Minister of State and President of the Council of Finances (1774). Up to his death (1781) he had in reality all the power of a prime minister.

[2] Jacques Turgot, Baron de l'Aulne, belonged to an old family which came originally from Brittany, and had settled in Normandy. He was born in 1727. He was counsellor of *parlement*, then, in 1762, intendant of Limoges, where his enlightened and benevolent administration made his name famous. Secretary of State for the Department of Marine (1774), comptroller-general in the same year, dismissed from office in 1776, he died five years later. Closely associated with the economist party, he left several works on political economy and on administration.

[3] Chrétien-Guillaume de Lamoignon de Malesherbes, of an illustrious family of Nivernais, which during two centuries occupied the highest posts in the magistracy. He was born in 1721, was counsellor of *parlement* (1744), chief president of the *Cour des Aides* * (1750), dismissed, and exiled in 1771. Re-instated in his office by Louis XVI, in 1774, he resigned in the following year. Secretary of State to the King's Household (1775-1776), Minister of State (1787-1788). He lived abroad until 1792, when he returned to France to offer his services to the king, whose defence

* The *Cours des Aides* were tribunals charged with judging and deciding as a final court of appeal all civil and criminal cases concerning taxes, *Gabelles* † and *Tailles.* ‡ That of Paris dated from 1355. This tribunal was the only one that had the right of interpreting the royal ordinances concerning the levying of taxes.—*Translator.*

† Salt tax. ‡ Villain-tax.—*(Translator.)*

M. de Castries,[1] M. de Calonne, a few Councillors of State, and several heads of administration. About the same time, I was introduced to the Duc de Choiseul,[2] Madame de Brionne,[3] Madame de Montesson,[4] Madame de Boufflers,[5] Madame de la Reynière;[6] on certain days, the best society in Paris met at the houses of these people.

My cold manners and apparent reserve, had induced some persons to say I was witty. Madame de Gramont,[7] who did not like the reputations which she had not made herself, was of service to me by seeking to embarrass me, at the time I first went into society. I was supping for the first time at Auteuil at Madame de Boufflers', and was seated at one end of the table, hardly speaking to my neighbour. Madame de Gramont, in a loud, harsh voice,

he pleaded before the Convention. Arrested in December, 1792, he mounted the scaffold with his daughter and his son-in-law (M. de Chateaubriand, the brother of the illustrious writer).

[1] Charles de la Croix, Marquis de Castries, belonged to an old family of Langue-doc. Born in 1727, he became lieutenant-general, Governor of Montpellier and of Cette (1758), Governor of Flanders and of Hainaut, Secretary of State to the Department of Marine (1780), Marshal of France (1783). He emigrated during the Revolution, commanded a division of the army of Condé, and died in 1801.

[2] Etienne François, Duc de Choiseul-Stainville (1719–1785), ambassador, then Minister-Secretary of State (1758–1770).

[3] Louise de Rohan, Canoness of Remiremont, daughter of Prince Charles de Rohan-Montauban, lieutenant-general. She became the wife of Charles de Lorraine, Comte de Brionne, Grand-Equerry of France.

[4] Charlotte Béraud de la Haie de Riou, Marquise de Montesson, born in 1737. She married, in 1754, the Marquis de Montesson, lieutenant-general. Widowed in 1769, she married secretly the Duc d'Orléans (1773). After the death of the Duc (1785), she lived in retirement. Arrested under the Terror, she was saved by the 9th Thermidor. She was very intimate with Madame de Beauharnais, afterwards Empress Josephine. She died in February, 1806. Madame de Montesson had written much, and has left numerous comedies and novels.

[5] The Comtesse Marie de Boufflers-Rouvrel, *née* de Campar-Saujon, was lady in waiting to the Duchesse d'Orléans. She became a widow in 1764. Imprisoned under the Terror, but more fortunate than her daughter-in-law, the Duchesse de Lauzun, she escaped the scaffold, and died in 1800.

[6] Suzanne de Jarente, daughter of Alexandre de Jarente, Marquis d'Orgeval, married on February 1, 1763, Alexandre Grimod de la Reynière, who from being a simple pork-butcher had risen to the post of *Fermier-général.** He made a considerable fortune, and built the superb hotel which now stands at the corner of the Rue Boissy-d'Anglas and of the Avenue Gabriel. This hotel, which served as the residence of the Russian, and afterwards of the Turkish, embassies, belongs to-day to the *Cercle de l'Union Artistique.* It is known that La Reynière had acquired the reputation of an epicure of the first order. The dinners given by him and his wife have remained famous.

[7] Béatrix de Choiseul-Stainville, daughter of the Duc de Choiseul, canoness of Remiremont. In 1759, she married Antoine, Duc de Gramont, Governor of Navarre. She mounted the scaffold in 1794 with her friend, the Duchesse du Châtelet.

* *Fermier Général.* The custom existed under the old Monarchy of conferring the farming of the taxes on financiers who paid a fixed sum for it.—(*Translator.*)

asked me, calling me by my name, what had so much struck me on entering the drawing-room, whither I followed her, to say: " Ah! ah!" "Your grace," I replied, "did not exactly hear what I said ; my words were not 'Ah! ah!' but ' Oh! oh!'" That wretched reply caused general hilarity ; I continued to sup, and did not say another word. On leaving the table, a few persons came up to me, and I received for the following days several invitations which enabled me to make the acquaintance of the persons whom I was most anxious to meet.

I had no occasion to do so at the house of my parents ; for they saw but few people, and especially few of those who shone on the scene where ministerial appointments were disputed. I preferred to go to my mother at the hours when she was alone : I could then better enjoy the graces of her mind. No one ever seemed to me to possess such fascinating conversation. She had no pretension. She spoke only by shades ; she never made a pun : that would have been too pointed ; puns are remembered ; she merely wished what she said to please—to please her hearers for the time being and be forgotten. A richness of easy expressions, new and always delicate, supplied the various needs of her mind. From her I have inherited a great aversion for persons who, in order to speak with more accuracy, use only technical terms. I have faith neither in the wit nor in the knowledge of those who do not know equivalent terms and are always describing : they are indebted only to their memory for what they know, their knowledge can therefore be only superficial. I am sorry that such a thought should have occurred to me whilst M. von Humboldt,[1] is in Paris, but it is written.

I spent my time in a very pleasant manner and did not waste it too much ; the circle of my acquaintances was widening. The relations which it was then considered good style to have with the wits of the day, came to me through a good lady named

---

[1] The two brothers, William and Alexander von Humboldt, both made their names famous—the former in literature and politics, the latter in science. The author here refers to Alexander. Born in 1769, he travelled a long time in America and in Asia, and published an account of his travels ; he is also the author of numerous scientific works and treatises, notably the *Cosmos*. Thanks to him, physical geography and botany made remarkable progress. He died in 1859.

Madame d'Héricourt,[1] whose husband had held the post of naval commissary at Marseilles. She loved wit, young people, and good cheer. Every week we had dinner at her house, and a most enjoyable one it was. The guests were M. de Choiseul, M. de Narbonne, Abbé Delille, de Chamfort, de Rulhière, de Marmontel,[2] who took turns with Abbé Arnaud,[3] Abbé Bertrand,[4] and myself. The gaiety that reigned there kept the pretentious in check, and I must state that in that company, where so much gaiety and presumption was brought together, jeering or slandering were never indulged in, in the space of five years.

Count von Creutz,[5] Minister of Sweden, who thought to please his master by pretending to be considered a wit in France, took great pains to have once a week at his table, the same persons who composed the dinner-party of Madame d'Héricourt. We went there three or four times, but Marmontel read so many tragedies that he drove away all the guests. As for me I held firm until he came to *Numitor*.

Readings after dinner were then the reigning fashion; they imparted special importance, and were reputed to give a select tone, to some houses. One seldom dined at the houses of M. de Vaudreuil,[6] M. de Lian-

---

[1] Louise Duché, daughter of a chief advocate-general in the *Cour des Aides* of Montpellier. She married, in 1741, Bénigne du Trousset d'Héricourt, a former naval commissary.

[2] Jean-François Marmontel, born at Bort (Limousin) in 1723. On the advice of Voltaire, his master and friend, he wrote for the stage, but failed completely. He found his vein only in moral tales, which had a prodigious success, and procured him the congratulations of nearly all the sovereigns of Europe. He was appointed Historiographer of France, and entered the Academy. He died in 1799.

[3] Abbé François Arnaud, born in 1721, at Aubignon (Vaucluse). He was one of the warmest supporters of the philosophical impulse of the eighteenth century, and acquired a certain celebrity by his works. He was a member of the French Academy. He died in 1784.

[4] Abbé Bertrand, born in 1755, at Autun. He studied astronomy, and was appointed Professor of Physics at Dijon. He was admitted to the academy of this city. He undertook with d'Entrecasteaux a voyage round the world, but he died on the way at the Cape of Good Hope (1792). He left various scientific treatises.

[5] Count Gustavus von Creutz was born in Sweden in 1736. Minister from Sweden to Madrid in 1753, and then to Paris, where he remained twenty years. His *salon* became one of the circles of society most sought by philosophers and literary men. In 1783, King Gustavus III. recalled him to Stockholm, and appointed him Senator and Minister of Foreign Affairs. He died two years after.

[6] Joseph de Rigaud, Comte de Vaudreuil, belonged to a very old family of Languedoc; he was born in 1740. He lived for a long while at Versailles, frequenting the *salon* of Madame de Polignac and the society of the queen. He was intimate with the Comte d'Artois, whom he accompanied in 1782 to the siege of Gibraltar.

court,[1] Madame de Vaines,[2] M. d'Anzely, without being obliged to hear either *Le Mariage de Figaro*, the poem known as *Les Jardins*,[3] or *Le Connétable de Bourbon*,[4] or some tales by Chamfort, or what was then called *La Révolution de Russie*.[5] It was an obligation rather strictly enforced on all the persons invited ; but then, the fact of being a guest at any of these houses, ranked one among the distinguished men of the day. I might say that many people whom I did not know spoke of me in good terms, simply because they had met me at some of these dinner-parties to which the right of making people's reputation had been granted.   In this respect, I was like the man spoken of by the Chevalier de Chastellux :[6]   "*He is doubtless a very witty man*," remarked the Chevalier to some one ; "*I do not know him, but he goes to Madame Geoffrin's.*"

I had also noticed that when one was anxious not to be classed among the *habitués* of open houses and thus to rank with the crowd, some advantage could be derived by affecting estrangement from, and even aversion for, some prominent member of society. My choice fell on M. Necker.   I persistently refused to go to his house. I said, rather boldly, that he was neither a good

He kept open house at his residence of Gennevilliers, and often received M. de Talleyrand there. He emigrated with the Comte d'Artois, took up his residence in London in 1799, returned to Paris at the Restoration, was created peer of France in 1814, and died in 1817.   His correspondence with the Comte d'Artois was published in Paris, 1889 (2 vols. 8vo.   L. Pingaud).

[1] François de la Rochefoucauld, Duc de Liancourt, born in 1747, was brigadier of dragoons ; Grand Master of the Wardrobe (1783), deputy of the nobility of Clermont to the States-General, lieutenant-general (1792).   He emigrated after August 10 ; he lived in retirement under the Empire.   At the Restoration he was created a peer, but his liberal opinions precluded him from obtaining public functions.   He died in 1827.   His funeral gave rise to tumultuous incidents.

[2] This was probably the wife of M. J. de Vaines, Receiver-General, Commissary of the Treasury (1733-1803).   He was often seen at the house of Marshal de Beauvau, and at that of Madame Geoffrin.

[3] "The Marriage of Figaro," a poem of Abbé Delille on the gardens of the Duc d'Orléans at Monceau.

[4] Tragedy of the Comte Jacques de Guibert (1743-1790), lieutenant-general. His name will remain known, not by his tragedies, but by an *Essay on Tactics*, of which Napoleon said " that it was fitted to make great men."

[5] "The Revolutions of Russia"—a work by Ruhlière.

[6] Talleyrand doubtless means here François-Jean, Marquis de Chastellux, born in Paris in 1734 ; he took service in Germany from 1756 to 1763 ; and, in 1780, went to America as major-general, and there formed an intimacy with Washington.   He was a friend of Voltaire and of the encyclopædists.   He wrote various works and was elected a member of the *Académie Française*.   His essay entitled *De la Félicité Publique* (1772), was praised by Voltaire.   He is the author of another essay entitled *Éloge d'Helvétius* (1774), and of an account of travels in North America (1780-1782).   He died in 1788.—(*Translator.*)

minister of finances nor a statesman ; that he had few ideas, no administrative system of his own, that his loans were badly conducted, onerous and injurious to public morals ; badly conducted, because they provided no sinking-fund ; onerous, because the rates of public bills of exchange neither required so high an interest as that paid for his loan, nor such delays as those, which, in order to make the fortune of Girardot's and of Germani's firms, were granted to thirty Geneva bankers; injurious to public morals, because his loans based on life-interest fostered and developed a kind of selfishness unknown to French manners before the days of M. Necker. I said that he talked badly, that he did not know how to argue, that he was always affected ; I said that the weakness of his constitution, which kept him in a continual state of fear, reflected upon all the faculties of his mind. I said that his pride did not come from his nature, but rather from his crooked mind, and want of taste ; I said that with his fantastic hat, his long head, his big body, burly and ill-shaped, his inattentive airs, his scornful demeanour, his constant use of maxims, painfully drawn from the *laboratory of his mind*, he had all the appearance of a charlatan. I said, I believe, a thousand other things that it would be useless to repeat, because to-day they are on everybody's lips.

Madame de Montesson's house, which was kept just on the verge of decency, was particularly agreeable. To amuse the Duc d'Orléans, Madame de Montesson had pieces played by her visitors, which she knew would please him ; and, in order not merely to amuse, but to interest him as well, she wrote several of these pieces herself. In the theatre, a special box was placed at the disposal of the mundane members of the clergy ; to which the Archbishop of Toulouse,[1] the Bishop of Rodez,[2] the Archbishop of Narbonne,[3] and the Bishop of Comminges,[4] had secured my admission.

---

[1] M. de Brienne.

[2] Jérome Champion de Cicé, born at Rennes in 1735. General-agent of the clergy (1765), Bishop of Rodez (1770), Archbishop of Bordeaux (1781), member of the Assembly of Notables (1787), deputy of the clergy to the States-General (1789), Keeper of the Seals (1789). He refused to take the oath to the civil constitution of the clergy, and emigrated (1791). Archbishop of Aix in 1802, he died in 1810.

[3] M. de Dillon.

[4] Charles d'Osmond de Médavy, born in 1723; Bishop of Comminges (1764–1785).

Curiosity, much more than a decided taste for music, took me also to all the learned and wearisome concerts that were given then, sometimes at the house of the Comte de Rochechouart, sometimes at M. de Albaret's, sometimes at Madame Lebrun's.[1] I was careful not to have an opinion on French music, or Italian music, or on that of Gluck. I was too young to reason as to the proportionate value of what fashion forced me to regard as a pleasure. If, however, I had been obliged to pass an opinion, I would have felt inclined to say that music being, in general, only a language which expresses, in an ideal manner, the sensations and even the sentiments that we experience, each country must have a style of music peculiar to itself, and which the taste of its inhabitants induces them to prefer to all others. But my ignorance saved me, and I never had, on this important subject, any quarrel with any one.

The position I had taken in society gave a sort of pre-eminence to my agency ; I performed its duties almost alone, because, a few months after our taking office, a rather too public adventure had deprived Abbé de Boisgelin,[2] my colleague, of the confidence of the clergy. The natural indolence of M. de Boisgelin and his passion for Madame de Cavanac (famous under the name of Mademoiselle de Romans, and also because she was the mother of Abbé de Bourbon[3]) had easily induced him to countenance my doing his work as well as my own.

I had surrounded myself with persons of learned and sound views : M. de Maunay,[4] afterwards Bishop of Trèves ; M. Bourlier,[5]

[1] Marie-Louise Vigée-Lebrun, born in 1755, was one of the most celebrated painters of the eighteenth century. She left France in 1789, and was received with distinction at most foreign courts. She died in 1842. She has left very interesting Memoirs.

[2] Abbé de Boisgelin was a cousin of the cardinal-archbishop. He perished in 1792, in the course of the massacres of September.

[3] Mademoiselle de Romans had, by Louis XV., a son who was christened under the name of Bourbon, a favour not accorded to any other natural son of the king. She however failed to obtain his legitimization. He was known afterwards under the name of Abbé de Bourbon, and died in the reign of Louis XVI. Mademoiselle de Romans married later M. de Cavanac (see the *Memoirs of Madame Campan*, vol. iii.).

[4] Charles Maunay, born at Champoix (Puy-de-Dôme) in 1745 ; Bishop of Trèves in 1802.

[5] Jean-Baptiste, Comte Bourlier, born at Dijon in 1731. He took orders, and the oath of allegiance to the civil constitution of the clergy. Bishop of Evreux in 1802, deputy to the *Corps législatif*, senator in 1812, peer of France under the Restoration, he died in 1821.

afterwards Bishop of Evreux; M. Duvoisin,[1] who became Bishop of Nantes, and M. Des Renaudes,[2] who was not socially the equal of the former. I am happy to acknowledge here all the marks of friendship displayed towards me by MM. Maunay, Bourlier, and Duvoisin, whom I have always been pleased to meet at all periods of my life. M. Des Renaudes left me to enter the house of Secretary of State, Maret[3]; his style of talent finding permanent employment in his new duties might have led him promptly to fortune · he was a man who excelled in making use of other people's ideas.

I was anxious not to keep for ever my post of agent-general of the clergy, but took all necessary precautions not to let any one suspect my ambition ; thus, in order to attract notice, I was busily engaged on works, which, without belonging exactly to my province, were not altogether foreign to the duties I discharged.

The abolition of the lotteries was one of my favourite ideas; I had investigated all the chances and all the consequences of that baneful institution. At the same time, I noticed that the clergy, being attacked and scoffed at by philosophers, were daily

[1] Jean-Baptiste, Baron Duvoisin, born at Langres in 1744, was a professor in the Sorbonne, a promoter of the *Officialité* * of Paris, chief-vicar of Laon. In 1792, he was exiled for refusing to submit to the civil constitution of the clergy. In 1802, he was appointed Bishop of Nantes, and took a part in the differences that arose between the emperor and the Holy See. He died in 1813.

[2] Martial Borge des Renaudes, born at Tulle in 1755, was chief-vicar to M. de Talleyrand at Autun, whom he assisted in the capacity of under-deacon at the Mass of the Federation. He was the confidential man of Talleyrand, who, it is said, entrusted him with the task of writing his speeches. Talleyrand's report on public instruction is entirely Des Renaudes' work. Under the Consulate, Des Renaudes was named Tribune. His name was struck out of the list of the Tribunate in 1802. Later on he was appointed *Censeur* †—a post which he preserved under the Restoration. He died in 1825.

[3] Hugues Maret, born at Dijon in 1763, advocate to the *parlement* of Burgundy. Sent to Naples in 1792, he was seized by the Austrians, and only set at liberty in 1795, being exchanged for the Duchesse d'Angoulême. Minister-Secretary of State in 1804, he was Minister of Foreign Affairs in 1811, and created Duc de Bassano ; Minister of War (1813). He was exiled in 1815 ; peer of France in 1831, he was for a while President of the Council (November, 1834). He died in 1839.

* The *Officialité* of Paris was the tribunal of bishops and archbishops. All students came under the jurisdiction of this court, which judged certain lay cases as well (tithes, marriage cases, heresy, and simony). The *official* only pronounced canonical penalties ; for cases requiring corporal punishment he sent the culprit to the secular courts. The *promoteur* fulfilled the functions of public accuser. M. P. Fournier has published a very interesting volume on the *officialité*. Paris. Plon. One 8° vol.—(*Translator.*)

† The censorship had been abolished in 1791 for the press as well as for books. Re-established, as a matter of fact, under the Directory, it was legally organized under the Consulate. A censorship was imposed by the Empire over each daily paper. The Restoration in proclaiming the liberty of the press re-established the censorship. Among the papers of which Des Renaudes was censor, *L'Ami de la Religion et du Roi* must be mentioned. In 1808, Des Renaudes was appointed councillor of the University for life.—(*Translator.*)

losing public regard. My object was that they should regain the esteem of the people, and for this purpose, I was anxious to hold them up to the eyes of the nation, as the protectors of strict morality. By inducing the clergy to submit to some pecuniary sacrifices in support of that principle, I should have served, not only public morals, but also the very order I had consented to join.

I was anxious that the clergy should propose to buy from the government the royal lottery, in order to suppress it; that is to say, that they should engage to furnish regularly every year, a gratuitous present representing as much revenue as the lottery produced for the royal treasury. The memorial to be addressed to the king to ask him to proscribe this baneful institution, might have been superb; I should have been most happy to have drafted it.[1]

The members of the clergy, upon whom I most depended to second my motion, declined to do so. It may be observed that my first political campaign was not very fortunate, a result which I dare to attribute to the fact that my proposals were far too radical for the men with whom I purposed to make use of them.

The amelioration of the condition of the clergy, as determined by the edict of 1768, appeared to me far from sufficient.[2] It was necessary to induce the clergy to propose an increase of salary; but in order to respect the interests of the chief tithe-owners as far

---

[1] For a long time, lotteries in France constituted a revenue for the State. The government collected the fees paid by the persons licensed to organize lotteries, and organized some official ones besides. The Order in Council of June 30, 1776, created the royal lottery of France. This was suppressed in the year II., re-established in the year VI., and not definitely abolished until 1836, in execution of the Law of Finances of 1832.

[2] The lower clergy had always been complaining of having hardly anything to live upon, while, on the contrary, the bishops and the commendatory abbots were enjoying considerable incomes. At different times the government had intervened to better their condition. An edict of 1768 insured a minimum salary of 500 livres * to a curate, and of 200 to a vicar. In 1778, the former received 700 livres, and the latter 250, increased afterwards to 350 livres (1785). This was the settled allowance, in contrast with which it is as well to cite the amount of income derived by certain chief tithe-owners, who often retained for themselves half, sometimes even three-quarters, of the total amount of the tithes. The Abbé of Clairvaux received thus 400,000 livres a year; the Cardinal de Rohan, 1,000,000; the Benedictines of Cluny, 1,800,000; the Benedictines of Saint-Maur, 1,672 in number, 8,000,000, and these were not exceptions.

* A French coin in use before the Revolution, and amounting to about tenpence.—(*Translator.*)

as was consistent with my objects, I followed the plan employed by M. de Malesherbes and M. de Ruhlière, when they pleaded the cause of the Protestants. In order to reach their end, they both maintained that the intentions of Louis XIV. had not been carried out. I maintained, even, that the principle which had served to establish the new rate of State allowance for the lower clergy, had been violated in deciding that the said allowance should, in no case, exceed five hundred francs. I had confined myself to requesting the redress of an error, of which, as I said, the higher clergy would surely have been glad to be informed. According to the value of the silver mark, of which I pointed out the growing depreciation and its low proportion to the price of commodities, the increase, to be fair, ought to reach seven hundred and fifty francs. To-day a thousand francs would be required to obtain what these seven hundred and fifty francs would then have easily procured. However, I did not succeed. The State allowance remained fixed at five hundred francs, and to-day, I believe, it still stands at about the same rate.

Another attempt on my part was no more successful. During a journey I made to Brittany I noticed that, in this country, many women were neither maids, wives, nor widows. They had, at some time or other, been married to sailors who had not returned home, but whose death had never been properly ascertained. The law forbade their marrying again. I employed all the arguments of theology, which, when handled with a little judgment, are elastic enough to serve any purpose, to show that it was desirable that, after a certain number of years, sufficient to prevent social scandal, these poor women should be allowed to marry again. My memoir was committed to M. de Castries, who thought it necessary to consult his friend, the Bishop of Arras, on the subject.[1] The latter saw, as a theologian, that my suggestion could be of no use to him, and, therefore, denounced it in the strongest terms. My memoir was thrown into the fire, and it

[1] Louis de Conzié, born in 1732, entered the army at first, and was officer of dragoons. Having embraced the ecclesiastical career, he was appointed Bishop of St. Omer in 1766, and of Arras in 1769. A violent adversary of the Revolution, he refused a seat in the States-General, and went over to England. He died in 1804, in London.

required no less an event than the Revolution to enable all these
Breton women—who I should think, were no longer young—
to marry again, if they chose.

The care I bestowed upon the private affairs of the clergy
and the success of some of my reports to the *Conseil des Parties*[1]
caused my superiors to overlook all the little reforms of general
utility which I endeavoured to rank with my duties. They said :
" It is the result of his youth ; with a little experience that will
soon pass off." Emboldened by the benevolent disposition
manifested towards me, I launched myself into an undertaking
which I managed to connect with the interests of the clergy,
although in point of fact, it was quite foreign to them. M.
d'Ormesson,[2] a very honest man, but one of the most wretched
comptroller-generals of the last century, had undertaken such
a series of unfortunate speculations that the government was left
without either money or credit. The uneasiness was general :
people anxious to withdraw their deposits, rushed in crowds to
the Bank of Discount,[3] the directors of which, in the interest
of a few bankers, preferred to solicit authorization to suspend
payment rather than diminish their rate of discount. M.
d'Ormesson having granted the authorization requested by the
directors, bank-notes obtained a forced currency, which necessarily caused them to fall in value.[4] The clergy possessed a

---

[1] The *Conseil des Parties* was a section of the Council of State or Council of the
King, the great administrative body of the kingdom. It decided the conflicts of
jurisdiction, interpreted the laws and ordinances, and pronounced on the cases which
the king " thought fit to bring before his council." It was composed of the chancellor, president, twenty-six counsellors-in-ordinary, and sixteen counsellors appointed
every six months.

[2] Henri Lefèvre d'Ormesson belonged to an old and illustrious family of magistrates. He was born in 1751, was Counsellor of *parlement* and Intendant of
Finances. Raised to be Comptroller-General in 1783, he failed completely in this
office, and was replaced by Calonne. He was elected Mayor of Paris in 1792, but
declined the post. He was afterwards Administrator of the Department of the Seine,
and died in 1807.

[3] *Caisse d'Escompte.* It was instituted by Turgot, with royal license in 1776 ;
its object was to discount at four per cent. all bills of exchange, and to bring general
interest in all transactions to the same rate. A sum of seventy millions (about
£2,800,000) having been exacted from its governors by Comptroller-General de
Calonne as reserve fund, seriously shook its credit. It was abolished on August
24, 1793, by decree of the National Convention.—(*Translator.*)

[4] The ordinance of March 24, 1776, authorized the creation of a bank named the
Caisse d'Escompte, which, without exclusive privilege, loaned money to the trade at
four per cent. In 1783, the Treasury being in a most critical situation, M. d'Ormesson
secretly borrowed six millions from this bank. The secret got abroad. Holders of

large number of them. Having alleged the necessity for watching the proceedings of the bank, I was enabled to attend the first meetings of the shareholders. Enlightened men thought with reason that the old regulations did not offer sufficient security. A commission was named to examine them; new regulations were agreed to, and I was selected to draw up the report to be read at the general assembly.

This was the first time that I was, strictly speaking, connected with public affairs. I prefaced my report by a speech in which I had applied myself to set forth all the advantages of public credit; I laid stress on its importance; I established the fact that all was possible to one who possessed a large credit; that credit alone suffices for all the needs of commerce, of large trading establishments, of manufactures, and so on. After having set forth all the advantages of credit, I spoke of the means of obtaining and of preserving it. I remember that, in this paper, I was so pleased to make known all the various uses of which credit is susceptible, that I made use of a host of expressions which are only employed to depict the most timid and delicate sentiments. An old banker, named Rillet, a regular Genevese, who listened to me with attention, learned with extreme pleasure, which he expressed by the roughest gestures, that, in paying exactly his bills of exchange, he did something so very fine that it could only be expressed in the language of imagination. He came to me, and begged me as he pressed my hands to allow him to copy that part of my speech. His enthusiasm became useful, for he repeated so badly what I had just said, that I deemed it quite out of place, and left it out in the printed text.

From the advantages of credit, and the means of obtaining it, I turned at last to the special institutions which facilitate, accelerate, and simplify all its transactions while hastening and ensuring its progress.

notes became uneasy, and insisted on their deposits being returned to them. D'Ormesson authorized the bank to suspend for three months the payment in cash of notes of more than 300 livres, and gave forced currency to bank notes. The panic increased; the payment of arrears was to be suspended. Calonne suppressed the forced currency; the bankers advanced to the bank the sums necessary for its payments; its credit was re-established, and it regained the greatest prestige.

The most important of these institutions was a bank, whose first object must be to maintain the low price of money, and to furnish it in abundance for all the needs of circulation. The crisis which the Bank of Discount had just passed through required that great changes should be introduced into its government; the changes I proposed were all adopted. The only article that met with any opposition was that in which I suggested that the assembly should not be composed of so many bankers, because their personal interest was opposed to that of the establishment which they were called to manage; nevertheless as the greater number of shares were in the hands of the bankers of Paris, it was foreseen that the article would be easily evaded, and it was adopted.

I am rather prolix: but when speaking of our recollections we speak of something dear to us : besides, when I began these memoirs, I fully made up my mind, rightly or wrongly, to disclose frankly my opinion on all that which, either as an act of administration or as a settled project, engaged my attention, or that of the public, for any length of time.

The different subjects with which I had been occupied had attracted to me the attention of men, who, by profession, were acquainted with all new ambitions. Foulon,[1] Panchaud, Sainte-Foy[2] Favier,[3] Daudé sought my acquaintance, and spoke of me as destined some day to direct the affairs of the State. It was indeed somewhat dangerous to be too closely connected with these men ; though also advantageous to be on good terms with them. Yet, to reach his goal with dignity, it was necessary for any one that the suffrages of polite society should

[1] Joseph François Foulon, born at Saumur in 1715. He was Commissioner of War under the ministry of M. de Belle-Isle. Having been appointed Intendant-General of the armies of Marshals de Broglie and de Soubise, he was afterwards Intendant of Finance (1771). In 1789, he was Councillor of State, and was entrusted with the supply of the troops destined to act against Paris. On July 14, fearing for his life, he tried to escape, but was arrested about sixteen miles from Paris, brought back, dragged to the Hôtel de Ville, and there assassinated.
[2] Diplomatic agent and secretary of the Comte d'Artois.
[3] Jean Louis Favier, born in 1711, was Syndic-General of the States of Languedoc. He afterwards entered diplomacy, and became one of the principal secret agents of Louis XV. Arrested at Hamburg by the order of the Duc d'Aiguillon, and conducted to the Bastille, he remained there until the accession of Louis XVI. He died in 1784. Favier has left a number of political writings. The most important—*Réflexions contre le Traité de* 1756 *—was composed for M. d'Argenson.

* "Considerations against the Treaty of 1756."

appoint him to the posts he wished to gain. As for me, I was in no hurry; I was instructing myself. I took journeys; I had done my best to form some idea of the constitution of the *pays d'états*,[1] and had easily convinced myself that that of Brittany, where Madame de Girac,[2] sister-in-law of the bishop of Rennes,[3] lived, was likely to procure me most information. I made several journeys thither. I enjoyed a certain reputation, but not being yet sufficiently acquainted with the world, I was happy to think that I had still some years before me during which I might share the life and pleasures of society, without being obliged to arrange any of the deep combinations required to satisfy the aspirations of a serious ambition.

All who sought office frequented some of the chief families of Paris, whose opinions and language they moulded. The house of Madame de Montesson was visited by the Archbishop of Toulouse, who also shared with M. Necker the sympathies of Madame de Beauvau.[4] It was at the house of

---

[1] One knows the difference which existed between the *pays d'états* and the *pays d'élection.* The former were the provinces which had preserved the right of being taxed by their provincial States (Brittany, Burgundy, Languedoc, Dauphiné, Franche-Comté, Lorraine, &c.). The others were those which, deprived of provincial States, were taxed by the *élus* (elect), that is, agents so-called, since the States-General had actually elected them, and who still preserved this name, although they had for a long time past been appointed by the king himself.

[2] The name of Madame de Girac reminds me that one day, she being indisposed, the people who had come to see her were making end-rhymes late in the evening, and that these were proposed : *jolie, folie, sourit, traces, esprit, grâces.* They urged me to fill them out ; I said that I had never made verses. They did not even give me a pencil. The second verse which came to me, and which is almost the history of my life, induced me to write on a card :

> " Et que me fait à moi qu'on soit belle ou jolie,
> A moi qui, par raison, ai fait une folie?
> Je ne puis que gémir lorsque tout me sourit.
> Et l'austère vertu qui partout suit mes traces,
> A peine me permet les plaisirs de l'esprit,
> Lorsque mon cœur ému veille au chevet des Grâces." *
>
> (*Prince Talleyrand.*)

[3] François Bareau de Girac, born at Angoulême (1732), was vicar-general of this city, then Bishop of Saint-Brieuc (1766), and of Rennes (1769). He refused to take the oath in 1791, and exiled himself. He returned to France under the Consulate, and died in 1820, having previously been appointed a canon of Saint-Denis.

[4] Marie Sylvie de Rohan-Chabot was born in 1729. She married Jean Baptiste de Clermont d'Amboise, Marquis de Renel, and, at his death, became the wife of Charles Just, Prince de Beauvau-Craon, grandee of Spain, and Marshal of France.

> * " What do I care if people be beautiful or pretty,
> I who, out of reason, indulged in folly?
> I can but lament, when all smiles upon me.
> And that austere virtue which everywhere follows my steps,
> Hardly permits me the pleasures of the mind.
> When my aggrieved heart watches by the pillow of the Graces."

Madame de Polignac,[1] and at the Hôtel de Luynes that M. de
Calonne found his supporters. The Bishop of Arras was next to
M. Necker in the eyes of Madame de Blot,[2] and of M. de Castries.
M. de Fleury was backed by Madame de Brionne. The
Baron de Breteuil[3] was second in many houses, first in none. M.
de Soubise[4] protected Foulon. The Hôtel du Châtelet had its
own ambition, and formed wishes for the appointment of the
Duc de Choiseul, for everybody except M. Necker was in favour
with Madame de la Reynière. Les Noailles spoke kindly of
M. de Meilhan,[5] but did not place him in the foremost rank.

I went almost everywhere, and to a mind somewhat accustomed
to observe, the sight offered by the upper classes of society, during

[1] Gabrielle de Polastron was married in 1749, to the Comte Jules de Polignac,
who was raised to the dukedom in 1780. She was long the friend of Marie-Antoinette.
Her *salon* was the centre of "the Queen's party"; she became governess of the
*Enfants de France.** She emigrated after the 14th of July, and died shortly after
at Vienna, leaving two sons, one of whom became the minister of Charles X.

[2] Pauline Charpentier d'Ennery, born about 1733, married in 1719 Gilbert de
Chauvigny, Comte de Blot, a brigadier-general. She was lady-in-waiting to the
Duchesse d'Orléans.

[3] Louis Auguste Le Tonnellier, Baron de Breteuil, born in 1738 at Preuilly
(Touraine); entered the Foreign Office when still quite a youth. When minister at
Cologne, he was initiated in the secret diplomacy of the king. Ambassador at St.
Petersburg (1760). Having returned to France, he was appointed State Minister of the
king's household and of Paris (1783). He re-assumed for a while the direction of
affairs in 1780. He emigrated in 1790, with powers from the king to negotiate with
foreign sovereigns; he returned to France in 1802, and died in 1807.

[4] Charles de Rohan, Prince de Soubise, born in 1715, lieutenant-general in 1748,
Marshal of France and Minister of State (1758). He died in 1787. He was married
three times—1st, to Anne de la Tour d'Auvergne, Princesse de Bouillon, who died in
1739, leaving a daughter, who married the Prince de Condé; 2nd, to the Princesse
Thérèse de Savoie-Carignan; 3rd, to the Princess Christine de Hesse-Rhinfeld.

[5] Gabriel Sénac de Meilhan, born in 1736, was first *Maître des Requêtes,†* then
Intendant of Aunis, of Provence (where the "*allées de Meilhan*" at Marseilles still
preserve his memory), and finally of Hainaut. He was commissary-general of the
War Department in 1775; he emigrated in 1791, resided in Russia on the invitation
of the Empress Catherine, and died at Vienna in 1803. Sénac de Meilhan wrote
many works, two of which have established his reputation as a writer: *Les Considéra-
tions sur l'Esprit et les Mœurs* (1787), and *Du Gouvernement, des Mœurs, et des Conditions en France avant la Révolution ‡* (1795).

* The graceful title given to the royal children of France under the old monarchy.—(*Translator.*)
† *Maître des Requêtes,* to the number of eight till the year 1344, but who were afterwards raised
to eighty-eight, had two principal duties. First, they sat in rotation for periods of three months at
the King's Court, where they drew up reports of the proceedings. Second, they administered justice
for three months in rotation at the Tribunal of the Courts. They had the right of jurisdiction over
all the officers of the king's household. In the first instance, they examined not only the cases of these
officers, but those of all the persons who had the right of *committimus.* Appeals from them were
made to the *parlements.* Sometimes, though very seldom, their decision in the cases sent before
them by the Council of State for final trial were without further appeal. These trials were generally
for forgery of official seals, or of letters patents, or infringements of the privileges of authors or
printers. They were also entrusted with making official inquiries in the provinces, whenever needed,
and from amongst them the *Intendants de province* (whose duties resembled somewhat those of a
high sheriff) were chosen.—(*Translator.*)
‡ "Considerations on Mind and Manners" (1787). "Government, Manners, Customs, and Social
Condition of France before the Revolution" (1795).

the ten years of which I speak, was curious indeed. People's pretensions had put everybody out of place. Delille dined at the house of
Madame de Polignac with the queen; Abbé de Balivière played
with the Comte d'Artois; M. de Vianes pressed the hand of M.
de Liancourt; Chamfort took the arm of M. de Vaudreuil; La
Vaupallière, Travanet, Chalabre, took a trip to Marly, and had
supper at Versailles at the house of Madame de Lamballe.[1]
Gambling and witty sayings had levelled all ranks. Careers,
that great support of hierarchy and of good order, were being
destroyed. All young men considered themselves fitted to rule
the country. They criticized all the measures adopted by the
ministers. The personal acts of the king and queen were
brought under discussion, and nearly always incurred the dis-
approbation of the *salons* of Paris. Young women spoke per-
tinently of all the branches of the administration. I remember
that at a ball, between two dances, Madame de Staël,[2] taught
M. de Surgère [3] what was meant by the kingdom of the *West;—*
Madame de Blot had an opinion upon all the officers of the
French Navy; Madame de Simiane,[4] said that there ought to be
no duties on Virginia tobacco. The Chevalier de Boufflers [5] who

---

[1] Marie Thérèse Louise de Savoie-Carignan, Princesse de Lamballe, was the
daughter of Prince Victor de Savoie-Carignan. Born in 1749, she married in 1767
the Prince de Lamballe, son of the Duc de Penthièvre. Having lost her husband
after a year's marriage, she spent a portion of her life near the queen, who appointed
her superintendent of her household. Having been arrested after the events of
April 10, 1792, she was murdered on September 2.

[2] Anne-Louise Necker, Baronne de Staël, was born at Paris in 1766. She was
the daughter of Necker. She found herself early in life in contact with all the most
distinguished people and learned men of the time. When twenty years of age, she
married the Baron de Staël-Holstein, Swedish Ambassador to Paris. Madame de
Staël resided in Paris during the whole of the Revolution, and took an active part in
public affairs. Relentless enmity sprang up between her and the First Consul.
Having been exiled to Coppet with orders not to leave that place, she managed to
escape after eight months of semi-captivity. She visited Vienna, Moscow, St. Petersburg, Stockholm, and London. Returning to France with the Restoration, she died
on July 10, 1817.

[3] The Vicomte Jean-François de la Rochefoucauld, Comte de Surgère, only
known under this last name, was the son of the Marquis de Surgère, a lieutenant-
general. He published under the title of *Ramassis* * several moral treatises (3 vol.
in 12), 1734–88.

[4] Probably Adélaïde de Damas, who married, in 1777, the Comte Charles de
Simiane, a colonel in the army, and gentleman-in-waiting to Monsieur, the Comte de
Provence, afterwards Louis XVIII., next brother to Louis XVI.

[5] At the age of twenty-four, the Chevalier de Boufflers, born in 1738, was appointed
a Knight of Malta. Brigadier-General in 1784, he was, in the following year, appointed
Governor of Senegal. Deputy of the States-General in 1789, he was one of the mem-

* *Miscellanies.*

possessed some letters from Prince Henry of Prussia[1] in his pocket-book, said that France could only regain her political preponderance by abandoning the alliance of Austria for that of Prussia. "There is much more learning in the *parlement* of Rouen than in that of Paris," said Madame d'Hénin.[2] "Were I in the king's place, I would do. . . such a thing," said M. de Poix.[3] "Were I the Comte d'Artois, I would say. . . to the king," said St. Blancard,[4] and so on with the others. This state of affairs would have changed in a moment, if the government had been stronger or more skilful ; if serious preoccupations had not totally gone out of fashion ; if the queen, less beautiful and above all less pretty, had not given way to all the whims and fancies of the time. Easy manners in sovereigns inspire more love than respect, and when troubles come, that love itself vanishes. Then an attempt is made to resort to authority, but it is too plain that this show of authority is only an effort, and a mere effort does not last. The government, not daring to follow up that which they undertake, fall again, of necessity, into a fatal indolence. Then comes the last expedient—a change of ministers ; that, it is thought, will remedy the situation ; it may content some families, please some persons, but that is all. At that

bers of the Constitutional Party. He emigrated in 1792, and lived at Berlin near Prince Henry of Prussia. He returned to France in 1800, and died in 1815. The Chevalier de Boufflers had married in 1768, the Princess Lubomirska. Later, at Berlin, he, having become a widower, married the widow of the Marquis de Sabran. The letters he exchanged with his second wife before his marriage have been published.

[1] Prince Henry of Prussia was a brother of the great Frederick. He obtained brilliant successes during the Seven Years' War. Very French in his tastes and manners, he often came to Paris, where he was received in all the *salons*. He died in 1802.

[2] Mademoiselle de Monconseil married, in 1766, Charles d'Alsace de Hénin-Liétard, born in 1744, known under the name of Prince d'Hénin. She was lady-in-waiting to the queen. The Vicomtesse de Noailles has penned a very pretty portrait of her in the *Vie de la Princesse de Poix*.

[3] Philippe de Noailles-Mouchy, Prince de Poix, peer of France, and grandee of Spain, born in 1752, was brigadier-general in 1788. Deputy of the nobility to the States-General, he adopted the constitutional principles, and was elected Commander of the National Guard at Versailles. He emigrated in 1791, returned to France in 1800, and lived in retirement until the Restoration. Lieutenant-General in 1814, he died in 1819.

[4] Charles de Gontaut, Marquis de Saint-Blancard (born in 1752) was, at the time Prince Talleyrand speaks of, a captain in the *Gardes françaises.** He emigrated in 1792, and commanded a brigade in the army of Condé. Having returned to France, he lived in retirement until the Restoration.

* A body of French troops under the old monarchy.—(*Translator.*)

time, France had the appearance of being composed of a certain number of families whose interests the government had to take into account. By such or such a choice they gratified the wishes of one of these families, and secured its influence ; then turning to another, they made use of it in the same manner. How could such a state of affairs endure ?

The power of what, in France, they call *Society*, was prodigious during the years which preceded the Revolution, and even during the whole of the last century. The light and varied ways peculiar to it, probably prevented our historians from noticing the origin, and following up the effects, of this strange result of modern civilization ; I have often thought of it : here are my ideas on the subject.

In countries where the constitution is lost in the clouds of history, the influence of society must be immense. When the origin of that constitution is recent and consequently still before us, this influence amounts to nothing. We see that Athens and Rome in antiquity, England and the United States of America in modern times, have never had, and have no Society.

The dramatic literature of the ancients, Plutarch, the letters of Cicero, those of Pliny, the chronicles of Suetonius, give us no idea of society circles. If we are to judge of Athens by the comedies of Aristophanes, or by the fragments of those of Menander, which have been preserved in the clever adaptations of Terentius, we see that the women lived in absolute retirement. The love-intrigues related in these comedies only apply to courtesans, or to young girls stolen from their parents by slave-dealers.

When every citizen took part in the management of public affairs, the only meeting places were the forum, the tribunal, and the stock-exchange. Ardent imaginations gave a few hours to artists' studios, or to the *salons* of famous courtesans. But this was not the general custom, it was only the amusement of a few. The Romans, by nature warriors and conquerors, always scorned those customs which make life more quiet and pleasant. If eloquence itself, which contributed so much to their glory, was not banished from Rome, it was merely because the Senate made use of it when discussing the great interests of the

State, and, in the forum, to defend the property and the lives of the citizens. They abandoned even the arts, fruits of their conquests, to slaves or to freedmen. The women of Rome never left the shelter of their homes ; it was indecent for any woman but a courtesan to show any talent.

The mingling of the two sexes in society was unknown to the ancients, and but a few years since it was still held in scorn by the customs of England and America.

Permitted in France, it has formed the essential and distinctive character of society : it was under the reign of Francis I. that women began to appear at court. Their presence had an immediate influence on manners, on politeness and on good taste.

Italy was ahead of us in the progress of social refinement. The courts of Naples, of Ferrara, of Mantua, the palace of the Medici, already presented models of urbanity, of politeness, even of elegance. Literature was in honour, the fine arts were successfully cultivated. But the political situation of Italy, the wars of which she was the seat, her division into small states, arrested the progress that would have been accomplished by the practical arts of life.

The carousals, the tournaments, that took place in France under Henry II. imparted more brilliancy, more grace, more nobility to gallantry, and made society more attractive than all the inspirations of the poets of Italy had done.

The court, during the reign of Henry III., degraded itself by adopting the frivolous and shameful habits of the sovereign, and besides, the sad agitations occasioned by the Reformation prevented the development of the character of the nation.

Henry IV., after all the early storms of his life, separated from his first wife, and perpetually quarrelling with the second, had no court. His courage, his vivacity, his happy sallies, his simple language, gay and brilliant, only exercised a personal influence on the customs of the nation.

Cardinal de Richelieu, after having attracted the heads of the great noble families to the court, was anxious to become its centre of attraction. With this object, he threw open his house at Rueil to the men and women whose intellectual abilities had most struck him. From that time dates the first social circle, apart from that of the court, which made itself famous. But the terrible power of the Cardinal detracted much from its pleasantness. A spark caused the bursting forth of the transient conflagration known as the *Fronde ;* this burlesque war, which had no other aim than to gratify the love of agitation entertained by its promoters, was hardly more than a social war, that is, a war between rival social circles.

This chaos ceased with the accession of Louis XIV. He enforced order ; at his voice all classes, all subjects, assumed their proper rank, without effort or violence. To this noble subordination we are indebted for the art of observing propriety —the elegance of manners and the exquisite politeness, which are the main characteristics of that splendid reign. By skilfully combining the aptitudes peculiar to each sex, and causing men and women to display their natural dispositions to mutual advantage, society reached a degree of splendour, the most insignificant details of which Frenchmen will always enjoy to learn. The *salon* of Madame de Sévigné is one of the monuments of our glory.

Society under Louis XV., had all the weaknesses of his reign ; it opened its sanctuary, a few men of letters slipped in. The effect of this was at first, to improve conversation and literature.

M. de Fontenelle and M. de Montesquieu, M. de Buffon, President Hérault, M. de Mairan, M. de Voltaire, all brought up under the influence of the century of Louis XIV., kept up in society that exquisite sense of propriety, that polite and yet free speech, that noble ease which made the charm and lustre of Paris gatherings. Such was the standard which one had to observe.

But under the reign of Louis XVI., every class of literature spread in society. Each writer altered his literary manner, confusion thus crept in, pretensions grew bold, and the sanctuary was broken into. As a result of all this, the general spirit of society underwent all manner of modifications. People wanted to know everything, to fathom everything, to judge of everything. Sentiments were replaced by philosophical ideas ; passions, by the analysis of the human heart ; the wish to please, by opinions ; amusements, by plans, projects, &c. . . . . Everything became unnatural. I pause, for fear I might make you feel too strongly the coming of the French Revolution, from which several years and many events still separate us.

The quarrel of the English with their colonies had just broken out.[1] Philosophers had sounded the question at issue in all its depths. They weighed the rights of peoples and of sovereigns. Old military men were of opinion that this quarrel was likely to bring war, young men saw something new in it ; women something of an adventure ; the mean, cavilling and thoughtless policy of the government made them responsible for all the excitement caused by these distant events. They had tolerated, or rather countenanced, the departure of M. de la Fayette,[2] of M. de Gouvion,[3] of M. Duportail.[4] Only the first of these names has fame handed down to posterity. When writing a novel, an author will endow the hero with an enlightened mind and noble impulses ; fortune does not take so much trouble : insignificant men often play the leading part in great events, simply because they happened to be on the spot.

M. de la Fayette comes from a noble family of Auvergne, not yet rendered illustrious until, under Louis XIV., the wit of a woman reflected some lustre on this name. He had married a young lady of the Noailles family, and was himself the owner of

[1] The Declaration of Independence of the United States was made on May 4, 1776. The cabinet of Versailles recognized the new republic, and signed a treaty of alliance with it (February, 1778). The rupture with England took place on the 17th of the following June.
[2] Gilbert Motier, Marquis de la Fayette, was born in 1757, at Chavagnac, near Brioude. At twenty years of age he fought for American independence. Member of the Assembly of Notables in 1787 ; deputy to the States-General. On the 15th of July he was elected Commander-General of the National Guards of the Seine. Out-lawed after the 20th June, 1792, he was obliged to take to flight, but was arrested by the Austrians, and remained five years imprisoned at Olmütz. He played no part under the Empire. Having been elected a deputy in 1814, he voted for the deposi-tion of the emperor. Still a deputy under the Restoration, he always sat with the Opposition. Elected Commander-in-Chief of the National Guards in 1830, he contributed to the accession of Louis-Philippe. He died in 1834.
[3] Jean-Baptiste Gouvion took part in the campaign in America as an officer of engineers. Greatly attached to la Fayette, he was, in 1789, appointed Major-General of the National Guard. Deputy of Paris in 1791, he sent in his resignation in 1792, and died in action near Maubeuge on the 11th of the following June.
[4] Duportail took part in the campaign of America as an officer of engineers. He was a colonel in 1783, was promoted to the rank of brigadier-general, and appointed Minister of War in 1790. Violently attacked in the Assembly, a writ of accusation was issued against him on the 10th of August. He remained concealed for two years, at the end of which time he succeeded in reaching America. He was returning to France in 1802, when he died at sea.

a large fortune. Had not some extraordinary event brought him to the front, he would have been passed by unnoticed. The qualities of M. de la Fayette were only such as to permit of his waiting patiently for promotion ; he was beneath the mark at which a man is reputed sensible and witty. His ambition, and his efforts to distinguish himself, did not seem his own, but rather to have been taught him. Whatever he does seems foreign to his nature ; he always acts as though he followed some one else's advice. Unfortunately no one will ever boast of having been his adviser at the most important period of his life.

The example of M. de la Fayette was followed by all the gilded and dashing youth of the nation. The young members of the French nobility, who had enlisted for the cause of independence, devoted themselves afterwards to the principles in defence of which they had shed their blood. They had seen the head of a great State rise from a humble private position ; they had seen the simple men who seconded him surrounded by public consideration. From this, it was but a step to the belief that services rendered to the cause of liberty are the only true titles to distinction and glory. These ideas, brought over to France, bore fruit all the quicker because all the prestige of the ruling classes, attacked by inferior men who had obtained an introduction to society, were daily vanishing from sight.

It is probable that I shall revert several times, in the course of these memoirs, to the considerations upon which, following too closely the order of the times, I allow myself to dwell at this point ; for they will surely present themselves, and with a more direct application, when I shall speak of the first years of the French Revolution.

Interest in the American cause was kept up in France by the account of all the deliberations of Congress published every week in a paper entitled *Le Courrier de l'Europe*. This paper, the first, I think, of specially political French papers, was edited by a man who belonged to the police : his name was Morande ; he was the author of an infamous libel which bore the title of *Le Gazettier Cuirassé*.[1]

[1] Charles Thévenot de Morande, born in 1748 at Arnay-le-Duc (Côte d'Or), where

Such Frenchmen who had gone to the colonies of America with military expeditions came home with magnificent descriptions of all the wealth that new part of the world contained. America was the sole topic of conversation. The peculiarity of the members of the aristocracy, in the time of my youth, was that everything that was new to them they believed they had discovered, and were, therefore, all the more fond of it. " What should we be without America ? " was on everybody's lips. " It gives us a navy," said M. Malouet ;[1] " It extends our commerce," said Abbé Raynal ;[2] " It procures employment for our excess of population," the men in office at the time were wont to say ; " It is the refuge of all restless minds," said the members of the government ; " that of all dissenters," said the philosophers, and so on. . . . No country seemed more profitable, none better fitted to develop the arts of peace. The only subject of conversation was the glory connected with the discovery of America. And yet (for

his father was an attorney. He came to Paris, where his life of dissipation and intrigue led to his being imprisoned for fifteen months at Fort l'Evêque.* On being set free, he went to England, and acquired some celebrity as a pamphleteer. His *Gazettier Cuirassé, ou Anecdotes scandaleuses de la Cour de France*† (1772) caused quite a sensation. He lived by extorting hush-money from various people, especially from Madame du Barry, who sent Beaumarchais to him to purchase his silence. He edited afterwards, under the name of *Courrier de l'Europe*, a periodical as disgraceful as his pamphlet. Having returned to France, he was imprisoned after August 10, for holding anti-revolutionary views ; he managed to escape, however, and died in 1803.

[1] Pierre-Victor, Baron Malouet, born at Riom in 1740, began life as an *attaché* of embassy at Lisbonne (1758). He afterwards entered the naval commissariat at Rochefort (1763) ; became sub-commissary in 1767, and was sent to San Domingo, and to Guyana after as commissary-general. Deputy of Riom to the States-General, he voted with the constitutional party ; emigrated in 1792, returned to France in 1801, was *Préfet maritime* at Antwerp (1801-1807), and Councillor of State (1810-1812). He was minister of marine under the provisory government, and died in the same year (1814). Malouet is the author of numerous works on the navy and the colonies. He has left most interesting memoirs, which have been published (2 vols. 8vo).

[2] Guillaume-Thomas Raynal, born at Saint-Geniez (Aveyron) in 1713 ; took orders, and came to Paris in 1747, where he won reputation both as a professor and a preacher. He eventually gave up his ecclesiastic appointments. He was one of the most daring philosophers of his time. *L'Histoire philosophique des Indes*,‡ which made his reputation, was burned by the public executioner's hand, and Raynal had to take refuge abroad. He returned to France in 1788, was elected a member of the *Institut* (1795), and died in 1796.

* Le For l'Evêque, which some people wrongly spell Fort l'Evêque, was the prison of the Bishop of Paris. It was situated in the middle of the Rue St. Germain l'Auxerrois, opposite the For du Roi. Louis XIV., having united all the private jurisdictions at the Chatelet in 1674, the For l'Evêque served from that time as a debtors' prison, and was destroyed about 1780.—(*Translator.*)
† " The Unimpeachable-Gazetteer; or, Scandalous Anecdotes of the Court of France."
‡ " A Philosophical History of India." It may be as well to note here that this work excited the enthusiasm of Bonaparte—then but a subaltern officer—who professed the greatest admiration for its author.—(*Translator.*)

let us examine things to the bottom) what has been the result of all our intercourse with the New World ? Do we see less misery about us ? Do subverters of the social order no longer exist ? Have not the glances we cast on distant countries diminished our love for our native land ? Are not wars more frequent, longer, more widely spread, more costly, through the fact of England and France having become sensitive and irritable on other parts of the globe ? The history of mankind furnishes us with the following sad result : that the spirit of destruction quickly repairs to all places with which intercourse has become easier. When a few Europeans cast themselves upon America, they at once found that vast continent too narrow for their ambition, and their interests clashing continually, they fiercely competed against each other until one of them became the master. To-day, when a discussion arises between the captain of a merchant-vessel and a director of the Hudson's Bay Company, all the States of Europe take up arms in the quarrel.

I know how much all I have just said is contrary to current ideas. Voyages around the world make the glory of some individuals, and even of the governments who order them. Learned men will not allow any of the discoveries of our great navigators to be attributed merely to chance ; they insist that previous knowledge enabled these bold pioneers to guess, or at least suspect, the existence of the new countries which enrich our maps. However, they must allow us to point out, that in our own days, when gravitation has become the ruling theory, when methods of calculation have reached their greatest perfection, it has been imagined that, in order to preserve the equilibrium of the earth, there must be a considerable continent at the antarctic pole; several expeditions, however, have been directed towards that point, and all their researches have, so far, proved almost useless. The unfortunate Louis XVI. held to that idea, and we ought to think it but natural that he, of all men, should have been induced to seek afar for other men.

But it seems to me of little interest to us to engage in such enterprises ; if it be absolutely necessary that they should be

carried out, we should leave this duty to the new rulers of the
ocean ; it does not concern us.

A correspondence which I closely kept up for several years
with M. de Choiseul-Gouffier, then ambassador in Constantinople, and M. Peissonel, consul in the seaports of the Levant,
fully convinced me of the many advantages we might still derive
in our days, by turning our political and commercial views
towards the old world.

When we consider the geographical position of this compound, solid, compact body which is called France, when we
follow its whole coast, we needs must be astonished that it has
not always looked upon the Mediterranean Sea as its own
domain. This basin, the entrance to which is accessible
only through an inlet a few miles wide, is closed in on all
sides by countries possessing little or no shipping. Possessing in herself, and in Spain, her ally, all the means
afforded by the fine harbours of Toulon and Marseilles, by
Carthagena, and numerous other ports, ... France can easily
acquire in the Mediterranean whatever degree of superiority she
may wish to possess. The immense advantage that might
result for her from such superiority has hitherto been overlooked.

A spirit of imitation and a sentiment of rivalry attracted us
to the ocean. It is a remarkable fact that all the schemes for
the naval greatness of France always required the spirit of
opposition to foster them. It has always required the prospect
of having to fight an enemy, or weaken some nation, to excite
our pride, rouse our courage, and develop our industry. I am
sorry to make the statement, but everything indicates that in
man, the power to hate is stronger than that of love to humanity
in general, and even than that of our personal interests. The
idea of greatness and prosperity without jealousy and rivalry is
too abstract for any ordinary mind to grasp it : ordinary minds
require some concrete object to which to apply their conceptions,
and, so to speak, measure them materially.

In order to palliate somewhat the sadness of these remarks,
let us attempt a compromise. Might not the natural rivalry
which exists between what is known of the new world and of

the old, afford a sufficiently large field to the men who are inclined to mischief?   Generous impulses would thus be left the hope of exciting the industry of the two continents, and of bringing them mutually to promote each other's happiness and prosperity.

I feel no restraint in discussing this question, for France is almost without colonies ; the ties that bound her to her former possessions are either broken or loosened ; we are thus free to choose the system which may appear most useful to us.

Have we any greater interest in resuming our former intercourse with the new world than in seeking new relations with the old ?   It is important that this political problem be solved. If it could be proved that farming is easier and not so expensive in the old world as it is in the new one ; that the produce is equally good, and that merchant shipping would not suffer by that new state of things, the solution would be complete.

In the first place, farming is easier, for since the abolition of the slave-trade, pronounced in England, at the Congress of Vienna and in the United States, it seems impossible that any people of Europe should again undertake such infamous traffic, and that planters should much longer be able to get coloured men, whose number is growing less every year, to till the soil of the West Indies and of the equatorial colonies.[1]   The instruments of agriculture being no longer the same, the latter must experience changes, and the bases of calculation upon which the riches of the American colonies were founded will necessarily become inexact. The cultivation of the soil in these hot climates being more diffi-cult and costly, the productions must decrease, and their price be

---

[1] The slave-trade was abolished but very late by modern civilized nations. During all the eighteenth century, England reserved to itself, by the treaty of Utrecht, the monopoly of importing negroes to all the Spanish colonies—that is to say, to nearly all South America.   When the English colonies had a proportion of twenty blacks to one white, it occurred to them to be indignant at the immorality of the traffic, and one of the first acts of the Union was the prohibition of the importation (1794), which was even punishable by death (1818). Denmark had preceded them (1792) ; England followed (1806). At the Congress of Vienna, a declaration was signed by all the powers, except Spain and Portugal, *stating that the slave-trade was repugnant to the principles of universal morals ; that it afflicted humanity and degraded Europe ; that, in consequence, negotiations should be opened between all the States to hasten the moment when it should be abolished everywhere.*   On his return from the island of Elba, Napoleon suppressed the slave-trade in all the French colonies, a decree which was confirmed by Louis XVIII.   For many years after, the slave-trade was to form the subject of delicate transactions between the cabinets of Europe.

proportionately increased. None of these inconveniences would be felt in the old world. In Africa, the instruments are there, they are numerous, they support themselves. If the soil requires more cultivation, the unoccupied population is so abundant that it easily supplies this need. We must no longer compare the work of blacks in America with that of blacks in Africa. It is white men in America who will hereafter be employed at labour beyond their endurance ; to obtain the same products a greater number will be necessary, and will they have this number ? In Africa they have them.

The second point of the problem resolves itself equally in favour of the Mediterranean. All the products of Africa are good. The sugar of Egypt is hard and grained ; in the process of refining it becomes as white as that of San Domingo ; and there is every reason to believe that we could obtain a very fine quality in the central parts of the regencies of Tunis and of Algiers. Abyssinia produces coffee which is superior to that of the West Indies ; if its culture were encouraged by an assured sale, all the kingdoms and islands of southern Asia would furnish it in abundance. The beauty of the cotton cultivated in Africa merely for local needs, proves that it would easily surpass that of Cayenne, of our other colonies and of the United States of America. Indigo is cultivated successfully between the 34th and 35th degrees of latitude, and could be easily obtained in this latitude in Africa.

It remains then to be seen if it would not be prejudicial to the great art of navigation, to give to commerce a new direction, which, at first sight, appears to tend to narrow the domain of science.

There would be no foundation for any fear in this respect. One cannot seriously believe that France, with the extent of coast which she has on the ocean, and the ports which she possesses, could allow herself to lose or be forbidden her competition in the navigation of the high seas. This supposition needs not even be discussed. The ocean, the seas of America and of India, must always remain open to all nations ; it is the great school where the art must be preserved and perfected. The principles of the great discoveries are fixed ; the development of which they are susceptible will necessarily follow. Except by a frightful revolution of the whole globe, the fruits of so many efforts, of so much work, of so many centuries, could not be lost for France, any more than for the rest of the world. It is not something less than what exists that I demand, it is something more. While England is so placed as to have greater advantages than France upon the ocean, France is so situated as to have greater advantages on the Mediterranean than has England. From this division, there would result even for commercial peoples, motives of emulation which would tend to maintain a sort of level between the industries of all civilized countries.

It is principally to commercial interests that I address myself, because I am disposed to believe that reason or rather lassitude will bring about a state of affairs in which so much attention will no longer be paid to the strength of the navy, and to the means it affords of securing the upper hand in war. I hope that some day this will become a secondary point of view, and that the principal object of a navy will be to foster trade, to increase comfort, and to contribute to the general prosperity.

However vaguely expressed these ideas may be, and although they only seem confined to a wish, they cannot be regarded as idle fancies, if we put aside what is too absolute and arbitrary in them and confine ourselves to considering them as subject to the obstacles which proceed from those events which always interfere with the progress of human schemes.

A little good, eagerly grasped, the enjoyment of which is always of short duration, is all human nature can boast of. Thus it suffices that a political view offer some advantage, that it be in principle conformable to nature, that it present little risk, little loss, few sacrifices, for it to be regarded as good, and for men to be able to place hope in it, without fear of being carried away by their own conceptions.

One would be more encouraged in taking this view, on looking back to the preceding epochs of our history. Thus it would be seen that in the time of the Crusades Europe was precisely on the way to these ideas. The commerce of Asia, liberty of communication with this rich part of the old world, were among

the secret motives of war on the part of the Western Powers
against the Califs of Arabia, against the Soudans of Egypt,
and the Sultans of Nicomedes. Religion served as a pretext for
politics, and politics could gain a glimpse already of the advantages of an exclusive navigation. With some success, prudently
managed, European colonies might soon have been seen forming
on the coasts of Egypt and Syria. And in the wars which would
have been sustained by the jealousies and rivalries of the
confederate princes, France, by her position, would have had
immense advantages that later she was not able to regain in the
struggle caused by the discovery of America. In our days, the
great difficulties of religion having been overcome, commercial
arrangements might further the interests of all the powers of the
East, which by themselves are not essentially maritime powers.

I ought still to indicate another strong consideration ; it is
That is why, at a time of my life when I had the power to
do so, I introduced into the treaty of Amiens—as a mere philosophical view, so as to give no umbrage to the powers—a few
provisions having for their object the civilization of the coast or
Africa.[1] If the government had followed the matter up ; if, instead of sacrificing all that remained of the fine army of Egypt,
to the vain hope of reconquering San Domingo,[2] one had
directed against the States of Barbary that imposing and
already acclimatized force, it is probable that my philosophy
would have become practical, and that France, instead of having
destroyed in a few months a fine army at San Domingo, would
now be firmly established on the African coast of the Mediterranean, thus sparing us the gigantic and disastrous continental
system.

I ought still to indicate another strong consideration ; it is

---

[1] The treaty of Amiens guaranteed the independence of Malta, its neutrality, and
opened its ports to vessels of all nations. An article excepted from this latter privilege
the ships of the Barbary states, *until by means of an arrangement procured by the
contracting parties, the system of hostilities existing between the aforesaid Barbary
States and the order of St. John, as well as the Christian powers, should have ceased.*
It is doubtless this latter provision which denoted on the part of its author certain
views on the Mediterranean that he mentions above.

[2] Since 1795, the island of San Domingo had been independent under the government of Toussaint-Louverture. The First Consul wished to re-occupy it ; his brother-
in-law, General Leclerc, was charged with the expedition (February, 1802). He was
victorious at first, and took possession of nearly all the island, but sickness decimated
his troops, and he himself died. After the breach of the peace of Amiens, the English
seconded the efforts of the blacks. The remnant of our troops were obliged to evacuate
the island, which has since remained independent.

that America has not yet taken her place in the political order, and that in regard to her, time has not yet furnished its proof. If, some day, she should become powerful enough to dare to consider as hers, all the lands grouped about the new continent, what an advantage would it then be for France to have turned her attention to the old world! By this means, also, she would have rendered an essential service to humanity, in preventing, or at least, in lessening the movement of emigration which is leading the present generation towards America. The inclination, almost imperceptible, which draws the European population towards the new world would have required perhaps this retrograding force. I am astonished that philosophers have not taken hold of this great question. It touches, in all its points, on their principles; the slave-trade, of itself, ought not to have led them to it. But since they have neglected it, it is probable that I am mistaken, and that leads me to believe that I do not even understand myself very well when I speak of Philosophers; I employ this term as some people do Nature when they have something vague to say, and the suitable expression is lacking. But, as I often mention the Philosophers, and as I credit them with and shall credit them with much influence on my time, I ought, in order to be clear, to explain, once for all, what I mean by the philosophers of the eighteenth century.

If the philosophers of the eighteenth century had formed a sect, their doctrine would be easy to understand; but modern philosophy has nothing in common with the spirit of a sect. The atheists and deists, to whom alone this qualification could be applied, hardly belong to our times. When one endeavours to fathom the depths of matters, one finds that the secret principle of all sects is political, and that everywhere they are all born from a spirit of independence and liberty, which, finding itself bound by established constitutions, and restricted by prevailing laws, comes out and breaks forth under forms that it tries to legitimatize by religion. It is, beyond doubt, the spirit of opposition to the established government which is the prime mover in all these new doctrines, which are spread afterwards with various modifications. All other causes, physical and moral, are only secondary and accessory.

In England, where the principle of political liberty is em-
bodied in the constitution of the State, sects are innumerable,
and little dangerous.

In Germany, a country divided into various small states, the
spirit of reformation has been perpetuated since Luther and
Calvin, and might have made great ravages, if the French Revolution had not alarmed all governments and dispersed inno-
vators ; those who remain, including Madame von Krudener,[1]
are only ridiculous.

I do not name either Spain or Portugal, because in respect
of philosophy, letters, and science, these two countries have made
no progress since the fifteenth century.

In France, the genius of the exact sciences, by the pride and
the real supremacy it has assumed, has annihilated the spirit of
sect by covering all systems with scorn. The introduction of the
philosophy of Bacon, of Locke and of Newton, completed by
M. de Laplace,[2] subjected all the devices of imagination to a
test which permitted it to make discoveries, but not to wander
beyond bounds.

The indecisions of Montaigne, resting his mind on what he
calls those two pillows so soft for a well-made head, ignorance
and heedlessness, prevented him from joining any of the previous
sects, or forming a new one. He discusses all opinions, adopts
none, and intrenches himself behind doubt and indifference.

Almost at the same time, Rabelais, in the attacks of his
railing, cynical and droll humour, had insulted all prejudices
and attacked all beliefs.

It appears to me that there is a great difference between
this style of philosophy, and that of the founders of sects. By
order of date, Montaigne and Rabelais are the oldest of our

[1] Julie de Wietinghoff, daughter of a rich Lavonian nobleman ; born in 1764 ;
married at eighteen Baron von Krudener, a Russian diplomatist. Madame von
Krudener had a restless youth. After 1804, she seemed entirely changed, devoted
to austerities, and to the conversion of sinners. In 1815, she became acquainted with
the Emperor Alexander, who grew attached to her, and over whom she had a great
ascendency. She wandered afterwards over Switzerland and Germany, disturbed the
cities by her predictions, and was often persecuted. She returned to Russia in 1818,
and died in 1824.

[2] P. Simon, Marquis de Laplace, born in 1749 at Beaumont-en-Auge (Calvados),
was at seventeen years of age Professor of Mathematics. A member of the Institut
from its foundation, Minister of the Interior after the 18th Brumaire, Senator (1799),
President of the Senate, peer of France (1815). He died in 1827.

French philosophers, but they are not the founders of schools. Their pyrrhonism threw into ideas a vagueness, an uncertainty, the results of which make them partly responsible for that confusion we have seen in the last century. Thus the writers who have come nearest to them have never pretended to be the exponents of any doctrine whatever. The disposition to doubt, and the spirit of sect are diametrically opposed.

The spirit of sect has perhaps less of inconvenience, because it is less general in its object, and because it takes possession of but few individuals, and, in France, for a short time only; for the frivolity of the nation does not permit any opinion of this nature to establish a lasting rule. Doubt, on the contrary, can extend itself to all, and endure a long time; it is so convenient that it takes possession of all; for is enlightenment ever sufficiently clear for it? and its danger lies in this, being the aim to which one tends; its advantage, in this being the point of departure. For then one is afraid of divining too quickly; one is afraid of simple outlines; intelligence contents itself with examining modestly in order to arrive slowly at causes: it thus rises by degrees from one abstract idea to another; from phenomena to phenomena, from discovery to discovery, and finally from truth to truth.

This method was not fully understood or faithfully followed until the eighteenth century, for up to this time France was wholly Cartesian. The schools, the Academy of Sciences, even Fontenelle and Mairan, were consistently faithful to Descartes. I remember, and perhaps I alone, that M. Duval,[1] my professor of philosophy at the Harcourt College, afterwards Rector of the University, had issued a little pamphlet against Newton; D'Alembert,[2]

---

[1] Pierre Duval, born in 1730 at Bréauté, a village of Normandy, was at twenty-two years of age Professor of Philosophy at the Harcourt College, principal of the same college, and Rector of the University (1777). There are numerous treatises left by him, in which he endeavours to refute the philosophical theories of the time, notably those of Buffon, Rousseau, and Holbach. He died in 1797.

[2] Jean Lerond d'Alembert was the son of Madame de Tencin and of the Chevalier Destouches, officer of artillery. Abandoned at his birth, he was taken and brought up by a family of working people. His name came from the fact that he was found on the steps of the church Saint-Jean Lerond, which is now destroyed. He soon made himself noticed by his love of science, entered the Academy of Sciences in 1744, and the French Academy in 1754. Closely associated with Voltaire and Diderot, he joined with them in the publication of the *Encyclopædia*. He died in 1783.

Maupertuis,[1] Clairault,[2] and Voltaire, all four very young, were the first apostles of the new philosophy. Thanks to them, the philosophy of Newton, or rather the system of Nature, has triumphed. Thanks to them once more the philosophy of Bacon was applied to science and shed the brightest light thereon. This was the most brilliant side of the philosophy of the eighteenth century; but its glory becomes obscured when one looks upon its moral influence, and, above all, upon its ravages in moral science.

Voltaire, it seems to me, has perfectly traced the character and mission of true philosophy.

"Philosophy," said he, "is simple ; she is tranquil, without envy, without ambition ; she meditates in peace, far from the luxury, the tumult and the intrigues of the world ; she is indulgent, she is compassionate ; her pure hand holds the torch which is to enlighten men ; she never makes use of it to kindle a conflagration in any place on earth ; her voice is feeble, but makes itself heard ; she says, she repeats : ' Worship God, serve kings, love mankind.' "

The beautiful character of this philosophy is found in all the writings of Locke, of Montesquieu, and of Cavendish.[3] These true sages, always prudent in their boldness, have constantly respected, and often strengthened, the eternal foundations on which the morals of mankind rest. But some of their disciples, less enlightened, and consequently less circumspect, have, by dint of researches, shaken all the bases of the social order.

When, in the senate of Rome, they were deliberating on the punishment merited by the accomplices of Catiline, Cæsar, reasoning in the philosophy of the eighteenth century, and presenting abstract principles in order to draw political conclusions

[1] Moreau de Maupertuis, born at Saint-Malo in 1698, died in 1759 ; officer of cavalry. He soon left the army for the study, and entered the Academy of Sciences in 1723. In 1736, he set out on a scientific expedition to the polar regions. Member of the French Academy in 1743, he left for Berlin in 1745, where King Frederic named him President of the Academy. It was there that he had his famous debates with Voltaire. They were published in 1856, under the name of *Life of Maupertuis*, by La Beaumelle, in a small volume, very interesting on account of certain letters of Frederick's contained in it.

[2] Alexis Clairault, born in 1713 at Paris, astronomer and mathematician, entered the Academy of Sciences at eighteen years of age. He died in 1765.

[3] Henry Cavendish, illustrious English physician and chemist, born at Nice in 1731, belonged to a younger branch of the family of the Dukes of Devonshire. He was admitted in 1760 to the Royal Society of London, and, in 1803, was associate of the Institute of France. He died in 1810.

from them, descanted at length upon the nature of the soul, and professed the dogmas of the Epicurean philosophy. Cato and Cicero arose indignant, and declared to the senate that Cæsar was professing a doctrine dangerous to the republic and to mankind. Now, this subversive and distressing doctrine that these great statesmen had the wisdom to discard, has been openly taught in the last century. Under the pretext of uprooting superstition, which was falling of itself, and of extinguishing fanaticism, which inflamed no heads but theirs, Helvétius,[1] Condorcet,[2] Raynal, Baron von Holbach,[3] sometimes with "the state of nature," sometimes with "perfectibility," ruthlessly broke all the ties of moral and political order. What madness to pretend to govern the world with abstract ideas, with analyses, with incomplete notions of order and equality, and with a purely metaphysical morality! We have seen the sad results of these idle fancies.

If such is the necessary outcome of analysis, I would say with good old La Fontaine to the imprudent philosophers who apply it to everything : *Quittez-moi votre serpe, instrument de dommage.*[4]

Your analysis may enlighten the mind, but it extinguishes the heat of the soul ; it dries up all sensitiveness, it withers the imagination, it spoils the taste. Has not Condillac,[5] your oracle, himself said, "*Nothing is more opposed to good taste than a philo-*

[1] Claude Adrien Helvétius, born in Paris about 1715, obtained at the age of twenty-three a place as *fermier-général.* He gave himself entirely to philosophy, and published in 1758 his book *L'Esprit,* condemned at the time by the Pope, the Sorbonne, and the *parlement.* His works—fourteen volumes—were published after his death, which took place in 1771.

[2] M. Caritat, Marquis de Condorcet, born in 1743 at Riblemont, near Saint-Quentin, of a noble family originally from Dauphiné. He was received into the Academy of Sciences at the age of twenty-six. Closely connected with the philosophers, he embraced with ardour the cause of the Revolution. Deputy to the Legislative Assembly and to the Convention, he voted with the Girondists. Proscribed on May 31, 1793, he remained concealed for eight months, but, leaving his retreat, was arrested and imprisoned. He poisoned himself a few days after in his prison (March, 1794). Condorcet had married Mademoiselle de Grouchy, sister of the Marshal of the Empire.

[3] P. Thiry, Baron von Holbach, celebrated philosopher, was born in 1723 at Hildesheim, in the Palatinate. He came to Paris in his youth, and embraced the most violent philosophical principles. He preached atheism openly. His best-known work, *The System of Nature,* was condemned even by Voltaire and Frederick II. He died in 1789.

[4] Lay aside your sickle, it is a dangerous tool.

[5] Etienne Bonnot de Condillac, born in 1715 at Grenoble, of a noble family. He took orders, but without exercising ecclesiastical functions ; was preceptor of the child of the Duke of Parma in 1757 ; member of the French Academy in 1768. Condillac has left several works, which have made him the head of the sensualist school. He died in 1780.

sophical mind ; this is a truth that I must own." If he had opened his hand wider, perhaps he would have let fall a few others of the same kind, which, to-day, contrary to his opinion, are professed in our schools.

All that I have just said leads me to think that the peculiar character of the philosophy of the eighteenth century lies in the use of analysis ; useful, when applied to physical sciences ; incomplete, when applied to moral sciences ; dangerous, when applied to social order.

Thus in all I have written and in all I shall write, the object to which the method of analysis shall be applied will point out, without my being obliged to remark it, whether the name of philosopher is to be taken in good or in bad part.

The importance which economic philosophers have enjoyed for nearly thirty years, demands that I should speak of them in a special manner.

The economists were a section of philosophers solely occupied in drawing from the administration all the means of amelioration of which they believed the social order was susceptible. They were divided into two classes : the one looked upon agriculture as the only creator of riches, and treated industrial labour and commerce as sterile, under the plea that they only created new forms and changes in the materials produced and created by agriculture. The doctrine of this first class of economists is called the doctrine of the nett result, and is set forth in the *Tableau Économique*.[1] The object of this work is to show the distribution of the riches produced by agriculture, and spreading thence into all the arteries of the social body. The consequences of these doctrines following the circulation of wealth, end in the theory of taxation, which eventually saddles agriculture exclusively.

The liberty of commerce is almost the only point upon which this first class of economists is in harmony with the economists about whom I am going to speak. The latter did not adopt the division of sterile classes ; they did not look upon the *Tableau Économique* as a strict or even sufficient demonstration of the

---

[1] The *Tableau Économique*, in which is set forth the physiocratic doctrine, is the work of the physician Quesnay, 1694-1774, founder and head of that school.

phenomena of circulation. They restrict themselves in this respect to some truths of detail. Their great principle is the general liberty of trade in the most extended sense. As for taxation, they accept modifications—they are not absolute.

The government rejected the ideas of the economists of any school whatever ; they preferred known and established principles. They feared changes which might interfere with the existing method of taxation, and with the regular flow of the revenue thus obtained into the royal treasury. Their fear of some diminution in the revenues of the State was such as to prevent their risking any means of increasing them. Such short-sighted and narrow views were necessarily prohibitive.

It was not yet known that a few incontestable principles of political economy, besides a reasonable use of public credit, constitute the whole science of financial administration. Public credit would have diminished the inconvenience which might have resulted from too strict an application of the principles of political economy ; the principles of political economy would have enlightened and moderated the enterprises of public credit. M. Turgot, in establishing the Discount Bank, appears to have foreseen the advantages of this beneficial alliance. He grasped the method which carries the greatest aid to all industries, by maintaining the price of money at a moderate rate ; but he went no farther. The modern art of procuring for the State, without raising taxes, extraordinary levies of money at a low rate, and of distributing the burden over a succession of years, was unknown to him, or, if he knew it, perhaps he perceived, in its application, future difficulties which the French administration, always too lax and inclined to abuse, might some day render dangerous. Besides, to borrow continually while paying debts as constantly, belonged to an order of ideas totally opposed to the pure doctrine of the economists. For, to issue and repay loans, requires the temporary use of moneys for that special object taken from a class of State revenues distinct from the land-taxes which are intended to meet a permanent and special expenditure. But, to attain that end, various articles of consumption should be taxed, chiefly those which, belonging to the comforts of life, are only in use among men who are in luxurious, or at least, well-to-do circumstances. In this class, the articles I speak of are measured by the resources of each consumer, and if the requirements of the latter become too great, too imperative, there is reason to believe that comfort would become more exacting and find compensation in the perfection of industrial production, the limits of which are unknown ; it is true that if it were limited, those financial administrations which had not foreseen it, would be in danger of finding themselves in trouble.

This prolific subject might lead me a long way, for it is full of charm for me. It recalls to me all that I learned in the conversation and in the memoirs of a man whose true value the English have acquainted us with. M. Panchaud has said a thousand times to M. de Calonne, M. de Meilhan, M. Foulon, M. Louis,[1] and myself: "*In the present state of Europe, out of the two countries, France and England, that which follows exactly the sinking scheme which I propose will see the end of the other.*" These were his own words. England adopted his doctrine, and so for thirty years has directed all the movements of Europe. M. Panchaud was an extraordinary man ; he had at once the most ardent, broad, and vigorous mind, and a perfect judgment. He had every kind of eloquence. If an equal and abundant proportion of perceptive and reasoning powers constitute genius, Panchaud was a man of genius. Of his generosity, candour, and gaiety, thousands of instances occur to me which it were pleasant to give here.

But, I must refrain, in order not to interrupt too long the order of ideas which I had prescribed to myself, and I fear I have already some cause for reproach for having spoken of the influence of the philosophers and the economists on the brilliant and ambitious portion of the clergy, long before I had explained

[1] Louis Dominique, called the Baron Louis, was born at Paris, November 13, 1757. He was destined for the church, and was counsellor-clerk in *parlement.* He was intimately associated with Talleyrand, whom he assisted as under-deacon at the Mass of the Federation. He was appointed minister to Denmark (1792); emigrated in 1793. Returned to France after the Consulate, he was *maître des requêtes* to the Council of State (1806), Councillor of State (1811), Minister of Finances in 1814, 1815, and, in 1818, Minister of State, member of the Privy Council. In 1822, he was deprived of all his posts. As a deputy, he took his seat in the Liberal party. In 1831, he was again Minister of Finances, was created a peer of France in 1832, and died in 1837.

what I meant by philosophers and economists ; so I am obliged now to ask my readers to recollect what I have said of the clergy, that it may well be understood what was the kind of spirit with which all orders of the State, all classes of society, were more or less, imbued. My remarks on the clergy apply equally to the magistracy, which, by its great civil prerogatives, has a direct influence upon all minds. It is constantly in operation ; it watches every act of life ; it gives security of property and of person; its power is immense ; consequently, those institutions which are assailed by the magistracy are as good as destroyed in the minds of the people. The new ideas took possession of all the youth in the *parlement.* To defend the royal authority was denounced as servile obedience. The majority which President d'Aligre [1] preserved for the court was every day diminishing, and was lost on the occasion of the quarrel between M. de Calonne and M. de Breteuil. Although M. d'Aligre could promise to the members of *parlement* who voted with him, the favour of M. de Miromesnil,[2] Keeper of the Seals ; of M. de Breteuil, Minister of Paris ; of the queen through M. de Mercy,[3] with whom he was intimately acquainted, he saw his majority melt away at the moment that he was at open war with the comptroller-general.

The first time it failed him was on a question which concerned the queen personally. The counsellors of this unhappy princess, blinded by their own passion, and wishing to serve hers, had carried before the tribunal, and given the greatest publicity to an affair known as that of the necklace, which ought to have been hushed up from the very beginning.[4] The decree passed by the *parlement* of Paris

[1] Etienne François d'Aligre belonged to an old family of magistrates originally from Chartres. *Président à mortier,* then first president of the *parlement* of Paris (1768). He gave in his resignation in 1780, went to England, then to Brunswick, where he died in 1798.

[2] Armand Hue de Miromesnil was born in 1723. First-President of the *parlement* of Rouen (1755). Keeper of the Seals under Louis XVI., (1774-87). He died in 1766, on his estate of Miromesnil in Normandy.

[3] François, Comte de Mercy-Argenteau, belonged to an old family of Lorraine. He was ambassador of the German empire in France, during the whole of the reign of Louis XVI. From 1789, Mercy took an active part in bringing about foreign intervention in favour of the king. He died in 1794. His correspondence with Marie-Antoinette and Marie Thérèse has been published.

[4] It is well known what this sad affair was, which did irreparable injury to the queen, although she was entirely innocent. The jeweller Boehmer had offered to the queen a magnificent necklace, worth 1,600,000 francs. She refused to accept it. A

ought to have made a profound impression on the queen, and to have enlightened her as to the character of the person upon whom she had bestowed her confidence. But fatality prevented this hard lesson from having the effect one might have expected ; she did not change her counsellors ; the Baron de Breteuil and the Archbishop of Toulouse only gained in power ; and the queen, again allowing herself to be carried away by the frivolous excitement which surrounded her, satisfied herself with speaking with scorn of Abbé Georgel,[1] with sharpness of MM. Fréteau,[2] Louis, Le Coigneux,[3] de Cabre,[4] and with showing displeasure towards those who were associated with Madame de Brionne and her daughters. This petty revenge was extended even to me, and I experienced some difficulty in obtaining the places to which I was naturally called. The affection of Madame de Brionne and her

lady of high birth, but of doubtful morality, Madame de la Motte-Valois wished to appropriate it. She succeeded in persuading Cardinal de Rohan, who had recently incurred the displeasure of Marie-Antoinette, that the queen had only refused the necklace in appearance, and in order to avoid the scandal of the excessive expense, but that she would be very grateful if he would secretly facilitate the purchase. The cardinal, convinced, bought the necklace on credit, and gave it to Madame de la Motte to give to the queen. Madame de la Motte hastened to sell it in England. The affair soon got abroad through the complaints of Boehmer who had not been paid. The cardinal and Madame de la Motte were arrested, and denounced to *parlement*, which acquitted the former and convicted the latter. They worded their verdict in such a manner as to throw a doubt on the innocence of the queen.

[1] Abbé Jean François Georgel, born at Bruyères (Lorraine) in 1731, was at first Professor of Mathematics at Strasbourg. Cardinal de Rohan took him to Vienna as secretary of the embassy. On his return, he was appointed vicar-general at Strasbourg. In the affair of the necklace, he rendered the greatest service to the cardinal by burning his papers and writing his defence. He was himself exiled to Mortagne ; he emigrated in 1793, returned to France in 1799, refused a bishopric, was named vicar-general of the Vosges. He died in 1813. Abbé Georgel left some memoirs extending from 1760 to 1810 (Paris 1817, 6 vols., in 8vo.).

[2] Emmanuel Fréteau de Saint Just, was born in 1745. Counsellor of *parlement* in 1765. In the affair of the necklace he took the part of the cardinal. He was imprisoned after the session of November 17, 1787. Deputy of the nobility to the States-General, he embraced the cause of the Third Estate ; he was twice President of the Assembly. He retired to the country after August 10. Arrested in 1794, he was guillotined on June 14th.

[3] Marquis Lecoigneux de Belabre was received as Counsellor to *parlement* in 1777. He was a descendant of the first president Lecoigneux, who lived at the commencement of the seventeenth century, and whose son was the celebrated Bachaumont.

[4] Abbé Sabatier de Cabre was Secretary of the Embassy at Turin. Minister at Liège (1769). Chargé d'affaires at St. Petersburg. Director of the consulates at the Ministry of Marine (1782). He was advisory clerk to the *parlement*. He embraced with ardour the cause of the Revolution. Arrested under the Reign of Terror, he escaped the scaffold and died in 1816. He must not be confounded with Abbé Sabatier de Castre, a journalist protected by Vergennes, who also played a certain part in parliamentary affairs (1742-1817).

daughters, the Princesse de Carignan and the Princesse Charlotte of Lorraine, indemnified me largely for all the opposition I experienced in my career. The beauty of a woman, her noble pride mingled with the prestige of an illustrious and famous race, so often near the throne either as enemy or as support, adds a special charm to the sentiments which she inspires. I thus remember the time of my disfavour at court with more pleasure than many of the fortunate circumstances in which I have been placed in life, and which have left no traces either in my mind or on my heart. I scarcely recollect that the queen prevented my profiting by a great act of kindness of Gustavus III.,[1] who had obtained for me a cardinal's hat from Pope Pius VI.[2] She told M. de Mercy to advise the court of Vienna to oppose the nomination of a French cardinal before the promotion of the *crown cardinals.*[3] Her wishes were fulfilled, the nomination of the Pope suspended, and, it is probable that since that time, my cardinal's hat has passed some years in French fortresses.

The new spirit introduced into the *parlement* having sown the seeds of discontent and ambition amongst the members composing this ancient body, intrigue penetrated everywhere. M. Necker, M. de Calonne, M. de Breteuil, each had their creatures who defended or attacked the measures of the minister whom they wished to sustain or overthrow. Each day saw the great magistracy farther estranged from the royal authority, to which in the best times of the monarchy, it had been constantly attached. Even *esprit de corps* no longer existed ; the demand of the States-General, made a little more than a month afterwards, is a proof of this. An alarming number of scattered opinions which

---

[1] Gustavus III., King of Sweden, son and successor of Adolphus Frederick. Born in 1746, he mounted the throne in 1771. He was assassinated in a conspiracy of the nobility, March 16, 1792. He left the throne to his son, Gustavus IV.

[2] Pope Pius VI. gave a cordial reception to the King of Sweden, Gustavus III., during a visit which the latter paid to Italy. He sought a means of being particularly agreeable to him, and accorded him the promise of a cardinal's hat for the Abbé de Périgord, for whom Gustavus III. had solicited it. It was entirely a favour, and all the more remarkable that it was bestowed upon a Protestant prince.—(*M. de Bacourt.*)

[3] The Pope has always reserved the exclusive right of naming the cardinals. Sometimes certain Catholic sovereigns, the King of France, the Emperor of Germany, the King of Spain, the King of Poland, the Stuarts, had obtained the right of naming, or rather presenting to the nomination of the Pope, who always sanctioned their choice, a certain number of cardinals, who were named, in consequence, *the cardinals of the crowns.* They were assimilated with the other cardinals, and represented their sovereigns at the papal elections.

did not always take their stand under the colour of any party, caused anxiety to the ministry on the registering of each law that the needs of the State appeared to require.

M. de Calonne braved this state of affairs, and insisted on bringing before the *parlement* a law on a very delicate matter which required a mass of information which he lacked.

The relative value adopted in gold and silver money in the recoinage of 1726, was no longer in conformity with the marketable value of gold and silver metal. A mark of gold in the ingot, of the same standard as the louis, sold for more than seven hundred and twenty *livres*, yet the same mark of gold made into louis yielded only thirty such coins, equivalent to seven hundred and twenty *livres*. It was necessary then to give to gold coin, in its relation to silver coin, a proportion more nearly approaching the value it had relatively to silver in the ingot. By the law of 1726, the proportion of gold to silver was from 1 to $14\frac{513}{1000}$ to from 1 to $14\frac{1}{2}$, very nearly. By the law of which I am now speaking, the proportion of gold to silver was raised to from 1 to $15\frac{477}{1000}$, or nearly from 1 to $15\frac{1}{4}$.

M. de Calonne had adopted with regard to this the opinion of M. de Madinier, a broker, who was better versed in commercial transactions, than in the power of management, which a government ought always to possess when it deals with money. It must be shown to the public, by figures, and a long time in advance, that the recoinage is done in its interests. In important affairs, the reproach of being slow contents everybody; it gives to those who make it an air of superiority, and to those who receive it an air of prudence. M. de Calonne was right, but his precipitation gave him the appearance of being wrong. Baron de Breteuil, Foulon, little Fornier, hawked about memoir after memoir ; Abbé de Vermond[1] gave them to the queen who sent them to the king. The *parlement*, having become an instrument of intrigue, made

[1] The Abbé Mathieu de Vermond was the son of a village surgeon. Born in 1735, he was received as doctor in the Sorbonne in 1757. He attached himself to the fortunes of the Cardinal de Brienne, was in 1769, sent to Vienna by Choiseul as reader to the future dauphiness. He managed to obtain the confidence of the empress and of the archduchess, and gained a great influence over them. He emigrated in 1790, and died soon after at Vienna.

remonstrances, which showed that there was in this body not so much light on these matters, as a disposition to put obstacles in the way of the comptroller-general. The legal motive for the recoinage was to reduce the quantity of fine gold which entered into the composition of pieces of twenty-four *livres Tournois*, to a value corresponding to that of a silver ingot, equivalent to four six-livre pieces.

In the recoinage of 1726, grave faults were committed. They had badly solved the problem of an exact proportion between the value of the two metals of which our money is made (a proportion easy to establish, but difficult to maintain). The valuation had been fixed at about one-sixth above the value of the metal. It is true that the greater number of the Mint directors had lessened this inconvenience, but by means of a grave fraud, by reducing the standard or the weight to such a degree that the remedy had become worse than the evil. Thus, besides the defect of proportion between the two metals, there was a defect of legal identity between louis of the same coinage. A new coinage was thus necessary ; but people did not do M. de Calonne the honour to believe that he meant to be just. They did not understand the diminution of weight which the new gold pieces were to undergo, although this was an indispensable condition for the re-establishment of the proportion between gold and silver, and although in the change of coins, compensation was allowed to the owners of the old money. The delivery of the new louis was to be preceded by the deposit of the louis of the previous coinage ; the delays for changing were prolonged far beyond the time necessary for the coinage, and, as a sequel to so many other financial expedients which were no better, it was supposed that the real object of the minister was to obtain the use of funds by a sort of loan from the owners of the old pieces of gold. Thus, although the proportion adopted by M. de Calonne was good, it furnished a pretext for censure which was made use of unscrupulously. He was able to establish the equilibrium (at least for a time) between two metals each intended to be recognized as a standard, but without having acquainted himself with the very intricate calculations which

justified the reform of the law of 1726, and consequently without
having put himself in a position to reply to all the objections
raised by sceptical or ignorant persons. He achieved his aim,
although he did not deserve all the credit of it.

Louis XVI., encouraged by the opinion of M. de Vergennes,
displayed a very strong will on this occasion. The remonstrances
of the *parlement* were without effect. Madame Adelaide, aunt of
the king, to whom Madame de Narbonne [1] had handed a very
learned memoir on this subject, was not even able to prevent
the exile of Foulon. This unfortunate man was banished to one
of his estates in Anjou, and returned a few years afterwards
only to be one of the first victims of the Revolution.

Unremitting firmness was not in the nature of the king,
and besides he was necessarily discouraged by the want of
harmony existing in his council. Matters became involved ;
public opinion gained strength ; it openly censured and protested. Its action was too powerful to be arrested or even
directed ; it was nearing the steps of the throne ; people
already spoke of the ministers as being popular or unpopular, a
new expression which, taken in the revolutionary acceptation,
would have degraded in their own eyes the counsellors of Louis
XIV., who only desired the esteem and consideration of the
king, but which flattered the republican vanity of M. Necker
because it gave him an influence of his own.

Ordinary expedients were exhausted : it was thought that no
more reforms could possibly be made, and yet the expenditure
exceeded the revenue by an enormous sum. The deficit of 1783
was more than eighty millions. M. Necker, whatever he may
have said in his official report, left it on retiring at nearly
seventy millions. Now that the infatuation he had aroused
has subsided, everybody acknowledges this as a fact. The bonds

---

[1] Mademoiselle de Chalus, married to the Comte de Narbonne-Lara, brigadier-
general. She was maid-of-honour to Queen Marie Leczinska, and subsequently to
the dauphiness. She was the mother of the Comte de Narbonne, Minister of War in
1791, spoken of above.

[2] The financial account handed in by Necker was published in January 1781. It
was the first time that "the secret of the finances was placed before the public," which
until then, was ignorant as to its payments to the State, and as to that which the
State expended. Thus the effect was prodigious. Necker, by this stroke of policy,
reconquered public opinion, and regained credit.

of the Receivers-General, that of the treasurers, of the registrars, which are made use of to make anticipated payments, were only negotiated at a fearful loss. The portions of the loans of M. Necker, which did not bear life-annuities, bore promise of such speedy repayment as to empty the royal treasury. For, in the year 1786, those repayments amounted to nearly fifty-three millions, and they were to increase from year to year until 1790.

This was no longer a time when the revenues of the State could be increased by abandoning the fiscal laws to the interpretation of companies, who knew how to extend their application even to its utmost consequences over property and industry. The four sous per *livre* levied by M. de Fleury was too great a burden for several provinces and was levied with difficulty. Offices only to be obtained by purchase were declined. The *parlement* was unwilling to register any more loans. The public funds were falling day by day. The Bourse of Paris received its impetus from speculations made on behalf of private establishments. They bought or sold shares of the Bank of Discount, of the India Company, of the water companies of Paris, of insurance companies, &c. As usual in times of calamity, gambling occupied the attention of all. The government tried to raise some money by obtaining an Order in Council authorising the creation of lotteries amounting to several millions ; but these weak means had limits, and now they were reached.

M. de Calonne, thwarted in all his operations, attacked on all sides, sapped by the intrigues of the Archbishop of Toulouse, but having still M. de Vergennes and the king on his side, believed he would be able to overcome all the difficulties which assailed him by resorting to a new method, the result of which was not to be devoid of success. He formed the project of summoning an Assembly of Notables ;[1] he hoped, by this unexpected appeal, to replace the national sanction, the registra-

[1] The Assembly of the Notables was a compromise imagined by the minister to obviate the necessity of convening the States-General. Calonne wished to impose a land-tax, but, foreseeing the resistance of the *parlement* and of the clergy, he was anxious to find support in the nation. The Assembly met on February 22, at Versailles, and broke up on the 25th of May.

tion of the *parlement*, which had been refused him, and to regain
the opinion of the public, before which he was confident he could
appear with advantage.

At the very first sitting of the assembly, he proposed the
formation of provincial assemblies throughout the kingdom, the
suppression of statute-labour, of provincial customs and of several
duties connected with the collection of taxes and disapproved by
public opinion, the reduction of the excise duties on salt, and the
freedom of the corn trade.

He boldly resolved to increase the deficit by the sacrifice of
ten millions on the product of the salt-duties, of twelve millions
on the customs and the duties connected with the collection of
taxes, of ten millions on the villein-tax, of seven millions to help
the clergy to pay their debts, the principal part of which would be
cancelled by the alienation of the sporting rights, and of the
honorary rights attached to its possession ; and, in addition, by
an expenditure of ten millions to replace the statute-labour, and
of six millions for the encouragement of agriculture, the arts and
commerce. He flattered himself that, as a compensation for so
many advantages, he would easily be allowed to raise or replace
a revenue amounting to from one hundred and ten to one
hundred and twelve millions.

He could already reckon on fifty of them in the regular receipt
of the two-twentieths of the net revenue of all the landed
property in France. The increase of this tax proceeded from
the proposal of M. de Calonne to destroy all the privileges of
corporations or of orders, all exemptions, all personal favours.
He gave to this new tax the name of *subvention territoriale ;*
and said that this would not be a new tax, since the charge for
those who were paying exactly the two-twentieths would not be
increased, and that it was only a matter of suppression of the
abuse of an unjust apportioning and of exemptions which those
who enjoyed them were ready to forego.

He estimated at twenty millions the revenue from the
establishment of the stamp duty.

The infeoffment of domains, and a better administration of
the forests was to yield ten millions.

In order to reimburse these sums at fixed periods, he issued an annual loan of twenty-five millions, which was only to be repaid after fifteen years.

He also submitted retrenchments amounting to fifteen millions.

This was indeed a vast plan, but it could not be carried out seeing that the Notables had no power to vote it; it was imposing as a whole; it presented the advantage of soothing the apprehensions of all those who had money invested in the funds, and of adopting by legal means ideas, which, for some time, had been circulating among the educated classes of society, and were beginning to penetrate the mass of the nation.

But M. de Vergennes was dead,[1] and the king was the only and feeble support for a minister who was openly attacking so many interests.

The clergy were subjected to a tax from which they had hoped their gratuitous donations had relieved them for ever. They maintained that, if they did not pay the twentieth under the name of twentieth, they paid its equivalent under the name of tenth; then leaving the question which concerned them, they attacked the *subvention* from a general point of view. M. de Calonne was unfortunately persuaded that the payment of taxes in kind would prove less difficult than a tax of fifty millions of money. He has set forth in one of his memoirs that the raising of taxes in kind is the easiest way to make the division proportional, to abolish arbitration, and to spare the tax-payers the cruel necessity of paying when there is no harvest. The Archbishop of Narbonne, the Archbishop of Toulouse, the Archbishop of Aix, the Archbishop of Bordeaux, all well-versed in this question, of which their tithes had taught them the weak side, showed that the expenses of this mode of taxation would be very great, that the difficulties to which it led were enormous, and that the time required to make a correct classification of lands would be a loss for the royal treasury.

The opinion of the higher clergy became that of the Notables and M. de Calonne was beaten upon that point.

One check leads to another, often indeed, to many.

[1] February 13, 1787.

M. de Montmorin,[1] the successor of M. de Vergennes, had as yet but little credit ; he had no opinion and was afraid even of being thought to have one. M. de Miromesnil, the Keeper of the Seals, found that the new enterprise was imprudent, and had compromised the royal authority ;—the Baron de Breteuil was bestirring himself—the Archbishop of Toulouse was still intriguing, and M. de Calonne, whose position the importance of affairs still made tenable, and who, at the conference held at the house of *Monsieur*,[2] had shown a prodigious talent, left the solid ground on which he had been standing, and no longer sought for means of defence, except in the intrigues of the court. The Comte d'Artois sustained his credit with the king ; Madame de Polignac placed at his disposal all the influence she still enjoyed over the queen. The poet Lebrun,[3] at M. de Vaudreuil's request, addressed him in beautiful verse.

All this might have had some influence in ordinary times, but it was of very little account in such ominous circumstances. M. de Calonne no longer spoke to the king with the same assurance. The Assembly of the Notables had been an expedient, and he needed an expedient for the Assembly of the Notables. He had none. When one fears others, and has no longer complete confidence in one's self, one only makes mistakes. What ruined him was the interruption of the session during the Easter vacation. The Notables left Versailles and came to Paris, where they were received by all circles of society ; the spirit of opposition they brought with them, strengthened by that which they found there, seemed to the king to represent the opinion of imposing numbers ; he was frightened at it. Since

---

[1] The Comte Armand de Montmorin Saint-Hérem, issue of a very old family of Auvergne, was born in 1745. He was ambassador at Madrid. Member of the Assembly of Notables, 1787. Secretary of State for Foreign Affairs, 1787. He was a partisan of the constitutional monarchy. Minister of the Interior *ad interim*, 1791, he resigned all his functions in November of the same year. Arrested on August 20, 1792, he was summoned before the Assembly, which issued against him a writ of accusation. He perished in the massacres of September.

[2] The title given in France to the king's eldest brother.

[3] Denis Écouchard-Lebrun, lyric poet, was born in 1729. He has written odes, epigrams and elegies, and made himself such a reputation that he was known under the name of Lebrun Pindar. But his character was not as high as his talent. After having lived for a long time on a pension from the queen, he joined the revolutionary party, incited the violation of the tombs of Saint-Denis, demanded, in another ode, the death of Marie-Antoinette, and ended by being the poet-laureate of the empire. He died in 1807.

the death of M. de Vergennes no one possessed enough influence over his mind to reassure him. M. de Calonne was dismissed.

In the long list of the ministers of the eighteenth century, I do not know in what rank, nor by the side of whom, history will place him ; but this is what I saw of him.

M. de Calonne had a free and brilliant mind, a shrewd and quick intellect. He spoke and wrote well ; his diction was always clear and elegant, he had the talent of embellishing what he knew, and of avoiding the discussion of that which he did not know. The Comte d'Artois, M. de Vaudreuil, Baron de Talleyrand,[1] the Duc de Coigny,[2] liked in Calonne the forms he had borrowed from them, and the intellect he made them believe they possessed. M. de Calonne was susceptible of attachment and fidelity to his friends ; but, in selecting these, he followed more the dictates of his mind than of his heart. Dupe of his vanity, he believed in good faith that he loved the men his vanity had sought. He was ugly, tall, nimble and well-shaped ; he had an intellectual countenance and a pleasant voice. In order to enter office, he had compromised or, at least, neglected his reputation. He was surrounded by worthless people. The public credited him with sense, but not with morality. When he obtained the post of comptroller-general, he seemed, in most people's eyes, but the clever steward of some ruined spendthrift. Great quickness of mind pleases, but does not inspire confidence ; it is generally thought that people so gifted display little attention and scorn advice. Most men like industry and prudence in their ministers. M. de Calonne was not encouraging in this respect ; in common with all brilliant minds, he displayed thoughtlessness and presumption in all he did. This was the salient characteristic of his nature, or rather of his way of proceeding. I will quote a remarkable instance of this. M. de Calonne had come to Dam-

---

[1] The Baron Louis de Talleyrand, uncle of the author, born in 1739, was ambassador to the King of the Two Sicilies in 1785, and died in 1799. He had married Mademoiselle Marie-Louise de Saint-Eugène Montigny, niece of de Calonne.

[2] Henri De Franquetot, Duc de Coigny, born in 1737. Governor of Choisy (1748), lieutenant-general (1780), first equerry to the king since 1771. He emigrated in 1791 ; became captain-general in Portugal. Returned to France in 1814, and was appointed Marshal of France and Governor of the Invalides. He died in 1821.

pierre,[1] to visit Madame de Luynes, on the day following that on which the king had decided to summon an Assembly of the Notables. He was intoxicated with the success of his report to the council of ministers. He read it to us, enjoining the greatest secrecy. This was at the close of the summer of 1786. A week before February 22, 1787, the very day of the opening of the Assembly, he wrote me a note, in which he pressed me to go and spend the week with him at Versailles, to assist him in revising some of the memorandums which he was to submit to the Assembly. He added that I should find all the material necessary to elucidate the points I should undertake to treat. He had written a similar letter to M. de la Galaizière,[2] to M. Dupont de Nemours, to M. de Saint-Genis, to M. Gerbier,[3] and to M. de Cormerey. We found ourselves all, on the same morning, in the study of M. Calonne, who handed us bundles of papers relative to each of the questions which we were to treat. From these we were to draft all the memorandums and bills, which were to be printed and submitted to the discussion of the Assembly eight days later. Thus, on February 14, not a line of this work had yet been written. We divided among us this immense labour. I took upon myself the memorandum and bill on corn ; I wrote them both without assistance. I worked with M. de Saint-Genis on the memoir relative to the payment of the debts of the clergy, and with M. de la Galaizière on that concerning statute labour. M. de Cormerey drew up the whole project relative to the abolition of the barriers.[4] Gerbier wrote paragraphs on all questions. My friend Dupont, who believed great good was to be accomplished, applied all his imagination, mind and heart, to the questions which came nearest to his views. We

---

[1] Dampierre, village of Seine-et-Oise on the Yvette, at some distance from Rambouillet. The château built by Mansart for the Duc de Lorraine, became afterwards the property of the de Luynes family.

[2] The Marquis Chaumont de la Galaizière, born in 1697, was Intendant of Soissons, and Chancellor of Lorraine (1737). Councillor of State in 1766, member of the Royal Council of Finances (1776). He died in 1787.

[3] Pierre Gerbier, a celebrated counsel to the *parlement* of Paris. He was born at Rennes in 1725. He was one of the few counsels who consented to plead before the commission instituted by Maupeou, during the interregnum of the *parlement*. He was nevertheless elected staff-bearer of his order in 1787. He died in the following year.

[4] These were internal customs which Calonne wished to do away with, and to restrict to the frontiers.

thus accomplished, in a week, with tolerable success, a task which the presumption and heedlessness of M. de Calonne had led him to neglect for five months.

The king, compromising with himself, had been weak enough to abandon his minister, but was more desirous than ever to carry out the projects which had been brought before the Notables, and he sought to find as a successor to M. de Calonne, a man whose own opinion would lead him to follow the plans proposed.

M. de Fourqueux [1] seemed the most suitable in this respect. His great simplicity, his ideas, his freedom from all intrigue, and his good reputation pleased the king. But his assent had to be obtained. M. de Calonne, who preferred him to any one else, and who feared that the choice of the king might eventually fall on the Archbishop of Toulouse, wrote to M. de Fourqueux. He instructed M. Dupont, who had had, through M. Turgot, M. de Gournay, and M. de Trudaine, [2] former relations with M. de Fourqueux, to carry the letter to him.

I only mention this insignificant detail because it led to a rather entertaining scene. While M. de Calonne was gathering up all the papers, which he foresaw he might need if his administration were attacked, his particular friends were awaiting him in the large drawing-room of the comptroller-general, where they were meeting perhaps for the last time. They had been there a long while .... no one spoke .... it was eleven o'clock in the evening .... the door opens .... Dupont enters precipitately and shouts in great excitement : " *Victory ! victory ! Mesdames* . . . ." Everybody rises and surrounds him, whilst he repeats : " *Victory ! M. de Fourqueux accepts, and he will follow all the plans of M. de Calonne. . . .*" The astonishment caused by this kind of victory, on Madame de Chabannes [3] Madame de

---

[1] Michel Bouvard de Fourqueux, Counsellor of *parlement* (1738), Attorney-General of the Court of Accounts (1769), Councillor of State (1769), Intendant of Finances. He was for a short time comptroller-general in 1787.

[2] Ch. de Trudaine de Montigny, born in 1733, was Intendant-General of Finances (1763). He declined the office of comptroller-general, and died in 1777. He had by his marriage with Mademoiselle Fourqueux, two sons who were guillotined in 1794.

[3] Marie-Elizabeth de Talleyrand, daughter of Daniel-Marie de Talleyrand, and aunt of the author. She married, in 1759, the Comte Charles de Chabannes La Palisse, colonel of grenadiers. She was lady-of-honour to *Madame.**

* The title given to the king's sister, to his brother's wife, and to his daughters; that of *Mademoiselle* being reserved to the king's grand-daughters.—(*Translator.*)

Laval, Madame de Robecq, and Madame d'Harvelay, greatly
scandalized Dupont, who loved M. de Calonne on account of the
provincial assemblies, and who did not know that these ladies
loved the provincial assemblies on account of M. de Calonne.
Vesmeranges,[1] who was also waiting, and who cared little, either
for the provincial assemblies or for M. de Calonne, but who
felt the greatest respect for the comptroller-general, left immediately for Paris, in order to prepare, ahead of everybody
else, the speculations which the nomination of M. de Fourqueux
was likely to render advantageous.

This new ministry was of short duration. M. de Fourqueux
soon grew discouraged, and the queen, at last, obtained the
nomination of the Archbishop of Toulouse, whose mind and
character were not on a level with the circumstances in which
France was now placed.

On entering office the latter made sacrifices to public opinion,
which, encountering only weakness, became each day more
exacting. Nothing could be obtained from the Assembly of
the Notables, but complaints and the advice to convoke the
States-General, and, in truth, I do not see how the Notables
could have done otherwise than as they did. All concession
on their part would have been useless, because they were really
without power to act ; and, had they done so, they would only
have made themselves odious to no purpose.

It was therefore a great mistake to have summoned them
without being previously sure of directing their deliberations.
For the competence of the *parlements* having been called into
question, or rather their incompetence being implicitly proclaimed by the mere fact of convening the Notables, they were
henceforth powerless. Thus they refused to do what was
asked of them, alleging that they had not the right to do so.
Their refusal was punished by exile, which made them popular ; they were recalled soon after, which making them
feel their importance more, could but induce them to avoid
compromising it. All these measures having served only to
show the limits of royal authority, without being of any assistance

---

[1] M. de Vesmeranges was intendant of the stations, relays, and post-houses of
France.

to it, there only remained the alternative of being self-sufficient, asking sacrifices from no one—which the deficit in the treasury rendered it impossible to do—or of convoking the States-General. The struggle of the Archbishop of Toulouse with the *parlements* was of sufficient interest to induce me to relate it in all its details, in the second part of these recollections, which I have specially devoted to it, and in which the Duc d'Orléans, whose political life was closely connected with the parliamentary opposition of this period, plays a leading part.

None of the operations of the Archbishop of Toulouse succeeded ; the influence which he had used to overthrow M. de Calonne was entirely his own. Although he deprived M. de Calonne of the *blue riband ;*[1] although he obtained for himself a cardinal's hat, the archbishopric of Sens, the abbey of Corbie ; although he made his brother Minister of War,[2] neither fear nor favour gave him a single supporter. Home opposition was becoming stronger, the foreign policy of France was annihilated ; Holland, so easy to defend, had just been abandoned.[3] The royal treasury was empty, the throne was deserted ; the diminution of the royal power was the reigning passion of the moment ; every subject considered himself too much governed ; yet, it is probable that at no other period in our history, were people subjected to a milder rule, and never did they, individually and collectively, so much trespass beyond proper bounds.

The political existence of every nation depends essentially upon the strict observance of the duties imposed upon each individual. If, at the same moment, all these duties cease to be performed, social disorder ensues. This was the position of France when the Archbishop of Sens left the ministry.

[1] That of the order of the Holy Ghost (*ordre du Saint-Esprit*), the highest order of chivalry under the old monarchy.—(*Translator.*)

[2] Louis Marie de Brienne, born in 1730, Lieutenant-General, Minister of War (1787-1788). He was guillotined May 10, 1794, with his two sons and Madame de Canisy, his daughter.

[3] Holland had re-established the stadtholdership in 1747, in the person of the Prince of Orange ; his tyranny irritated all parties, and in 1784, the states deprived him of the greater part of his authority. The prince, supported by a fraction of the nobility and of the populace, called England and Prussia to his aid. The states claimed the intervention of France, which had not failed them in 1785, after their quarrel with the emperor. But the Cardinal de Brienne did not dare to assemble an army on the frontier. The Dutch were crushed by the Prussian army, and delivered to the fury of the victorious faction (September, 1787).

The Protestants were stirring themselves and manifested alarming confidence in M. Necker.

All classes were ready to embrace enthusiastically the new ideas. All the men who had been to college or to an academy, looked upon the application of what they had learned or read there, as conquests to be made by the human mind. Each state wished to be regenerated.

The clergy, who ought to be as immovable as dogmas, had been the first to propose great innovations. They had requested the king to convene the States-General.

The *pays d'états*[1] only saw in their treaties of union with France, a means of opposing all the general measures proposed by the government.

The *parlements* seditiously abdicated the power which they had exercised for centuries, and called from every direction for representatives of the nation.

The administration itself, which until then had cherished the honour of being appointed by the king to represent him, now found its obedience humiliating, and wished to be independent.

Thus, all the bodies of the State were diverging from their first destination, each one had broken its bonds, and had entered on a declivity which, deprived as they were of experience, light and support, must necessarily draw them into the precipice ; therefore, from this time everything presents the character of fatality.

Affairs were in this state when, in spite of his personal repugnance, the king felt obliged to recall M. Necker, who, by works flattering prevailing ideas, and published at carefully studied intervals, had managed to keep constantly the attention of the public upon him.[2] He might, perhaps, in ordinary times have worked some good ; I do not know, personally I do not believe it, but I am sure, that, in 1788, the king could not have

---

[1] Certain *pays d'états*, Brittany for instance, at the time of their union with France had made some formal reservations, and exacted the maintenance of all their rights and privileges.

[2] Necker resumed the direction of public affairs on August 25, 1788. During his retirement he had published a new report on the finances, which appeared in 1784, under the name of *Administration des Finances* (3 vols. 8vo.), of which he sold nearly 80,000 copies. He had also published his correspondence with M. de Calonne (1787, 4").

made a worse choice. At the time of a purely national crisis, to put at the head of affairs a foreigner, a commoner from a little republic, professing a religion which was not that of the majority of the nation, only endowed with moderate talents, full of himself, surrounded by flatterers, without personal consistency, and consequently needing to please the people, was indeed to place one's trust in a man who could only overcome the difficulties of the situation, and that badly, by summoning a meeting of the States-General. It had been shown in every possible way that the latter were dreaded, yet the only reason which made them dreaded was ignored. The nature of the danger had been misunderstood; therefore nothing was done to prevent it, and, on the contrary, it was made inevitable.

The States-General were composed of deputations of the three orders of the State, so that no one was, or could be, a member except by election. All that could be hoped or feared was consequently subject to the result of the elections, which itself depended upon the method according to which they should be carried on.

It was evident that a coalition of the three orders against the throne was a thing morally impossible; that if it were attacked it could not be by the first order nor by the second, nor as long as these two existed; but by the third, after it should have annihilated the two others, and that its first blows should be directed against these. It was equally evident that the first and second orders having nothing to gain over the third, had consequently no interest in attacking it, and could have no desire to do so, while the third, being very differently situated with regard to the two others, was naturally the only one to be feared and against which it was necessary to be forearmed. In this state of affairs, the only end to secure was the preservation of legitimate rights, and it was evident this could not be attained except by proportioning the force of resistance of the first two orders to the force of aggression of the third, and that it was necessary that the former should be made as great and the latter as feeble as possible.

There were two methods for this.

The number of deputies from each order might be so fixed

that the most important members of this order in rank and
fortune should suffice to fill the deputation, and the right to elect
or the right of being elected might be so restricted that the choice
should, of necessity, fall upon them.   In this way, there were
reasons to believe that, in the deputations of the first two orders,
class-feeling would not be weakened by any opposition ; that the
deputation of one would feel as interested in defending that of
the other as its own ; that, in case of attack, the aggressors could
have no secret intelligence in their ranks nor find there auxiliaries ; and, that in the deputations of the third order, the fear of
losing, outweighing the desire of acquisition, would cause the
spirit of preservation to prevail over that of domination.

     It still remained (and this would have been the best plan) to
substitute for the first two orders a peerage composed of
members of the episcopacy and of heads of noble families of
the oldest nobility, greatest wealth and lustre, and limit the
election to the third order which would have formed a separate
assembly.

     Many people, after the Revolution broke out, sought a
method by which it might have been averted, and, with
this object, they imagined various remedies corresponding with
the causes to which they ascribed it ; but, at about the time
when the Revolution broke forth, it could only be prevented
by one of the two methods I have just indicated.

     M. Necker adopted neither the one nor the other.   He fixed
the number of deputies in such a manner that each of the first
two orders was to elect three hundred members, which was far
too many to avoid the necessity of extending the choice to the
inferior ranks which it was advisable to exclude.[1]

     On the other hand, almost unlimited latitude was left as to
the right to elect or to be elected, which put the higher clergy
and nobility in the minority, in the deputation of their order ;
and caused the third order to be composed almost exclusively
of barristers—a class of men, whose method of thinking, necessarily resulting from their profession, render them generally very
dangerous. But the greatest of all mistakes was to authorise the

---

[1] The States-General were composed of 1,145 deputies—291 for the clergy, 270 for
the nobility, and 584 for the Third Estate.

third order to itself elect as many deputies as the other two together. As this concession could only be useful to it in the case of a fusion of the three orders into a single body, it could not have been done without presupposing this fusion, and con- senting implicitly to it. The attempts the third estate would make to obtain the fusion were thus rendered legitimate before- hand, its chances of success increased, and absolute prepon- derance in the body in which the three orders were to be blended was assured to it.

There was in M. Necker a something which prevented his foreseeing and therefore of fearing the results of his own measures. He persuaded himself that he possessed an all- powerful influence over the States-General, that the members of the third order, above all, would listen to him as to an oracle, would only see with his eyes, would do nothing except by his advice, and would not use, against his will, the weapons he had put into their hands. An illusion which was to be of short duration. Precipitated from the height where his vanity alone had placed him, and from which he flattered himself that he ruled events, he had to lament in retirement the evils he had not wished to cause, and to deplore the excesses which horrified his probity, but which, had he been more skilful and less presumptuous, he might have spared France and the world.

His presumption rendered him absolutely incapable of seeing that the movement then taking place in France, was the result of a passion, or rather of the errors of a passion, common to all men, vanity. In the majority of nations it exists only in a subordinate form, and only constitutes one shade of the national character, or else it is apparent only in a single object, while with the French, as formerly with the Gauls, their ancestors, it mingles with all, it rules in everything with an individual and collective energy which makes it capable of the greatest ex- cesses.

In the French Revolution, this passion did not figure alone ; it awakened others which it called to its assistance, but these remained subordinate ; they took its colour and spirit, acted in accordance with it and to further its ends. It so far gave the

impulse to and directed the movement of the French Revolution, that one may really say this great event was born of vanity.
Directed towards a certain aim, and confined to certain limits, the passion of which I speak, binds subjects to the State; it animates and vivifies it ; it then takes the name of patriotism, emulation, love of glory. By itself, and apart from its direction towards a determined end, it is only the desire for pre-eminence. One can desire pre-eminence for his country ; one can desire it for a body of which one is a member, one can desire it for one's self, and, in this case, one may desire to obtain it in a single thing or in several, in the sphere where one is placed or outside of that sphere. One can, in short, but not without madness, desire to have it in everything and over all. If circumstances are such that, with the generality of the members of a State, this desire bear upon social distinctions, the inevitable consequence will be that the greater number will wish only for those titles of distinction that each of them may flatter himself that he has, or has acquired, to the exclusion of all those which by their nature can only be the privilege of a very small number ; thus from the desire for pre-eminence will proceed the spirit of political equality. This is precisely what happened in France just before the Revolution. As *revolutionarily* set forth by Abbé Siéyès,[1] in his essay on privileges, it was a natural and necessary consequence of the situation in which France then was.

---

[1] Emmanuel Joseph Siéyès was born at Fréjus in 1748. He took orders, and was vicar-general at Rennes, played a certain part in the philosophical movement, and became acquainted with all the writers of the time. He was a member of the provincial assembly of Orléans. In 1789, he published his celebrated pamphlet, *What is the Third Estate?* of which 30,000 copies were sold in a few days. Deputy of Paris, he became one of the most influential members of the Third Estate. He was elected president (June, 1790); member of the administration of the Department of Paris (February, 1791). He declined at that time the archbishopric of Paris. In 1792, he was elected to the Convention, of which he became president. He voted for the death of the king. He held aloof during the Reign of Terror, was appointed, in 1795, a member of the Council of the Five Hundred, and sent as minister to Berlin, in 1798. He entered the Directory (1799), and became the head of it. He attached himself to Bonaparte, and prepared with him the *coup d'état* of the 18th *Brumaire*. Provisory consul, he presented his famous constitutional project, was replaced by Cambacérès, and entered the Senate. He was, in 1814, one of the promoters of the downfall of the emperor, was created peer of France during the Hundred Days, and was exiled in 1816. He returned to France in 1830, and died in 1836. He had entered the Institut in 1795. Member of the French Academy in 1804, his name was cancelled from the list of this learned body in 1816.

The State, although nominally divided into three orders, was really so only into two classes—the nobles and the plebeians ; a portion of the clergy belonged to the first, and the rest to the second of these two classes.

All pre-eminence in social order is founded on one of these four things—power, birth, riches, and personal merit.

After the ministry of Cardinal de Richelieu and under Louis XIV., all the political power became concentrated in the hands of the monarch, and the orders of the State no longer possessed any.

Industry and commerce gave riches to the plebeian class, which developed all sorts of merit.

Only one title of pre-eminence thus remained : birth.

But, as nobility had been conferred for a long time on the purchasers of venal offices, birth itself could be obtained for money, thus lowering it to the level of riches.

The nobles themselves lowered it still more, by taking as wives the daughters of enriched *parvenus*, rather than poor girls of noble blood. Nobility could not fall below riches, without poverty degrading it ; and the greater number of noble families were relatively or absolutely poor. Degraded by poverty, it was still more so by riches, when it had, as it were, sacrificed itself to them by these misalliances.

In the Church and episcopacy, the most lucrative dignities had become the almost exclusive portion of the aristocracy. In this respect, the principles constantly followed by Louis XIV. had been abandoned. The plebeian, that is to say by far the most numerous section of the clergy, was therefore interested in seeing that, in its order, not only merit should always prevail over birth, but even that birth should count for nothing. In the noble class, there was no fixed hierarchy : the titles which ought to have served to indicate the rank had no constant value.

Instead of one nobility, there were seven or eight ; that of the sword, and that of the magistracy, of the court, and the provincial nobility, the ancient and the recent nobility, the higher and lesser nobility. Each of these pretended to be superior to the others, which themselves claimed to be its equals. Beside these pretensions, the plebeian raised his own claims, almost equal to those of the simple gentleman seeing how easily he could obtain this title. Often quite superior to a gentleman in wealth and talents, the plebeian did not believe himself inferior to the nobles whom the simple gentleman considered as his equal.

The nobles no longer inhabited their feudal towers ; war was no longer their sole occupation. They no longer lived exclusively with nobles like themselves, with their men-at-arms, or with the tenants of their estates. Another style of life had given them other tastes, and these tastes other needs. Often unoccupied, and making pleasure their only business, everything which was a resource against weariness, all that added to their enjoyment, became necessary to them. The plebeian, rich and enlightened, being no longer dependent upon them, having indeed no need of them, I have already said so, lived with them as with his equals.

When I spoke of the upper French society at the time of the Revolution, my object was to make known all the heterogeneous elements of which it was then composed, and to point out the results which such inconsistency of manners must necessarily bring about. I have reached the time when love of equality began to manifest itself without fear and with open face.

In polished times, the culture of letters, of the sciences, and of the fine arts, constitutes professions followed by men who generally belong, by their personal merit, to all that is most elevated ; and, by their birth or fortune to all that is most inferior in civil society. A secret instinct must induce them to raise the advantages they possess to the level of, if not above, those of which they are deprived. Besides, their aim is, in general, to secure celebrity. The first condition for this is to please and to interest, to succeed in which there is no safer way for them than to flatter the ruling tastes and the prevailing opinions, which they strengthen by flattering. Manners and public opinion tended to equality ; thus these men became its apostles.

While there were few other riches than landed property, and this was in the hands of the nobility, while industry and commerce were the callings of inferior men, the nobles scorned them, and, because they had once scorned them, they believed it their right and even their duty to scorn them always (even when relating themselves by marriage, which it shocked them to do, with the men who followed those callings), and by this, they incensed the pride of the plebeian class, who felt that one could not scorn their industry without scorning themselves.

From among the ruins of its former existence, the nobility had preserved certain privileges, which, in their origin, were only a compensation for charges which they alone supported, but which they had ceased to support. When the cause existed no longer, these privileges appeared unjust ; but their injustice was not that which made them most odious, it was rather by reason of the fact that not on the quota but on the form of the tax, they established a distinction in which the plebeian class saw less a favour to the nobles than a slight to itself.

These sentiments in the plebeian class proceeded from the spirit of equality, and served to encourage it. He who would not be considered as an inferior, either claims or aspires to be treated on a footing of equality.

I ought to say besides, that that portion of the army so imprudently sent to the aid of the English colonies struggling against their mother-country, was imbued in the New World with the doctrines of equality. It returned full of admiration for these doctrines and perhaps with the desire also to put them into practice in France ; and, by a sort of fatality, it was even this very time that Marshal de Ségur [1] chose for reserving for the nobles all the officers' promotions in the army. A host of articles appeared denouncing the measure which closed to all who were not nobles, a career in which Fabert [2] Chevert, [3] Catinat, [4] and others,

---

[1] Philippe Henry, Marquis de Ségur, belonged to an old family of Guyenne. Born in 1724, he entered the army at fifteen, was badly wounded at Raucoux, and at Lawfeld ; lieutenant-general (1760) ; wounded again at Clostercamp. Governor of Franche-Comté (1775), Minister of War (1780-1787), Marshal of France (1783). Imprisoned under the Reign of Terror, he escaped death. In 1800, he received a pension from the First Consul, who treated him with all the honours due to his high dignity. He died in 1801.

[2] Abraham Fabert issued from a Lorraine family. He entered the army, and took part in all the campaigns of his time. He became Marshal of France in 1654, and died in 1662.

[3] François de Chevert, born in 1695 at Verdun. He enlisted at nine years of age ; at eleven he was appointed lieutenant in the regiment of Carné, lieutenant-colonel in the campaign of Bohemia, where he made his name illustrious by the taking of Prague, and later, in defending this city. Brigadier-general (1744), lieutenant-general (1748), Grand Cross of the Order of St. Louis. He died in 1769.

[4] Nicolas de Catinat de la Fauconnerie, born in 1637. He left the study of the

plebeians like themselves, had covered themselves with glory. The lucrative professions being forbidden to the poor nobility, it had been thought advisable to offer them this compensation. Only this side of the question had been considered. But this measure, substituting evidently birth for personal merit, in what was the proper domain of merit, offended both reason and public opinion. For, in order to indemnify the nobles for the loss of advantages which the plebeian class already looked upon as a prejudice humiliating to them, on the latter were inflicted an in-justice and an affront. This measure completed the estrange-ment of the troops already disaffected by the introduction of a foreign discipline which exposed them to a treatment, which, from the earliest times had been considered in France, as ignominious.[1] It seemed as though it were wished not to be able to depend on our brave soldiers at the time of the greatest danger, and, in fact, their assistance failed when it was most needed.

Thus all tended to injure the noble class : that which had been taken from it, and that which had been left to it, the poverty of some of its members, the wealth of the others, their vices and even their virtues.

But all this, as I have said before, when speaking of the second ministry of M. Necker, was the work of the government, at least as much as the result of the general evolution of human things. It was not the work of the plebeian class, which merely profited by it. Equality had come, so to say, to meet the plebeians. To resist its advances would have required in the greater mass of men, a moderation and foresight of which but few privileged individuals are capable.

Equality once established between the two classes by new manners and accepted by public opinion, could not fail to be

law for the army. He became lieutenant-general in 1688. In the following year he conducted, in Savoy and Piedmont, a campaign which has remained famous (victories of Staffarde and of Marsaille). Marshal of France (1699). Minister Plenipotentiary at Turin (1695). Again at the head of the army of Italy (1701), he commanded afterwards in Alsace, and died in 1712.
    [1] Lieutenant-General Comte de Saint-Germain, having been called to the Ministry of War, tried to re-establish discipline in the army. But he wished to introduce into France the corporal punishments in vogue with the Germans and the English. Public opinion was aroused against this innovation, and the Comte de Saint-Germain lost all the favour he commanded when he took office (1776).

established by law as soon as the occasion should present itself.

At the very opening of the States-General, the deputation of the third order began the attack against the two others. Its leaders were men, who did not belong to the Third Estate, but had joined it out of spite at a disappointed ambition, or from the desire to open, by means of popularity, a road to fortune. They might perhaps have been easily led ; the need of it was not felt until success would no longer have been of any use.

Whoever is called upon to join any public body, should prove his fitness to become a member of it and produce the titles which justify his appointment. But to whom should he prove it ? Evidently to those whose interest it is that no one should introduce himself into this body by means of sham or incomplete titles, and who have no interests contrary to those of that body, if it be already formed ; and, if it be not, to those of the majority of the members who are appointed to form it, and to none other. Reason says this, and the policy of all peoples has been at all, times consonant with this principle.

The deputation of the third order, however, claimed that the members of each deputation ought to prove their competency before the three orders, and that to effect this they should assemble in the same hall ; in other terms, that they should verify their qualifications in common. This pretension once admitted, this order would have said to the other two deputations: By admitting the consequence, you have necessarily admitted the principle, and this verification of powers supposes that the three deputations form but a single body ; a single body admits only of deliberation in common, and of individual vote ; the three deputations forming but a single body, there are no more orders, for orders cannot exist except as separate and distinct bodies : where there are no longer orders, the titles and privileges which constitute them must cease. This is what this deputation wished to achieve, but, not daring to proceed openly, it took a round-about way.

Without foreseeing, perhaps, all the consequences of its pretension, or denying them, it insisted ; and, while discussing and

deliberating, it proclaimed itself a National Assembly,[1] representing thus, implicitly, the two other deputations as simple
conventicles, and pointing them to popular hatred as foreign
to the nation and as being its enemies.

I was a member of the deputation of the order of the clergy.
My opinion was that the States-General should be dissolved ;
but that, being obliged to take things as they were, they should
be convoked anew, according to one of the plans I have indicated
above.   I submitted this advice to the Comte d'Artois, who was
then displaying kindness, and,—if I may dare to quote one of the
expressions he made use of,—even friendship towards me.   My
advice was thought too risky; it was an act of force, and there
was no one about the king to wield force.   I had, in the evening,
several interviews at Marly, all of which proved useless, and
convinced me that I could be of no service, and that, in this
case, it would be folly to think of anything but self.[2]

The composition of the States-General evidently reducing
the two first orders to mere ciphers, there remained but one
reasonable course to take, it was to yield without being forced to
do so, and while there would still be some credit in doing it.
This might prevent matters being carried to extremes ; it compelled the third order to be circumspect, and enabled the other
two orders to retain some influence over the common deliberations, and to gain time, which often means to gain everything ;
and if there was still a chance to recover lost ground, this was
the only one.   I did not hesitate, therefore, to join the men who
set this example.

The struggle became prolonged, the king intervened as
mediator, but failed.   He ordered the deputation of the third
estate to separate, and is not obeyed ; so as to prevent their
meeting, the hall in which they held their sittings is closed.   They
meet in a tennis hall, and take oath not to separate until they
have made a constitution, that is to say until they have destroyed
that of the kingdom.[3]   Then it occurs to arrest by force the

---

[1] Sitting of June 17, 1789.   The Third Estate proclaimed itself a National
Assembly, on the motion of Legrand, deputy from Berry, and not on that of Siéyès,
as is generally believed.

[2] See the Appendix, page 104, containing M. de Bacourt's account of these interviews.

[3] June 20, 1789.

movement which the government had failed to foresee, and the instrument of force escapes from the hands which try to make use of it. On the same day, the whole of France, cities, villages, hamlets, are under arms. The Bastille is attacked, taken or thrown open in a couple of hours, and its governor slaughtered.[1] Popular fury is vented on other victims.[2] From this moment the government is powerless, there are no longer any States-General ; they have given place to a single and all-powerful assembly ; and the principle of equality is sanctioned. Those who have advised the employment of force, those who have set it in motion, those who have been its leaders, think only of their own safety. A number of the princes leave the kingdom, and emigration commences.

The Comte d'Artois had been the first to give the signal for it ; his departure caused me much grief. I loved him ; it needed all the force of my reason to keep me from following him, and to enable me to resist the entreaties made to me on his behalf by Madame de Carignan, to join him at Turin. It would be a great mistake for any one to conclude from my refusal that I blamed those who emigrated ; I did not blame them, but I blamed the emigration. Nearly all the *émigrés* were actuated by a noble sentiment and by a deep devotion to the royal cause ; but emigration was a false step. Whatever may have been its motive, whether the fear of danger, offended self-love, the wish to recover by force of arms what had been lost, or the idea of a duty to fulfil, it appeared to me under all these aspects, but a poor calculation.

There could have been a necessity for emigrating, only in the case of a personal danger against which France could have offered no refuge, or no sufficiently safe refuge, that is to say, in case of general danger for the nobles. This danger did not exist then ; it might be prevented, while the first effect of emigration was to

---

[1] Bernard Jourdan de Launay, issued from a noble family of Normandy, born in 1740 at the Bastille, of which his father was governor ; he also filled this post as successor to M. de Jumilhac. The part he played during the attack of July 14 is well known ; how, having been compelled to surrender, he was massacred with several of his officers, in spite of the efforts of Hélie and of Hulin, the leaders of the assailants.

[2] Besides the governor de Launay and his soldiers, the people massacred the *Prévôt des Marchands*,* Flesselles, and, a few days after, the intendant Foulon and his son-in-law, Bertier de Sauvigny, intendant of Paris.

* Provost of the Merchants—an office similar to that of Lord Mayor in England.

create it. Not all the nobles, nor even the majority of them, were able to leave the kingdom. Age, sex, infirmities, lack of money and other causes, not less powerful, were an insuperable obstacle to a large number. Only a portion of them, then, could go abroad, and this absent portion must inevitably compromise those who remained. Objects of suspicion, which soon degenerated into hatred, the nobles who could not leave the country, must, through fear, swell the number of the ruling party, or become its victims.

The only loss with which as yet the spirit of liberty threatened the nobility, was that of its titles and privileges. By emigration this loss was not prevented, while by it the French aristocracy ran the risk of adding to this loss a still greater one, that of their estates. However painful for the nobility the loss of their titles and privileges may have been, it was incomparably less so than the situation to which they were going to be reduced by the simple forfeiture of their revenues. The loss of titles alone could be softened by the certainty that it was not irreparable, and by the hope that it might even be repaired. In a great and ancient monarchy, the spirit of equality, carried to its utmost conse- quences, is a disease essentially transient, and this disease might have been less severe and of much shorter duration had it been less combated. But property once lost could not be as easily restored as titles ; it might have been transferred, and have passed through so many hands as to make it impossible ever to recover it, and even dangerous to attempt to do so. The loss of property would then be an incurable disease, not only for the nobles, but for the entire State, the natural organization of which could be but imperfectly restored as long as one of its essential elements no longer existed, except partly. For nobility, an essential element of a monarchy, is not a simple element, and birth without wealth, or wealth without birth does not constitute, politically speaking, a perfect nobility.

One could scarcely delude one's self so far as to believe that what the entire class of the nobles, with the means of action and influence that remained to it, had failed to defend and preserve, could have been recovered with the mere help of that portion of the nobility which had emigrated. All its hope would then reside in the help of foreigners. But was there nothing to be feared from such assistance? Could it be accepted without suspicion, if it were offered, and could it be implored without scruples? The greatness of the injury received was not sufficient to excuse those who called to their assistance the help of a foreign force. An act of this nature can be justified only by a concurrence of extraordinary circumstances; it should have been required by the vital interests of the country itself; to resort to it, all other means must have previously failed; the success of such intervention must have been certain, and there must have been undeniable proofs that neither the country, its integrity nor its future independence would thereby be injured. But what certainty could there be as to the next action of the foreigners, having once crushed the Revolution? What certainty was there that they could crush it? Was there a certainty of receiving real assistance, and was it wise to trust simply in hopes? Why go to meet assistance which perhaps would not be forthcoming, when, even with the certainty of its coming, reason advised to keep quiet and await its arrival? And, while waiting for it, one could, if the social need of the country demanded it, co-operate with this assistance in a more efficacious manner; the chances of success would be thus increased, and nothing be compromised; while, in going to seek assistance, one compromised all, relations, friends, fortune, and the throne with them; and not only the throne, but the life of the monarch as well, and that of his family, which, perhaps one day, on the brink of the abyss, or already in the abyss, could only account for its misfortunes, by crying out: "*Behold, see where emigration has led us.*"[1]

Thus, far from deserving to be regarded as the accomplishment of a duty, the emigration needed to be excused, which it could be only by the immensity of a personal danger from which

[1] I can say that the positive opinion of Louis XVI. in this respect is found in *Memoirs* I have read, and of which M. de Clermont-Gallerande is the author. They are written in his hand, and are now in the possession of the Marquis de Fontenille. In them, M. de Clermont* gives an account of the mission he had been charged by the king to fulfil at Coblentz. He was instructed to describe to the king's brothers the personal danger in which his life had been placed by the emigration (*Prince Talleyrand*).

* Charles, Marquis de Clermont-Gallerande, was the issue of a noble family of Maine. Born in 1744, he became brigadier-general, took part in the defence of the Tuileries on August 10, and was long imprisoned under the Terror. It was he who, under the Consulate, delivered to Bonaparte the letter by which Louis XVIII. invited him to re-establish him on the throne. Peer of France in 1814, he died in 1823. His *Memoirs* were published in 1825 at Paris (3 vols. 8vo).

there was no other way of escaping. These views, if another order of things should some day be brought about, will, I hope, be generally shared by the men who may perhaps still have to struggle against the revolutionary torrent.

I resolved, therefore, not to leave France, until constrained to do so by personal danger ; to do nothing to provoke it, not to struggle against a torrent which must be allowed to pass ; but to hold myself in a position enabling me to save those who could be saved, to raise no obstacle between opportunity and myself, and to hold myself in readiness for it.

The deputies of the third order before triumphing over the two others had been engaged in drawing up a declaration of rights in imitation of that made by the English Colonies, when they proclaimed their independence. They continued to prepare it after the fusion of the orders. This declaration was nothing more than a theory of equality, a theory which may be summed up as follows :

" There is no real difference, and there ought to be no permanent distinction, between men, other than that which proceeds from personal merit. The distinctions which are inherent to the tenure of offices are accidental and ought to be temporary, in order that the right which each citizen has to pretend to them, need not be illusory. All political power proceeds from the people and returns to them. To them alone belongs the sovereignty. What they wish is the law, and nothing is law but what they wish. If they cannot exercise the sovereignty themselves, which is the case when their numbers are too great for assembling together, it must be exercised by representatives of their choice, who can do all which they could do themselves, and whose power is therefore without limit."

The incompatibility of an hereditary monarchy with such a theory was flagrant. However, the Assembly wished, in good faith, to preserve the monarchy and to apply to it the republican theory which found universal support. It did not suspect that it was difficult to conciliate them ; ignorance is so presumptuous, and passions are so blind. By the boldest and most insolent of usurpations, the Assembly arrogates to itself this sovereignty which it attributes to the people; it declares itself constituted, that is to say invested with the right to destroy all that exists, and to substitute in its place all that may please itself.

It was a sad certainty that if the government wished to dissolve it, it would not obey, and that no one was in a position to force it to obedience. To argue against it would have served no purpose. In restricting one's self to contesting the power it claimed, one did not prevent its acting; to protest against its acts was a measure full of danger, and unlikely to have the desired effect. But the king could say to it :

"You hold as a *principle* that the sovereignty belongs to the people. You hold in *fact* that it has delegated to you the exercise of it in its plenitude. I have my doubts upon that, to say the least. It is necessary, above all, before going any further, that this question be decided. I do not pretend to make myself the judge ; neither can you be ; but this people is a judge that you cannot challenge. I will interrogate it ; let its answer be our law."

All the probabilities are, that if skilfully handled, the people, at a time when revolutionary ideas had not yet tainted the masses, and when what have since been called revolutionary interests did not yet exist, would have disclaimed the doctrines and disapproved the pretensions of the Assembly. Nothing then would have been easier than to dissolve it. Being thus condemned, these doctrines and these pretensions would have been so for ever. If the people, on the contrary, had sanctioned them by their votes, they would then have been subjected to all their consequences, and justly subjected to them, having been able to preserve themselves and not having willed to do so ; and no share of responsibility would have rested on the monarch. From · an appeal to the people, there would have followed, it is true, the necessity of recognizing him as sovereign, if he so declared himself ; and this, it will perhaps be said, was a thing to be avoided at any price. But the appeal to the people at the stage which was reached, would not have created this necessity ; it would, on the contrary, have presented the sole chance which still existed, of avoiding it, in rendering it, from being present and absolute as it was, contingent and simply possible. The Assembly attributed to itself a power, ascribing its foundation to

the sovereignty of the people, and which could have no other.
This sovereignty was therefore acknowledged as soon as this
power was acknowledged, and there was an absolute necessity
for acknowledging it, unless the Assembly could be forced to
retract or to dissolve (two things equally impossible), or the
people could be led to pronounce against its decisions, which
could not be done without making them the judge.   In this case,
the people, would, as I believe, have fulfilled the hopes placed in
them,—or would have betrayed these hopes.   In the first supposition he would have crushed the evil at its birth, and caused
the Revolution to prove abortive ; in the second, he would
have rendered inevitable that which could only have been prevented by his own interference, which would not have extended,
but have simply revealed the magnitude of the evil.   The
advantage of such a course would have been to make it no
longer possible to entertain any delusion as to the real nature
of this evil ; it would no longer have occurred to anybody to
check it by means that were only calculated to aggravate it.   It
would have been felt that, until it had passed through all its
phases of development, there was no remedy to be expected from
within ; its contagiousness would have become plain to all, and
Europe would not have rocked herself, as she did, in a false and
pernicious security.   Thus, even by the worst supposition, the
appeal to the people would have been a step of the greatest
utility, without any admixture of inconvenience.   Why then was
it not resorted to ?   From prejudice, perhaps, or from passion,
for indeed prejudices and passions were not all on the one side ;
perhaps, also, because this remedy did not occur to any of the
men who formed then the councils of the king.

   After a few attempts at force, abandoned almost as soon as
conceived, they trusted entirely to intrigue to destroy a power
that they had allowed to become too strong to be restrained,
or even directed, by so feeble a means.   The Assembly was
therefore left almost to itself.   In the midst of the passions
which agitated it, it soon lost sight of all the constituent principles of society.   It no longer knew that there is for civil society
a necessary mode of organization without which it could not
exist.

Fascinated by the chimerical ideas of equality and of the sovereignty of the people, the Assembly committed endless faults.

The king was styled first representative, delegate of the people, and chief of the executive power ; none of which titles were his, none of which expressed the functions which he ought to fill as monarch.

The right to convene, adjourn and dissolve the legislative body was taken from him.

That body, having risen to be a power, became permanent, and was to be renewed at fixed periods. It was to form but a single house.

Every Frenchman of age, who was in receipt of wages and who had not been sentenced to penal servitude or other igno-minious punishment, was eligible or an elector, according as he paid fifty francs in yearly taxes, or only three francs.

The elections had to be carried out by a medley of all professions.

The nomination of the bishops, judges, and public officials was ascribed to the constituencies.

The king had only the power of suspending provisionally public officials. The right of dismissing them from public service was vested in the general power of the electors. The judges were only appointed for a time.

The initiative in making peace or war rested solely with the sovereign ; but the right to declare the latter or to sanction peace was reserved for the legislative power.

In the army, a scale of promotion by grades was established, which deprived the king of two-thirds of his power of nominating.

The king could reject the proposals of the legislature, but with this restriction, that what three successive legislatures should adopt, should become law, notwithstanding the refusal of the king to sanction it.

Such were the constitutional laws imposed upon political and civil society in France by the Assembly ; these laws only left a semblance of what had been royal power.

The men who had been the most anxious to destroy this royal power perceived at last that they had gone too far, and attempted to retrace their steps ; they succeeded only in losing their popularity. The torrent formed by ignorance and passion was so violent that it was impossible to stem it. Those who foresaw its ravages most clearly, were compelled to confine themselves as much as prudence allowed, to playing a passive part.

This I resolved to do on most questions. However, I felt that I ought to speak on several matters relative to State finance. I opposed the creation of paper money, and the reduction of the interest on the national debt. I established, in a rather extensive essay, the principles on which I believed a national bank should be founded. I proposed the establishment of uniformity in weights and measures. I charged myself, also, with the report of the Constitutional Committee on Public Instruction.[1] To accomplish this great work, I consulted the most learned men, and the most prominent scholars of the time, amongst whom I may mention M. de Lagrange,[2] M. de Lavoisier,[3] M. de la Place, M. Monge,[2] M. de Condorcet, M. Vicq d'Azyr,[3] and M. de la

[1] The following is a brief statement of the part played by Talleyrand at the Constituent Assembly : He proposed the nullification of the imperative mandates (July 7, 1789) ; was elected member of the Committee appointed to draft a constitution (July 13) ; urged the suppression of tithes (August 11) ; caused the adoption of certain articles in the declaration of rights (August 21) ; proposed proper measures to insure a loan (August 27) ; proposed to apply the wealth of the clergy to the needs of the State (October 10) ; presented a police regulation for Paris (November 5) ; proposed to make an inventory of the properties of the clergy (November 7) ; was appointed to examine the state of the Bank of Discount (November 26) ; rendered an account of this examination (December 4) ; proposed to consider the Jews as citizens (January 28, 1790) ; proposed an address to the people to induce calmness (February 9) ; elected President of the Assembly by 373 votes against 125 for Siéyès (February 26) ; proposed a method for the conveyance and sale of the national lands (June 13) ; opposed the issue of 2,000,000,000 of francs * of paper money (September 18) ; reported on the rights of registration (November 22) ; speech on the re-coinage of money (December 12) ; caused the adoption of a project of law on the unification of weights and measures (March 26, 1791) ; reported on a decree of the Department of Paris relative to religious freedom (May 7) ; drew up a report on public instruction (September 10).

[2] Joseph-Louis Lagrange, born at Turin in 1736 of French parents, was at eighteen years of age the first mathematician of Europe. In 1766, Frederick II. called him to Berlin as President of the Academy. He came to Paris in 1786, entered the *Institut* in 1795, was appointed senator under the Empire, and died in 1813.

[3] Laurent Lavoisier, born at Paris in 1743, entered the Academy of Sciences at twenty-five years of age, and obtained, soon after, the post of *fermier-général*. He was the first chemist of his time. Arrested under the Terror, he was guillotined on May 8, 1794.

[4] Gaspard Monge, born at Beaune in 1746, was at first professor at the School of Engineers at Mézières. He entered the Academy of Sciences in 1780. Minister of Marine after August 10, he was appointed a member of the *Institut*. He accompanied Napoleon, later, to Egypt, and became President of the Institute of Cairo. Napoleon appointed him senator and Comte de Péluse. He died in 1818.

[5] Felix Vicq d'Azir, born at Valognes in 1748, studied medicine, and opened, in

* £80,000,000.

Harpe.[1]   All assisted me.   The reputation this work has acquired demanded that I should name them.

A circumstance occurred, in which, in spite of all my repugnance, I thought it necessary to come to the front. Here are the motives which decided me.

The Assembly pretended to regulate alone and by civil law that which until then had been regulated only by a concourse of the spiritual and temporal powers and by canonical and civil laws. It made a particular constitution for the clergy,[2] exacting from all the ecclesiastics in function an oath to conform to it, under pain of being considered as resigning. Nearly all the bishops refused to do so, and their seats being considered vacant, the constituents nominated people to fill them. These newly elected bishops were only too ready to dispense with the institution given by the Court of Rome ; but they could not do without the episcopal character which could only be conferred upon them by men who had received it. If no one should be found to confer it upon them, it was greatly to be feared, not that all religion would be proscribed, as came to pass a few years after, but, what seemed to me more dangerous seeing that it might have been more lasting, that the Assembly, by the doctrines it had sanctioned, might soon force the country into Presbyterianism, more in accord with the ruling opinions, and that France could not be drawn back to Catholicism, whose hierarchy and forms are in harmony with those of the monarchical system. I lent, therefore, my services to consecrate one of the newly-elected bishops, who in his turn, consecrated the others.[3]

1773, brilliant lectures on anatomy. Member of the Academy of Sciences (1774), and of the French Academy, where he succeeded Buffon. First physician to the queen (1789). He was the last chancellor of the old Academy (June, 1793), which was suppressed on August 8 following. He died June 20, 1794.

[1] J.-Fr. de la Harpe, born in Paris in 1739, *littérateur* and critic. The literary lectures he was entrusted with at the establishment that Pilâtre des Roziers had just founded under the name of *Lycée*, made his reputation. La Harpe was arrested under the Terror, and proscribed on Fructidor 18. He died in 1803.

[2] The civil constitution was voted by the Assembly on July 12, 1790. It is known that it reduced the number of dioceses, decreed the election by the people of bishops and curates, and suppressed the canonical institution. This was the origin of the schism which divided the Church of France into sworn and unsworn clergy.

[3] Talleyrand had been chosen as consecrating prelate, and with him Gobel, Bishop of Lydda, and Miroudot, Bishop of Babylon. On February 24, 1791, Talleyrand consecrated the first two constitutional bishops—Expilly, Bishop of Finistère, and Marolles, Bishop of Aisne—in the Church of the Oratoire, Rue St. Honoré.

This done, I gave in my resignation of the bishopric of Autun, and I thought only of abandoning the first career I had followed ; I put myself at the disposition of events, and, provided I remained a Frenchman, all else contented me. The Revolution promised new destinies for the nation ; I followed its course and ran my chances. I devoted to it the best of all my energies, being resolved to serve my country for herself, and I placed all my hopes on the constitutional principles that were believed to be so nearly attained. This explains how and why, at several periods, I entered, and re-entered public life ; it also throws light on the part I have played.

APPENDIX.[1]

Note of M. de Bacourt on the interviews of Prince Talleyrand with the Comte d'Artois.

WE wish to add to this passage some details which M. de Talleyrand had neglected or perhaps forgotten.

It is a positive fact that at the time to which this passage relates, M. de Talleyrand had several interviews with the Comte d'Artois, in which he sought to convince the prince of the necessity for taking forcible measures, and while maintaining the concessions which the king had already made, to repress with vigour the popular agitation which was manifesting itself daily, and which had already caused bloodshed in the streets of the capital. The most important, and the last of these interviews, took place at Marly on the night of the 16th to the 17th of July, 1789, that is to say, a few hours before the prince left France. When M. de Talleyrand presented himself at the residence of the Comte d'Artois, this prince had already retired, but nevertheless received him for an interview which lasted more than two hours. M. de Talleyrand exposed anew all the dangers of the situation, and begged the prince to make them known to the king. The Comte d'Artois was much affected, arose and repaired to the king, and, after quite a prolonged absence, returned to declare to M. de Talleyrand that nothing could be effected with the king, who was resolved to yield rather than to cause a single drop of blood to be shed by resisting the popular outbreaks. "As for me," added the Comte d'Artois, " my decision is made ;

[1] See page 94.

I depart to-morrow, and I leave France." M. de Talleyrand entreated the prince in vain to renounce this resolution, representing to him the difficulties and dangers it might bring on him in the present, both concerning his rights and those of his children in the future. The Comte d'Artois persisted, and M. de Talleyrand concluded by saying to him : " Then, Monseigneur, it only remains for each of us to think of his own interests, since the king and the princes desert theirs and those of the monarchy."— " Indeed," replied the prince, " that is what I advise you to do ; whatever happens I shall never blame you ; and you may always rely on my friendship."—The Comte d'Artois emigrated on the morrow.

In the month of April, 1814, M. de Talleyrand, having become President of the Provisory Government, found himself in a position to announce to the Comte d'Artois, who was then at Nancy with his attendants, awaiting the issue of events, that Louis XVIII. was called to the throne, and that the prince himself was invited to return to Paris to take charge of the government as lieutenant-general of the kingdom. He charged the Baron de Vitrolles[1] with this mission, and as the latter was about to leave, and while the despatch for the prince was being sealed, Talleyrand told the baron the story of the interview of the night of July 16, 1789, while walking up and down the *entresol* of his hotel in the Rue Saint Florentin. After which he said to him, " Do me the favour of asking the Comte d'Artois if he recollects this little incident."

M. de Vitrolles, after having delivered his important message, did not fail to put to the prince the question as requested by

---

[1] Eugène d'Arnaud, Baron de Vitrolles, was born in 1774 at the château of this name in Provence. His family was one of the oldest in the country. He was the grand-nephew of the illustrious *bailli* de Suffren. He emigrated in 1790, and entered as volunteer in the army of Condé. He returned to France in 1797 after the 18th Brumaire, he was struck off the list of the *émigrés*, thanks to the intervention of General Bernadotte, who, when a sergeant in the regiment of the Royal Marines, had been his fencing master. M. de Vitrolles was mayor and councillor-general under the Empire. In 1812, he was appointed inspector of flocks—a post which had just been created for inspecting and favouring the breeding of merinoes in France. M. de Vitrolles took a leading part in the first Restoration. To his personal action was perhaps due the decision of the allied sovereigns to march on Paris, which brought about the fall of the Empire. Minister of State in 1814, royal commissioner at Toulouse in 1815, he was arrested by the order of Napoleon, and remained in prison during the period of the Hundred Days. He was a Member of the *Chambre introuvable,** and deprived in 1818 of his post of minister. In 1827, Charles X. appointed him minister at Florence, and peer of France in July, 1830. M. de Vitrolles did not support the monarchy of July. He died in retirement in 1854. He left interesting memoirs on the Restoration, which are well known.

* The *Chambre introuvable*—This was the name given to the Chamber elected in 1815, on account of the exaggeration of its royalist opinions. It could scarcely have been anticipated that the imperial constituencies should return such a parliament. On learning the composition of this Chamber, which he was to dissolve ten months later, Louis XVIII. was delighted and said several times: "Chambre introuvable ! Chambre introuvable !" It exceeded indeed his most sanguine hopes.—(*Translator.*)

M. de Talleyrand ; to which the Comte d'Artois replied, "I recollect the circumstance perfectly, and M. de Talleyrand's account is exact in every particular."

Having been informed that M. de Vitrolles had related this anecdote to several persons, we thought it advisable to appeal to his memory and to his loyalty. To justify this expression " loyalty," it must be told that M. de Vitrolles, after the Revolution of July, 1830, had ceased all intercourse with M. de Talleyrand, and expressed himself very severely in regard to him. This will explain the tone of hostility and of bitterness which pervades M. de Vitrolles' letter, which we insert here. We think that for the reader, as for us, this hostility will only further confirm the sincerity of M. de Vitrolles' declaration, and the authenticity of the passage in the memoirs of M. de Talleyrand. The slight divergence which will be observed between the account given to us by M. de Talleyrand and that of M. de Vitrolles' letter will explain itself naturally as the effect of the time that had elapsed since the occurrence, and which had modified the recollections of the two narrators. It, nevertheless, remains a fact, that in July, 1789, M. de Talleyrand believed that the progress of revolutionary events might be arrested, that he had the moral courage to say so, and to propose to undertake to check it. He is not the only one, perhaps, who boasted of so doing afterwards ; we think we have proved that his boast, at least, was not unjustified. Here is the letter of M. de Vitrolles :—

THE BARON DE VITROLLES TO M. DE BACOURT.[1]

PARIS, *April 6th,* 1852.

SIR,

You are good enough to consider as of some value the testimony I might furnish respecting a particular incident in the life of Prince de Talleyrand ; I think I cannot better comply with your wishes than in transcribing here what I wrote many years ago, in connection with the events of 1814.

When His Majesty the Emperor of Russia and the Prince

---

[1] Adolphe Fourier de Bacourt, born in 1801. He entered diplomacy in 1822, and was sent in 1830 to London. M. de Talleyrand noticed him there, and attached him to his person. In 1835, he was appointed minister at Carlsruhe, and then at Washington, 1840. Ambassador to Turin in 1842, he resigned in 1848. He had been appointed a peer of France. During the early portion of his career, Bacourt had made, at the Hague, the acquaintance of the Comte de la Marck, who entrusted to him his correspondence with Mirabeau. He published it in 1851. He undertook afterwards the publication of the present memoirs. (It is known that Prince de Talleyrand had left the care of their publication to the Duchesse de Dino, his niece, and, in case she died, to M. de Bacourt.) He died in 1865. He left memoirs, published since by his niece, the Comtesse de Mirabeau.

de Talleyrand were convinced that the presence of the king's brother endowed with the powers of lieutenant-general of the kingdom was necessary, and I was about to leave with the object of inducing *Monsieur* to return to Paris, I had several conferences on this subject with the President of the Provisory Government. In a last interview, at the moment of departure, we had talked of the conditions and ceremonies for the reception of *Monseigneur.* After a moment's silence, Prince de Talleyrand said, with his wheedling smile, and in a tone which he endeavoured to make careless and almost indifferent :—

"I beg of you to ask the Comte d'Artois if he recollects "the last occasion on which I saw him ; it was in the month "of July, 1789. The court was at Marly. Three or four of " my friends, struck like myself with the rapidity and the violence " of the agitation which was stirring all minds, resolved with me " to acquaint the king, Louis XVI., with the real situation of " affairs, which the court and the ministers seemed to ignore. "We requested His Majesty to be so kind as to receive us ; " we desired for his good as for our own that this audience " should be kept secret. The reply was that the king had "charged his brother, the Comte d'Artois, to receive us ; the " appointment was made for Marly, in the pavilion occupied by "the Comte d'Artois alone. We arrived there at midnight."

M. de Talleyrand named to me the precise date, and the names of the friends who accompanied him : they were members of the National Assembly and of that minority of the nobility who were in the Third Estate ; I recollect neither the date nor the names.

"When we were in the presence of the Comte d'Artois," continued M. de Talleyrand, "we exposed to him in all frank- " ness the situation of affairs, and of the State, as it appeared to " us. We said to him that it was a great mistake to believe that " the agitation which was stirring all minds could easily be " calmed. It was not by delays, caution, and a few concessions, " that the dangers which menaced France, the throne, and the " king could be averted. It was by an energetic display of the " royal authority, wisely and skilfully employed. We know the " ways and the means and the position which would enable us to " undertake this, and guarantee our succeeding, if the con- " fidence of the king should entrust us with it. The Comte " d'Artois listened to us attentively, and fully understood us, " though he was, perhaps, inclined to think that we were exag- " gerating the danger of the situation and our importance in " remedying it. But, as he said to us, he had only been " instructed by the king to hear us, and to report to him what

" we wished to make known to him ; he had no answer to give
" us, and no power to engage the will or the word of the king.
" When we had reached this point, we begged of the Comte
" d'Artois permission to add, that if the application we now
" made conscientiously and in good faith was not appreciated, if
" it had no effect and led to no result, *Monseigneur* must not
" be astonished if, not being able to resist the torrent which
" threatened to carry all before it, we should support the new
" state of affairs. . . . Ask, I pray you, of *Monsieur,*" repeated
M. de Talleyrand, "if the conversation of that night has left
" any trace in his memory.   It was almost at the very time
" when he left France."

I admired the subtilty of this mind, which found, in one of
its recollections, an explanation, an excuse, and almost a jus-
tification of all his revolutionary life ; he could have found many
others to serve him in very different and even contrary circumstances.   In listening to this story, which was related with a sort
of indifference and unaffected simplicity, I took the liberty of
doubting whether what might remain in the memory of *Monsieur*
would be entirely consonant with the words I had just heard.
However, when, at Nancy, I remembered the request of M. de
Talleyrand, *Monseigneur* said to me, without entering into any
detail, that he had not forgotten this circumstance, and that all
I had repeated to him was the exact truth.

I hope, Sir, that this testimony will meet with your expecta-
tions.   I thank you for having offered me this opportunity of
giving you the assurance of my highest regard.

BARON DE VITROLLES.

END OF THE FIRST PART.

PART II.

THE DUC D'ORLÉANS.[1]

General considerations on the importance of private *Memoirs* and reliable biographies to history—Lineage of Louis-Philippe-Joseph, fifth Duc d'Orléans—His early years and dispositions—His education—His frivolity and dryness of heart—His marriage with Mademoiselle de Penthièvre—Associates of the Duc d'Orléans—M. de Voyer—Abbé Yvon—M. de Lille—M. de Voyer's philosophy—M. de Voyer and M. de Maurepas—The Prince de Lamballe—The Marquis de Conflans—Cruel indifference of the Duc d'Orléans—M. de Biron—The *liaisons* of the Duc d'Orléans—The Princesse de Bouillon—The Marquise de Fleury—The Princesse de Lamballe—Madame de Sillery, Comtesse de Genlis—Her influence over the Duc de Chartres—Her literary productions—Count de Cagliostro—The Chevalier de Luxembourg—Speculations of the Duc d'Orléans—Outrageous proceedings of this prince towards his treasurer, Séguin—The Duc d'Orléans wishes to become grand-admiral—He is appointed colonel-general of hussars—Mademoiselle Arnould, the famous actress—Journey of the Duc d'Orléans to England and to Italy—He falls seriously ill — Grand-master of the freemasons — Debauchery and depravity of the Duc d'Orléans—Agitation in France—Forebodings of the Revolution—The deficit—M. de Calonne summons an assembly of the Notables—Intrigues of the Duc d'Orléans against the king—The Marquis Ducrest—Ambition of the Duc d'Orléans—Measures taken by

---

[1] The second house of Orléans descends from Philippe I., Duc d'Orléans, junior son of Louis XIII. Louis-Philippe-Joseph, of whom we are about to speak here, is the fifth prince of this house. His mother was a Princess de Bourbon-Conti. He was born in 1747. All his life he carried on a systematic opposition to the Court, and became, in 1787, the leader of all the malcontents. Exiled in 1787, Deputy to the States-General, he was one of the first to go over to the Third Estate. He became a member of the Jacobin Club. The part he played in the Convention is well known. He died on the scaffold, November 6, 1793. He had married Louise de Bourbon-Penthièvre, daughter of the Duc de Penthièvre and of Marie Thérèse d'Este, who was one of the most virtuous and most distinguished ladies of her time. Imprisoned in 1793, she was saved by the *coup d'état* of Thermidor 9, and exiled to Spain (1797). She returned to Paris in 1814. The Duc d'Orléans had three sons: the Duc de Chartres, afterwards King Louis Philippe, the Duc de Montpensier, and the Comte de Beaujolais.

the Archbishop of Toulouse against the *parlements*—M. and Mdme. de Sémonville—A loan of £16,000,000—General discontent of the people —Louis XVI. refuses to allow the Duc d'Orléans to go on a visit to England—Differences between the Queen and the Duc d'Orléans— Trianon—The Duc d'Orléans becomes the head of all malcontents—M. de Limon's ability—Abbé Sabatier de Cabre—The *lits de justice*—The Marquis de Lamognon—The edict of 1787 and the Protestants—The sitting of November 19, 1787—M. d'Espreménil—Public protest of the Duc d'Orléans against the king's orders—Lepelletier de St.-Fargeau—Imprisonment of the Abbés Fréteau and Sabatier—Exile of the Duc d'Orléans—Popular outburst of sympathy on this measure being known—Intervention of the *parlement* of Paris—Energetic attitude of Louis XVI.—The Duc d'Orléans forgiven by the king—Struggle between M. de Brienne and the *parlements*—Stringent measures of the government—Premonitory symptoms of the Revolution—Riot in the Faubourg St.-Antoine—M. de Laclos—Abbé Siéyès—Project of reforms drawn up by the Duc d'Orléans for the States-General—Judgment of Prince Talleyrand on the political part played by the Duc d'Orléans—The origin and causes of the Revolution.

THE private memoirs and lives of celebrated men are the source of true history ; as compared with tradition, which is always credulous and even superstitious, they serve to criticize its accounts or to support them, and help with it to give history the character of authenticity to which it lays claim.

By this means the times of Henry III., Henry IV., Louis XIII., and of Louis XIV., have become well known, and the history of these reigns has been received with more confidence. The following period, though nearer to the days we live in, has not, up to the present, been so favourably treated ; it has not furnished us with such abundant sources of information. It seems that traditions alone founded the historical facts generally believed with regard to these times.

The *Siècle de Louis XIV.*, by M. de Voltaire, is a production *sui generis*. It belongs to the style of memoirs by its simple, natural tone, and the mention of a few anecdotes, but it often rises to general views of a lofty and superior order. It is evident that M. de Voltaire did not intend to write the history of the reign of Louis XIV., and that he wished to confine himself to sketching in broad outline the chief events of that reign.

A well-written life of M. de Colbert or of M. de Louvois

would give a correct idea of what the government of that great king was. A work of this kind on the ministry of the Duc de Choiseul would acquaint us with the spirit which prevailed at court and in the administration under the reign of Louis XV. I have thought that a picture of the life of the Duc d'Orléans would give the features and the colour of the weak and transient reign of Louis XVI.; that it would set forth in a tangible manner the general laxity of public and private manners under that reign, as well as the degradation in the form of government and in the habits of the administration; that a work undertaken with this view, would faithfully depict the character of an important period of French history.

In the lapse of three centuries, at very nearly equal intervals, the form of government in France has been threatened by outbreaks, each of which bore a particular stamp. The first two, the *Ligue* and the *Fronde,* hastened the development of national greatness and power ; there was something grand and noble in the audacity and in the methods of the Guises and of Cardinal de Retz : it was the seduction of that time.

As for the last outbreak, that which we have just witnessed, it has been but a frightful catastrophe. The Duc d'Orléans who made himself conspicuous in it, only joined in it from his love of disorder, his contempt for decency, and his self-abandonment ; such were the glory, the taste, and the intrigues of those days.— I now enter upon my subject.

I cannot say what part the different parties who ruled in France from the beginning of the Revolution will ascribe to the Duc d'Orléans, when they depict, each for his own apology, the great scenes of that Revolution. Provided that they attribute to him only wrongs which can result from the most extreme weakness of character, the facts of the case, though not correct, will be at least probable. His entire life would prove it. The circumstances in which he was placed, changed often, but he, as a child, as a young man, or as a man of mature age, was always and invariably the same.

Although I can furnish the most curious and least known details concerning the life and character of the Duc d'Orléans, I would allow all recollection of them to be lost to my memory if

they were merely meant to gratify curiosity, but it struck me
that they might serve some useful end ; I therefore collected
them.

In a country where some elections still take place, it is
advisable to furnish the characteristic signs by which the men
who ought to be removed from the theatre of affairs may be
recognized.   The Duc d'Orléans is a remarkable instance of this.
Any man who, in youth, affects deep contempt for public
opinion, and whose habits, besides, are so depraved that he does
not respect himself, will, when he advances in years, not know
any other limit to his vices than the sterility of his own imagination or of that of the persons who surround him.   Were it not
important to know exactly the degree of consanguinity which
existed between Louis XVI. and the Duc d'Orléans, there would
be no need for me to say what were the advantages the first
prince of the blood of the House of Bourbon could boast.   It
is by placing the latter in the midst of all the advantages he
enjoyed, it is by confronting him with all his obligations, that
his character will be better understood.   It will be seen what he
trampled under foot, what ties he broke, what sentiments he
smothered, what position he degraded.

It was a powerful title to the love of the French to be
descended from Henry IV.   France was accustomed to revere
in the first prince of the blood, the first of subjects, one who
was great enough to protect, though not to oppress her, who
was more powerful than any other individual, but less powerful
than the law, and than the king, who was the living representative of the law.   He was one of the most natural channels by
which the private beneficence of the king could descend
upon the people, and the gratitude of the people ascend to
the throne.[1]

It need not be expected that I shall give full details as to the
first years of the Duc de Chartres.   I will not imitate those who
endeavour to seek in the babblings of a child the horoscope of his
vices and of his virtues.   I leave that to persons who write with
a system ; I have none.

---

[1] There is here in Talleyrand's own manuscript a blank of eight leaves, for which
we have vainly sought explanation.

The Duc de Chartres, having passed from childhood, entered upon his education, but then his governesses were men, for there was little difference between his nurses and his first teachers, other than the difference of woman's weakness and man's complaisance. Yet when speaking of him, people often remarked, "If he is not very well brought up, he will at least be good. The Orléans are good." That goodness of which people felt so sure, led the prince's tutors to devote as little attention to his character as to his studies. As he had a very elegant figure, they sought to have it developed by physical exercises. Few young people could ride a horse as well and with as much grace as he. He was a good fencer and a good shot ; at the ball he always attracted notice. All the members of the old Court of France who are still alive repent having applauded him as he danced the *Béarnaise* dressed as Henry IV., or other aristocratic steps in the holiday dress worn by young people at the court of Louis XIV. Although in the defence of his petty interests, and in his intercourse with children of his age, he displayed a certain accuracy of judgment, he learned absolutely nothing. He began to study a few sciences, and a few languages, but never could master even the rules of orthography, with which, to-day, every woman in France is conversant. His master of mathematics told me, however, that he believed the prince had some aptitudes for that science. But he was too changeable for any one to attempt more than to acquaint him very superficially with the different branches of knowledge; his attention got too easily tired ; he only listened until such time as he began to have a faint grasp of what was being taught him ; from that moment, he made no progress. No salient feature could as yet be detected in his character, it was, however, easy to notice that he found a sort of mischievous pleasure in annoying persons who approached him, a species of gay, meddlesome, naughty wickedness that the benevolent called waggishness.

It was remarked that, in his early youth, he never showed gratitude either towards his relatives or his masters, and that he never had any attachment for his playfellows. Although these are, in children, purely negative faults which do not characterize any definite propensity, they foretell great coldness of heart.

Among the persons who assisted in his education, I only dare to mention the Comte de Pont, M. de Chateaubrun,[1] and M. de Foncemagne ;[2] I only name these gentlemen, because they have, by themselves, just claims to public esteem.

The Duc de Chartres was impatient to reach the age of independence, and that impatience was not dictated, as is the case with noble-minded young men, by the wish to try for himself the honourable pursuits of life, but simply by that to escape the irksome eye of his tutors, and follow the impulse of his bad inclinations. That moment, which ought to be fixed for each individual according to the disposition of his mind, the stamp of his character, the employment he has made of his time, is, in general, wrongly calculated among the French. They leave almost no interval between childhood, and the instant when a young man enters without guide upon a world of which he is ignorant. This sudden withdrawal of all control is still more harmful for princes. Slaves of the care with which they are surrounded, they remain children up to sixteen years of age, and all at once they are told that they are even more than the rest of men ; they are not yet fit to be free, and already they command. Astonished at their new power, impatient to abuse it in order to ascertain its properties, they find themselves surrounded only by seductions. Their most faithful servants fear to warn them, lest the warning should displease them, and a host of others try to be agreeable to them by all possible means.

Everything was to be feared from such concurrence of circumstances, with the nature already noticed in the Duc de Chartres. If he had been armed with some principle that had made a profound impression upon his heart, there might have been some prospect of discovering its effects in those calm moments when every man communes with himself. He would thus, at least, have given to his tastes the conventional limits of public opinion. If he had felt a strong attraction

---

[1] Jean-Baptiste Vivien de Chateaubrun born at Angoulême in 1686. First *maître d'hôtel* of the Duc d'Orléans. He wrote several tragedies, which secured his election to the Academy (1753). He was appointed under-governor to the Duc de Chartres, and died in 1775.

[2] Etienne de Foncemagne, born at Orléans in 1694. He made himself known by some historical treatises. Under-governor of the Duc de Chartres (1752), he died in 1775.

for any science whatever, his intellect would have sought to extend itself, his attention might have been governed. If only he had been truly in love, his mind, always active to please, would not have been worn out, or depraved by lack of occupation ; his heart would have rejected all the defects which are obliged to vanish before a true sentiment. Simple happiness which guards itself against the dangers of a restless imagination, self-abnegation which produces all our generous sentiments, would, without doubt, have developed some solid qualities in the Duc de Chartres.

But his cold heart deprived him of the illusions of youth, while his inattentive mind knew not how to fix itself upon serious matters. Unbridled in his taste, making of his pleasures a rampart around himself, even against love, he began life by the abuse of everything, and displayed constancy only in his excesses.

In 1769, he married Mademoiselle de Penthièvre. She was good, fair, fresh, sweet, and pure ; she pleased him so long as she was for him a new woman. A few days after, on the occasion of the first appearance of the Duc and Duchesse de Chartres at the opera the most dashing girls of Paris were able to lay aside the widows' costumes which they affected to wear there.

On entering society, the Duc de Chartres formed an intimacy with M. de Voyer,[1] the leader of the corrupt men of his time A large fortune, the reputation of possessing some business abilities, a rather brilliant conversation on military subjects, and a very witty mind, gathered around Voyer young men of unruly passions, men whose reputation was lost, bad characters and intriguers of all conditions. Abbé Yvon,[2] better known by the protracted persecution he had to bear than by some articles he

[1] Marc-Réné, Marquis de Voyer, son of the Comte Voyer d'Argenson, Secretary of State at War. Born in 1722, he became lieutenant-general, Governor of Vincennes, and died in 1782.

[2] Abbé Yvon, born in 1714 at Mamers, never discharged any ecclesiastical function, and was always in open contest with the Sorbonne. He made his first appearance in literature in the *Encyclopædia*, where he wrote the articles : *Soul, Atheist,* and *God.* Suspected of having taken part in the thesis sustained by Prades in the Sorbonne, and condemned by that learned body, he fled to Holland. Returning soon after, he was appointed historiographer to the Comte d'Artois, and died in 1791. The Abbé Yvon has left a large number of works on theology.

contributed to the *Encyclopædia*, especially by the article "Soul," which brought on him that persecution, had initiated Voyer in high metaphysics, whose language he had adopted even for the most familiar conversations.   It was always "*the soul . . . space . . . the link of beings . . . abstractedness . . . matter . . . composed of points . . . simple . . . without extent . . . indivisible,* &c.*" All these words, never explained, pronounced at intervals, with gestures, reticent and mystic forms, prepared the young adepts to believe.   They were then taught that every sentiment is but ridiculous . . . that scruples are but a sign of weakness . . . that justice is a prejudice . . . that our interest, or rather our pleasure only, ought to determine all our actions, &c. . . . . They naturally dispensed with proofs.

One evening, at a supper-party, M. de Lille,[1] an officer in the regiment of M. de Coigny, and a man of sense, strongly attached to his friends, a little susceptible, perhaps too familiar, but, on the whole, a very good lad, not feeling sufficiently convinced *that justice was absolutely a prejudice,* allowed himself to make some objections.   "It is my fault, my dear De Lille," said M. de Voyer, modestly ; "if you still have some doubts, it is because I did not go back far enough.   I was wrong, I ought to have taken the question from its origin . . . Listen, it is only a word . . .   Everybody knows that existence is for us the idea of the permanence of a certain collection of sensations which (follow me well) in similar or nearly similar circumstances, re-appear constantly the same . . . . You understand, De Lille ?   If they are not just exactly the same, they only show changes which are subject to certain laws which govern the universe, &c. . . . .   You understand me well, do you not ?   You see the sequel and the consequence of all this for a man like yourself, my dear De Lille, it is not necessary to develop it farther, &c ! ! ! "

By what means, if he would preserve his self-love, could a young man avow himself incapable of understanding this mysterious language?   He must, indeed confess himself convinced.   M. de Lille was sensible enough not to understand the sophism, but he had not the courage to say it ; and it was

---

[1] M. de Lille, officer in the regiment of Champagne, born at Saint-Mihiel, is the author of a collection of light poetry.

not until ridicule dared to attack the corruption which was the only thing in France that, until then, had been sacred to him, that M. de Lille related this conversation, and some others, which the oddness of the expressions had caused him to remember.

In the midst of that shapeless rubbish of metaphysics, this new sect only taught a few much truncated maxims, and a few sententious suggestions, with a gilt of seductive learning.

The fundamental principle of M. de Voyer's doctrine, however, was simple. He denied the existence of morality, sustaining that to say one must seek sanction in one's conscience was, for men of sense, but a word, with nothing real in it ; and that thus, it did not exist for all those, who, by their mind and nature, were inaccessible to remorse. As a deduction from this, frankness, sincerity, confidence, natural integrity, all the honourable affections, were accused and denounced as silly.

The source of true pleasures being thus dried up, these must of course be replaced by monstrous propensities. Among the initiated, at twenty, all illusions were already destroyed. Their organs thus depraved had need of strong emotions. Corruption alone could furnish them : and indeed it reigned over all these young, ruined imaginations, and when it reigns, it is with over-ruling authority. Sacrifices do not soften its sway ; the more it obtains, the more it exacts ; candour, fidelity, uprightness, are its first victims.

When one is but an adept, he is obliged to believe : M. de Voyer, who was an innovator, availed himself of the right of leaders of sects, and did not believe in the doctrine he professed ; this is proved by a host of details on his life and death. He always expressed the most absolute scorn for public opinion, and the judgments of the public were his torment.—"Good company," he said, one day, "will fall into the contempt it deserves."—And he was distressed to find that the houses of some of the members of that good company, which he thus despised, were closed to him. The total disregard of every kind of feeling enforced on him by the part he affected to play, sometimes compelled him to take precautions in order that no one should come to know the assistance he afforded to some unfortunate families. At "The Elms,"[1] on his estate, chiefly in the most out-of-the-way districts, he did much good. He never spoke of the court except with derision, any more than of the favours it granted and of the vile characters who solicited them, yet he indirectly requested for himself the honour of the blue riband[2] which, of all the rewards accorded by the king, bore the plainest imprint of favour. It was at Marly, the habitual seat of fêtes and pleasures, that Louis XVI., with the severity of honest manners and the brusqueness which timidity and probity combined produced in him, reproached him with his corruption, in the presence of all the court. Astonished at the first moment, M. de Voyer could find no reply. Having, however, collected himself a little he called on M. de Maurepas in order to acquaint him with what had occurred and to beg him to obtain for him some sort of apology. He had little to congratulate himself about the choice of his intermediate, from whom he could only obtain the following words : " *We shall never be able to teach politeness to the king.*" That insulting word *politeness*, the refusal of the " blue riband," the harsh expressions of the king, wounded him deeply, and all who knew him intimately, his wife for instance, had no doubt that sorrow was the cause of his death, which occurred soon after.

The Duc de Chartres, who only knew in M. de Voyer that side of his character which he displayed, submitted completely to the yoke imposed upon him by the society of the former. He lost all the natural sentiments by which he might have been able to reclaim himself. And it is from that time, from that second education, given at the age when men are the disciples of all that surrounds them, that really dates the corruption of the Duc d'Orléans. Until then, he only had unfortunate tendencies ; then, he was imbued with pernicious apologetic maxims, and contracted habits which he never gave up. If one would explain his entire life, it is necessary to go back to this period. If acquainted with the poison with which he was impregnated, one would no longer be surprised at his fatal errors. Thus, in making known the

---

[1] Château and land belonging to the d'Argenson family, near Tours.
[2] The riband of the order of the Saint Esprit (Holy Ghost), the highest order of the old monarchy. It had been created by Henri III.—(*Translator.*)

doctrine of M. de Voyer, I have pictured the Duc d'Orléans completely, I have revealed the secret of his life, and the motive of his actions. However different they seem to be, the same principle reappears in all. There never was a man more completely a slave to his belief. What ravages have been produced in the present generation of Frenchmen by that system, known among the disciples under the name of *désabusement*, which, until the eighteenth century, shut up in the hearts of a few depraved men, awaited these days to dare to shine forth as an opinion which could be professed, like a system of philosophy! This phenomenon of audacity merits attention.

The history of the French people has paid too little heed to the great faults of the human mind, as if there were not a necessary bond between its errors and its crimes. Has not morality, for example, everything to gain, when it can reconcile the opinions of the Duc d'Orléans with the different acts of his life? He believed there was nothing just but that which was comfortable for him: he was always ignorant of the fact that man depends for his happiness on the happiness of other men ; he failed to recognize this reciprocal need of services, that powerful motive of general and private benevolence. All the pleasant gifts which nature only confers on us for noble purposes, he subjected solely to personal intrigues, directed against credulous and inexperienced innocence. Called to an immense fortune, he did not see in the good he wished to do to his fellow-creatures the guarantee of that which he received from them ; his narrow egotism did not permit him to believe that, in this exchange, more would be returned to him than he would give. In early youth, when one calculates sentiments, one does it badly, or rather one only calculates upon them because one has none. In the continual change of inclinations that caprice causes to spring up, and which leads the soul from ardour to indifference, and from indifference to another caprice, there is no place for friendship. Thus the Duc d'Orléans loved no one. Some young, indulgent persons, who took this indifference for meekness, had an attachment for him. He made them the companions of his pleasures, comrades of his debauches, but never felt any real friendship for them. One of his first associates was the Prince de Lamballe: the latter's constitution was too weak to admit of his bearing long the kind of life led by his brother-in-law.

The death of young princes is never believed to be natural. This death made the Duc d'Orléans so prodigiously rich, and he made so bad a use of his fortune, that, in several works, he has been accused of having contributed to it in a more direct manner than by sharing the orgies of the deceased. But there is nothing to prove this allegation. I ought even to say, as the result of very reliable inquiries, that there is nothing to justify the suspicion at all. It is quite enough to say that the Prince de Lamballe was the most intimate companion of the Duc d'Orléans, that he was corrupted by him, that he died of it, and was not even the object of a regret.

A much longer intimacy left no more traces on the heart of the Duc d'Orléans. In 1788, after twenty-five years of association, he showed the most cruel indifference when he lost one of his principal companions, the Marquis de Conflans,[1] a man who always attracted general notice for his beauty, his noble bearing, his figure, his skill, and by his faults when he was in bad company, by his aptitudes when he was with military men, by the shrewdness of his mind when he spoke of serious things, and, at all times of his life, by the freedom of his tastes, his feelings, and his aversions. M. de Conflans was suffering from a disease which was to cause him to die suddenly ; he would not however believe himself to be ill, and went into society as usual. On the day of his death, he was to dine with the Duc d'Orléans and a few other noblemen, at the house of M. de Biron [2] at Montrouge. They were waiting for him, the Duc d'Orléans more impatiently than the others, because he wished to go to the theatre. At four o'clock every one was present, when one of M. de Conflans' people brought the message that he had just died. All who were in the room expressed their regrets according to their close or distant relations with the deceased. The only words uttered by the Duc d'Orléans were : " Lauzun,

[1] Louis-Gabriel, Marquis de Conflans d'Armentières, born in 1735, son of Marshal de Conflans. He was brigadier-general.
[2] The Duc de Lauzun who had reassumed his family name at the death of Marshal de Biron, his uncle (1788).

as we do not expect any one now, let us dine, in order to be in time to see the beginning of the opera."

The study of the human heart does not explain how so barren a soul could inspire the sentiment of friendship; and I regard it as incredible that the Duc d'Orléans should have been sincerely loved. M. de Biron, from his childhood until his death, had for him the most tender feelings. It is certainly not to the Duc d'Orléans that one can attribute the honour of these sentiments; it is to M. de Biron alone that it belongs. M. de Biron was courageous, romantic, generous, and witty. The similarity of their ages, a position almost equally brilliant, mutual sympathy, and a certain analogy of mind had caused an intimacy to spring up between them. It very soon required courage to love the Duc d'Orléans, generosity to defend him. The exercise of these two qualities rendered the Duc d'Orléans dearer to M. de Biron, and his romantic nature furnished him afterwards with all the fancies which his inward soul needed, to cultivate this sentiment. On the occasions when M. de Biron, reduced by his prodigality to be always in difficulties, was in pressing need of money, he did not believe that the Duc d'Orléans, although enormously rich, could lend him any, since he did not offer it; and it was by this same logic of illusions that he maintained that the Duc d'Orléans, having entered on political life, had no secret thoughts, no personal intentions, no part in the Revolution, since he had never made any confidence to him on this subject.

I do not speak of the other intimacies of the Duc d'Orléans with the Vicomte de Laval,[1] M. Sheldon, M. de Liancourt, M. Arthur Dillon,[2] M. de Fitz-James, M. de Saint-Blancard, M. de Monville,[3] &c. . . . These acquaintances all vanished at different

---

[1] Mathieu Paul Louis de Montmorency-Laval, known under the name of Vicomte de Laval, born August 5, 1748. He was at that time colonel of the regiment of Auvergne, and became brigadier-general in 1788. He died in 1809.

[2] Arthur, Comte de Dillon, born in Ireland in 1750. The family had been for a century in the service of France. He took, as colonel, an active part in the American war, became brigadier-general, and Governor of Tabago. Deputy from Martinique to the States-General, general-in-chief of the Army of the North, he was guillotined in 1794. Dillon had married the Comtesse de la Touche, cousin of the Empress Josephine.

[3] The Baron Thomas Boissel de Monville, born in 1763 at the Château of Monville (Normandy) of a noble family of this province. Counsellor of *parlement* in 1785,

times. Pleasure, which alone had formed them, is not a bond strong enough to last through a whole life. Those transient friendships, lead me, against my will, to speak of the throng of mistresses who occupied a part of the life of the Duc d'Orléans ; they were the source of so few incidents, however, that I do not feel bound to add the long list of their names. My task will be only too well filled in saying that all the tastes, all the caprices, all the fantasies of which his senses, at first imperious, afterwards impoverished, had need in order to be gratified or excited, were resorted to by the Duc d'Orléans.

I should like now to dwell here upon sweeter images, in speaking of the women of a more elevated character, who attached themselves to the Duc d'Orléans. This prince some-times reappeared in society, but always as in an enemy's country, where he sought victims. The Princesse de Bouillon,[1] the Marquise de Fleury,[2] the Princesse de Lamballe, each believed herself loved by him, and proved to him that they loved him. Their delicacy became, for his depraved mind, a new form of libertinage, which satiated him like all the others. He soon abandoned them, but with a publicity, which, happily, produced a contrary effect to that which the Duc d'Orléans expected. The public treated them with indulgence ; it pitied them, and they afterwards made him forget their errors.

When speaking of the women who only figured for a while in the life of the Duc d'Orléans, I could not name Madame de Sillery ;[3] she deserves a special mention.

he was one of the most active members of the opposition, and embraced with ardour the principles of the Revolution. Under the Empire, he lived in retirement. Peer of France in 1814, he died in 1832. Monville was a distinguished *savant.* He practised mechanics and manufactured several agricultural machines.

[1] Marie-Christine von Hesse Rheinfelz-Rothenburg, married in 1766 to Jacques de la Tour d'Auvergne, Prince de Bouillon, born in 1746.

[2] Claudine de Montmorency-Laval, born in 1750, married in 1768 to André, Marquis de Fleury.

[3] Felicité Ducrest de Saint-Aubin, Marquise de Sillery, Comtesse de Genlis, born in 1746 near Autun. She married in 1762, Charles Brulart, Comte de Genlis, born in 1737, captain in the navy, who took the title of Marquis de Sillery on inheriting his property some years afterwards. M. de Sillery, later Deputy to the States-General, was guillotined with the Girondists, October 31, 1793. His wife, who retained all her life the name of Comtesse de Genlis was appointed lady-of-honour to the Duchesse de Chartres in 1770, governess to Madame Adelaide, and afterwards *tutor* of the young princes d'Orléans. She emigrated with Madame Adelaide in 1792, retired to Switzerland and then to Berlin. She returned to France in 1800, where she was very well received at the Consular Court. Madame de Genlis wrote much. She

When one is a combination of ambition and moderation, of communicativeness and of reserve, of rigidity and complacency, one is certainly a person whose life and intimacy must offer extraordinary contrasts. It was by opposite means, and which she never separated, that Madame de Genlis succeeded in all that her ambition desired. Being young, pretty, without relations, it was by risking morning calls to men that she found a husband ; later, she affected the height of prudery, in a regular career of gallantries ; with the same pen, she wrote *The Knights of the Swan*, and *Lessons in Morals for Children ;* [1] on the same desk, she composed a church book for Mademoiselle de Chartres and a speech to the Jacobins for the Duc d'Orléans. All her life presents the same contrasts. Mademoiselle de Saint-Aubin—that was her name—had an elegant figure but devoid of nobleness ; the expression of her face was very lively ; she had little dash in conversation, little charm in the habitual usage of her mind, but possessed at her fingers' ends all the advantages that can be given by instruction, observation, reserve, and the tact of the world. When she had, for better or worse, married the Comte de Genlis, it became necessary for her to make the acquaintance of her husband's family, who, as she knew, were not well-disposed towards her. Talents, affected timidity, and time enabled her, however, to reach her aim. She managed to be invited at Sillery. In a few days, she succeeded in winning the favour of M. de Puysieux,[2] one of the most wearied men of his time, and in disarming the sour old temper of Madame de Puysieux. She felt indeed that she was then truly in society ; and, moving in it, for the first time, consequently brought all her methods into play ; she showed herself caressing, attentive, gay without blundering, and was even able to be continually complacent, with a shade

left a number of novels, and works on education. Under the Empire, she wrote every other week in different periodicals, at the request of Napoleon himself. She left, besides, interesting memoirs. She died in 1830.

[1] "Les Chevaliers du Cygne"—"Leçons de Morale pour les Enfants." The former is not exactly intended to be placed in the hands of school-girls. (*Translator.*)

[2] Louis Brulart, Marquis de Puysieux and de Sillery, born in 1702, first entered the army, was afterwards ambassador at Naples (1735), Secretary of State for Foreign Affairs (1747–1751), Minister of State up to 1756. He died in 1770. He was the great-uncle of the Comte de Genlis and proprietor of the estate of Sillery.

of compassion. This first success was of great use to her ; a few doors were thrown open to her ; she obtained to be introduced to the Duchesse de Chartres, who, by the protection she accorded her, destroyed in a very short time all the little oppositions of society which still existed. The Duc de Chartres found her charming, told her this, and was quickly listened to, for Madame de Genlis, to avoid the scandal of coquetry, always yielded easily. A few years of care, indulgence and retired life, gave her such an ascendency over the Duc de Chartres, that it has been supposed that she had a kind of influence over his actions, or rather over the events of his life. So skilful a conduct had its reward ; she succeeded in being appointed governess or rather *tutor* of his children. One can only see in this choice of the Duc de Chartres, the intention to appear peculiar, and to mark plainly his scorn for accepted usages.

Madame de Genlis, proved, in the first works she published, that she was capable of directing all that part of the education which pertains to the mind. Their exceptional nature made of the eldest son of the Duc d'Orléans, and of his daughter *Mademoiselle* two superior beings.[1] Tried, fortified, instructed and ennobled by misfortune, they showed themselves simple and great when they entered upon their natural destiny.

The best works of Madame de Genlis, with the exception of *Mademoiselle de Clermont*, date from this time, and if to-day she has fallen in reputation, and follows, without glory, in her quality of woman of letters, a singular and ill-considered path, it is because, intoxicated by her first successes, she yields to her pride and no longer consults her judgment ; it is because she wishes to manage the jealous independence of the public, as she managed formerly the obedient submission of her pupils ; it is because she cannot soften her morality to subjugate the public, as she has formerly done to subjugate all who were around her. I cannot resist remarking upon two things : one, that to command is so necessary to Madame de Genlis, that when she has no more princes to domineer, she takes by chance the first comer to make a pupil of him ; the other, that, in spite of the rigidity of manners she advocates, and the morality she professes

---

[1] King Louis-Philippe and Madame Adelaide.

in her writings, one always meets in her later novels, something of the freedom of her earlier manners ; there is always in them some *amours* or some illegitimate children. For whom, with what object, does she still write ? It may be, perhaps, only from love of fame ; she was more sensible in her youth.

All the youth of the Duc d'Orléans was spent without plans, without projects, without result, without discretion. All he did bore the stamp of irreflection, frivolity, corruption, and deceit. To instruct himself he went to see the experiments of Préval ; he ascended in a balloon ; he assisted Cagliostro[1] and the Chevalier de Luxembourg[2] in their fantasmagoria ; he went to the Newmarket races and to other fashionable places.

To increase his fortune, which was already immense, he made speculations on the lands of the Palais-Royal,[3] the dwelling of Louis XIII., Anne of Austria, Louis XIV., and finally of *Monsieur*, by whom it became an appanage of the House of Orleans.

Later, in a moment of suspicion, after having announced

---

[1] The history of this celebrated adventurer could form a novel made up of the most curious adventures. Born at Palermo in 1745, his real name was Giuseppe Balsamo. He travelled all over Europe, procuring resources by most disreputable means. He had a certain knowledge of medicine and of chemistry, which enabled him, in working skilfully upon popular credulity, to acquire an universal reputation as a magician and healer. He came to France, where he took the name of Comte de Cagliostro. He found a protector in the person of the Cardinal de Rohan. His house became the meeting-place of all Paris, who ran to witness the prodigies of the skilful charlatan. Compromised in the affair of the necklace,* he was exiled and went over to England ; he then resumed his wandering life, and ended by settling in Rome in 1789. He was arrested by order of the Inquisition, and accused of practising freemasonry. Condemned to death, his sentenced was commuted, and he died in prison in 1795.

[2] Anne de Montmorency-Luxembourg, known in his youth under the name of Chevalier de Luxembourg, was born in 1742, was named Captain of the Guards (1767), Marshal of Camp (1784). He died in 1790. He had accepted the title of Grand Master of the lodge of Egyptian freemasonry, founded by Cagliostro.

[3] The Palais-Royal was built between the years 1629 and 1636, for the Cardinal de Richelieu, by the architect Lemercier. It was called then the Palais-Cardinal. Richelieu left it by will to Louis XIII. (1643). Under the regency, Anne of Austria came to live there with Louis XIV. It was then that it took the name of Palais-Royal. Louis XIV. gave it, in 1693, to his brother the Duc d'Orléans. In 1763, it was burned and re-built by the architect Moreau, who designed it as we see it to-day. Louis-Philippe (grandson of the Regent) increased its dimensions considerably by buying all round a large belt of lands. The Palais-Royal, having become the Palais National under the Revolution, was used as the residence of the members of the Tribunate. In 1814, it was returned to the family of Orléans. Under the Second Empire, it became the dwelling of Prince Napoleon.† It is now devoted to the sittings of the *Cour des Comptes* and of the *Conseil d'État*.

* See footnote 4, p. 59, Part I.
† Prince Jérôme Napoleon, son of King Jérôme of Westphalia and of Queen Catherine of Wurtemberg. By the death of the " Prince Imperial," he has become the head of the Bonaparte family —(*Translator.*)

some days beforehand to Séguin, his treasurer, his wish to see for himself the state of his treasury, he had him arrested in his presence, carried away the keys, and seized by this means all the money which Séguin, forewarned, had borrowed from his own friends, in order to replace momentarily that which he had invested in private speculations.

A spark of ambition made him desirous of appearing in the squadron of M. d'Orvilliers,[1] hoping thereby to acquire a title to the extremely lucrative reversion of grand-admiral that belonged to his father-in-law, the Duc de Penthièvre. He did not, however have this post, and doubts were raised as to his bravery.[2] To prove his courage, he had himself applauded at some of the theatres and crowned under the windows of Mademoiselle Arnould.[3] Paris amused itself then in a satirical but very unjust song at his expense.

Some journeys to England, a run to Italy, remarkable only for the rapidity with which it was performed; the glory of being elected Grand-Master of the freemasons;[4] after a rather serious illness, a *Te Deum* sung by the lodge of the *Nine Sisters*;[5] some

---

[1] Louis Guillouet, Comte d'Orvilliers, born at Moulins in 1708. He entered the navy, became vice-admiral in 1764, and lieutenant-general. In 1777, he fought the battle of Ouessant, which, although indecisive, was glorious for French arms. He resigned in 1779, retired to a convent, emigrated in 1789, and died in 1791.
[2] To make up for his disappointment, the king appointed him to the office of colonel-general of Hussars.
[3] Sophie Arnould, a celebrated actress of the Opera (1744 to 1803).
[4] The Duc d'Orléans was elected Grand-Master in 1771, in which office he succeeded the Comte de Clermont. It was he who suppressed the Grand Lodge of France, and replaced it by the Grand-Orient. I give here, as a curiosity, the acceptance of the Duc : " In the year of great light, 1772, third day of the moon of Jiar, fifth day of the second month of the Masonic year, 5772 ; and since the birth of the Messiah, fifth day of April 1772. In virtue of the proclamation made in the Grand Lodge, assembled on the twenty-fourth day of the fourth month of the Masonic year 5771 by the very high, very mighty and very excellent prince H.S.H. Louis-Philippe-Joseph d'Orléans, Duc de Chartres, prince of the blood, as Grand-Master of all the regular lodges of France. And of that of the sovereign council of the emperors of the East and of the West, sublime mother lodge of Scotland, on the twenty-sixth of the moon of Elul 1771, as sovereign Grand-Master of all the councils, chapters and lodges of the great orb of France ; an office which the aforesaid S.H. has willingly accepted for the love of the royal art, and in order to concentrate under a single authority all the masonic operations. In witness whereof, the aforesaid S.H. has appended his name to the report of acceptance."
[5] The lodge of the Nine Sisters was founded in 1776 by several men of letters and of European fame. This rather profane name (the nine Muses) caused a deal of trouble to the founders. Their lodge was even, for a time, erased from the list of the order. It was nevertheless the most brilliant lodge of the day, Franklin, Helvétius, Roucher, Voltaire himself, being members of it. In 1827, it amalgamated with the lodge of *Saint-Louis de France*, but kept its original name.

pleasures, or rather disorders of all kinds at Mousseaux,[1] filled the following years.

The Duc d'Orléans was approaching the age when, with the greater number of men, the passions of youth begin to weaken and to yield to the sway of a new tyrant. Nevertheless, he did not yet display symptoms of ambition, which latter is, doubtless, more backward in hearts withered by depravity and shrunken by combinations of personal interest.

An agitation which spread all over France, was, however, beginning to manifest itself, and could already be heard in all parts of the kingdom—those dull and distant rumblings, the forerunners of volcanic outbreaks. The French people had been called, by the government itself, to consider the situation of the finances, and to hear the statement of the fortune of the State. A light so new to their eyes had caused a lively sensation and made a profound impression. An entirely new power was created in France, that of public opinion. It was not the clear and firm opinion which is the privilege of nations who have long and peaceably enjoyed their liberties and the knowledge of their affairs, but that of an impetuous and inexperienced people, who are only the more presumptuous in their judgments and more decided in their will. It is this formidable instrument that M. de Calonne dared to undertake to handle, in order to adjust the old springs of the government. He summoned the Notables; he divided them into commissions, over each of which presided a prince of the royal family or a prince of the blood. The presidency of the third commission fell to the Duc d'Orléans. He only made himself noticed by his indifference and lack of application. Diligence at the sessions would have required the sacrifice of his pleasures or of his habits for a considerable time, and this he was not capable of making. He began by absenting himself from the evening sittings, and ended by neglecting the day meetings, to which he

---

[1] The hamlet of Mousseaux or Monceau, now a district of Paris, belonged formerly to the parish of Clichy. The fermier-général de la Reynière had acquired the lordship of Monceau, where he possessed the château of Belair. The Duc de Chartres became in turn its purchaser. He built on it a country seat called *La Folie de Chartres*, and designed around it a magnificent park. The Convention declared the Parc Monceau national property. Later, the Emperor gave it to Cambacérès. Louis XVIII. returned it to the Orléans family, which kept it until the passing of the decree of 1852, which made it definitively a national property.

came very late, and sometimes not at all. He pushed his frivolity
to the extent of going, during one of the sessions, to a hunt in
the woods of Raincy. The deer which he pursued was captured
in the ditches of the Faubourg Saint-Antoine, under the eyes,
and to the great scandal of, the Parisians.

His partisans, not very numerous, thought to excuse his conduct
by remarking that, at least, he was no party to the intrigues,
which, after having scandalised the Assembly of the Notables,
had ended in annihilating all the hopes its meeting had given rise
to. This negative praise was not flattering; for was there no
other part for the Duc d'Orléans to play, on this memorable
occasion, but that of an intriguer? It was more than a century
and a half since France had seen her king summon so important
a council. The greatest lords, the first magistrates, the wealthiest
landowners of France, had met together to give their advice on
the principal questions of the administration. It was meant
thereby to oppose the power of a stronger and more enlightened
opinion to the resistance of the *parlement*, to attack the Colossus
of ecclesiastical privileges, to cause the yield of the public rates and
taxes to balance the expenditure of the State by changing the
whole system of taxation, to pass long desired uniform laws on
the removal of the *barrières*, on statute labour, on the freedom of
the corn trade, and many other impediments to national prosperity. It is easily conceived that the men or the organizations
threatened by these reforms would have done their utmost to
render them impossible, and that the swarms of ambitious men
whose aim it was to secure office, took possession of this vast field
to carry on their struggle. But that a prince of the blood, so
foreign to interests of this nature, should not have experienced
the noble temptation to crush all these petty intrigues under the
weight of his independence, that he should have viewed with
indifference all these symptoms of rebellion, that he should have
calmly looked on the dangers of the king, whose weakness was
so obvious and was so cruelly relied on, I cannot conceive, nor
can I account for it at all. He was bitterly reproached for it by
the nation, which took only too much interest in those debates,
and which had already lost too much of its former frivolous
character, to excuse a prince of the royal blood, scandalously

parading his indifference : and the murmurings of the public were not slow in conveying to him all the severity of this judgment.

To thwart its effect, the advisers of the prince acknowledged the necessity of a prompt proceeding and obtained his assent to it; but it must be easy of execution and require but little following up : it was necessary that the part to be performed should be in proportion to the person who was to perform it.

The Duc's chancellor was the Marquis Ducrest,[1] one of those adventurers whom the caprice of fortune sometimes raises to the top of the tree, and who think they deserve such favour. This man was venturesome to foolhardiness and confident even to imprudence. He had reached this post through the influence of his sister, Madame de Genlis, and he sustained the importance of his place with the adroitness of a charlatan, rather than with the skill of a business man. The affairs of the Duc d'Orléans had the reputation of being well conducted, and this reflected some credit on M. Ducrest. Financial projects were then the mania. M. Ducrest thought fit to draw up a memorial on the finances of the State, in which he proved easily that they had, up to that time, been badly administered, and proposed, in order to re-organize them, to follow the plans he had put into practice in the administration of his master's fortune. It was arranged that the Duc d'Orléans should deliver this memorial to the king, and he consented more willingly to doing this than to discussing the arguments set forth in it. It was enough for him that the plan should have publicity and should give him, with little trouble, the appearance of displaying zeal. This scheme was at first successful. The king received the memorial, and did not allow its contents to transpire ; this was a treatment which its author did neither wish nor anticipate. Piqued by this silence, the Duc composed a second memorial in which he no longer restricted himself to criticizing the operations of the ministry, but openly attacked the persons of the ministers, and above all, the Archbishop of Toulouse. As to the point in hand, he did not

---

[1] Charles Louis, Marquis Ducrest, born in 1743. He was the brother of Madame de Genlis. He served first in the navy, then in the army, where he was appointed colonel of grenadiers in 1779. He was for some time chancellor of the Duc d'Orléans, with whom he quarrelled later. He emigrated to Holland, and died in 1824. He left some works on political economy and various scientific treatises.

hold himself solely to the restoration of the finances, he went directly to the root of the evil, and expressed the wish of bringing back to the king the hearts of the French, which had been estranged by the faults of the government. He proposed, in order to accomplish both these ends at once, to establish councils at the head of each of the sections of the administration, and by this means to weaken the authority of the ministers. But, at the same time, he wished for a supreme chief, a principal leader at the head of the council, and declared himself ready to consent to play this leading part provided that he was entrusted with unlimited power, and supported by all the means public opinion could devise to strengthen this power. He asked, in consequence, that the title and post of superintendent of finances, an office which had not been conferred since the disgrace of Superintendent Fouquet, under the reign of Louis XIV., should be re-established in his favour. The easy indulgence of Louis XVI., to whom the Duc d'Orléans delivered this second memorial, would only have repaid with scorn this unwarrantable piece of impertinence. Chance did men justice by divulging it. A copy of this document was found on the person of the Comte de Kersalaun, a Breton nobleman whom the governor of Brittany had had arrested in connection with matters relating to his jurisdiction, and the secret thus spread abroad enabled people to appreciate the modest talents of the chancellor, and the prudence of his master.

   This discovery exposed both to many jokes in verse and in prose, of which we only cite the following epigram, as it may serve to indicate the ruling tendencies in France, at this period of the life of the Duc d'Orléans :—

> " Par tes projets bien entendus,
> Modeste Ducrest, à t'entendre,
> A la reine, au roi, tu vas rendre
> Les cœurs français qu'ils ont perdus.
> Sans miracle cela peut être ;
> Hélas ! ils n'ont qu'à le vouloir.
> Mais, en preuve de ton savoir,
> Fais-nous avant aimer ton maître." [1]

---

[1] " Thanks to your well-concerted plans,
If we are to believe you, unassuming Ducrest,

This first attempt to reconquer public favour having proved a failure, the confidants of the Duc d'Orléans did not lose courage, and only considered themselves warned to arrange matters better in future.

Occasions could not be rare at a time when the position of affairs was changing and becoming more intricate every day. The progress of ideas, more rapid even than that of events, was prodigiously accelerated.

At the beginning of that same year, a meeting of Notables had, as I have already said, surprised everybody, and in the month of July following, the name of States-General was uttered in the *parlement* of Paris itself with more enthusiasm than surprise. The courts of justice everywhere abdicated their old pretensions, to decide the amount of taxes to be raised. They refused to register the edicts, and sent back the tax-laws to be discussed by the States-General. The court, astonished at this language, tried to intimidate the *parlements;* that of Paris was transferred to the city of Troyes, and for other difficulties, the *parlement* of Bordeaux removed to Libourne.[1] This severity had not been of long duration. The obstinacy of the magistrates had not been inflexible; half-way measures and intrigues, in which M. and Madame de Sémonville[2] (then Madame de

> You will win back to the queen, and the king,
> The French hearts they have lost.
> Without miracle, too, that may be ;
> Alas ! they have only to wish it.
> But first make us love your dear master,
> And your power, perhaps, then we will credit."

[1] The *parlement* of Paris was exiled to Troyes, August 15, 1787, as a result of the deliberation it had held on August 7 preceding, to protest against the *lit de justice*, where the edicts on the stamp-duty and on the territorial subsidies had been registered by force. It was recalled on August 19 following ; the ministry had decided to agree to these two edicts. As to the *parlement* of Bordeaux, it had been exiled to Libourne, at about the same time, for having protested against the creation of provincial assemblies. It had even forbidden the assembly of Limousin to meet again.

[2] Charles Louis Huguet, Marquis de Sémonville, born in 1759, was received as counsellor at the *parlement* of Paris in 1778. In spite of his opposition to the court, he retained the favour of the king, was charged with negotiating the reconciliation of Mirabeau, and later, that of the Girondists. Minister at Geneva in 1791 ; minister at Florence in 1793, where Danton sent him to negotiate the setting at liberty of the royal family, he was arrested with his colleague, Maret (the future Duc de Bassano), and suffered thirty months' captivity. On the 18th Brumaire he was named minister to Holland. Senator in 1805, he took no part in politics under the Empire. Peer of France in 1814 ; grand referendary of the court. He kept aloof during the Hundred Days, took up his functions again in 1815, and kept them until 1830. He then made some efforts to save the Bourbon monarchy. Nevertheless, he retained his office under

Montholon) appear for the first time, in different capacities, had brought about a temporary reconciliation ; but it was only a truce, and even though the measures taken seemed more conciliatory, public opinion gradually assumed a more menacing aspect. The ears of the ministers became familiar with the name of States-General ; they entered into new engagements on every occasion ; the efforts of the ministry were directed only to putting off the meeting of this assembly until the year 1792. This delay they must gain, and, in the meantime, face the taxes, pay off the sums about to fall due, or already so, and meet extraordinary expenses ; and for so many needs, the ministry mentioned no other resource than that of a loan open for five successive years, and whose capital was to reach four hundred millions.

In order to palliate the effect of this enormous demand, they spoke on the one hand of reforms, economies, and ameliorations ; while on the other, they added to the bursal edict a law favourable to the non-Catholics, a law that the government believed conformable to the prevailing ideas and calculated to rally many supporters. It had certainly never stood in greater need of them. The critical mind prevailed everywhere ; everybody prided himself on being an opponent, it was the general disposition ; it animated all the corporations, it prevailed in all the writings ; all men vied with each other as to who should attack a ministry that no one dared to defend, and which, after all perhaps, had no more dangerous enemy than its own incapacity. So it was easy to win victories over it, and, whatever might be the issue of this contest, to have public opinion in one's favour.

The friends of the Duc d'Orléans pressed him to aspire to that easy success, by which various other interests could be satisfied at the same time. He was not without experiencing some resentment at having been met with a refusal, the last time he had asked to be authorized to go to England ; for the princes of the blood could not go out of France without the permission of the king. Political reasons, easy to be conceived, placed all

the new government.   He died in 1839.   Sémonville married Mademoiselle de Rostain, widow of the Comte de Montholon.   His step-son was General de Montholon, who accompanied Napoleon to Saint Helena.   One of his step-daughters married General Joubert, and on her second marriage, Marshal Macdonald.

the members of the reigning house in a sort of dependence on its head for all the important actions of their private life,—a sort of legitimate subjection, inasmuch as it is useful for the public good, and, in truth, very easy to support when so many enjoyments make up for it. The Duc d'Orléans in vain affected to ignore the cause of that refusal which had so offended him ; it was none the less obvious to observant eyes. Some scandalous reports were circulating in France as to his conduct during his first two journeys, and Louis XVI., as the friend of decency and good manners, wished to spare him a new occasion for indulging his disorderly conduct and parading it before the eyes of a neighbouring nation.

Perhaps this refusal to the Duc d'Orléans was dictated, in some measure, by the dread of the influence of the examples and habits of a free country. Such a fear was puerile at this period of history, and insulting to English liberty, for it would have been a good thing for the Duc d'Orléans to acquire a taste for and understand the principles of it. He would thus have learned to know what true liberty is, and have understood that each individual has duties to perform, that the most eminent in the social scale must set the example of respect to the king, and that it is a crime to sacrifice public interest to one's own resentments. Those of the Duc d'Orléans were more particularly directed against the queen, and they were kept up by a constantly increasing series of society quarrels. Sharp words were bandied about on both sides, and courtiers were not wanting to report them to those at whom they were aimed.

Such miserable wranglings only had too great an influence on the fate of the unfortunate queen. Why was it, that from the height of this throne where her beauty alone was rivalled by her greatness she should ever have consented to take part in quarrels which she ought to have ignored ? Sovereigns are doomed to reign without relaxing ; they should never permit themselves to forget the importance of their private actions, for they can never cause them to be forgotten by those who surround them, and their negligence simply gives birth to hatred, their least preference to jealousy, and their slightest offence to implacable resentment.

The Duc d'Orléans saw himself each day farther removed
from that familiar society of which the queen had given the
first example to the court of France, and of which Little Trianon
was the ordinary rendezvous. To several fêtes in this delightful
garden, to that,[1] among others, which the queen gave there for
the archduke, her brother, the Duc d'Orléans was not invited.
It is true that no prince of the blood was favoured on this
occasion. Disagreements of another character likewise kept the
Prince de Condé[2] and his family away from the parties given at
Little Trianon. At the gates of this charming retreat, the
queen felt that she could lay aside the chains of her grandeur.
Queen at Versailles, she believed she paid there her debt to the
august rank she occupied ; privately at Trianon, she wished
to be there only the most amiable of women and to know only
the sweetnesses of intimacy. Seeing that no one had absolutely
a right to the favour of being admitted to these little excursions,
it was only the more desirable, and the more calculated to excite
the desire of being invited. The Duc d'Orléans could not conceal
his envy, even under the cloak of indifference. At one of these
fêtes, he planned with some ladies of the court as little in favour as
he was, the means of mingling with the people admitted to look
at the illuminations ; and, having thus penetrated into the
garden, he avenged himself, for not having been invited, by such
loud jeering and noisy gaiety that the queen was informed of it,
and keenly hurt.

These little fits of animosity had so irritated the Duc
d'Orléans that it was not difficult to lead him on to more serious
measures of opposition. The sway of fashion alone would
have sufficed to decide him. What was there to be feared in a
faction which the pettiest bailiwick of the kingdom joined with
impunity, and of which the courtiers professed the principles even
in the very antechambers of the king. The Duc d'Orléans had

[1] Fête given to Joseph II., at Trianon, on the occasion of his visit to France,
June 13, 1777,
[2] Louis-Joseph de Bourbon, Prince de Condé, son of the Duc de Bourbon, who
was first minister under Louis XV., and fourth descendant of the great Condé. Born
in 1736, he took an active part in the Seven Years War, emigrated in 1789, and
became the chief of that body of *émigrés*, who took from that time the name of Army
of Condé. He retired to England in 1801, re-entered France at the Restoration, and
died in 1818. He had married the daughter of the Marshal Prince de Soubise.

only to present himself, in order to be proclaimed leader of the malcontents at a time when everybody was, or affected to be, one. This position was often presented to his imagination by the men who had succeeded in gaining his confidence. It belongs to my subject to make them known, for what would history be if it painted but the surface alone, without ever penetrating into the inner life of men who have played a prominent part, and without disclosing the motives which caused them to act ?

I have already sketched the character of Chancellor Ducrest, who held the first place in the house of the Duc d'Orléans. M. de Limon,[1] had, under M. Ducrest, the duties and the title of Intendant of Finances. He was a business man, adroit beyond measure ; he had had the management of the pecuniary interests of *Monsieur.* The estate of the former Duc d'Orléans had just been proved ; it was of enormous value, but involved, and the co-heirs raised all sorts of difficulty. M. de Limon succeeded in clearing this chaos, and making the brother and the sister[2] satisfied with each other and with himself. By this service, he secured the confidence of the Duc d'Orléans ; and he was not a man who would not make the most of it for himself. While following the litigation relative to the estate, he had made the acquaintance of the chief members of the *parlement* of Paris, who, being then engaged in higher politics, had willingly welcomed the intendant of a prince whose name could give weight to their opinions. As for M. de Limon, he had detected some hope of making himself necessary, and he cultivated carefully his new acquaintances, in order that no one could dispute with him the part of medium between the prince and the *parlement.*

M. de Limon found himself powerfully aided by Abbé Sabatier de Cabre, one of the most stirring members of the *parlements* of that time. A friend of Madame de Sillery, it had been easy for the abbé, who attracted general notice by a rare effrontery, a seducing imagination, a sort of eloquence, abundant, fantastic and fertile of abuse, to gain access to the

[1] The Marquis Geoffroy de Limon was comptroller-general of the Duc d'Orléans. Deeply devoted to this prince, he assumed, during the Revolution, a rather equivocal attitude. It is even pretended that he wanted to have the Comte d'Artois poisoned. After having been a fervent patriot, he emigrated, and became a firm royalist. He it was who drew up the manifesto of the Duke of Brunswick. He died in 1779.

[2] *Madame,* the Duchesse de Bourbon.

intimacy of the Duc d'Orléans. He pleased the latter, and soon succeeded in leading him on. Though enjoying no esteem in the *parlement*, he possessed some influence there. His fellow counsellors had accused him of having been the spy of the last ministry ; he cleared himself by harassing the new one. It was he who, on July 16, 1787, suggested, in the meeting of the courts, the convocation of the States-General ; and this bold novelty had been greatly instrumental in drawing attention to him.

What an advantage for a man of this stamp if he could succeed in drawing the Duc d'Orléans into a series of undertakings, respecting which his incapacity would each day increase his dependence ! Sabatier understood that he must above all smooth the difficulties before the prince, that he must not hope to conquer his frivolity, but rather confine himself to exacting little from him in order to conciliate all his failings. So the prince had merely to rehearse the part arranged by the abbé for his appearance on the stage of public affairs. The loan of four hundred millions of which I have already spoken furnished the occasion for it. It is from then that the part taken in public affairs by the Duc d'Orléans ought really to be dated.

In order to better understand this incident, it is necessary to make known a few of the forms observed then in France, when the government had need to borrow. The edicts which created the loans, and which determined its conditions, had the character of laws, and, like other laws had to be transcribed on the registers of the *parlements* of the kingdom. This formality, which sanctioned the engagement of the State, secured the lenders. But to produce such powerful effects, was simple form sufficient ? Could the mere act of a material transcription constitute a public obligation, and mortgage the revenues of the State ? Was not then the registering in the *parlements* an approval of measures included in the edict ? And does not the right of approval suppose that of disapproval ? Was not the registering a witness of the national consent ; and could this consent be sufficiently expressed by a mechanical operation, blind and perfectly passive ? All these questions recurred without ceasing, and being always eluded, never made clear, were an inexhaustible source of debates and intrigues. At each new loan, a struggle was necessary against a resistance into which the magistrates were drawn by their natural propensity, for their power being purely negative, they could only exercise it by refusals. Besides, they had not, and could not have, any acquaintance with the needs of the State, nor with its resources. It was only, then, by general reasons that they could be convinced, and to give value to these general reasons, there must be found means of persuasion for each magistrate. This duty was entrusted to the first president ; and when he met with too many difficulties, the king was told he must display his authority. It was then that he summoned a *lit de justice.*

This kind of assembly, of which one can form no adequate idea from the name it bears, was, in fact, the annihilation of the remnant of liberty and of justice, which had taken refuge with the resistance offered by the *parlements.* Thus M. de Fontenelle was justified in saying that a *lit de justice* was a bed where justice slept. Whether the king came himself to sit in the courts of the *parlement,* or whether he obliged its members to call personally with the registers at his palace, the ceremony reduced itself to a reprimand pronounced by the monarch and commented upon by the chancellor. The advocate-general of the king arose next to expose and often to blame the motive of the edicts, concluding, nevertheless, that they must receive without delay the character of laws. For, it is to be remarked that the presence of the king did not deprive the advocate-general of the liberty of expressing his opinion, though it imparted a certain direction to his summing-up. When all these speeches were delivered, the king ordered the transcription of the edict on the register of laws, and after this act of authority to which the magistrates had no means of offering resistance, there remained to them no other resource than that of remonstrance, a species of tardy warning having a direct action on public opinion, and often hindering the progress of affairs.

It is also necessary to bear in mind that the *lits de justice* were the corruption of an ancient French custom according to which the kings had formerly rendered justice in person, in the bosom of the *parlement*, and in the midst of the princes of their blood, and of the peers of their kingdom. At these royal sittings, all the judges gave their opinions; the king had only his own vote and delivered a verdict as expressed by the majority. But his presence at the trial of private cases gave weight to the measure there adopted—that was the greatest defect of this exercise, otherwise so respectable, of the functions of royalty. It was understood later, that if justice is the debt of kings, this debt is better discharged when they do not discharge it personally. Thus the king no longer attended the trial of cases; but he had retained his right of sitting in the midst of the judges. He only made use of it, as a rule, to enjoin personally the registering of some laws, and to overcome any opposition to it : this visit was named a *lit de justice* ; the direct result of this institution was that even in the matter of taxes and loans, the king was sole and absolute legislator ; for the co-operation of the *parlements* could always be reduced to a purely passive action ; and in fact, they had no part in the making of the laws, the passing of which they had no right to propose, nor to prevent.

The only counterpoise to the royal power consisted in the national manners, and in public opinion, which gives force to the law in well-constituted countries, and which, in purely despotic countries, fills the lack of institutions. This impalpable force was certainly most real in matters of loans ; for the government might indeed call for capital, and it is confidence, and well-founded confidence which brings it. The Archbishop of Toulouse, Minister of Finances, recognized this truth ; the need of more than four hundred millions to assess on the five years to follow, was each day more fully demonstrated to him. He understood, at the same time, that if this loan were only registered by force, it would be announced under too unfavourable auspices and would never be covered. The *lits de justice* had become odious. He could not count upon a free consent ; he feared the results of a consent too openly wrenched. He felt the need of bringing authority into action, and, at the same time, of dissimulating this action. He thought then of getting the king to hold a sitting in the *parlement* of Paris ; a sitting which should be a compound of a *lit de justice* and of the old royal sessions. Of these he borrowed the name which was not dis-credited, and the mode of suffrage, which permitted each member of *parlement* to give his opinion, and develop his arguments. He retained the essential parts of the *lits de justice*, the right to enforce the registering, without regard to the plurality of votes or the wish of the majority.

On November 19th, 1787, the king presented himself at nine o'clock in the morning at the *parlement.* The Duc d'Orléans was there, and the other princes of the blood, with the exception of the Prince de Condé, who was then occupied in holding the estates of Burgundy. The king brought with him two edicts, one of which related to the creation of the loan of four hundred millions, and formed the principal object of the session, while the second, which was on the civil condition of the non-Catholics, had only been conceived in order to throw some favourable light on the *bursal* edict.

The king opened the session by a speech divided into two parts ; in the first, he announced that he had come to consult his *parlement* of Paris on two great acts of administration and of legislation. He developed very little of the purpose of these, leaving, as was customary, to his Keeper of the Seals, the care of the details and of the explanations. In the second part, he took occasion to reply to the remonstrances that the *parlement* of Paris had addressed to him in favour of the *parlement* of Bordeaux, which had been punished by a re-moval to Libourne for having raised difficulties relative to the registering of a law on the provincial assemblies. The king, in this part of his speech, employed a tone of authority, which being affected and not even sustained during the little time he spoke, served only to make perceptible by its variations, the hesitations of his character.

The Keeper of the Seals[1] spoke after him ; his discourse embraced a vast plan ; he commenced by attacking directly the

[1] The Keeper of the Seals was then Chrétien François, Marquis de Lamoignon, cousin of the illustrious Malesherbes. Counsellor to the *parlement* of Paris, then first president of that court, he was exiled in 1772 ; he was appointed Keeper of the Seals in 1787, in the place of De Miromesnil ; he drew up and presented to the *parlement* the edicts relative to the stamp duty and to a territorial tax. He resigned in 1788, and died in the following year. His son was peer of France under the Restoration. With him the family of Lamoignon became extinct.

demand made by the *parlement* for an immediate convocation of the States-General. Without a positive refusal, he seemed to oppose to this demand some maxims on the absolute power ot the king, which rejected the demand and made it depend entirely upon the king's will. His constitutional system was drawn from the most absolute doctrines ever professed by French ministers at any period in our history.

From these principles which he gave as a peremptory response to the demands and the decisions of the *parlements*, the Keeper of the Seals passed to the examination of the proposed laws. He descanted on the value of the ameliorations already or- dered by the king, his measures of economy, the retrenchments, which he desired to make in his personal pleasures rather than on the establishments devoted to the defence or to the splendour of the State. He presented as a work of genius the skilful conception of a loan of four hundred millions which would suffice at the same time to extinguish other more onerous debts, to make useful improvements, to fill the deficit in the revenue, to meet the foreseen and unforeseen expenditure during five years, and even the cost of a war,—for which it was said every measure had been taken,—if such a misfortune should break out, in spite of the justified hopes the king entertained of its being deferred for a long time by the wisdom and firmness of his negotiations. (It was thus that the minister dared to describe the conduct of the court of France towards Holland during the course of the year 1787.)

This description of the benefits of the present administration led finally to the new edict on the non-Catholics.[1] The Keeper of the Seals called attention to the great advantages that this increase of population would give to industry ; the benefit accruing to society from new citizens ; the laws at last re- conciled with nature and manners. But all could see the object of this philanthropy adopted for the circumstance, and no one would have thought of irritating the minister by adjourn-

---

[1] The edict of 1787 on the Protestants returned to them a civil status which they had lost after the revocation of the edict of Nantes. It is known that the registers relative to births, marriages, and deaths were held solely by the curés, so that the Catholics alone profited by them. As to the Protestants, their marriages were not recognized, and their children were considered as illegitimate by law.

ing these benefits of a tolerant legislation, provided the sanction of the loan which was to bring four hundred millions into the public treasury had been voted without delay.

After the Keeper of the Seals had finished his exposition of the subject under examination, the deliberation followed its course, and took the usual form of sessions of *parlement*. The *rapporteur* of the court was first listened to on the subject of the edict for the loan. This *rapporteur* was one of the magistrates charged with examining all the laws that the government sent to the *parlement* for registering. This magistrate was always chosen by the ministry among the oldest judges who formed between themselves a privileged section called the *Grand' Chambre*, which they entered only by length of service according to their order of reception. The title of *rapporteur* of the court was not that of an office, but of a place of trust ; it was the road to ambition and to fortune ; it was conferred almost always on an ecclesiastic, because, of all the means of recompensing and enriching a man, the easiest and the cheapest was to give him abbeys. It was in this post that Abbé Terray[1] commenced his reputation and his fortune ; after him, an exception was made by giving this post to M. d'Ammécourt, *protégé* of the house of Orléans. M. de Calonne, who suspected M. d'Ammécourt of serving the minister unfaithfully, because he wished to become minister himself, dismissed him. Abbé Tandeau succeeded M. d'Ammécourt ; he had not the astonishing ability, the great aptitude for affairs, the very composed appearance of that magistrate ; but the essential part of the office was to repeat faithfully the instructions received from the council, to reply to the questions which might be asked by a few explanations, too trivial to really enlighten, but sufficient to appease the pretensions of the large number, more eager for consideration than for enlightenment. Such was on this occasion the report of Abbé Tandeau, a long and fastidious comment on the edict. He concluded by saying that the extreme im-

---

[1] Joseph Terray, born at Boen (Forez) in 1715. He was at first counsellor of *parlement*, and took always in parliamentary struggles the part of the court. He was recompensed by being named *rapporteur* (1775). Comptroller-general in 1769, he became all powerful, after the downfall of Choiseul, with Maupeou and d'Aiguillon Exiled by Louis XVI., he died in 1778.

portance of such a loan would induce him to ask to have a commission named to examine the edict and make a report on it, if the presence of his Majesty did not apprise him that he had come into the bosom of his *parlement* to seek there a definitive opinion.

After the speech of the *rapporteur*, the discussion was opened : each member in his turn was invited by the first president to give his opinion. The Duc d'Orléans in a very few words advocated the rejection of the edict. This was the first action in which he openly declared himself against the court.

Those orators whose talent and character caused them to be listened to ordinarily with more interest, redoubled their efforts on this day to make themselves noticed by the king and to produce an impression upon him. The presence of the sovereign indicated nothing likely to intimidate courage and discard the truth ; he was said to have come to the Court of Peers in order to obtain the opinion of his natural counsellors. What a glorious success for the magistrates, if, by power of word, they should succeed in withdrawing the king from the seductions of mediocrity, striking his mind with the light of reason, in touching his heart by the picture of the evils from which France was suffering, and which she did not attribute to him.

M. d'Espresménil's [1] object was, above all, to achieve this latter point. He was reputed the first orator among the members of the *parlement* opposed to the court, and he did not deceive the hopes of his party. On this important occasion, his speech was a special appeal to the personal feelings of the king. He begged him to put aside the advice of his minister, the settled opinions of his council, to weigh without prejudice the truths he was about to hear, and to allow himself to be influenced

---

[1] Jean Jacques du Val d'Espresménil, born at Pondichéry, January 30, 1746, was the son of Jacques d'Espresménil, Governor of Madras. His mother was the daughter of the illustrious Dupleix. Having come to France at five years of age, young d'Espresménil was received as counsellor of *parlement* in 1775 ; he put himself at the head of the opposition. He it was who provoked the resistance of his colleagues to the edicts of Brienne suppressing all the *parlements*. Arrested for this, he was detained some time in the island of Sainte-Marguerite. Deputy of the nobility to the States-General, he became one of the firmest defenders of the monarchy, and when he found his efforts powerless, he left the assembly never to re-enter it (1791). He was nearly murdered, August 10. Imprisoned at the Abbaye, he escaped by a miracle from the massacres of September. Arrested anew a few months after, he was guillotined in 1794. His wife shared the same fate.

by the convictions they would carry with them. He entreated him to believe himself in the bosom of his family, surrounded by his children, and not to restrain the emotions that this sweet situation ought to awaken in his paternal heart.

Each orator seized the points that were most suited to his usual views, and to the nature of his talent. The austere Robert de Saint-Vincent,[1] recapitulating all that had been said by the Keeper of the Seals and the *rapporteur* of the court, on the actual sum of the charges of the State and the insufficiency of the revenues, on the eventual ameliorations and a recognized deficit, on the future economies and a present poverty, found that the loan had no other guarantee than an enormous deficit ; that they could not, without fraud, mortgage for a new debt the old taxes already given as a guarantee for the preceding loans ; and that the *parlement* would share in the responsibility of this crime if it sought the confidence of the lenders, by covering, by the credit of its registering, the bottomless abyss into which they would precipitate their capital.

M. Fréteau, whose too ready elocution was nourished by a badly arranged knowledge, astonished the king and the assembly by the comparisons with which his memory furnished him. He attacked directly the irregularity of the double position of the Keeper of the Seals, who, while still in possession of the office of first president of the *parlement* of Paris, came into the midst of this court to fill there the functions of minister, drawing up projects of law in the council, and pretending to deliberate on these same projects in the *parlement*, accumulating thus sanction with initiative, the partiality of a maker of projects with the impartiality of a magistrate. He concluded with proposing nothing less than excluding M. de Lamoignon from the sitting when they should come to count the votes. Abbé Lecoigneux established the same motive of exclusion against M. Lambert,[2]

---

[1] Robert de Saint-Vincent (1725-1799) was the issue of an old family of magistrates. Counsellor to *parlement* in 1748, he always displayed hostility to the court, notably in the affair of the necklace. He emigrated at the Revolution, and died in 1799.

[2] Charles Guillaume Lambert, born in Paris in 1727. Counsellor of *parlement*, Councillor of State, member of the Council on Finances, member of the assembly of the notables. Deprived of his honours in August, 1788, he was re-instated in August, 1789. On October 19, 1790, the Assembly decreed that he had lost the confidence

comptroller-general, who had none the less taken his seat as honorary counsellor.

Abbé Sabatier, whom I have already named as one of the counsellors of the Duc d'Orléans, flattered the king by encomiums which rendered only more cutting the bitter satire which he pronounced against the ministers. He insisted on his favourite project, the convocation of the States-General. He dwelt upon the incapacity of the *parlements* to win and retain the public faith for the future, and insisted that the assemblies of the nation should meet and re-seize the conduct of their affairs, and put an end to the depredations for which they alone possessed the remedy.

A few speakers spoke in favour of the edict. The court was not without partisans in this numerous assembly. Foremost among those who declared for it, was the Duc de Nivernais,[1] who, at the time of the affairs of 1771, had made himself noticed by his opposition to the plans of Chancellor Maupeou. Men rarely keep their energy to the end of their career. Courtiers age early, and nearly all the men who age early become courtiers.

Seven hours were devoted to this discussion, to which the king listened with sustained attention, and often with manifest interest. He had, above all, to guard himself against the impression apparently produced upon him by the discourses of MM. d'Espresménil, Sabatier and Fréteau. But, in this respect he had been well trained.

After having heard all the speakers, the moment was come to collect the votes, and to count them, when the Keeper of the Seals was seen to rise, approach the king, take his orders, and return to his place. Then the king pronounced these words : " I ordain that the edict providing for . . . be transcribed on

of the nation. He retired on December 4 following. Arrested in February, 1793, he was guillotined a few days after.

[1] Louis-Jules Mancini-Mazarin, Duc de Nivernais, was the grandson of the Duc de Nevers, who was the nephew of Cardinal Mazarin. Born in 1716, he married Mademoiselle de Ponchartrain, sister of M. de Maurepas. He had by her a daughter, who married the Comte de Gisors, son of the Marshal de Belle-Isle, killed at Crevelt in 1758. Nivernais followed at first the career of the army, and fought in the campaigns of Italy (1734), of Bohemia (1742), of Bavaria (1745). He was afterwards ambassador at Rome, then at Berlin (1756), and at London (1762). Under the Revolution, he declined to emigrate. Imprisoned during the Terror, he was delivered on the 9th Thermidor, and died in 1798.

the registers of my *parlement,* to be executed according to its form and tenor."

It was now that the Duc d'Orléans was to appear upon the scene. But better to understand the proceeding agreed upon for him, it is necessary to pay attention to the expressions employed by the king. The formula he had just used would have been the proper formula, if the session had been really a royal session, that is to say, if the deliberation had been completed by the call for the votes, and if the king had not ordained anything except as a consequence of the known and stated wish of the majority. But it was precisely this essential characteristic of all deliberations of an assembly which was lacking in this. They had discussed freely, but had not taken the votes. It is believed, that if a minister, more courageous and more skilful, had dared to count the votes, the result would have been favourable to the edict. It is certain that all measures had been taken to secure a majority. They had chosen the moment of the year when the vacations of the *parlement* were strictly finished, but a well-known custom prolonged them far beyond the legal term. So great a number of members were absent, that of six presidents there were only four at the session, while the Archbishop of Toulouse had not failed to notify in advance those upon whom he relied. Besides, they had swelled the numbers of the assembly beyond measure, with ordinary counsellors, who seldom made use of their right of entrance ; *maîtres des requêtes,* dependent by reason of their situation, had been chosen, and who were still more dependent by their character or their ambition. In spite of so many precautions, the ministers had not dared to make an appeal to the majority which they would have been so happy, however, to see prevail, and the sitting ended in a regular *lit de justice,* infallible sign of terror for the support it had wished to attract. One cannot avoid remarking the imprudence and timidity displayed on this occasion.

The ministers had thought to remedy all by not having the king pronounce in the order of registering, the characteristic words of a *lit de justice* : *by my express command.* In withholding these words, they flattered themselves that they would impose upon the public, and believed that they could maintain that the king had held a royal session. Therefore, to deprive them of this subterfuge was to deal them the finishing stroke ; this was exactly the master-stroke that the counsellors of the Duc d'Orléans had managed for him. Hardly had the king finished speaking than the Duc d'Orléans arose and said : " If the king holds a session of *parlement,* the votes ought to be collected and counted . . . if it is a *lit de justice* he imposes silence upon us." He stopped then, and the king not replying, he continued thus : " Sire, allow me to lay at your feet, my protest against the illegality of your orders." It is necessary to revert to the ideas then ruling in France, to the principles of authority then in force, to grasp the effect which must have been produced by the first instance of a prince of the blood making a protest in the midst of *parlement,* and attacking as null and void, in the presence of the king himself, the orders he had just given.

The whole history of the monarchy offers nothing like it. Princes of the blood had been seen to resist with arms in hand the power of the king ; they had never been seen to try to impose constitutional limits to his authority.

The king, surprised and embarrassed, said with precipitation : " That is legal." And he gave orders for the reading of the second edict to be proceeded with on the instant. As soon as it was finished, he arose and went out with his two brothers, after a sitting of eight hours and a half, which had greatly disturbed him, and furnished him with many causes for uneasiness.

The princes and peers, and with them the Duc d'Orléans, arose and accompanied him according to custom, then returned immediately to take up again the deliberation which recommenced with more heat. The partisans of the court wished to break up the sitting, and to adjourn for a week to give time for minds to calm down. They represented that *Messieurs* (this was the parliamentary expression) were exhausted with fatigue and that they had need of repose.

M. Lepelletier de Saint-Fargeau,[1] who, in spite of his ex-

---

[1] Louis Michel Lepelletier, Comte de Saint-Fargeau, belonged to an ancient family of magistrates. Born in 1760, he was successively advocate-general, then *président à mortier* in the *parlement* of Paris. Deputy of the nobility to the States-General, he was at first a prominent defender of the monarchy. Alone with the Comte de Mirepoix, he refused to unite with the Third Estate, in spite of the order of the king (June 27,

treme youth, was already *président à mortier*, proposed also an adjournment, but only until the morrow. This advice was appropriate to the feebleness of his mind and the pusillanimity of his character, which caused him constantly to try to propitiate all parties, until republicanism, becoming dominant in France, fixed his resolution. He little expected then to merit one day as a republican the honours of a martyr and the laurels of apotheosis.

On this day, he was strongly opposed by Abbé Sabatier, who, classing together the two dilatory opinions to destroy them at the same time, maintained " That *Messieurs* ought to have hunger and thirst only for justice, and that they ought to consecrate to it the remainder of the present day, not being assured that the morrow would be at their disposal." In pronouncing these words he tried to give to his accents a somewhat prophetic character. Abbé Sabatier then invited the Duc d'Orléans to draw up his protest in writing, and for fear the memory of the prince might not be accurate, he found in his own and suggested to him the expressions, *that he believed he had heard him utter.* With this aid the Duc d'Orléans did what was asked of him, and had it written on the registers of the *parlement,* that immediately after the order of the king to register the edicts he had risen and made the following protest :

" Sire, I beg your Majesty to permit me to lay at your feet, and in the midst of the court, the declaration that I regard this registering as illegal, and that it would be necessary for the security of the persons who are accounted as participating in it, to add that they did so by the express command of the king."

After a little debate, the resolution proposed by Abbé Sabatier prevailed, in these terms :

" The court, considering the illegality of what has just passed at the royal sitting, in which the votes were not counted in the manner prescribed by the ordinances, so that, *in short,* the deliberation was not completed—declares that it wishes to be understood as taking no part in the transcription ordered to be

1789). After July 14, he suddenly changed his colours, and enrolled himself in the most advanced revolutionary party. Deputy of Yonne to the Convention, he displayed most violence in the trial of the king ; he demanded his being put on trial, voted his death, and refused the appeal to the people. On January 20, following, he was assassinated at the Palais-Royal by a former body-guard named Pâris. He was given a solemn funeral service at the Panthéon.

made on the registers, of the edict regarding the establishment of
loans, gradual and successive, for the years 1788, 1789, 1790,
1791, and 1792, and puts off the deliberation of other matters to
the next sitting."

They closed the sitting at eight o'clock in the evening. The
Duc d'Orléans had carried off all the honour of this day, and it
must be acknowledged that all had been planned and conducted
with great skill by him and by his friends.

The minister, who had only been able to resort to trivial
means to sustain the already tottering royal authority, found his
ends defeated by the protest of the Duc d'Orléans, and by the
resolution of the *parlement*, which exposed to the broad daylight
the *ruse* employed by the government, and proved its weakness.

While all was thus succeeding with the Duc d'Orléans, in the
interior of the *Palais de Justice*, agents stationed outside were
publishing the proceedings of the sitting, and proclaiming the
name of the prince of the blood who had shown himself so good a
citizen. The people besieged the *Palais* in crowds, and could
be heard speaking of the pluck and success of the Duc
d'Orléans. When he appeared to enter his carriage, the waves
of this fickle people carried him there, overwhelming him with
the most flattering applause. The liberator of his country could
not have had a more splendid triumph. He whom they had
greeted a few days before with sarcasms, was to-day covered
with blessings. Such are the judgments of that throng that one
pretends to honour by the name of the people.

Unfortunately, the Duc d'Orléans sought no purer incense ;
this one was just to his mind ; as he had not been capable of
making true sacrifices to public opinion, so he was not able, either
to detect the value that ought to be attached to this opinion,
when it is exalted by those who proclaim it.

The cries of joy of an ignorant populace flattered his passion
against the court, and fortified him in his scorn for public opinion
by showing him how easily it could be conquered.

The Archbishop of Toulouse and the Keeper of the Seals,
indignant at seeing that their stratagems had become snares
against themselves, united all their efforts to excite the anger
of the king and to represent to him the non-execution of their

measures as a public misfortune. " A prince of the blood," they said, " who ought to have sustained the throne, and who had dared to sap its foundations, even to the point of supposing limits to the authority of the king and to say it in his presence ! Judges bold enough to accuse of prevarication the ministers, that is to say the trustees of the confidence of the master, the agents of his will ! Such an excess of audacity merited punishment. The exile of the one, the detention of the others, were examples necessary in order to put a stop to similar scandals."

It was by such discourses that this feeble minister drew the king into measures, which, being the outcome of passion, could only induce all ambitious persons of the same stamp, as abbés Fréteau and Sabatier, to wish for a light persecution. The ministers of Louis XVI. were ignorant of the fact that arbitrary power has not the right to punish with moderation those who resist it, and that it is doomed by its nature either to tolerate or to crush its enemies.

The first alternative would have been more consonant with the character of the king ; the second might well have tempted the ministers, but they knew that they were not strong enough, either with the king or in the eyes of the nation, to take it. They thought they had done much in suggesting the exile of the Duc d'Orléans, and in proposing to have counsellors Fréteau and Sabatier carried off to prison. They took the first to the citadel of Doullens, and the second to the château of Mont Saint-Michel, a kind of isolated tower on a rock washed by the waves of the sea.

It was Baron de Breteuil, Minister of Paris, who went, on the 20th of November, at six o'clock in the evening, to notify to the Duc d'Orléans the order for his exile. This minister was specially entrusted with the distribution of the *lettres de cachet,*[1] when they were drawn up against one of his brother-ministers or against a prince of the blood. It was customary for the minister to go in person to give the information, and this mission drew upon him, sometimes, receptions which bore the impress of the

---

[1] Literally sealed letters. Originally they only conveyed the king's orders on State business. Since the sixteenth century, however, they were subscribed by a Secretary of State, and solely employed to notify to the authorities the decision of the king to have persons of rank sent to prison without any trial, and often for imaginary offences. —(*Translator.*) .

temper of the disgraced ones.   Here, the position was so much
the more delicate that Baron de Breteuil owed his fortune
to the protection of the house of Orléans.   His uncle, Abbé de
Breteuil,[1] had been chancellor of the late Duc d'Orléans, who
had loaded him with riches and kindness, and had opened to the
nephew the road to favour and high offices.   The king's letter,
which the latter handed to the Duc d'Orléans, contained the
order to go that very night to his Château at Raincy,[2] in order
to arrive on the following day at that of Villers-Cotterets,[3] which
was about eighteen leagues distant.   The prince received this
injunction with ill-humour, and took care to make the bearer of
the order feel it.   After having given an hour to a few private
arrangements, he called for his horses, and entered his carriage.
The baron who, according to his instructions, was to accompany
him, prepared to take a seat by his side, when the prince stopped
him saying : "What are you doing?"   The baron showed his
orders.   " Oh, well," replied the prince, " get up behind," and he
started.   The baron, without taking any notice of this passing
cloud (that is the expression he used when relating this little
incident) entered his own carriage and followed as best he could.

The news of the exile of the Duc d'Orléans spread quickly
in Paris.   The garden of the Palais-Royal, all the adjacent
streets and places were filled with people, and resounded with
cries of " *Long live the Duc d'Orléans !* "   On the 21st, in the
morning, the chambers of the *parlement* reassembled, and decided
to send the first president to the king to ask him to *recall to his
presence the august prince whom he had removed, and to return to
the court two members whose zeal alone had dictated their
opinions.*   At noon the *parlement* was summoned to Versailles,

---

[1] The Abbé Théodore de Breteuil, born in 1710, prior of Saint-Martin des Champs,
at Paris, chancellor of the Duc d'Orléans.   He died in 1781.

[2] Le Raincy, near Bondy, about nine miles from Paris, had been at first an abbey.
In the seventeenth century, Jacques Bordier replaced it by a magnificent château,
which belonged afterwards to the Princess Palatine.   It became, in 1750, the
property of the Duc d'Orléans.   It was sacked during the Revolution, and entirely
destroyed in 1848.

[3] Villers-Cotterets, chief place of the Canton of Aisne.   In the thirteenth century,
Charles de Valois possessed there a château which was destroyed during the war of
the Hundred Years.   Francis I. had another built by the side of the old one, which
became one of the favourite residences of the court.   It was acquired in the seventeenth century by the family of Orléans.   This château is used to-day as a kind of
workhouse.

and the king gave orders for the resolution taken on the preceding 19th to be erased from the registers. The speech which
he delivered on this occasion is worth being preserved.

"I have ordered you," said he, "to bring to me the minutes
of the resolution taken by you on Monday last, after my leaving
the *parlement.* I cannot allow it to remain on your registers,
and I forbid you to replace it in any other manner.

"How can my *parlement* say it has taken no part in registering the edicts, which I only pronounced after having listened
during seven hours to the advice and opinions of those of the
members who wished to give them, and when it was certain for all
as for myself, that the majority of the votes were in favour of the
registering of my edict, and requested me to hasten the meeting
of the States-General of my kingdom. I have already said that
I would convoke them before 1792, that is to say, at the latest
before the end of 1791. My word is sacred.

"I approached you with confidence, in this ancient method, so
often employed by the *parlement* of the kings, my predecessors
and it is at the moment when I have so deigned to hold council
in your midst, on an object of my administration, that you try
to transform yourselves into an ordinary tribunal, and to declare
illegal the result of this council by invoking ordinances and
rules which concern only tribunals in the exercise of their
functions.

"The claims of my *parlement* ought to come to me only in
the form of respectful representations or remonstrances. I dis-
approve always of resolutions, which declare their opposition
to my will, without expressing any motives for it."

After this speech, remarkable for the principles it sets forth,
and by the formal promise of the States-General it contains,
the first president[1] obtained the permission to have the representations heard which had been resolved upon that same
morning, relative to the exile of the Duc d'Orléans, and to the
detention of the two counsellors.

The king replied in these few words : "When I remove from
my person a prince of my blood, my *parlement* ought to believe
that I have strong reasons for so doing. I have punished

[1] The first president, d'Aligre.

two malcontents with whom I had good reason to be dissatisfied."

They expected such a cold reply; it did not prevent the *parlement* from making a fresh attempt. Its example was followed by all who had the right to raise their voices, and to cause representations to reach even to the foot of the throne. All the *parlements* emulated with each other in making remonstrances; all demanded the recall of the prince and of the two magistrates. The princes and the peers were forbidden to attend the sittings of the *parlement*, which were almost permanent and drew the attention of the people. Experience had taught that importunity was a method not without efficacy with a feeble government.

In the sitting of the 22nd of November, the *parlement* had also resolved to send the registrar Isabeau to congratulate the Duchesse d'Orléans, and to express the concern they felt at the exile of her husband. This princess had already departed for Villers-Cotterets. On arriving at the place of his exile, the Duc d'Orléans had hastened to beg the *parlement* of Paris not to take any notice of him. He knew well that in affecting to claim this silence for himself, he would only attach the popular party more strongly to his cause, and he was sure that the zeal of the *parlement* for his interests would not be slackened. But it must not be possible that the entreaties of that body should be attributed to his instigations, otherwise, they would be more likely to embitter the king than to appease him. The latter could not, without compromising his authority, remit so promptly the punishments he had imposed.

The peers submitted unwillingly to the prohibition which had been laid upon them to enter *parlement*. They met secretly at the Hôtel de Luynes, to draw up an address in favour of the exiled prince. Similar requests, as I have said, came from all parts. And yet the Duc d'Orléans little merited the interest he inspired. Little impressed by the *éclat* of his *rôle*, he complained with bitterness of the privations it imposed upon him. Never had lighter privations been supported with less patience and less courage. If the Parisians could have read to the depths of the heart of their new idol, they would have been strangely surprised to find what little devotion they were recompensing by so much homage.

The orders of the king forbade the Duc d'Orléans to receive in his exile other visits than those of his family and of persons attached to his service. It had been desired to avoid the immense concourse of visitors which would not have failed to gather around the exile to honour his retirement, and above all to brave the dissatisfaction he had incurred. However, Villers-Cotterets was anything but a solitude. All the relations of the prince, among whom must not be forgotten the generous Madame de Lamballe, considered it a duty to gather about him ; his children had joined him. His attendants and those of the Duchesse d'Orléans formed a numerous society. At this period of his life he was intimately acquainted with Madame de Buffon,[1] a young and pretty person, whose disinterestedness and extreme devotion have won the indulgence of all who have known her. Once a week, she repaired to Nanteuil,[2] a small city situated at equal distance from Villers-Cotterets and Paris ; it was there the Duc d'Orléans went to see her.

With these resources, in a magnificent dwelling, in the midst of all the distractions procurable by an immense fortune, it would only have required a very ordinary dose of moderation to have been happy. But the prince's position appeared to him unbearable, and it is impossible to deny that, at this time, blind vengeance became the ruling passion of his heart. This is the secret of the second portion of his life.

While those ideas of vengeance were fermenting in his head, he nevertheless used every means to obtain his liberty. The Parisians, who wished to justify their enthusiasm, related that he had rejected the means of return and of reconciliation offered by the Archbishop of Toulouse. According to them, the Duc d'Orléans had refused to re-enter into favour before the two counsellors were recalled, and also before the motive of the

---

[1] Mademoiselle de Cépoy, married in 1784 to Louis-Marie, Comte de Buffon, son of the illustrious *savant*, who was decapitated in 1794. The relations existing between the Duc d'Orléans and Madame de Buffon determined a separation (1789) between her and her husband, and this was converted into a divorce (1793).

[2] Nanteuil, chief seat of the Canton of Oise ; 1,600 inhabitants ; fifteen miles from Senlis.

severity which had been employed towards them, should have been made known positively to all three.

These rumours were credited by those who were on good terms with the inmates of the Palais Royal, where all mention of the vain efforts of the Prince de Condé and of the Duc de Bourbon [1] in the exile's favour was carefully avoided. The king had received those princes with kindness. He had not disapproved of the interest they had shown for the Duc d'Orléans, but, pressed by them to explain himself on the duration of the exile, he contented himself by replying : " Believe me, I am a good kinsman."

The same newsmongers, as fortunate in invention as in reticence, abstained also from speaking of the letters in which the Duc d'Orléans had directly solicited his pardon. In these letters, he had not blushed to put forward motives surely much more humiliating than any prayer. It was not on the legitimacy of his conduct nor even on the purity of his intentions that he based his request. In order to move the king, he had sought the most extraordinary means. Thus, he laid weight on the necessity of resuming and superintending the work commenced at the Palais Royal, the suspension of which caused great prejudice to his interests ; he spoke also of the neglect into which these had fallen through the illness of M. de Limon, the intendant of his finances. In order to try everything, he spoke of his health and of that of the Duchesse d'Orléans, saying they could not do without returning to Paris. Finally, he laid weight on the retirement of his Chancellor Ducrest, as an expiatory sacrifice which ought to be recompensed by a return of favour, or at least by a generous forgetfulness of the wrongs of which this "imprudent favourite had rendered himself guilty."

It was true that M. Ducrest had just given in his resignation, and the letter that accompanied it had been circulated in public.

[1] Louis Henry-Joseph, Duc de Bourbon, was born August 13, 1776. He was the son of the Prince de Condé. He took no part in public affairs under the reign of Louis XVI. He emigrated at the beginning of the Revolution, and commanded a corps of the army of Condé. He retired afterwards to England. During the Hundred Days, he tried without great success to raise the Vendée. He was appointed, under Louis XVIII., grand master of the king's household. He put an end to his life, August 27, 1830, at Chantilly. He had married his cousin, the Princesse Louise d'Orléans, and was the father of the unfortunate Duc d'Enghien.

According to that letter, the resignation was purely voluntary; the faithful servant had perceived that he was injuring his master, and his attachment for him required him to separate from him. Too much hatred had attached to him as the author of the memoranda handed to the king by the Duc d'Orléans, for him to hope that he could do the latter any good. He flattered himself that the vengeance of his enemies being satisfied, they would seek no other victim. All this was intermingled with phrases on the success of his administration. Neither the resignation of Chancellor Ducrest, nor his letter, nor that of the Duc d'Orléans, had touched the heart of the king, and severity prevailed still in his resolutions. The Duc d'Orléans did not even obtain a written answer; but the Comte de Montmorin, Minister of Foreign Affairs, was instructed to see him, to exhort him to patience, and to say to him that the king did not write in order to spare himself the chagrin of refusing him.

The *parlement*, where princes and peers had at last obtained permission to reappear, did not cease to insist on the recall of the two exiled counsellors and of the prince. All the month of December was passed in waiting, and soliciting replies from the government. The Prince de Condé and the Duc de Bourbon attracted notice by their assiduity at the sittings of the *parlement*, and if they appeared to agree with the ministers on some points, they could not be reproached with failing on every occasion to speak in favour of the three exiles. After some weeks rigour at last ceased. The king resolved to trust to mercy, and was pleased to accord to the Duchesse d'Orléans that which he had refused to the entreaties of the *parlement*.

The Archbishop of Sens (M. de Brienne had exchanged the Archbishopric of Toulouse for that of Sens,) thinking he had obtained a truce by this concession, prepared with the Keeper of the Seals a new judiciary organization, the effect of which was to suspend the functions of all the sovereign courts of the kingdom at the time when it should be-come law. Sanction was to be given to this new project in an assembly summoned under the name of plenary court, in which the edicts that the minister had proposed to the *parle-ment* were to be registered. But M. de Brienne had neither the intellect nor the energy required by projects so vast and circumstances so grave.[1] The measures taken by the ministry, and the mysterious silence they kept, caused great uneasiness to all the magistrates. They made all sorts of attempts to discover the projects of the government. They succeeded : MM d'Espresménil and Goislard[2] obtained a copy of the edicts and some documents which related to them. They had them printed and distributed, without the ministry having even had knowledge of the discovery that had just been made. In an assembly of the chambers convened immediately, and at which the Duc d'Orléans was not present, after all the peers and members of the *parlement* had taken an oath not to recognize as a court officer any except those present, and to reject at the risk of their lives all propositions tending to retard the convocation of the States-General, they declared that if violence made it impossible for the court to watch personally over the constituent principles of the French monarchy, they would confide this duty to the hands of the king, the princes of his blood, and the States-General.

The ministry, informed of what had passed, decided to have those magistrates arrested whom they supposed to have discovered and published their projects. M. d'Espresménil and M. Goislard took refuge in the *parlement*. A detachment of the armed force that was in Paris followed after them. After some hours they gave themselves up into the hands of M. d'Agoult,[3] who

[1] Brienne undertook to destroy the *parlements.* On May 8, 1788, the king ordered the *parlement* to Versailles, and the Keeper of the Seals, Lamoignon, read the following edicts :—The first instituted under the title of *Grands Bailliages*, new courts of justice which were to decide all civil and criminal cases below 20,000 livres. The *parlements* were only cognizant of cases above that figure, as also of those concerning ecclesiastics and nobles. The second edict reduced considerably the number of counsellors of *parlement.* The third suppressed all extraordinary tribunals. The fourth abolished the previous question. The fifth, and the most important, instituted a plenary court, charged with verifying and registering the laws for the whole extent of the kingdom. This court was composed of the Chancellor or of the Keeper of the Seals, of the great chamber of the *parlement* of Paris, of the princes of the blood, the peers, the grand officers of the crown, various dignitaries of the Church and of the army, a certain number of members chosen in the Council of State and the *parlements* of the provinces. The court had the right of remonstrance, but the king reserved to himself that of dictating his orders at *lits de justice.* Finally, the sixth edict published an interdict against all existing *parlements*, and forbade their assembling on any public or private case.

[2] M. Goislard de Monsabert was a young counsellor of *parlement.*

[3] Antoine Jean, Marquis d'Agoult, born at Grenoble in 1750 of an old family of Dauphiny. Lieutenant of the body-guard (1781), colonel (1783). He emigrated in

commanded the expedition, and who had declared that he would take them away by force, if they would not follow him. M. d'Espresménil was taken to the island of Saint Marguerite. I ought to observe, for the sake of the history of the odd freaks of the human mind, of which it is always well to take account, that that same d'Espresménil—just as in the assembly of the clergy held at that time, the Bishop of Blois, like M. de Thémines—they both being then leaders of the opposition against the court, and decided advocates of the States-General, —made himself conspicuous, during all the time of the constituent assembly, by sentiments, opinions, and intrigues directed against the new order of things which he had himself produced.

The Archbishop of Sens after having tried for twenty-four hours a kind of bankruptcy, and having, for some days, resorted to a certain severity against the *parlements*, renounced all his plans, and, promised to summon a meeting of the States-General, in order to gain time, but he did not gain any, and was obliged to retire, leaving the court enfeebled, public opinion informed of its own strength, and, in one word, the Revolution commenced.

The Duc d'Orléans had no influence on the last movements of the *parlement*, and his name was hardly mentioned at the States-General. I shall not therefore dwell on the events which marked this important period.

The government had itself proclaimed the limits of its power and invited the public, by an appeal made to all enlightened men, to devise itself the best method of convoking the States-General. Was it not imprudent to agitate France by political discussion of all kinds and without fixed principles to start with? In fact, the first cause of the disorders excited by the assembling of the States-General lay here.

The first symptoms of these disorders broke out in the Faubourg St. Antoine, and everything goes to prove that the Duc d'Orléans was not a stranger to them. A manufacturer named

1791, and joined the army of Condé. He remained attached to Louis XVIII. during all his exile, and only returned to France in 1814. He died in 1828, peer of France and Governor of the Château of Saint-Cloud.

Réveillon,[1] a very respectable man, gave employment to a large number of workmen. I do not know what calumny was circulated among them concerning him who gave them their means of livelihood. At the same time money was distributed to them; and the crowd having mixed with them, the number increased, and the riot became so serious, that it was necessary to employ the French and the Swiss Guards to restore order. The same amount of money, twelve francs, that was found on each of the rioters killed or arrested, proved already that some one of a superior class, had directed that outbreak; the confessions made by several of those poor wretches allowed it to be no longer doubted that the sedition had been brought about by the agents of the Duc d'Orléans. The depraved character of that prince made him enjoy any tumult whatever; he was delighted to agitate, to make a noise, to create embarrassment, but he dared not do any more.

This disturbance had been brought about by M. de Laclos,[2] who had been for some time attached to the person of the Duc d'Orléans as " secretary of his commands." M. de Laclos had been introduced in Paris to a few houses by the Vicomte de Noailles,[3] who had known him in garrison; his ambition, spirit, and

[1] Réveillon was a stained-paper manufacturer of the Faubourg St. Antoine. He had been accused of having used harsh and unfriendly language to his workmen, which had provoked a furious riot (April 28, 1789). His house and factory were destroyed. The riot was quelled, but not without much bloodshed.
[2] Pierre-Ambroise Choderlos de Laclos, born at Amiens in 1741, was captain of engineers in 1778. He formed an intimacy with the Duc d'Orléans, and became "secretary of his commands." He was actively concerned in the intrigues of the party of the prince at the outbreak of the Revolution. He was a member of the Jacobins' Club, and edited its journal. After the flight to Varennes, he moved the deposition of the king, and drew up with Brissot the petition of the "Champ de Mars." He became brigadier-general in 1792. Imprisoned on two different occasions during the Terror, he was, later, sent to the army of the Rhine as general of brigade. In 1803, he was inspector-general of artillery at Naples, when he died. Laclos has left also a literary reputation. He is the author of a few light poems and several novels, the best known of which is entitled *Liaisons Dangereuses.*
[3] The Vicomte Louis Marie de Noailles was the second son of Marshal de Mouchy. Born in 1756, he became colonel of the Chasseurs d'Alsace, and joined in the expedition to America. Deputy of the nobility of Nemours to the States-General, he warmly adopted the new ideas, joined the Third Estate, and proposed the abolition of feudal rights (August 4). President of the constituent assembly in 1791, brigadier-general in 1792, he was defeated at Gliswal. He emigrated soon after. In 1803, he returned to France, again took service as general of brigade, and was killed in sight of Havanna whilst capturing an English frigate. The Vicomte de Noailles had married his cousin Anne, granddaughter of Marshal de Noailles. She was guillotined July 22, 1794, with her mother, the Duchesse d'Ayen, and her grandmother, the *Maréchale* de Noailles.

bad reputation had caused the Duc d'Orléans to regard him
as a man whose support it was by all means good to have
in stormy circumstances. *Un Éloge de Vauban*, the immoral
novel entitled *Liaisons Dangereuses*, some works on tactics,
several newspaper articles which had proved the flexibility
of his opinions, as of his talent, had induced the Duc d'Orléans
to entrust him with the draft of the instructions he wished to
give to the different persons who were to represent him in the
bailiwicks of his appanage. M. de Laclos had written on this
occasion a sort of code in which all the philosophical ideas of the
time, treated of in separate articles, did not seem sufficiently
veiled to the Duc d'Orléans. This not suiting him, he sought
another compiler. Abbé Siéyès was suggested to him as the
man who had reflected most upon the questions which, it
was supposed, the States-General would discuss. In a meeting
which took place with Siéyès at the house of M. de Biron at
Montrouge, the Duc d'Orléans showed to the abbé the draft of
M. de Laclos, and asked him to make such changes in it as he
thought suitable. Abbé Siéyès, who, owing to the disposition of
his mind, was usually little pleased with the work of others, found
that nothing could be preserved, and drew up a new project
which the Duc d'Orléans adopted and had printed.[1] My opinion
is that, from that time, there were no further relations between

[1] (Paris, 1789, 1 vol. 8vo.) This document is very interesting; the fact that it
emanates from the first prince of the blood gives it much more value. In it, the author
indicates first the principal articles to insert in the *cahiers*,* namely, individual and
political freedom ; privacy of letters ; inviolability of property ; periodical vote of
taxes, and their equal distribution ; responsibility of ministers ; divorce. Passing next to
the regulation of the assemblies, he requests his representatives to take notice only of the
present instructions, without paying any attention to the regulation joined to the king's
letters of convocation. He deplores that the ministry "by an inconsistency worthy of
the enlightenment which has always distinguished them," should have adopted the
mode of deliberation by separate orders. "The only important deliberation is that
of the Third, for it alone has the general interest in view, it alone is the depositary of
the powers of the nation, and it feels that it is about to be entrusted with its
destinies." And farther on, he adds: "The duty of the States-General will then be
to attack the despotism of the *aristocrats*, and the unlimited prerogatives of the royal
power, to draw up a declaration of the rights of man, and to establish a constitution
on the following bases : A national assembly elected in the third degree ; the parish
assemblies will elect cantonal assemblies, which in their turn will elect provincial
assemblies, which will choose from their midst the national representatives. All the
deputies will be subject to dismissal by their constituents." It must not be forgotten
that the estates of the Duc d'Orléans, where those instructions were scattered, had
the extent of three or four French Departments.

* The instructions given by the constituencies to their deputies with regard to the reforms that
were most needed.—(*Translator.*)

the Duc d'Orléans and Abbé Siéyès, and that this was the
only time they met. But, as those instructions caused considerable stir, and their author was known, it was supposed, at
different stages of the Revolution, that there was a secret bond
between Abbé Siéyès and the Duc d'Orléans. There never
existed, perhaps, two men more incompatible, and nothing
would prove it better than to show Siéyès as he is. I will
try to make a sketch of him.

Siéyès has a mind vigorous in the highest degree ; his heart is
cold and his soul pusillanimous ; his inflexibility is only in his
head. He can be inhuman, because pride will prevent his
drawing back, and fear will bind him to crime. It is not out
of philanthropy that he professes equality, it is out of violent
hatred against the power of others. It cannot be said, however, that the exercise of power suits him, for he would not
be at his ease at the head of any government, but would like
to be its only thinking and ruling spirit. Exclusive, domineer-
ing, he does not confine himself to a continuous and regular
action ; disdainful of that which is known, he wishes to go beyond
it. Obstacles make him indignant, he scorns every compromise.
What he calls a principle, is in his hands a brass sceptre, which
does not bend either to the imperfections of nature, or to the
weaknesses of mankind. He is equally ignorant of the virtues
and of the faults which are inherent in a feeling mind. His
resolution once taken, no affection can stop it. Men, in his
eyes, are but pawns to be moved about ; they occupy his
mind, but awake nothing in his heart. When he draws up a
constitution, he treats the country for which it is intended as
a place whose inhabitants never felt or saw anything.[1]

The only feeling that has any influence over Siéyès is that
of fear. At the Convention he feared death ; since then, the
fear of the vengeance of the house of Bourbon rules him.

Siéyès is regular in his habits, methodical in his conduct,
obscure in his dealings. His private life offers nothing philo-
sophically remarkable. In his tastes, he is somewhat choice ;
he is difficult to serve, to lodge, to furnish. He is not covetous,
but he is not lofty enough to despise fortune ; his pride, even,

[1] Allusion to the constitution proposed by Siéyès in the year VIII.

THE DUC D'ORLÉANS. 161

has not been strong enough to prevent that foible detracting, from his political consideration. He has no mental ability; he cannot argue, because he only knows how to prescribe. He converses badly; he has no desire to convince, he wishes to subjugate. His humour is sad : it is possible that a natural indisposition which forbids him intercourse with women contributes to this; and yet he does not disdain to jest with them ; then, he has a kind of grace ; he can smile, and resort to waggish banter, which is measured and rather cutting, but he never stoops so far as to be amiable. Proud and timid, he is necessarily envious and defiant ; so he has no friends, but has submissive and faithful followers.

Siéyès may be a leader of opinion ; he will never be a leader of a party. His mind is more superb than active. He is all of one piece ; if one does not do as he wishes, he sulks in his corner, and consoles himself that he is looked at there. He has not a happy countenance ; it bears the imprint of a hard and meditative character. His look has somewhat of superiority, of haughtiness, and only lights up when he smiles. His pale complexion, his figure without precision in its form, his slow and gentle walk, all his outward appearance in short, seems plain as long as he does not speak, and yet he does not speak well. He only says words, but each word expresses a thought and indicates reflection. In a serious conversation, he is never captivating, but he imposes.

Does all I have just said apply to a man who could have submitted his character, his temper, his opinions, to those of a prince; who could have the complacencies of accessory ambition ? No one will think so.

I have felt obliged for once to destroy by means of reasons drawn from the essence of their characters, the generally established opinion that the Duc d'Orléans had any concerted relations with Siéyès. It is equally true that there was not, between him and any of the remarkable men of that time, any other association than that brought about naturally by private meetings, entirely foreign to all personal combinations.

After the instructions given to his bailiwicks, the Duc d'Orléans ceased to be politically an active person ; his feeble character, his equivocal and unsettled position prevented his becoming so. After the crime of his vote, he was no longer of importance, people had no further need of him ; he remained simply in the ranks, and as that was not his place, he was there a cipher, was disgraced and killed.

What becomes then of the opinion, so positively accredited, that the Duc d'Orléans was the prime author of the Revolution ; that his name served for the rallying of a numerous class of citizens; that he was encouraged by the ambition of a few turbulent minds, to raise his eyes to the throne. This opinion cannot be held before the picture of his life. For immorality, extreme frivolity, want of reflection, and weakness, suffice to explain his agitations as well as his inaction. Furthermore, the impulse once given, the rapid and violent excitement of minds prevented, at every stage of the Revolution, the development of private ambitions. All ideas tending, from the beginning, to establish equality and to weaken all power, lofty ambitions were necessarily discountenanced. It was not until very much later, after terrible tests, that there began to be felt the need of a leader to modify the state of things which existed ; it was then that Bonaparte appeared. The Duc d'Orléans was, doubtless, not the last person to perceive the disposition of minds which I have just indicated. That is why he always concealed the real aim of his ambition. He was not, as I have said, either the principle, the object, or the motive of the Revolution. The impetuous tide carried him along with the others.

The Duc d'Orléans fell back upon himself, his tastes, his needs. Hence the secret thought which led him, after October 6, 1789, to undertake the disgraceful journey to England for which men of all parties have reproached him.[1] From that

[1] The Duc d'Orléans was accused of having been concerned in the events of October 5 and 6. The court and a portion of the *bourgeoisie* arose against him. La Fayette took upon himself to echo these recriminations—indeed, these menaces ; so much so that the prince, being intimidated, left for England on a fictitious mission, in spite of all that Mirabeau could do to restrain him. Immediately, the *Châtelet* opened, on the events of October, an inquiry destined to prove the culpability of the prince. The latter returned suddenly to Paris on July 7, 1790. On August 14 following, the court of the *Châtelet* delivered its report to the Assembly. It concluded by asking that he should be arraigned, but the Assembly refused to authorize the prosecution.

moment dates the disappearance of his enormous fortune, which having been put into a form more easy of handling, left even fewer traces than did the superb gallery of pictures of the Palais-Royal, so scattered to-day. The free cash of the Duc d'Orléans passed all to England by indirect means and through secret agents, who, on account of their obscurity, were enabled to be unfaithful, and to enjoy the proceeds of their theft. Such is the opinion of the men who were then at the head of affairs.

If historians make it a point to seek the men to whom they can award the honour, or address the reproach of having made, directed, or modified, the French Revolution, they will give themselves unnecessary trouble. It had no authors, leaders, nor guides. It was sown by the writers who, in an enlightened and venturesome century, wishing to attack prejudices, subverted the religious and social principles, and by unskilful ministers who increased the deficit of the treasury and the discontent of the people.

It would be necessary, in order to find the real origin and causes of the Revolution, to weigh, analyze, and judge questions of high speculative politics, and especially to submit to a profound and skilful examination, the question of the struggle between philosophical ideas and prejudices, between the pretensions of the *mind* and those of *power*. For, if we were to take into consideration only the sole results of that Revolution, we should soon fall into error, and end by mistaking M. de Malesherbes for Mirabeau, and M. de la Rochefoucauld for Robespierre.

END OF THE SECOND PART.

PART III.

THE CONVENTION, THE DIRECTORY, THE CONSULATE, THE EARLY YEARS OF THE EMPIRE.

1791—1808.

Dangers threatening the royal family—Talleyrand goes to London with a letter of Louis XVI. to the King of England—Defeat of the French troops under the Duc de Biron—August 10—Abolition of royalty—Could the royal family have been saved in 1792?—Talleyrand entrusted with a scientific mission to England—The Marquis of Lansdowne—The Marquis of Hastings—Doctors Price and Priestley—George Canning—Samuel Romilly—Jeremy Bentham—Lord Henry Petty—Charles Fox—The responsible authors of the Revolution—The Alien Bill—Lord Melville—William Pitt—Talleyrand expelled from England—Starts for America—Nearly shipwrecked—Stay at Falmouth—General Arnold—Lands at Philadelphia—M. de Beaumetz—William Penn—The Moravian brethren—The spirit of enterprise in America—General Hamilton—American commercial competition and its results—Talleyrand at Chénier's request is authorized to return to France—Starts for Hamburg—Madame de Flahaut and Talleyrand—Returns to Paris—Elected a member of the *Institut*—Madame de Staël—Talleyrand and Barras—Talleyrand appointed Minister of Foreign Affairs—Why he accepted office—Carnot and Barras—Talleyrand's first letter to Bonaparte—Treaty of Campo-Formio—Lord Malmesbury—Fructidor 18—First interview between Bonaparte and Talleyrand—Catherine of Russia and the French Revolution—The Directory and Europe—Moreau—Talleyrand retires from the Cabinet—Siéyès and the Directory—Bonaparte in Egypt—Brumaire 18—Bonaparte appointed First Consul—Talleyrand takes office again—Paul I. and Bonaparte—Marengo—Treaty of Lunéville—The United States and the French Republic—Lord Cornwallis and Joseph Bonaparte—Treaty of Amiens—The *Concordat*—Talleyrand's secularization—Bonaparte's blunder—Annexation of Piedmont to France—England declares war—Pichegru's death—Assassination of the Duc d'Enghien—Proclamation of the Empire—Napoleon emperor and king—The camp at Boulogne—The Austrian campaign—Napoleon at Schœnbrunn—Austerlitz—Napoleon and the Faubourg St. Germain—Talleyrand created Prince de Bénévent—Treaty of Presburg—Count

von Haugwitz—Fox and Talleyrand—Lord Yarmouth and Lord Lauder-
dale—Prussia and Hanover—Battle of Jena—Treaty of Tilsit—Napoleon
and Poland—War with Russia—Battle of Eylau—Battle of Friedland—
The interview of the three emperors—Napoleon and the Queen of
Prussia—Napoleon's return to Paris—Talleyrand appointed Vice Grand
Elector—Retires from the Ministry— His apology for doing so—Napo-
leon's designs on Spain—Defeat of Junot—Capitulation of Baylen—The
Erfurt interview — Talleyrand and the Czar Alexander—Failure of
Napoleon's projects against Austria.

WHAT was left of the royal prerogatives after the vote of the
Constituent Assembly was but a shadow, growing daily fainter.
It was, therefore, of paramount importance to save from further
ruin the frail power of the king, which all efforts made in view of
restoring to it its lost reality only tended to diminish. The men
who still affected to be afraid of it, such as it was, only sought a
pretext to complete its destruction. The great point would have
been not to have offered them any. They were not satisfied
that the king should imitate the reed, that withstands the fury of
the wind, simply because it is incapable of offering any resistance
to it : they wished his supporters both at home and abroad to
indulge in utter inaction, and to abstain from expressing any
opinion he might have been accused of sharing. But who could
be induced to adopt such unspirited policy ? The revolutionary
impulse was given and stirred all classes.

The cabinet of the time,[1] of which M. Necker was no longer
a member, then understood the necessity for royalty to obtain
a promise from the chief courts of Europe either to disarm, or
not to arm at all.[2] The leaders of the second Assembly, known

---

[1] This was the *Feuillant* ministry—the first ministry of the king under the new
constitution (November 1791—March 1792). It was thus composed : Justice, Du
Port ; Foreign Affairs, De Lessart ; Taxes and Public Revenue (Finances), Tarbé ;
Marine, Bertrand ; Interior (Home Department), Cahier de Gerville ; War Department, Narbonne.

[2] The *Feuillant* ministry had no warlike intentions. Thus the aim of all the
negotiations it then began with the various courts of Europe was to prevent the
breaking out of hostilities. The policy of the French cabinet was to win over
Prussia and England, in order to oppose them to Austria. M. de Ségur was sent to
Prussia (December 22, 1791). At the same time, M. de Narbonne sent off young
Custine to the Duke of Brunswick, in order to offer him the post of commander-in-
chief of the French forces. In England, M. de Talleyrand (the author of these
Memoirs) was officially entrusted with the negotiations (January 12, 1792). M. de
Lessart was also endeavouring to keep on good terms with Spain (Bourgoing's mission
to Madrid, February, 1792) ; he reassured the Emperor as to the consequences of the
reconciliation which it was sought to bring about with England (Lessart's letter to M.

under the name of Girondists, had insisted on this step under the belief that the king's ministry would decline to take it. Their hopes were deceived. M. de Lessart,[1] who was then Minister of Foreign Affairs, took up the suggestion, and proposed that I should go to England in order to open negotiations on the subject. I had been anxious to leave France for some time ; I was tired and disgusted, and sure though I felt that my mission had little chance of success, I accepted it. The king wrote to the King of England a letter of which I was the bearer.[2]

In 1790, war would have been useful to royalty. In 1792, it would only have upset the throne ; that is the reason why the revolutionists wanted it. They thought (as one of them, Brissot de Varville,[3] subsequently confessed) that, if war were once declared, the king, having the direction of the operations, would be left at their mercy, by being obliged to employ only those means that it might please them to place at his disposal, and that they would thus be enabled to urge to rebellion both the army and the masses, by holding the sovereign responsible for disasters which, owing to their own action, had been rendered inevitable ; an infamous calculation which subsequent events proved to have been made with the utmost skill. This hateful machination could, perhaps, have been thwarted by calling upon the armed

de Noailles, ambassador to Vienna, January 16, 1792), and tried to prevent all interference on the part of the Imperial Diet (M. Barbé-Marbois' mission, January 1, 1792).

[1] Antoine de Valdec de Lessart, born in 1742. Was successively *maître des requêtes* (1768), comptroller-general (December 1790), Minister of the Interior (January, 1791,) and Minister of Foreign Affairs (November, 1791). On Brissot's motion, the Assembly decreed his arrest and trial, March 2, 1792, when he was arrested and taken to Orleans, the seat of the national High Court of Justice. He was massacred at Versailles (September 9, 1792) on his way back to Paris, where he had been recalled by Danton's orders.

[2] Talleyrand was also the bearer of a letter from M. de Lessart to Earl Grenville. He had instructions to secure the neutrality, or, if possible, the alliance of England. He started on his mission, January 12, 1792, in the company of the Duc de Biron, and returned to Paris on March 9 in the same year. (See Sorel's *L'Europe et la Révolution Française*, Part II., Vol. III.).

[3] Jean-Pierre Brissot was the thirteenth child of a Chartres innkeeper. He was born in 1754, and soon added to his name that of Ouarville, or Warville, the village where he was brought up. Having come to Paris he founded, in 1782, *Le Patriote Français*, a journal in which he advocated new ideas with vigour and talent. Having been elected a member of the Commune of Paris in 1791, and deputy to the National Assembly and to the Convention, he became in a couple of years one of the leaders of the Girondist party, which for some time was master of the situation. He, at first, endeavoured to save the king, whose death he eventually voted, subject to an appeal to the people. He was proscribed with all his friends after the trial of the Girondist party, and guillotined May 31, 1793.

émigrés[1], who everywhere threatened the frontiers, to withdraw and by placing all the troops on a footing of peace. This course, however, was not adopted, or rather the steps resorted to were so full of indecision as to render them utterly useless ; as to the king, his natural weakness led him—in order to remove all suspicion of his conniving with the foreigners—to be induced to propose to the assembly a declaration of war which that body hastened to accept. The fate of monarchy was then sealed. The events which took place on the frontier[2] served as a pretext for the outrages of June 20, and, shortly after, for the crime of August 10, which the great regard I had for the Duc de la Rochefoucauld,[3] enabled me to witness. In compliance with a letter he had written to me, I had come back to Paris in order to share the noble and praiseworthy dangers, which the popularity of Pétion,[4] then Mayor of Paris, who, in accordance with a decision of the administrators of the Seine department, whose colleague I was, had been temporarily removed from office, caused us to face. I may add that the marks of approval given us by the queen, when, on the Federation day, we passed under

---

[1] The name given to the members of the aristocracy who, at the time of the Revolution, left France and fought in the ranks of the foreigners, but especially in what was termed the "army of the princes," under Prince de Condé.—(*Translator*).

[2] The defeat of the Duc de Biron, and running away of General Dillon's troops on the Belgian frontier (April 30, 1792).

[3] Louis-Alexandre, Duc de la Roche-Guyon and de la Rochefoucauld d'Enville, Born in 1743, he at first entered the army. As a member of the Assembly of Notables. he was elected deputy of the nobility to the States-General, where he showed himself favourable to new ideas and voted the chief reforms of the Assembly. He was appointed President of the Paris department in 1791 ; but after the events of June 20, 1792, he resigned that post and left Paris. Having been recognized at Gisors, he was stoned to death by the infuriated mob.

[4] Jérôme Pétion de Villeneuve was born at Chartres in 1753. He was practising as a barrister in that town, when he was elected deputy of the third estate * to the States-General. He soon acquired a great influence in the Assembly and in the clubs. In November, 1790, he was elected President of the Assembly. In June, 1791, he was appointed to fetch the king back from Varennes, and on November 14th of the same year, he was raised to the post of Mayor of Paris. His native town sent him as deputy to the Convention, of which he was subsequently elected President. He eventually sided with the Girondists. He voted for the death of the king. Having been banished and arrested on May 31, he managed to escape, reached Caen and endeavoured to organize the insurrection in the west. After the disaster at Vernon (July, 1793), he disappeared from the scene, and wandered in the south for nearly twelve months. In June, 1794, he was found dead in a field near Saint-Emilion in the Gironde department.

---

* The States-General were a meeting of the three states; the clergy, the nobility, and the third state (chosen from the upper middle classes). The States-General only assembled on solemn occasions. Their chief function was to decide as to the opportunity of raising new taxes, in order to meet the financial embarrassments of the State.—(*Translator*.)

the balcony where she was with the king, further excited the populace against us.

After the events of that day, and the rout of the Prussians in Champagne,[1] the Revolutionists flattered themselves that they had abolished monarchy for ever. They were blinded by their fanaticism ; but not less so the men who were of opinion that royalty could soon be restored, and Louis XVI. replaced on his throne by force. At this stage, it was no longer a question that the king should reign, but that he himself, the queen, their children, his sister should be saved. It might have been done. It was at least a duty to attempt it. At that time, France was only at war with the Emperor,[2] the Empire,[3] and Sardinia. Had all the other States concerted themselves to offer their mediation by proposing to recognize whatever form of government France might be pleased to adopt, with the sole condition that the prisoners in the Temple[4] should be allowed to leave the country and retire wherever they liked, though such a proposal, as may be supposed, would not have filled the demagogues with delight, they would have been powerless to reject it. Indeed what pretext could they have alleged to substantiate their refusal ? Would they have said to France : " General peace is offered us, but we wish for a general war, in which we shall stand alone against all Europe. . . . Our independence is recognized, but we wish to call it in question and cause it to depend on the chances of war. . . . We are not denied the right of governing ourselves as we think best. Nobody thinks of forcing a king on us, but we want to murder the one who did reign over us, in order that his rights may go over to his heirs,[5] who are indeed no longer in our power, and whom all Europe will recognize although we do not."

So little were the demagogues inclined to general hostilities, that they hastened to make pacific declarations to all the govern-

---

[1] The victory of Valmy, September 20, 1792.
[2] The Emperor of Austria was the head of the Holy Roman Empire, of which the German States were an integrant part.—(*Translator.*)
[3] Austria and the various German States.—(*Translator.*)
[4] It is well known that Louis XVI., Marie Antoinette, Madame Elizabeth, and the royal children, were imprisoned in the Temple.—(*Translator.*)
[5] The Comte de Provence (afterwards Louis XVIII.), and the Comte d'Artois (afterwards Charles X.), brothers of Louis XVI., both left France at the outbreak of the Revolution.—(*Translator.*)

ments with which France was still at peace. Indeed, very few amongst them thirsted after the blood of Louis XVI. ; and if they shed it afterwards, that was owing to special reasons, not one of which would have existed had Europe embraced the course indicated above.

The royal family might therefore have been saved. A war of twenty-two years, which threatened all the thrones, and upset many, which, by having re-established a few, though not on sufficiently secure bases, now threatens civilization itself, might thus have been averted. The revolutionary government (the barbaric expression of polygarchy could be suitably employed here) would have come to an end much sooner in France, where foreign wars and victories could alone sustain it.

After August 10, 1792, I solicited a temporary mission to London from the provisory executive. As the object of my mission, I chose a scientific question with which I was somewhat entitled to deal, seeing that it related to a motion previously made by me in the Constituent Assembly. My aim was to establish for the whole kingdom a uniform system of weights and measures. After the exactitude of this system had been vouched for by the most competent men of Europe, it might have been adopted by the different nations. It was therefore advisable to confer with England on the subject.

My real object was, however, to leave France, where it seemed to me useless, and even dangerous, to stay any longer, but I wished to leave the country with a regular passport, in order that it should not be closed to me for ever.

As in France, the tide of political passions ran high in the various cabinets of Europe. It was thought that if she were attacked on all sides, France could not resist. Only dreaming of success, they decided to wage war against her. The advantages they expected to reap by their victory were such as to cause them to lose sight of the dangers of the royal family. It was then that the Republicans, seeing war inevitable, took the initiative in declaring it, in order to show that they were not afraid of it.

I resided in England during the whole of the dreadful year 1793 and a portion of 1794. There I was welcomed with the utmost kindness by the Marquis of Lansdowne,[1] whom I had known in Paris; he was a nobleman of lofty views, gifted with abundant and lively powers of elocution. He was still free from the infirmities of old age. Some people brought against him the common-place accusation of being *too clever;* an accusation by means of which, in England as well as in France, people keep at a distance all the men whose superiority gives them umbrage, and this is really the only reason why he never was in office again. I saw him often, and he kindly sent me word every time he received the visit of some distinguished person whose acquaintance he thought I should be pleased to make. It was at his house that I met Mr. Hastings,[2] and the doctors Price,[3] and Priestley;[4] there, I also formed an intimacy with Mr. Canning,[5] Mr. Romilly,[6] Mr. Robert Smith, M. Dumont,[7]

---

[1] William Petty, Marquis of Lansdowne, Earl of Shelburne, was born in 1737, and at first joined the army. In 1761, he entered the House of Lords. Two years later, he was appointed a member of the Privy Council. Having been Chief Secretary of State, he was appointed First Lord of the Treasury in 1782; a post which he resigned in the following year. Until his death, in 1804, he remained a friend of France and bitterly opposed to Pitt's policy.

[2] Francis Rawdon, known successively under the names of Earl of Huntingdon, Earl of Moira, and Marquis of Hastings, was born in 1754. He was descended from a Norman family settled in Ireland. He entered the House of Lords in 1782, and always voted with the Whig party. He was successively Governor-General of the East Indies and Governor of Malta. He died in 1816.

[3] Richard Price, an English philosopher and political writer, was born in 1723. He studied finances, and, in 1772, he proposed, for sinking the public debt, a new system which was applied with success by Pitt. He was on intimate terms with the chief members of the French philosophical party, especially with Turgot, and displayed sympathy towards the Revolution. He died in 1791. Talleyrand is therefore mistaken in asserting that he had seen him during his journey to London, seeing that he only visited the English capital several months after Dr. Price's death.

[4] Joseph Priestley, famous English scientist and philosopher, born in 1733. His political and religious opinions compelled him to emigrate to America, where he died in 1804. He had been elected French citizen and honorary member of the Convention.

[5] George Canning, born in London, in 1770, from parents of Irish descent. In 1792, he had already distinguished himself as a speaker at public meetings, and was considered as one of the most prominent members of the Whig party. In 1793, he suddenly changed his political creed, was elected a member of the House of Commons in 1794, and became one of the most ardent supporters of Pitt. He was appointed Secretary of Foreign Affairs in 1807, and had to resign this post in 1809, in consequence of a duel with his colleague, Lord Castlereagh. In 1814, he was sent as ambassador to Lisbon. He again became Chief Secretary of Foreign Affairs in 1822, and died in 1827.

[6] Samuel Romilly, a famous English jurist, was born in 1757. He often visited France, and was on intimate terms with the chief writers and statesmen of the time. He entered the House of Commons in 1815, and was loud in his protests against the imprisonment of Napoleon. He died in 1818.

[7] Pierre Dumont, a Swiss writer, born at Geneva in 1759. He was a Protestant minister. Civil war compelled him to leave his country, and he travelled successively

Mr. Bentham,[1] and Lord Henry Petty,[2] the son of Lord Lansdowne, who at this time, was already looked upon as one of the hopes of England. All the friends of Mr. Fox,[3] with which gentleman I had, on several occasions, been on intimate terms, did their best to render my stay in London as pleasant as possible. My mornings were spent in penning down my impressions of the previous day, and when, after my return to France from America, my friends forwarded to me all the notes taken during the time I resided in England, I was extremely surprised to notice that they could be of no service to me for the work I am now writing. It would now be impossible for me to relate the events of this period, I do not recollect them ; their connecting link is lost for me.

Besides, my absence from France during the most terrible years of the Revolution left me in ignorance of the details of its dreadful events ; I could scarcely, at that distance, discern their broad outlines. On the other hand, I turned away from these hideous scenes, in which so much abject spirit was mingled with so much fierceness, too often to be able to depict them. The reign of Henri IV. and that of Louis XIV. are known to us in all their details, but recent events appear confused and problematical, even to the very men who played a part in them ; they followed each other with such rapidity, that each in turn almost stamped out the recollection of what had occurred before.

in Russia, in England, and finally in France, in 1788. Here he met the chief leaders of the Revolution, amongst whom Mirabeau, concerning whom he left some interesting memoirs (Geneva, 1831), and Talleyrand. He went back to Geneva in 1814, and died in 1829.

[1] Jeremy Bentham, an English writer and moralist, born in 1747, died in 1832.

[2] Henry Petty, Marquis of Lansdowne, son of William Petty, Earl of Shelburne and Marquis of Lansdowne, was born in 1780. In 1802, he was elected member of the House of Commons. In 1806, he was appointed Chancellor of the Exchequer ; entered the House of Lords in 1809. In 1827, he was Home Minister in the Cabinet of Mr. Canning, and, shortly after, held the same office in the short-lived Cabinet of Lord Goderich. In 1830, he re-entered the Cabinet as Lord President of the Council, resigned in 1834, held the same office again in 1835, and remained in that position until 1841. In 1846, he again resumed office as Lord President of the Council, and retired to private life in 1852.

[3] Charles Fox, born in 1748, was the son of Lord Holland, Secretary of State under George II. At the age of nineteen, he was elected member of the House of Commons, and appointed Lord of the Treasury. Having been removed from office in 1774, his powers as a speaker won for him the position of head of the Whig party. In 1782, he was appointed Chief Secretary of Foreign Affairs. He always displayed sympathy towards France and the Revolution, and showed himself a decided adversary of Mr. Pitt's policy. In 1806, he again took up office as Chief Secretary of Foreign Affairs, and died a few months after.

Perhaps also the mob leaves too slight an imprint on its work ; its deeds have but a transient effect, and the character of the men who serve it is such as to make no impression on one's memory. Having lived in obscurity until such day as they appear on the scene, they return to it as soon as their part there is played.

I confess that it would not cause me the slightest concern if the details of this awful calamity were to leave no trace in men's minds, for they are of no historical importance. Indeed, what teachings could men derive from deeds performed without aim or plan, and which were merely the outcome of ruthless and unruly passions ?

Teachings of all kinds are rather to be sought in the knowledge of the facts preceding the catastrophe, and for the investigation of which every material exists ; this knowledge will disclose the numerous and weighty causes of the revolution ; this is the truly profitable way of unfolding men's actions, for it bears with itself lessons equally useful to sovereigns, to the upper and to the lower classes. I have recorded in these memoirs all the events which occurred in the time closely preceding that dreadful upheaval, with which I was privately acquainted ; I advise my contemporaries to do likewise, and I feel sure that they will succeed better than I have done. The study of those already distant days possesses, it seems to me, the invaluable advantage of cautioning us against every form of intolerance. When considering the last twenty years of the old monarchy, there is no man of any elevation of mind and good faith who, on remembering what he did or said, what he wrote, what he blamed or approved, will not find some fault with himself—if this man possessed any influence at all : I might almost add that no one knows all the examples—good or bad—he must have set. I thus deny that it is in the power of any of the men I have known, whether princes or simple subjects, to decline all share of responsibility in the subsequent outbreak.

I do not mean to say that the amount of harm caused by the want of foresight of these men was the same in every case, but simply that it is in no one's power to ascertain and point out exactly the share of reproach deserved by each. The times in which we live, the circumstances in which we are placed, alter, or at least modify, the spirit of all our actions. What, in certain cases, may appear but natural and excusable, will deserve blame in others. Thus, I only insist on this appeal to the conscience of all Frenchmen, that I may eradicate all feelings of hatred and intolerance, and replace them by meekness and urbanity, so long banished from our beautiful country.

It was not my intention to stay long in England. Though being nominally an outlaw in France, I yet did not wish to place myself in the category of *émigré*, which I really was not. However, the English Foreign Minister thought it advisable to emphasize his zeal for the general cause by displaying at first his antipathy towards the *émigrés*. With this object, he availed himself of the Alien Bill,[1] which he had wrenched from Parliament, to send me orders to leave the country within twenty-four hours. Had I acted on the first impulse, I should have started off at once, but my dignity required of me to protest against the unjust persecution of which I was the victim. In consequence, I applied to Mr. Dundas,[2] to Mr. Pitt,[3] and to the king himself; being unable to obtain satisfaction in any quarter, I had but to submit, and therefore went to sleep on board a ship which, I had been told, was the first to start for the United States. The state of the weather and some business which the captain had to transact detained us nearly a fortnight in the Thames. In the meantime, a friend of Mr. Dundas came on board to invite me to put up—until such time as the vessel could start—at a house of his, near the river-side, but I declined his pressing offer.

---

[1] The first Alien Bill was passed in 1782. In 1793, Lord Grenville obtained from Parliament a Bill placing the French refugees under police supervision, and giving to the authorities necessary powers to expel them. This is the bill applied to Talleyrand in 1794.

[2] H. Dundas, Lord Melville, was born in 1741 from a noble Scotch family. Sent to Parliament by the city of Edinburgh, he always was one of the staunchest advocates of Pitt's policy. He was appointed successively Chief Comptroller for India in 1783, Home Minister in 1791, Chief Secretary of War, Lord of the Privy Seal, and first Lord of the Admiralty in 1804. He died in 1811.

[3] William Pitt, second son of Lord Chatham, was born in 1759. At twenty-two he was Member of Parliament ; at twenty-eight, Chancellor of the Exchequer ; in 1783, he resigned, but re-entered office again at the close of that year as First Lord of the Treasury. Pitt was the moving spirit of the coalitions against France. The treaty of Lunéville, in 1801, compelled him to retire from office, but the breach of the Peace of Amiens brought him back at the head of affairs. In 1805 he brought about the third coalition, and died in 1806.

I then experienced some satisfaction in refusing people's services: unjust though persecution may be, there are compensations in it. I never fully ascertained what my feelings really were at the time, though the fact is I was somewhat pleased. It seems to me that, in these days of general misfortune, I should almost have regretted not being persecuted too.

We sailed at last. On the second day of our voyage, after having but just left the Thames, we met with a violent storm. I was then between England and France, which, indeed, constituted one of the most critical positions in which any one could be placed. I could see France. . . . my head was in danger there . . . . I ran no immediate risk by returning to England, but it would have been far too repugnant to me to solicit the hospitality of a government who had tried to wound me.

Fortunately, the danger we were running was noticed on shore, and induced some Falmouth lightermen to brave the fury of the sea and come to our assistance. With their help, we managed to reach the harbour. Whilst our ship,—all the rigging of which was much damaged,—was being repaired, a rather striking incident added an impression of a special kind to the many I was to experience in the course of this voyage. The innkeeper at whose place I had my meals, informed me that one of his lodgers was an American general. Thereupon, I expressed the desire of seeing that gentleman, and, shortly after, I was introduced to him. After the usual exchange of greetings, I put to him several questions concerning his country, but, from the first, it seemed to me that my inquiries annoyed him. Having several times vainly endeavoured to renew the conversation, which he always allowed to drop, I ventured to request from him some letters of introduction to his friends in America.—" No," he replied, and after a few moments of silence, noticing my surprise, he added, " I am perhaps the only American who cannot give you letters for his own country. . . all the relations I had there are now broken. . . I must never return to the States." He dared not tell me his name. It was General Arnold ![1]   I

---

[1] General Arnold had been sentenced to death during the War of Independence for having furnished the English with information concerning the positions held by the United States troops.

must confess that I felt much pity for him, for which political puritans will perhaps blame me, but with which I do not reproach myself, for I witnessed his agony.

We left Falmouth with a favourable wind. All the passengers were on deck, and, looking in the direction of the shore, they all said, with evident pleasure : " I still see the land." I was the only one who felt relieved on seeing it no longer. The sea, at this moment, possessed special charms for me ; the sensations I derived from it were particularly suited to my disposition.

We had been sailing for several weeks, when one morning, the word I feared, " Land ! Land !" loudly shouted by the people on board, roused me from my sleep. The captain, the crew and the passengers all displayed the most lively joy. On reaching the deck, I saw the pilot who was to take us up the Delaware, and, at the same time, noticed an out-bound ship steering round the headland. Having ascertained from our pilot that this ship was bound for Calcutta, I there and then despatched a boat to her captain, in order to inquire whether he had room for one more passenger. The ship's destination was of no consequence to me ; she was going on a long voyage, and my object was, if possible, to avoid landing. Unfortunately, the captain being unable to accommodate me, I had no choice left but to submit to being taken to Philadelphia.

On landing in that city, my mind was totally indifferent to the novelties which, as a rule, excite the interest of travellers. I had the greatest trouble in rousing my curiosity. I met in Philadelphia M. Casenove, a Dutch gentleman whom I had known in Paris. M. Casenove was a man of a rather enlightened, though slow, mind, and of a timid and most careless nature. Both his qualities and his defects made him very useful to me. As he never pressed me to do anything, and himself felt interested in but few things, I had no occasion to resist him. Meeting with neither opposition, advice nor direction, my instinct alone guided me ; thus I was led gradually to contemplate more attentively the grand sight under my eyes.

Only twelve years had elapsed since the United States had ceased to be a colony, and the years of their independence had been lost as far as progress in material prosperity was concerned,

owing to the inefficiency of their first constitution.   The bases
of public trust not having been properly defined, a paper-money,
more or less discredited, roused everybody's cupidity, encouraged
deceit, disturbed all transactions, and caused the institutions
which had been rendered necessary by the recent independence
of the country to be lost sight of.   It was only in 1789, at the
time of the new federal constitution, that property in the United
States began to rest on truly solid foundations, that social
guarantees securing the safety of foreign intercourse were shaped,
and that the government of the young nation was admitted to
rank with older powers.

This is the true date of the foundation of the United States.

I was still haunted by my love for the sea, and I almost
forgot I was no longer sailing on it, when I found myself in that
vast country, where whatever I saw reminded me of nothing
I had seen before.

Intending to tire myself, I made up my mind to leave
Philadelphia, and therefore proposed to M. de Beaumetz [1] and to a
Dutch gentleman, of the name of Heydecoper, to travel inland
with me.   They both accepted, and I must confess that I was
pleased with the undertaking from the beginning.   I was struck
with astonishment; at less than a hundred and fifty miles distance from the capital, all trace of men's presence disappeared ;
nature in all her primeval vigour confronted us.   Forests old as the
world itself ; decayed plants and trees covering the very ground
where they once grew in luxuriance ; others shooting forth from
under the *débris* of the former, and like them destined to decay
and rot ; thick and intricate bushes that often barred our progress ; green and luxuriant grass decking the banks of rivers ;
large natural meadows ; strange and delicate flowers quite
new to me ; and here and there the traces of former tornadoes
that had carried everything before them.   Enormous trees, all
mowed down in the same direction, extending for a considerable distance, bear witness to the wonderful force of these terrible
phenomena.   On reaching higher ground, our eyes wandered,

[1] M. de Beaumetz was born in 1769.   He was a member of the Sovereign Council
of Artois.   As deputy to the States-General, he voted with the Constitutional party.
He emigrated in 1792, went to England, and thence to the United States and to
India, where he died.

as far as the sight could range, over a most varied and pleasant picture. The tops of trees and the undulations of the ground which alone interfere with the uniform aspect of large extents of country, produce a peculiar effect. In the face of these immense solitudes, we gave free vent to our imagination ; our minds built cities, villages and hamlets ; the mountain forests were to remain untouched, the slopes of the hills to be covered with luxuriant crops, and we could almost fancy we saw numerous herds of cattle grazing in the valley under our eyes. There is an inexpressible charm in thinking of the future when travelling in such countries. Such, said I to myself, was the place where, not very many years ago, Penn [1] and two thousand emigrants laid the foundations of Philadelphia, and where a population of eighty thousand [2] people is now enjoying all the luxuries of Europe. Such was also the seat now occupied by the pretty little town of Bethlehem,[3] whose neat houses and wonderfully fertile environs, due to the energy of the Moravian brothers, excite the admiration of all visitors. After the peace of 1783, the city of Baltimore was but a fishing village ; now spacious and elegant dwellings have there been built everywhere, and dispute the ground with trees whose stumps have not yet been removed. It is impossible to move a step without feeling convinced that the irresistible progressive march of nature requires an immense population to cultivate some day this large extent of ground lying idle now indeed, but which only wants the hand of man to produce everything in abundance. I leave to others the satisfaction of foretelling the prospects of those countries. I confine myself to noticing that it is impossible to walk a few miles away from seaside towns without learning that the lovely and fertile fields

[1] William Penn, born in London in 1644. He was the son of Admiral Penn. Having become a Quaker, he was subjected to numerous persecutions, and imprisoned three times. A state bond of £16,000 having been bequeathed to him, he received in exchange the country west of the Delaware. There, he founded, in 1681, a colony called after him Pennsylvania ; he built Philadelphia, and gave to his possessions a constitution which became the basis of that of the United States. He returned to England, where he died in 1718.

[2] Philadelphia is now the second city of the States as regards commercial importance. In 1874 it had already a population of 920,000 inhabitants.—(*Translator.*)

[3] Bethlehem, a small town in Pennsylvania, distant about sixty miles from Philadelphia. It was founded in 1741, by the Moravian brethren, a religious sect dating from the fifteenth century, and whose members are the descendants of the old Hussites. In order to escape oppression and persecution, a number of them had sought refuge in America.

N

we now admire were, but ten, but five, but a couple of years ago, mere wildernesses of forest. Similar causes must produce similar effects, especially when acting with ever increasing power. The population of the States will therefore daily reclaim some fresh portion of these fallow spaces, the area of which far surpasses that of the ground at present cultivated.

Having sated myself with these ideas, or rather impressions, my mind being neither free nor active enough to induce me to write a book, I returned to city-life, wishing at the same time that a considerable portion of the capital that took refuge in America, might there be devoted to clearing and tilling the ground on a large scale.

A new nation, whose manners, without going through the slow process of civilization, takes pattern from the already refined ways of Europe, stands in need of the teachings of the grand school of nature, for agriculture is the basis on which all States are founded. It is, I admit with the economists, agriculture that forms the chief wealth of the social state, that teaches respect for property, and warns us that we are blind to our own interests whenever we interfere with those of other people ; it is agriculture that clearly points out to us the indispensable correlation existing between the duties and the rights of men ; by binding the tiller of the soil to his field, it binds men to their country. The first attempts at agriculture teach us the necessity of the division of labour, that marvellous source of all manifestations of public and private prosperity ; agriculture goes deeply enough into the hearts and interests of men to induce them to see in a numerous family so much additional wealth ; while, by teaching resignation, it subjects our intellect to the supreme and universal rules that regulate the world. From all this, I infer that agriculture alone can put a stop to revolutions, because it is the only pursuit that usefully employs all the capabilities of men, that imparts to them calmness and moderation without indifference, that inculcates respect for that experience which enables men to control the results of their new experiments ; which, in short, furnishes constant proofs of the grand results to be obtained by simple regular work, and which neither hurries nor delays in anything.

In times of revolutions, rashness is regarded as skill, and exaggeration as greatness. To put a stop to them, circumspection must replace audacity, and greatness will then lie in moderation, and skill in prudence. A government, which is the friend of liberty and averse to disturbing the tranquillity of the world, must strive to act with moderation. An agricultural nation settles down, it does not wish for conquests. Commerce, on the other hand, always longs for increase of territory.

After the French Revolution, commercial transactions with foreign countries met with too many obstacles to enable them to become the chief pursuit of the country, and therefore to exercise any influence on the manners of the French people ; but if, in consequence of the excitement and vain dreams subsisting in men's minds, the nation, as there is too much reason to fear, turns its views to speculation in public funds, that will indeed be a very great evil, because in operations of this kind deceit is too much resorted to, and the attending ruin or fortune too rapid.

The American government allowed itself to be too easily influenced by the geographical situation of the States ; it gave too much encouragement to the spirit of enterprise, for, in order to increase its population, America annexed Louisiana ; it will now be obliged to annex the Floridas. Commerce requires ports and harbours from the Sainte-Croix river, near the Saint-Lawrence, to the Gulf of Mexico, yet nine-tenths of the five hundred millions of acres composing the territory of North America are still untilled. Too much activity is devoted to business, and not enough to farming ; and that first impulse given to all the ideas of the country unsettles its social establishment. You need only travel a bare hundred miles inland to see people paying in kind for whatever they buy, whilst others draw bills on the first markets of Europe : the contrast is too shocking ; it is the symptom of a social disease.[1]

I saw, sixty miles from Boston, six thousand feet of timber

---

[1] It must be borne in mind that the author of these Memoirs was travelling in the States as far back as 1794, and therefore long before the great influx of emigration that induced so many German and Irish agricultural labourers to go to America, where they performed the task pointed out to the Americans by Prince Talleyrand.—(*M. de Bacourt.*)

exchanged for a bullock, and, in Boston itself, twenty pounds paid for a Florence straw hat.

At Frenchman's Bay, on the border of the Eastern States, a violent storm having compelled me to stop at Machias,[1] I entered into conversation with the man at whose house I was staying. It was indeed the best house in the district, and, as people say in this country, the landlord was *a most respectable man.* Having exhausted the chapter relative to the value and price of land, I asked him whether he had ever been to Philadelphia. He replied that he had not yet done so. He was a man of about forty-five years of age. I scarcely dared to ask him whether he knew General Washington. " I have never seen him," he said. " If you should go to Philadelphia," I went on, " you will be pleased to see that great man ? " " Why, yes, I shall ; but," he added with an excited countenance, " I should very much like to see Mr. Bingham, who, they say, is so wealthy."

Throughout all the States I met with a similar love for money, very often quite as coarsely expressed. The country was too soon acquainted with luxuries. The latter are, indeed, ridiculous when men can hardly provide themselves with the necessaries of life. I recollect having seen in the drawing-room of Mrs. Robert Morris, a hat manufactured in the birth-place of the master of the house, carefully laid on an elegant Sèvres china table, bought at Trianon by some American. An European peasant would scarcely have consented to wear such a hat.

On the banks of the Ohio, Mr. Smith possessed a residence known in the country by the name of *log-house.* The walls of it were formed with rough trees. The drawing-room contained a pianoforte enriched with most beautiful bronzes. M. de Beau-metz having opened it, Mr. Smith said to him, " Please do not attempt to play, for the man who tunes it lives a hundred miles from here, and he has not come this year."[2]

---

[1] Machias, small trading port in the State of Maine.
[2] Several incidents connected with this journey left impressions that are yet present to my mind. To kill time is not so easy as people generally think, especially when one's mind is active and full of apprehension as to news from one's country. Under such circumstances, impressions can only be produced by material facts. To be riding through a large wild forest, to lose one's way in it in the middle of the night, and to call to one's companion in order to ascertain that you are not missing each other : all this gives impressions impossible to define, because each incident reflects comically

To us, inhabitants of old Europe, there is something awkward in all the luxury displayed by Americans. I grant that our luxury often shows signs of improvidence and frivolousness, but in America, luxury only denotes defects which prove that refinement does not yet exist there, either in the conduct of life, or even in its trifles. I must be pardoned for dwelling at some length on America. I was so lonely when there, that many reflections, which would otherwise have found their vent in conversation, now come rushing to my pen.

During the two winters I spent either in Philadelphia or in New York, I availed myself of the opportunity thus afforded me to see the chief personages whose names the American Revolution has handed to history, especially General Hamilton,[1] whose mind

on the others. When I cried, "So-and-so, are you here?" and my companion replied, "Unfortunately, I am, my lord," I could not help laughing at our position. That "Unfortunately, I am," so pitifully uttered, and that "my lord," in allusion to the Autun bishopric, sounded most ludicrous. Once, in the heart of Connecticut, after a long day's ride, we stopped at a house where the people consented to give us bed and supper. The food supply was fortunately better than we usually found it in American houses. The family was composed of an elderly man, his wife, about fifty years of age, two grown-up boys, and a young girl. The meal consisted of smoked fish, ham, potatoes, strong beer, and brandy. In a very short time, the beer and brandy had the effect of enlivening the conversation. The two young fellows, who were rather elevated, spoke of a journey they were about to undertake ; they were going beaver-hunting for a few weeks. They spoke of their future expedition in such glowing terms that they roused our interest and curiosity to such a degree that, after drinking a few glasses of brandy, M. de Beaumetz, M. Heydecoper, and myself, were dying to join them. This would have been a novel way of spending or wasting a few weeks. At each question that we put to our hosts, they filled our glasses. From that evening's conversation I learned that the fur of beavers is good only in the fall of the season ; that, to shoot them, one must lie in wait and hold out to them spears baited with split-up wood ; that, in frosty weather, the hunters attack the little dens the beavers build for themselves, thus causing the timid beasts to plunge under the ice, but, as they cannot long remain under water, they soon come up to breathe at holes purposely made in the ice, when they are captured by the foot. All this was sufficiently interesting to induce Beaumetz, either because of his love of sport, or because he felt more merry than we did, to propose that our hosts should allow us to accompany them on their expedition. They both gave their assent, and we were, without further formality, enrolled in the brotherhood of the Connecticut beaver-hunters. Having mutually pledged our word, each of us reached his bed as best he could. When morning came, the effect of the brandy having passed off, and sleep becoming imperious, we began to think the various implements each was to carry too heavy. I believe that the provisions alone weighed about forty pounds ; we also began to realize that spending a couple of months in woods or marshes was really too much of a good thing, so we endeavoured to quash the agreement made the night before. We got free with a few dollars, and resumed our journey, feeling rather ashamed of what we had done. (Prince Talleyrand.)

[1] Alexander Hamilton was born in 1757 in the island of Nevis (East Indies), of Scotch parents. When still very young, he took an active part in the War of Independence, and was appointed Colonel. The State of New York sent him to the Congress which framed the Constitution. Colonel Hamilton was one of the warmest supporters of the federative system. In 1789, Washington appointed him Minister of

and character placed him, I thought, on a par with the most
distinguished statesmen of Europe, not even excepting Mr. Pitt
and Mr. Fox.

As I remarked above, I had noticed, whilst travelling in the
States, that agriculture was less encouraged than commerce, that,
having to choose between two sources of prosperity, government
had chosen that the scale should fall in favour of commerce, and,
still more recently, had emphasized this intention, by adding to
all the real wealth of their country the fictitious one procured by
all the banking establishments, which have sprung up everywhere
in the States, and which serve exclusively the ends of commerce.
Such an impulse once started, vanity and cupidity could not fail
soon to denounce prudence, moderation, or simple probity, as
narrow views.   By overthrowing the barriers formerly raised
by the metropolis, which centralized all the products of its
colonies on its own markets, and set its own rules to their
speculations, the United States take able advantage of the
position and power that their independence has obtained for
them.   They send to all the markets of the old world unexpected quantities of all sorts of goods, the arrival of which,
by altering prices, brings about commercial crises impossible to
avoid.   The chief cause of all these perturbations proceeds from
the great distance existing between the eastern and southern
ports of the States, whence thousands of ships loaded with
similar products start every year, on almost the same day, bound
for all the ports of Europe.   Thus, for a long time to come, the
commerce of America to Europe will be left to chance.

During the long evenings of my stay in the States, always
thinking of my unfortunate country, whose troubles so deeply
afflicted me, I often considered what her future prospects were
likely to be.   I then sought the means of removing, or at least
of diminishing, the obstacles which prevented the establishment
of mutually advantageous commercial relations.

I fully realized how idle the wanderings of my imagination
were; yet they pleased me.   To put off conjectures, as reason

Finances.   He resigned this post, from his own free will, in 1795.   In 1798, when
war was on the point of breaking out with France, Hamilton was appointed General.
He was killed six years later (1804) in a duel with Colonel Burr, Vice-President of
the United States.

dictated, until such time as the expected quarrel of Spain with her colonies should be settled,[1] was to delay one's hopes too long, for only after the issue of this quarrel can the maritime . and commercial interests of the great powers assume a regular course. Thus my hopes of regulation were daily disturbed by all the events taking place under my eyes.

In 1794, I witnessed the return of the first American trading expedition to Bengal ; the shipowners connected with it were largely repaid for their outlay, and in the following year, fourteen American vessels started for India from different ports, in order to obtain a share of the enormous profits secured by the English company. There is a sort of hostility in the sudden appearance of American competition. This competition immeasurably increases the risks of commerce, and thus skilful combinations are seldom rewarded by compensating results. All this has come in times when the growth of population in all civilized countries, is adding daily to the ordinary stimulus of human passions that of the fresh wants it creates.

All these considerations make it exceedingly difficult to foresee the future, and well-nigh impossible to direct its course.

Yet everything seems easy to a man driven from his country and obliged to put up at an inn or reside in indifferent lodgings : it does not seem quite so easy to him who is quietly seated under his own roof. I therefore took advantage of the disposition of mind into which my narrow quarters threw me to indulge in high politics and set the world to rights. Having, like a good member of the Constituent Assembly, waived the question of the characters of men, I had recourse to a philosophical spirit, and devised a new general code of the law of nations, which, after having established the balance of the interests of nations and of individuals, should unite them for the political and reciprocal benefit of the powers, and introduce liberal equality into their habitual intercourse. I even fancy that I was on the point of applying the system of the economists on free trade and the abolition of customs, which must needs be com-

---

[1] This settlement was the emancipation of the Spanish colonies, of which Mexico was the first to throw off the yoke of the metropolis, in 1810. In 1824, Spain possessed no longer any territory on the continent of America.

prised in my speculative ideas, when, at the very moment I was
engaged in trying to solve the problem, a new tariff of customs,
. adopted by the American Congress, on the motion of my friend
Hamilton, came into force.[1]   The early conversations I had had
with the learned general dwelt on this branch of the American
administration   " Your economists," he said to me, " made a grand
dream, but it is the chimerical exaggeration of people whose
intentions were good.   Theoretically," he added, " their system
might perhaps be contested and its unsoundness exposed ; but
we must leave them their pleasant illusions ; the present state of
the affairs of this world suffices to prove that, at least for the
nonce, their plan cannot be carried out ; let us be satisfied with
this fact."   I did not make a very firm stand in favour of the
economists, yet I could scarcely make up my mind to accept the
idea that there could exist " liberal " combinations that did not
result in mutual advantages for all commercial nations.   Philan-
thropic conceptions rush to the mind when one is an outlaw.

Mr. Hamilton did not seem to me to reject so peremptorily
the possibility of all industries being, some day, permanently
divided among the nations of the world.

Europe, said I to him, is acquainted with, and cultivates, all
branches of art, and excels in the manufacture of all articles of
luxury, as in everything that tends to make life more pleasant
and agreeable.

The new world possesses a kind of wealth peculiar to itself:
its crops will always surpass those of any rival nation in
quantity.

Might not, therefore, the distribution of these two modes of
applying men's abilities serve, at least for a considerable time to
come, as the measure and basis of the relations that must necessarily spring up between nations, some of which daily require to
buy the most usual necessaries of life at a moderate cost, whilst
others are anxious to acquire all that tends to make life more
pleasant and agreeable ?

Might not this natural balance furnish a vast ground for

---

[1] There is a curious coincidence between this fact and that of these Memoirs
appearing at almost the very moment of the adoption of the bill of Major McKinley,
which seems to prove that the traditions of American economists of the early school
still possess numerous advocates in the States.—(*Translator.*)

intelligent exchange which, being ruled by international conventions, would constitute the commercial intercourse of the
different powers ?

" Your idea," Mr. Hamilton said to me, " will only be practical
the day when—and it is perhaps not very remote—great markets,
such as formerly existed in the old world, will be established in
America.

" There were four chief markets concentrating all the products
of the world : that of London, which, notwithstanding our commercial successes, will yet be the first, for a long time to come ;
that of Amsterdam, which, if things do not mend in Holland,
will soon be removed to London ; that of Cadiz, which will
eventually pass into the hands of our northern or southern ports ;
and that of Marseilles, which owed its flourishing state to Levantine trade, but is now on the eve of being lost to you Frenchmen.

" As for us, we only need two markets, but they are indispensable to us : one for the Northern and one for the Southern
States.

" When these large markets are established, commerce will
be able to resume its regular course ; commercial enterprise will
no longer rely on sole hazard, it being the interest of each
market to render public the real price and quality of the various
goods finding their way to it ; excessive fluctuations will be
thereby avoided, thus keeping within reasonable bounds the
losses and gains of all speculations. Then, will sailors of all
nations bring in all confidence their cargoes to the various ports
of the world."

I admired the spirit of general order always apparent in the
private views expressed by Mr. Hamilton respecting the prosperity
of his country. I do not know whether they will ever be realized,
but if they do, it will only be when the intrusive and invading
spirit of America will have ceased to alter the general relations
of the American people with other nations, and when, by a
judicious regard for its own interests, it will endeavour to
conquer its own country by turning to every possible advantage
the vast extent of territory belonging to it.

I had acquainted myself with almost all I wanted to know in
America ; I had been spending nearly thirty months in that

country,[1] without any other aim than that of being away from either France or England, and impelled by the sole interest of seeing with my own eyes the great American nation whose history is only beginning.

The uncertainty in which the news from Europe left my future prospects, induced me to launch in a speculation which, being carried on with skill and economy, might have proved most profitable. I made up my mind to go to the East Indies on board a ship I had chartered, and in the cargo of which several important Philadelphia firms and some Dutch capitalists had an interest. My vessel was loaded; and I was about to start, when a decree from the Convention, permitting me to return to France, reached me. This measure was quite unsolicited by me; it had been taken on the initiative of Messrs. Chénier,[2] and Daunou,[3] whom I scarcely knew, and to whom, however different their political opinions may be from mine, I shall always bear gratitude.[4] It was necessary to take advantage of this decree, or else to give up for ever the hope of returning to France. M. de Beaumetz, whom I had taken into partnership in my speculation, went to

---

[1] During his stay in England and in America, Prince Talleyrand kept up with Madame de Staël * an interesting correspondence recently edited by the present Duc de Broglie (the editor of these Memoirs) in the January and April numbers of the *Revue Diplomatique* (1890), under the title of *Lettres de M. de Talleyrand à Madame de Staël, extraites des Archives du Château de Broglie.*

[2] Marie Joseph Chénier, born in Constantinople in 1764. He was the junior brother of André.† He at first entered the army, but left it to devote his time to literature, and wrote several republican and revolutionary plays which gave him a certain reputation. As Deputy of the Department of Seine-et-Oise to the Convention, he voted for the death of the king. He was President of the Assembly in August, 1795, and was subsequently elected a member of the "Five Hundred." After Brumaire 18, he became a member of the Tribunate. Under the Empire, he was appointed Inspector of Public Education, was dismissed in 1806, and died in 1811.

[3] Pierre Daunou was born in 1761. He joined the Order of the Oratorians, but gave up his ecclesiastical functions after his election to the Convention by the Department of Pas-de-Calais in 1792. He protested against the trial of the king, and voted in favour of banishment. Having been arrested with seventy-three of his colleagues on October 31, 1792, he was imprisoned for a whole year. After Thermidor 9, he was appointed President of the Convention. He was, subsequently, a member of the "Five Hundred" and of the Tribunate, from which he was removed in 1802. He took no share in politics under the Empire. He became a Deputy under the Restoration, was appointed peer of France in 1839, and died in 1840.

[4] As mentioned here by Prince Talleyrand, the decree of the Convention permitting his return to France was proposed by Messrs. Chénier and Daunou, but at the pressing request of many of his friends, amongst whom was Madame de Staël.

* See footnote (2), p. 47.
† The author of remarkable poems. His royalist opinions caused him to be arrested during the Terror. The revolutionary tribunal sentenced him to death. He was guillotined in 1793.— (*Translator.*)

India instead of me and died in that country. I much regretted to part with M. de la Rochefoucauld,[1] for whom I had much affection, and with Mr. Hamilton, who will always occupy a foremost place in my recollections. Having taken leave of my friends, I took passage on board a wretched Danish vessel bound for Hamburg.

Before re-entering France, I was anxious to know what was going on there. Madame de Flahaut,[2] who was then at Hamburg, seemed to me hardly disposed to furnish me with the desired information, for, when I was still coming up the Elbe, she sent me word by M. de Riccé, who was simple enough to deliver the message—not to land but go back to America. Her reason for so doing, she told M. de Riccé, was that it being rumoured that she had been on rather intimate terms with me, she feared that my presence should be an obstacle to her marriage with M. de Souza, the Portuguese Minister. However, I thought I could, without any impropriety, take no notice of the extraordinary reasons alleged by M. de Riccé, and spent a month in Hamburg, in the society of persons who did, no more than I did myself, interfere with the marriage of Madame de Flahaut with that dear M. de Souza. In Hamburg, I met Madame de Genlis, whom I found exactly the same as I had known her at Sillery, at Bellechasse and in England. The unchangeableness of compound natures proceeds from their suppleness.

From Hamburg, I went to Amsterdam, where I spent a fortnight, thence to Brussels, where I stayed long enough to reach Paris only in the month of September 1796, as it had been my intention.

A national institute of arts and sciences[3] had been founded

---

[1] The Duc de la Rochefoucauld-Liancourt.

[2] Adelaïde Filleul, born in Paris in 1761, married, when very young, the Comte de Flahaut, a brigadier-general, who was guillotined in 1793. She had left France in 1792. After Thermidor 9, she wished to return to France, but had to stay at Hamburg, where she made the acquaintance of the Marquis José de Souza-Bothelo, who was then Portuguese Minister to Denmark, and whose wife she became in 1802, he having just been appointed Minister to France. The Marquis de Souza lost his appointment shortly after, but resided in Paris until his death (1825). Madame de Souza wrote several novels, which made her reputation. She died in 1836.

[3] All the academies had been done away with in 1792. The Convention inserted in the Constitution of the year III. a clause providing for the foundation of a national institute "entrusted with the care of collecting the various discoveries and improving arts and sciences." A bill passed in 1795, regulated the organization of this institute,

in Paris: the very organization of this institute was sufficient to gauge the spirit then reigning in France. It had been divided into four sections, of which that of physical sciences ranked first, whereas that of moral and political sciences only came next. During my absence, I had been elected a member of the latter. To pay my debt as academician, I read, at two public sittings closely following each other, a couple of papers which attracted a certain notice. The first of these papers related to the United States, the second dealt with the necessity for France to secure colonies.[1] I had also prepared a third paper on the influence of society in France, but, as it was based chiefly on my recollections, my friends did not think it suited to a time when France was ruled by the Directory. So I left it unfinished.

Having paid my literary debt, and perceiving no element of order and no guarantee of stability in the various political factions whose struggles I witnessed, I took care to keep aloof from active politics. Madame de Staël, who had already resumed a certain influence, closely insisted on my going with her to Barras,[2] one of the members of the Directory. I demurred at first; I could not call on a member of the Directory, without asking to see all the other Directors, and chiefly those[3] who had been my colleagues in the Constituent Assembly. The reasons alleged to justify my refusal did not seem valid. Besides, they had to be conveyed through Madame de Staël, who, being anxious

which was divided into four sections, comprising altogether 144 full members and 144 associate members. The Institute only resumed its old name of academy in 1816.
[1] These two papers were published in the *Recueil des Mémoires de l'Institut*, section of moral and political sciences, vol. ii., first series, 1799. In the first, headed *Sur les Relations commerciales de l'Angleterre et des Etats-Unis*, Germinal 5, year V. ("The Commercial Intercourse of England with the United States"), the author's object was to prove that England did not lose anything by the declaration of independence of her great colony, and that she will always find in America a regular market to buy her goods and adopt the overgrowth of her population. The second was headed, *Sur les Avantages à retirer des Colonies nouvelles* ("Advantages to be derived from New Colonies"); it was read Messidor 25, year V. The main idea in it is that, as a consequence of the revolution, it is necessary, in order to preserve its results, to apply the forces of the country to a new field of activity, and that, in the present state of affairs in France, the government ought to endeavour to supply all agitators and malcontents of all parties with vast territories to colonize.
[2] The Comte Paul de Barras, born at Fox-Emphoux, in the Var Department, was a captain in the army in 1789. Having been sent to the Convention, he voted for the death of Louis XVI. In February, 1795, he was appointed President of the Convention. He was elected a member of the Directory at the time of its foundation, and only left it on Brumaire 18, when he retired to private life. He died in 1829.
[3] La Réveillère-Lépeaux and Rewbell.

that I should be personally known to Barras, so managed matters that the Director sent me a note inviting me to dine with him at Suresnes on a certain day. I had no alternative but to accept. On the appointed day, I was at Suresnes at about three o'clock in the afternoon. In the dining-room, which I had to cross to reach the drawing-room, I noticed covers laid for five persons. Much to my surprise, Madame de Staël was not invited. A man who was rubbing the floor, showed me a cupboard containing a few odd books, and told me that the Director—the title given to Barras in private life—seldom came home before half-past four. Whilst I was engaged in reading I do not recollect what work, two young men came in to ascertain the time by the drawing-room clock, and seeing that it was only half-past three, they said to each other, "We have time to go for a swim." They had not been gone twenty minutes, when one of them returned asking for immediate help ; I ran, with all the persons in the house, to the riverside. Facing the garden, between the high road and the island, the Seine forms a kind of whirlpool in which one of the young men had disappeared. The watermen of the neighbour-hood soon rowed to the spot, and two of them most courageously dived to the bottom. However, all the efforts made to save the unfortunate fellow proved vain. I went back to the house.

The corpse of the young man was only found the next day caught in weeds, at a spot distant more than six hundred yards from the place where he had disappeared. The drowned was named Raymond, Lodève was his birthplace. Barras was very fond of him ; he had brought him up and, since he had been appointed a Director, he had made him his aide-de-camp. I was alone in the drawing-room, not knowing exactly what to do. Who was to tell Barras the misfortune that had just befallen him ? I had never seen the Director. My position was really unpleasant. A carriage drove up. On opening the door, the gardener said : "M. Raymond has just been drowned, yes, Citizen Director, he has just been drowned." Barras crossed the front yard, and rushed upstairs to his room, crying out aloud. After waiting some little time, one of his servants told him I was in the drawing-room. He sent me word to excuse his not coming down, and requesting me to sit down to dinner at once. The secretary who accompanied him remained upstairs. Thus, I was alone at Barras' table. A quarter of an hour having elapsed, a servant came to request me to go up to the Director's room. I felt thankful for his supposing that, under the circumstances, the dinner served to me could have no attraction. I felt quite upset. As I entered his room, he took hold of both my hands and embraced me ; he was weeping. I said to him all the kind things which the position in which I saw him and that in which I was myself, could dictate. The sort of embarrassment he, at first, displayed with me, an utter stranger to him, gradually disappeared, and the share I took in his trouble seemed to do him good. He begged of me to go back with him to Paris ; I readily accepted. From that day, I never had any occasion to regret having made his acquaintance. He was a man of an excited and impulsive nature, easily carried one way or the other : I had known him scarcely a couple of hours, and yet might have almost supposed I was the person he liked best in the world.

Shortly after my first interview, the Directory wished to make a change in the Ministry.[1]   To this Barras consented with the condition that his new friend should be appointed " Minister of Foreign Relations." He defended his proposal with great warmth, and so effectively that it was adopted ; at ten o'clock the same night, a gendarme called for me at the club named *Salon des Étrangers*[2] and handed to me the decree appointing me Minister.

The absolute character of all the measures taken by the Directory, the pressing requests of Madame de Staël, and above all this, the belief I had that I might possibly work some good, caused me to dismiss all idea of declining the post. On the following day, I therefore called at the Luxembourg,[3] in order to thank Barras : after which, I went to the Foreign office.

Under my predecessor, Charles de Lacroix,[4] all State matters

<hr/>

[1] During the summer of 1797, the cabinet was entirely modified.   Talleyrand took the Foreign Office, Lambrecht the Justice, Letourneux the Home Department, General Schérer the War Office, Admiral Pléville le Pelley the Marine Department, Sotin was head of the Police Department, and Ramel remained Minister of Finances.

[2] Strangers' or Foreigners' Club.

[3] The residence of Marie de Medici.   After passing through different destinations during the Revolution, it became the official residence of the executive during the Directory.   It is now devoted to the sittings of the Senate.—(*Translator*.)

[4] Charles de Lacroix de Constant was born in 1754 ; in 1789, he was chief clerk

concerning his department were previously settled by the Directory. Like the previous secretary, my duties were confined to signing passports and other administrative documents, and to forwarding to the proper quarters the despatches or communications already drafted by the executive ; yet, I often delayed these communications, which delay enabled me to soften their terms, when the impulse under which they had been written had passed away. All business relative to home affairs was kept from me. I imparted dignity to my odd situation, by trying to convince others, and myself to a certain degree, that all progress towards true order at home would be impossible so long as we did not have peace abroad, and adding that, since I had been called upon to contribute to its restoration, I ought to devote myself entirely to this object.

It has come to my knowledge that some people, not in the days I speak of, but since the Restoration, considered that it was wrong to accept office in times of crisis and revolution, when it is impossible to work absolute good. Such judgment always appeared to me most superficial. In the affairs of this world, we must not simply consider the present. *That which is,* in the majority of cases, has but a very small importance, whenever we lose sight of the fact that *that which is* produces *that which shall be ;* thus indeed, as we frame the present, so will the future be shaped ! If we consider matters, without prejudice and, above all, without envy, we plainly see that men do not always accept office so as to gratify their personal interests, and I might add that it is no mean sacrifice on the part of a political man to consent to being the responsible *editor* of other people's lucubrations. Selfish and timorous people are incapable of so much abnegation ; but, I repeat it, it must be borne in mind that, by declining official posts, in times of upheaval, one simply affords greater facilities to the enemies of public order. He who accepts does so, not to second the advocates of a state of affairs to which he is opposed, but in order to so modify their action that it may

---

in the General Comptroller's office. Having been elected to the Convention, he voted for the death of the king. He was subsequently a member of the "Anciens," Minister of Foreign Affairs (1796), Ambassador to Holland (1797), Prefect of the Bouches-du-Rhône, and afterwards of the Gironde. He died in 1808. He was the father of Eugène Delacroix, the famous painter.

be profitable to the future. "*En toute chose il faut considérer la fin,*"[1] said good old La Fontaine, and that is not a mere apologue.

I must not omit to state that Admiral Bruix,[2] for whose character, intellect, and talent I had the greatest esteem, was to be appointed Minister of Marine ; I was thus entering upon office with a colleague as unacquainted as I was myself with the ways of the Directory, and with whom I could deliberate as to what good might be done and what evil prevented.

To give a clear conception of what I have termed the ways of the Directory, I think it will be sufficient to relate the incidents that marked the first council at which I was present. A quarrel took place between Carnot[3] and Barras; the latter charged his colleague with having destroyed a letter which ought to have been submitted to the Directory. They were both standing. Carnot, putting up his hand, said : "I give you my word of honour that that is not so !" "Do not raise your hand," replied Barras, "blood would drip from it." Such were our rulers, and my task was to try to obtain the re-admission of France to the councils of Europe, whilst such men were in power. Difficult though this great undertaking was I did not hesitate to confront it.

Nearly all the enemies France had had since the beginning of the Revolution, had been compelled to seek safety in peace, which most of them bought and paid for with territorial cessions or pecuniary considerations.[4] Austria, defeated both in Italy

---

[1] In all things the end should be considered.

[2] Eustache Bruix was born at San Domingo in 1759 ; in 1789, he was a lieutenant in the navy ; in 1798, he was appointed Rear-Admiral and Minister of Marine, and died in 1805.

[3] Lazare Carnot was born at Nolay, in the Department of Côte d'Or, in 1753 ; in 1789, he was an officer of artillery. He sat in the Legislative Assembly and in the Convention, where he voted for the death of the king. Having been appointed a member of the Committee of Public Safety, he was entrusted with the organization of the army and the direction of the war. Having been elected a member of the *Conseil des Anciens* by fourteen Departments, he was appointed a Director. Having been banished on Fructidor 18, he took refuge in Geneva. Under the Consulate, he was Minister of War, and afterwards member of the Tribunate. In 1814, he was appointed General of Division and Governor of Antwerp. He took office as Minister of the Interior during the Hundred Days, was exiled at the Second Restoration, and died at Magdeburg in 1823.

[4] The following is the chronological list of the treaties which brought the war of the first coalition to an end :—With the Grand Duke of Tuscany, Paris, February 9, 1795 ; with Prussia, Basel, April 5, 1795 ; with Spain, Basel, July 22, 1795 ; with

and in Germany, and seeing her territory invaded on both sides and her capital threatened by General Bonaparte, had already signed the preliminaries of Leoben with her victor, and was now engaged in negotiating the definitive treaty, that of Campo-Formio.

I became Minister of Foreign Affairs [1] during the time that elapsed between the signing of the preliminaries of peace and the conclusion of the definitive treaty. On learning my appointment, General Bonaparte wrote to the members of the Directory to congratulate them on their choice, and also sent me a very nice letter. From that day, we kept up a close correspondence.[2] All the young victorious general did, said, or wrote was so full of originality, so striking, skilful and daring as to justify building great hopes on his genius. A few weeks after writing his first letter to me, he signed the treaty of Campo-Formio (October 17, 1797).

On the other hand, England had sent Lord Malmesbury [3] to France with proposals of peace ; but in this, she was not sincere. The English Cabinet was then forced to feign entering on negotiations with us, in order to overcome its difficulties at home.[4]

Hesse-Cassel, Basel, August 28, 1795 ; with Sardinia, Paris, May 15, 1796 ; with Wurtemberg, Paris, August 7, 1796 ; with the Margrave of Baden, Paris, August 22, 1796 ; with the King of the Two Sicilies, Paris, October 11, 1796 ; with Parma, Paris, November 5, 1796 ; with the Pope, Tolentino, February 19, 1796 ; with Venice, Milan, May 16, 1797 ; with Portugal, August 20, 1797 ; with the Emperor, Campo-Formio, October 17, 1797.

[1] July 18, 1797.

[2] The following is the first letter written to Bonaparte by Talleyrand :—

"PARIS, *July* 24, 1797.

"I have the honour to inform you, General, that the Executive Directory has appointed me Minister of Foreign Affairs. Fully alive to the fearful responsibility my duties lay on me, it is necessary that I should seek confidence in the fact that your glory cannot fail to facilitate the negotiations I may have to carry out. The mere name of Bonaparte will remove all obstacles.

"I shall diligently acquaint you with all the views the Directory may instruct me to bring to your knowledge, and fame, which quickly spreads all your achievements, will often deprive me of the pleasure of informing the Directors of the manner in which you have carried out their views." (Unpublished official correspondence of Napoleon Bonaparte with the Directory, the Ministry, &c. Paris, 1819. 7 vols. 8vo.)

[3] James Harris, Earl of Malmesbury, was born in 1746. In 1768, he was Secretary of Embassy ; in 1771, he was appointed Minister at Berlin ; in 1777, he went to St. Petersburg in the same capacity ; in 1783, he was sent to the Hague ; in 1788, he entered the House of Lords. After his missions to France, he retired to private life. He died in 1820.

[4] As early as 1796, Pitt had made overtures of peace, and sent Malmesbury to Paris. The negotiations were broken off on December 19, 1796. In the following

Such were the relations of France with foreign countries when I joined the ministry.

At home a faction was plotting the overthrow of the existing order of things, to replace it by what? Nobody ever knew or ever will know; for this faction was not numerous, and was composed of Republicans and of former members of the Constituent Assembly and of the National Convention, who may have been united by common hatred, but who could certainly not work any plan together.

At any rate, what soon became evident was the weakness of this faction, easily overcome, and whose real or pretended leaders were, in the course of a few hours, arrested for the most part, charged with plotting against the established government, convicted without being heard, and transported to Cayenne,[1] by virtue of what was then termed a law.

Civil war continued to desolate the western provinces, where the Republicans were masters of nearly all the towns. This war,—the organizers of which handed to their families the proud title of *Vendéen*, afterwards replaced and spoilt by that of *Chouan*,—was then confined within limits beyond which some vainly endeavoured to extend it. It had become more irksome than dangerous for the government.

The words of Republic, Liberty, Equality, Fraternity, were everywhere inscribed on all the walls, but the ideas and feelings they expressed were nowhere to be met with. From the highest authorities to those of the lowest rank, there was scarcely one that was not most arbitrary in its formation, its composition and mode of action. All was done with violence, and, as a natural consequence, nothing could last.

The young general Bonaparte, who, for the last two years, shone so brilliantly on the stage of the world, refused to be swamped amongst the crowd of single generals; he wanted to hear his name bruited abroad more yet, and to continue to attract all looks upon himself. Besides, he feared a situation in

year, Malmesbury returned to Lille (July 4), and began fresh negotiations, which, however, also failed.

¹ This was the *coup d'état* of Fructidor 18, year V. (September 4, 1797), made by the Directory with the assistance of the army against the Councils, where the elections of the previous May had sent an anti-revolutionist majority. The greater portion of these elections were quashed, and sixty-five Deputies transported to Cayenne.

which he would be defenceless against the very dangers to which his fame might give birth. Ambitious enough to wish to be head of all, he was yet not so blind as to think this possible for him in France, at least not without a concurrence of events which, at that time, could not be regarded as close at hand, or even as probable.

England in the time of Cromwell had but one army. Cromwell, who had selected all its officers, had only his own creatures among them. Outside the army he had no rival in fame. Two hours' fanaticism, skilfully employed, sufficed to put the troops into the state of mind he wished. Finally, the Long Parliament, which had concentrated all power within itself, had played its part;[1] all parties had grown tired of its tyranny ; they all desired its overthrow.

These circumstances were all lacking in Bonaparte's case. But if he had not yet the chance of ruling, as Cromwell, in his own country, it was, on the other hand, not impossible that he might cut out for himself a sovereignty elsewhere, provided France first furnished him with the means.

After having signed the peace with Austria at Campo-Formio, and paid a short visit to Rastadt, the place agreed upon with the empire[2] for treating of the peace (for, after the example of the old Romans, the French Republic had adopted the principle of never comprising two of its enemies into the same peace), he went to Paris to propose the conquest of Egypt to the Directory.

I had never seen him. At the time of my nomination to the Ministry of Foreign Affairs he had written to me, as I have already mentioned, a long letter, carefully compiled, in which he wished to appear under a different character from that which he had hitherto played on the stage of public life. This letter is

---

[1] The Long Parliament is the name given in England to the last Parliament convened by Charles I. Having assembled in 1640, it lasted more than twenty years. In 1648, Cromwell dismissed all members who were hostile to his own policy, and in 1653, he dissolved it. Recalled in 1659, and nicknamed *The Rump.* This Parliament broke up in 1660.

[2] Since the treaty of Campo-Formio, a congress had met at Rastadt (Grand Duchy of Baden) to regulate the questions still under discussion (navigation of the Rhine, indemnities to dispossessed princes, &c.). Reassembled at the beginning of 1798, it was suddenly interrupted by war at the beginning of the following year.

sufficiently interesting to make one wish it to be inserted at the end of these *Memoirs*.[1] The evening of the day on which he arrived in Paris, he sent me an aide-de-camp to ask at what hour he could see me. I replied that I awaited his leisure ; he fixed the next day at eleven a.m. I informed Madame de Staël of this ; she was in my drawing-room at ten o'clock. There were also some other persons whom curiosity had attracted thither. I remember that Bougainville [2] was there. The general was announced, and I went to meet him. While crossing the room, I introduced Madame de Staël to him, but he bestowed very little attention upon her. Bougainville was the only one whom he condescended to notice, and to whom he paid a few compliments.

At first sight, he seemed to me to have a charming face ; so much do the halo of victory, fine eyes, a pale and almost consumptive look, become a young hero. We entered my study. Our first conversation was full of confidence on his part. He dwelt in kind terms on my appointment as Foreign Secretary, and insisted on the pleasure it afforded him to correspond with a person of a different stamp from that of the directors. Almost abruptly he said to me, " You are the nephew of the Archbishop of Rheims, who is with Louis XVIII." (I noticed that he did not then say with the Comte de Lille [3]) ; and he added, " I *also* have an uncle who is an archdeacon in Corsica,[4] it was he who brought me up. In Corsica, you know, an archdeacon is like a bishop in France." We soon returned to the drawing-room which had become filled with visitors, and he said in a loud voice : " Citizens, I appreciate the attentions paid to me ; I

[1] This letter has not been found among the papers of the Prince de Talleyrand.
[2] Louis Antoine de Bougainville, born in 1729, was at first secretary of embassy, and afterwards an officer of Dragoons. He was thirty-four years old when he entered the navy. In 1766, he undertook round the world a voyage which lasted three years. He left the navy in 1790, entered the Institute (1796), was made a senator under the empire, and died in 1814.
[3] That was the name adopted by Louis XVIII. during the emigration.
[4] Joseph Fesch, born in 1763, at Ajaccio. He was, in 1789, archdeacon of the chapter of that town. Having protested againt the civil constitution of the clergy, he retired from the chapter, put aside his ecclesiastical functions, and became *commissaire des guerres* to the army of Italy (1795). After the 18th of Brumaire, Fesch resumed his ecclesiastical duties, became Archbishop of Lyons (1802) ; cardinal, and was sent as envoy extraordinary to Rome (1804). He was recalled in 1808. Peer of France during the Hundred Days, he retired to Rome at the Restoration and died in 1809.

waged war as well as I could, and as well as I could, made peace. It now rests with the Directory to turn the latter to the happiness and prosperity of the Republic." We then went together to the Directory.

The hesitations and jealousy of the Directory caused a certain annoyance to Bonaparte during the first weeks of his stay in Paris. I gave a fête to celebrate his victories in Italy and the glorious peace he had signed. I spared no trouble to make it brilliant and attractive ; although in this, I experienced some difficulty on account of the vulgarity of the directors' wives, who of course enjoyed precedence over all other ladies. My apartments had been decorated as tastefully as possible, and everybody congratulated me.

"*All this must have cost you a lot, Citizen Minister ?*" Madame Merlin,[1] the wife of the director, said to me.

"*Not a fortune, Madam,*" I replied, in the same tone.

The next day numerous other jokes, most of which were quite authentic, were going their round in Paris.

The Directory were then contemplating an expedition to Ireland[2] ; its command, at first intended for Hoche,[3] who died in the meantime, was afterwards offered to General Bonaparte, but it did not suit his views. This expedition, whether a success or a failure, could evidently not last long, so that the young general would, on his return, have found himself exactly in the same situation as he actually was. The army he would have led to Ireland he could not have used as a tool to further his own projects ; and, besides, he could have had no hope of establishing himself firmly in that country.

Nor did he think of obtaining supreme power in Egypt, nor indeed in any country he might have conquered with a French

---

[1] Merlin de Douay (1754-1838), former member of the Constituent Assembly and of the Convention. In 1795, he became Minister of Justice, then Minister of General Police, and finally a director after the 18th of Fructidor ; he was chief president of the Court of Cassation, under the Empire.

[2] The Directory intending to attack England at home, Ireland seemed to offer a propitious field of operations ; a rising of her inhabitants might be expected. A first attempt to land troops on that island had failed in January 1797. A second expedition started in August. General Humbert landed with 1,100 men in the bay of Sligo, was victorious at Killala and at Castlebar, but was defeated at Ballinamuck and obliged to surrender.

[3] Hoche died suddenly, September 18, 1797. He was then commander-in-chief of the armies of "Sambre-et-Meuse" and of "Rhin-et-Moselle."

army. He did not yet anticipate that his army would be satisfied with achieving victories that would only benefit him, and consent to letting him take a crown, and still less placing it on his head. The more so, that the troops over which he possessed most command, and which, for this very reason, he most wished to take with him, were composed of the very men with whom he had just been campaigning in Italy, and whose republican fanaticism he had himself aroused and carefully kept up. All he expected from them was that they should enable him to appear in the eyes of the Christians of the East and of all Greeks, as a liberator ready to break their fetters ; as for the ultimate realization of his ambitious dreams, he trusted to the number, the energy and gratitude of these same Greeks, but above all to some unforeseen chance. Such hopes, if they could have been suspected, would not have been likely to promote the success of his negotiation with the Directory. He therefore affected to have but one aim in view—to further the interests of France. He spoke of Egypt as of a colony alone worth all the colonies France had lost, and whence deadly blows could be struck at the English power in India. He sometimes, however, allowed his impetuous imagination and natural loquacity to carry him beyond the limits of prudence, and talked of returning to Europe by way of Constantinople, which was not exactly the road to India ; so that it did not require much penetration to guess that if ever he took Constantinople, the result of his victory would not be to consolidate the throne of the successor of the Kalifs or to substitute a *republic one and indivisible to* the Ottoman Empire.

Yet the Directory were so struck with the importance of getting rid of a man who caused them such umbrage and whom they felt powerless to keep in check, that they eventually yielded to Bonaparte, agreed that an expedition should be sent to Egypt, appointed him to the command of the troops composing the expedition, and thus paved the way for events they were most anxious to prevent.

I must state here succinctly what was the situation of Europe towards France at the time of Bonaparte's departure.

The Empress Catherine of Russia had been the first to

declare against the French Revolution, but all her policy had been limited to making her opinions publicly known by means of despatches which her ministers were instructed to show in the different courts to which they were accredited. I saw a great number of these letters in the hands of the Prince of Nassau.[1] She had carefully abstained from joining in a war, the result of which was necessarily to weaken her neighbours and, as a matter of course, to increase her relative power. Having no fear that French principles should contaminate her subjects, but justly afraid of the efforts made by Poland to shake off her anarchy, she had taken advantage of the moment when France, Prussia, and Austria were fighting together to plot the dismemberment of that kingdom, a portion of which she had already added to her dominions, leaving the rest to Austria and Prussia.[2] She died soon after (November 17, 1796).

It is impossible to tell what her successor, Paul I., who had inherited the disease of his father, Peter III.,[3] would have done, but for the invasion of Egypt by France. At any rate, this invasion became for him a decisive and peremptory pretext.

Since the time of Peter I., Russia had never ceased to consider European Turkey as a prey which was eventually to fall to her, which she was to absorb gradually, being unable to do so all at once. This prey would have slipped from her for ever if, through a revolution, Greece had recovered her independence ; and the invasion of Egypt not only caused Russia to fear this revolution, but pointed out to it as being inevitable.

Paul I., instead of the natural enemy of the Turks, at once became their ally ; he entered into a league with England. Austria joined them all the more readily that she had laid down her arms against her will, and that, since the peace of Campo-Formio, France had caused her much justifiable alarm.

---

[1] The Prince Otto von Nassau-Siegen, born in 1745, accompanied Bougainville on his voyage round the world (1766–1769). On his return, he took service in France, went afterwards to Spain, where the title of grandee and the rank of general were conferred on him. In 1787, he went to Russia, was appointed head of a naval squadron, and entrusted with sundry diplomatic missions to Vienna, Versailles and Madrid. Vice-admiral in 1790, he was defeated by King Gustavus III. He then retired to private life, came to Paris in 1802, and died in 1809.

[2] This was the third and final dismemberment of Poland (February 11, 1795).

[3] Through debauchery and excesses of all kinds, Peter III. had brought on himself epileptic fits.—(*Translator.*)

Some dispute which had arisen between the Vaudois and the senate of Bern, their sovereign, afforded a pretext to the Directory for sending troops to Switzerland, to both places at once, and change the confederation into a *republic one and indivisible*.[1]

Under some other pretexts the Papal States had been invaded by French troops, the Pope Pius VI. taken as a prisoner to the Chartreux convent of Florence, and thence to Valence, in Dauphiny, where he died ; his government replaced by what was then called a *republican* administration.[2]

The King of Naples, justly afraid, but whom prudence should have advised to keep quiet and bide his time, having rashly, and against the advice of the court of Vienna, begun hostilities with inexperienced and undisciplined troops, had to take refuge in Sicily, abandoning his kingdom of Naples, which the French Directory soon transformed into a Partheno-pean republic.[3]

The Directory could then, if they had wished it, have made of Italy a bulwark for France by forming but one single state with the former fine country. But, far from doing so, they felt much provoked on learning that the fusion of the new republics into one was secretly prepared in Italy, and they opposed this fusion with all their might. They wanted republics which made them odious to monarchies, but they wanted only small and weak republics, in order to occupy militarily their territories under the guise of protecting them, but in reality to rule them and feed their troops at their expense, which made them odious to these very republics.

All these upheavals taking place in the immediate neigh-

---

[1] The Swiss cantons were not all then independent as to-day The canton of Vaud, for instance, was subject to the authority of Bern. It rose in insurrection against the latter and was crushed. Many Vaudois then took refuge in France. They all pretended that Switzerland was in the hands of the Federalist party, which was itself serving the ends of Austria, and solicited the intervention of the Directory. Switzerland was invaded (February 1798), and the republic of Leman proclaimed with a constitution similar to that of France.

[2] On December 27, 1797, a riot had broken out in Rome, General Duphot had been killed in the course of it. On February 10 following, General Berthier became master of the town. Five days later, the Roman republic was proclaimed by a popular vote, at the instigation of the Directory.

[3] January 1799. Ferdinand IV., son of Charles III., King of Spain, was then reigning at Naples. He had married Marie-Caroline, daughter of the Empress Maria-Theresa.

hood of Austria, modified too much her relative situation for her to witness them peaceably.

Her first object in taking up arms again was to break off the negotiations of Rastadt : in this she succeeded ; but it is unfortunate for her that to this rupture of negotiations should have been added the assassination of the French plenipotentiaries.[1] After this event it was but natural to expect a furious renewal of hostilities.

The Directory were not wanting in soldiers to wage the war ; but, since the proscription of Carnot (Fructidor 18), they had no one capable of directing the military operations ; and of all their renowned generals, Moreau[2] alone was in France. But he was accused, if not of having been implicated in the anti-revolutionary plans of his friend Pichegru,[3] at least of having known them, and of having only disclosed them when too late. For this reason, he was so much in disfavour with the republicans, that the Directory would not have dared to entrust him with a command however much inclined they might have felt to do so. By authorizing Moreau to enlist as a simple

---

[1] Roberjot, Bonnier and Debry : the latter was the only one to survive his wounds.

[2] Victor Moreau, born at Morlaix in 1763, was in 1787, prevost of the school of law. He took service as a volunteer in 1792, became general in the following year and commanded successively the army of the Rhine (1796), the army of Italy (1799), and again the army of the Rhine (1800). He was very hostile to the First Consul ; he was implicated in the conspiracy of Georges Cadoudal,* arrested, tried and sentenced to two years' imprisonment. Bonaparte commuted this sentence into banishment. In 1813, Moreau returned from America, where he had been residing, served in the Russian army as field-marshal, and was mortally wounded at Dresden August 25.

[3] Charles Pichegru (1761–1804) was a non-commissioned officer of artillery in 1789. In 1793, he was appointed general commander-in-chief of the army of the Rhine, took the command of the army of the North in 1794, and conquered Holland. He allowed himself to give way to the solicitations of the royalist party, and plotted with the chiefs of Condé's army. Having aroused the suspicions of the Directory, he lost his command in 1796. Having been elected, in 1797, a member of the *Conseil des Cinq-Cents*, he became the leader of the anti-revolutionary party, which, on Fructidor 18, led to his arrest and transportation to Guyana. He managed to escape, however, a short time after, reached England, joined in Cadoudal's conspiracy in 1803, was arrested in Paris and strangled himself in his prison.

* Georges Cadoudal, one of the most famous and gallant leaders of the royalist rising, known under the name of *Chouannerie*, was born at Kerléano near Auray, in Morbihan (Brittany). His father was a small landowner and had him brought up at the college of Vannes. A fervent Catholic and loyal royalist, Cadoudal was the first to organize the insurrection in Vendée, in 1793. Though often crushed by the Republican troops, he always managed to escape, soon to appear again elsewhere at the head of his followers, until at last General Brune annihilated them completely at the battle of Grand-Champ, January 26, 1800. Bonaparte, admiring Cadoudal's indomitable energy and courage, sent him a safe-conduct and had him summoned to his presence, when he endeavoured to win him over. But Cadoudal declined every offer, although he bound himself not to take up arms again. Having been implicated in the plot of December 1800, when Bonaparte miraculously escaped the explosion of an infernal machine in the Rue St. Nicaise, Cadoudal was arrested with many of his accomplices and executed June 10, 1804.—(*Translator.*)

volunteer in the army of Italy, they considered they had done much.

The presence of Moreau at the army of Italy did not prevent it being thoroughly beaten and routed at the very beginning of the action. Macdonald,[1] who was coming up from the heart of Italy with thirty-five thousand men, in order to reinforce it, was crushed at *Trebia*.[2]

All these sham republics raised by the Directory, vanished as soon as reverse befell French arms, and, but for the precaution previously taken by the Directory to retain in trust all the fortresses in Piedmont, all the French troops would have had to evacuate Italy. By rallying in and around these places the scattered remnants of the armies of the Republic, Moreau succeeded in stopping the progress of the enemy.

When the Directory revolutionized Switzerland, they did not suspect that they were re-opening an inlet, closed for centuries, by which foreigners were one day to enter France, and bring about thither the great change so much dreaded by the revolutionists. The Directory must even have experienced it themselves, but for the blunder of the Archduke Charles,[3] who evacuated Switzerland in order to besiege Philipsburg in vain, and only left behind him a body of Russian troops, thus enabling Masséna to win the victory of Zurich,[4] which was all the more extolled in Paris, that it was indispensable to the safety of France.

The Directory shared the fate of all despots. So long as their armies were victorious, people hated their rule but feared their power. But as soon as the hour of defeat came, that government met with universal contempt. The press attacked it, lampoon-writers held it up to ridicule, everybody denounced it.

---

[1] Alexandre Macdonald (1765-1840), was born of Irish parents, took service in Dillon's Irish troops, became general of division in 1795, governor of the Papal States in 1798. He fell out of favour in 1804, again took service in 1809, became marshal of France and Duc de Tarente after the victory of Wagram. In 1814, he became a member of the House of Peers, and high-chancellor of the Legion of Honour in 1816.

[2] June 17, 18, and 19, 1799.

[3] The Archduke Charles was born in 1771 ; he was the son of the Emperor Leopold. He became field-marshal of the German empire in 1795, and Minister of War in 1802. Generalissimo of the Austrian armies in 1805 and 1809, the Archduke Charles was one of the first captains of his time, and the most formidable of Napoleon's adversaries. He died in 1847.

[4] Masséna was then commander-in-chief of the army of Helvetia. The battle of Zurich, where the Russian army was destroyed, was fought on August 26, 1799.

Naturally, the members of the ministry were not spared ; this offered the opportunity I was looking for of resigning my post. I had then ascertained that what little evil I could prevent was but insignificant, and that, only later, could any real good be worked.

The intention I had had for a long time of resigning had induced me to take certain precautions. I had acquainted General Bonaparte with my resolution before his departure for Egypt ; he fully approved the reasons which had led me to take it, and kindly used his influence with the directors to solicit for me the appointment of ambassador to Constantinople, in the event of it being possible to come to some understanding with the Porte, or else the authorization of joining him at Cairo, where, there was reason to believe, negotiations might have to be opened with the agents of the Sultan.[1] Having obtained that authorization, I sent in my resignation, and retired to the country, near Paris, whence I watched the course of events.[2]

The staunch demagogues, who had, for some time past, resumed an alarming attitude, agitated, and threatened to bring about a new Reign of Terror. But their clubs, which they had re-opened, and which Fouché[3] closed as soon as he deemed it advisable, were not to cause the overthrow of the Directory : the Directory fell by the fault of its own members.

Siéyès was envoy extraordinary and plenipotentiary minister of the Republic in Berlin, when he was elected a member of the Directory. His return to Paris was awaited with such impatience that the time he required to take leave of the Prussian court, start on the journey and reach the capital seemed intolerably long to his colleagues of the government. They credited him with possessing infallible means to remedy the critical situation of France at home and abroad. He had scarcely alighted than

---

[1] This is what Napoleon said subsequently, concerning his relations with Talleyrand, before his departure for Egypt : "It had been agreed with the Directory and Talleyrand, that immediately after the departure of the expedition sent to Egypt, negotiations should be opened with the Porte concerning the object of this expedition. Talleyrand was even to be the negotiator *and to start for Constantinople twenty-four hours after the expeditionary corps to Egypt had left the port of Toulon.* This promise, expressly claimed and positively given, had been forgotten, not only did Talleyrand remain in Paris, but no negotiation took place." (*Mémoires de Napoléon dictés à Saint-Hélène au général Gourgaud,* vol. i., p. 62.)

[2] July 20, 1799.

[3] Fouché had been appointed minister of police, on Barras' motion.

everybody begged of him to divulge those means. The most influential among the members of both assemblies[1] assured him that he had but to speak, and that, in all in which they can help him, they will strongly assist him. Before proposing anything, Siéyès desired to see everything with his own eyes, to examine and to ponder. The result of his investigations was that nothing useful could be accomplished with the colleagues he had. There and then three of them were removed. Among their successors two were but regular ciphers, the third was devoted to him.[2] Siéyès then no longer complained of the men, it was, he urged, absolutely necessary to modify the institutions. Five rulers were too many ; three would be sufficient. The name of Directory had become hateful ; it must be replaced by some other appellation. It was, above all things, indispensable that the government should comprise among its members a military man possessing the confidence of the army, as unless a government be supported by the army, it is powerless to do any good.

Moreau, having been sounded as to whether he would accept the post of member of the government, declined all but military functions. General Joubert was then thought of, and, in order to enable him to win the desirable fame he did not yet possess, he was sent to Italy with a command. On arriving, he fought imprudently the battle of Novi,[3] and was killed at the beginning of the action, thus causing all the hopes built on him to vanish. The situation remained as intricate as ever, and goodness knows how matters would have ended, but for an event which the Directory least expected.

After the conquest of Egypt, Bonaparte had followed up the execution of his plans by attempting that of Syria. But Acre stopped his progress. Although he had lost all his siege guns, captured by English cruisers, on the way from Egypt to Syria, he insisted on attacking the Turkish stronghold. After furiously

[1] The *Conseils des Anciens* (Council of the Elders) and the *Conseil des Cinq Cents* (Council of the Five Hundred).—(*Translator.*)
[2] This change of directors constituted what is known in history as the *coup d'état* of Prairial 30 (May 1799), aimed by the assemblies against the Directory. Director Treilhard was removed, and Gohier appointed in his stead. Lareveillère-Lépeaux and Merlin were called upon to resign, being replaced by Moulins and Roger Ducos. The latter was entirely devoted to Siéyès.
[3] August 15, 1799.

storming the place three times, he was, however, compelled to withdraw and bring his troops back to Egypt, where the English threatened to land. His magnificent hopes were thus vanishing ; that even of holding his own in Egypt was becoming anything but certain. He was haunted by the fearful apprehension of being reduced to leave the country only through a capitulation, which would have left him the reputation of being but an adventurer. Fortunately, the vicissitudes of the French arms in Italy relieved him from his perplexity, by giving him the rashness of doing what otherwise he never would have dared to attempt. Without any authority to do so, he handed his command to Kleber, left Egypt, escaped from English cruisers, and landed at Fréjus.[1]

As anticipated by him, the political parties of France saw in him not a man who was to account for his conduct, but one whom circumstances rendered indispensable, and whose favour it was necessary to win.

At first, some people thought that Barras, the author of Bonaparte's fortune, who of all former directors was the only one still in office, was so far mistaken in his judgment of the young general and had so much overrated his own influence over him, as to flatter himself that he could induce him to play the part of a Monk ; but Bonaparte who, even if he had been able to do so, would have declined it, was really not at that time in a position to play such a part.

He could not, therefore, hesitate long, between such a proposal, supposing it was made to him, and the offer not exactly of supreme power, but of a position that enabled him to aspire to it.

A great number of his supporters would doubtless have preferred to see him appointed simply a member of the Directory, but matters had reached such a point, that everybody was obliged to be satisfied with whatever Bonaparte might wish, and the very nature of things made him master of the situation. As a director, he could not have carried out his ambitious designs.

It was therefore agreed that the Directory should be replaced by three provisory consuls who, with the assistance of two committees from the *conseils*, would have to draft a new consti-

[1] October 9, 1799.

tution to be submitted to the approval of the primary assemblies, for the sovereignty of the people was a dogma which nobody was, then, dreaming of putting into question.[1]

This plan having been arranged, the council of elders, according to the rights conferred on them by the constitution, and under the pretext of the excitement existing in Paris, transferred the seat of the legislature to St. Cloud. By so doing, it was hoped to check all obstacles to the measures that had been concerted. The two most influential members of the Directory (Siéyès and Barras), the majority of the council of the elders and a portion of the council of the Five Hundred, were in favour of this step. On Brumaire 18 (November 9, 1799), the Directorial guards under the command of Augereau, who had been appointed to it since Fructidor 18, a host of general officers and other military men of all ranks, as also a few sightseers, amongst whom I was, repaired to St. Cloud, in order to attend the sitting.

Notwithstanding this display of force, the council of the

[1] A few days before Brumaire 18, my house was the scene of an incident, the whole interest of which lies in the circumstances that attended it. General Bonaparte, who was then residing in the rue Chantereine,* called on me, one evening, to talk about the preliminaries of his intended *coup d'état.* I was then living in a house in the rue Taitbout, which, I believe, has since been known as number 24. It was situated at the back of a yard, and, the first floor of it communicated with rooms overlooking the street. We were engrossed in conversation in the drawing-room which was lighted by a few candles ; when, at about one o'clock in the morning, we heard a great noise in the street ; it sounded like the riding of carriages and the stamping of horses, such as might be produced by an escort of cavalry. Suddenly the carriages stopped in front of my house. General Bonaparte turned pale, and I quite believe I did the same. We at once thought that people had come to arrest us by order of the Directory. I blew out the candles, and went on tiptoe, to one of the front rooms whence I could see what was going on in the street. Some time elapsed before I could ascertain the real cause of all this uproar, which, however, turned out to be simply grotesque. As in those days, the streets of Paris were hardly safe at night, all the money of gambling-houses was collected, at closing-time, and removed in cabs, for which, in this case the proprietor had obtained from the police that an escort of *gendarmes,* which he himself paid, should, every night, accompany the cabs as far as his residence which was in the rue de Clichy, or thereabout. On the night in question, one of these cabs had met with an accident exactly in front of my door, thus causing the whole party to stop on their way for about a quarter of an hour. We laughed a good deal, the general and I, at our panic, which however was but natural on the part of people acquainted as we were with the disposition of the Directory, and the violent measures they were capable of resorting to.—(*Prince Talleyrand.*)

* In 1680, it was but a small lane known under the name of " Ruellette aux marais des Porcherons " (Little lane of the swineherds' swamp). In 1734, it was called " Ruelle des postes," changed afterwards to that of "rue Chantereine." There, Bonaparte possessed a residence, where he came to live on re-entering France, after the treaty of Campo-Formio. From this circumstance, that street received the name of " rue de la Victoire." In 1816, it resumed its former name of rue Chantereine, and in 1832, it reassumed the name of rue de la Victoire, which it preserves to this day. It is situated not far from the Opera.—(*Translator.*)

Five Hundred offered such opposition to the proposed modification of the constitution, as to jeopardize the execution of the plan in view, although its object was merely to substitute one form of *polygarchy* for another (I am always obliged to make use of this barbaric expression, for want of any equivalent). Thus it is easy to imagine what would have happened to him who had manifested any desire to play the part of Monk ; he would have had against him nearly all the men to whom the success of the *coup d'état* of Brumaire 18 was, more or less, due.

At last, both persuasion and threats having been brought to bear, the motion was carried. The Directory was dissolved, Siéyès, Roger Ducos,[1] and Bonaparte were appointed consuls, and the committees who were to draft the project of constitution were all that remained of the Councils. Ten or twelve days later, I again became Foreign Secretary.

The overthrow of the Directory could not fail to please, or at least, be indifferent to all the foreign powers friendly with France. There being no reason to fear any modification in their disposition, no special steps were needed to inform them of the change of government. As for hostile powers, the only hope of altering their attitude towards France lay in fresh victories. Though no negotiations had to be carried on abroad, yet at home a most important and delicate negotiation was being proceeded with, and although I had nothing to do with it in an official capacity, it could not be either foreign or indifferent to me.

It became necessary either to re-establish monarchy or else to have made the 18 Brumaire in vain, thus postponing to an uncertain and perhaps indefinite date the hope of a restoration of monarchical institutions. Re-establishing monarchy did not mean raising the throne again. Monarchy has three degrees or forms : it is elective for a time, elective for life, or hereditary. What is called the throne cannot belong to the first of these three forms, and does not necessarily belong to the second. Now, to reach the

---

[1] The Comte Roger Ducos, born in 1754, had been a member of the National Convention, where he voted for the death of the king. He was elected a member of the Council of the Elders, of which he became the president in 1796. On Prairial 30, he was appointed one of the Directors. On Brumaire 18, he gave active support to Bonaparte, became a consul *pro tempore*, and was appointed a senator under the empire, in 1814 ; he was appointed a peer of France, during the Hundred Days, was exiled in 1815, and died at Ulm in 1816.

third, without passing successively by the two others, unless
France were in the power of foreign forces, was a thing absolutely impossible. It might, it is true, not have been so, if Louis
XVI. had lived, but the murder of that prince had put an insur-
mountable obstacle in the way

The passing from polygarchy to hereditary monarchy could not
be immediate, the result being, as a necessary consequence, that
the re-establishment of the latter and the re-establishment of the
house of Bourbon could not be simultaneous. Thus it was
indispensable to pave the way for the restoration of monarchical
institutions without having regard for the special interests of
the house of Bourbon, which time might bring back, if it so
happened that he who was to occupy the throne proved himself
unworthy and deserved to lose it. It was necessary to make a
temporary sovereign who might become sovereign for life, and
eventually hereditary monarch. The question was not whether
Bonaparte had the qualities most desirable in a monarch ; he
had unquestionably those which were indispensable to again
accustom France to monarchical discipline, as she was still
infatuated with every revolutionary doctrine ; and no one
possessed those qualities in the same degree as he did.

The real point was how could Bonaparte be made a temporary
sovereign ? If one proposed to appoint him sole consul, one
betrayed views which could not be concealed with too much
care. If, on the other hand, one gave him colleagues equal to
him in rank and power, one remained in polygarchy.

They remained in polygarchy if they established a legislative
body, either permanent, or which was to sit at fixed dates without
previous summons, and to prorogue itself. If this body, though
divided into two distinct assemblies, could alone make the
laws, they remained in polygarchy. In short, they remained in
polygarchy if the high officials, and chiefly the judges, were to
continue to be named by the electoral assemblies. The problem
to be solved was, as may be seen, very intricate, and bristling
with so many difficulties that it was almost impossible to avoid
arbitrary measures ; and they were not avoided.

Three consuls were created, a first, a second, and a third
consul, unequal in rank, and whose respective duties were such

that, with some interpretations (that Bonaparte knew better than any one how to give when his own power was at stake), the First Consul was almost alone invested, by that very fact, with the share of authority which, in limited or constitutional monarchies, is in the hands of the sovereign. The only essential difference was, that, instead of limiting his power to the sanction of the laws, he was also entrusted with proposing them, a plurality of power which proved fatal to himself.

In order to render the power of the First Consul still more effective, I made, on the very day of his installation, a proposition which he readily accepted. The three consuls were to meet every day, and the ministers were to acquaint them with the affairs of their respective departments. I pointed out to General Bonaparte the fact that all matters connected with foreign affairs, being essentially secret, should not be discussed in council, and that it was necessary that he should himself alone decide all questions of foreign policy, which the head of a government should have entirely in his hands and manage. He fully grasped the utility of that advice ; and as, when organizing a new government, everything is easier to settle, it was agreed, from the very first day, that I should work only with the First Consul.

The first act of General Bonaparte, in quality of First Consul, was to write to the King of England a letter in which he expressed the wish for a prompt reconciliation between the two countries. He made a similar advance to the Emperor of Austria. These two attempts led to no reconciliation, and could not lead to any, but they had a happy effect upon the internal peace of the country, because they announced dispositions which ought to be agreeable to the people, in revealing as a skilful statesman the great general who had become the head of the government This done, the refusal of the two cabinets being well proved by a failure to reply to those letters, which were not even honoured with an acknowledgment,[1] Bonaparte no longer thought of anything but taking measures to go to meet the enemy on a field of battle, where he was to find none but Austrians.

Paul I., discontented with Austria, by whom he believed him-

---

[1] Lord Grenville and Herr von Thugut both replied to M. de Talleyrand to reject the propositions of the First Consul.

self to have been betrayed,[1] had recalled his troops from Germany. The First Consul, availing himself of this circumstance, collected the few Russian prisoners who were in France, had them newly clothed, and sent home without ransom. He directed one of the officers who commanded them to offer to the Emperor Paul the sword of La Valette found at Malta. It is known that the Emperor of Russia had taken the order of Malta under his special protection.[2] Touched by these delicate proceedings, the Emperor Paul, who got easily prejudiced, directed General von Sprengtporten,[3] to make overtures of peace to France ; these overtures were followed up by M. de Kalitcheff, and led to a definite treaty, which I negotiated and signed with M. de Markoff.[4]

[1] Souwaroff had just conquered Piedmont, and, by the orders of his master, had written to the King of Sardinia to invite him to return to his possessions. Austria, which coveted Northern Italy, was stirred by that measure, and the Aulic Council, which had the direction of the military operations, rid themselves of this troublesome ally by sending him to Switzerland. The Russian army suffered cruelly in crossing the Alps, and was destroyed at Zurich. The Emperor Paul and Souwaroff were much irritated against the Austrians, whom they accused of being the cause of this disaster, and the Russian troops were recalled.

[2] The intervention of the Czar Paul in the affairs of the order of Malta is one of the singularities of the history of that time. The relations between the two powers date from 1795. The order possessed great wealth in Poland. This wealth being included in the territories fallen to Russia after the division of 1795, the Grand-Master, Prince de Rohan, endeavoured to negotiate an arrangement with Catherine. The Emperor Paul, having in the meantime ascended the throne, took the affair to heart, entered into relations with Malta, and was inflamed with a lively admiration for the old and glorious traditions of the Knights of St. John. On January 4, 1797, there was signed an instrument by the terms of which the possessions of the order in Poland were transferred to the grand priory of Russia. Seventy-two commanderies were created in one year. The Czar and his son became Knights of Malta. After the taking of the island by the French, the Czar, on the request of the grand priory declared himself protector of the order (September 1798), and two months after, the place of Grand Master having become vacant, a fraction of the order had the idea of offering it to the Czar. Paul solemnly accepted this new dignity. Bonaparte profited skilfully by these circumstances to conciliate Russia, and to detach it from Germany. It was then that he sent to the Czar the sword of La Valette, the Grand Master, found at Malta ; or, according to another authority, the sword of the Grand Master Villiers de l'Ile-Adam, that Leo X. had given to that illustrious warrior as a remembrance of his fine defence of Rhodes. When Malta was taken by the English, Paul claimed it in quality of Grand Master (September 1800). But the English refused formally to cede this important post, and a rupture ensued. The death of Paul (March 1801) terminated this curious episode. His successor, Alexander, did not claim the island, and the matter ended there. (Consult the *Memoirs* of Abbé Georgel.)

[3] Baron Joram von Sprengtporten, a Swedish general, and one of the authors of the Revolution of 1772, passed afterwards into the service of Russia. He became governor of Finland, after the conquest of that country by Russia, and died in oblivion.

[4] October 8, 1801. Arcadi Ivanovitch, Count Markoff, was, under the reign of Catherine, first counsellor of foreign affairs. Having fallen into disgrace under Paul I., he was recalled by Alexander, and appointed ambassador at Paris in 1801. He incurred the enmity of Bonaparte, who demanded and obtained his removal. On

M. de Markoff had made his first appearance in public life under the reign of the Empress Catherine, and had been sent later to Paris, as one of the most skilful business men of Russia. He appeared to me a bad-tempered man, without instruction, but witty. His temper bore then upon his own government, which is very convenient for the minister of foreign affairs of another country. While the Emperor Paul lived, business relations were easy and agreeable, but, at the accession of the Emperor Alexander, M. de Markoff became arrogant and insupportable. It was with him that I treated the important matter of the secularizations in Germany.[1]

Carnot, member of the Directory, having escaped from Cayenne, where he had been so cruelly exiled, with so many others, on Fructidor 18, had for some time been holding the post of minister of war. His first care, on taking office, was to assemble two armies, one on the Rhine, the other at the foot of the Alps. General Moreau had the command of the first ; Bonaparte with the second rushes upon Italy by a new route, and, without losing a cannon, crosses Great St. Bernard, May 20, 1800. He falls, without warning, upon the Austrians, and, after several fortunate encounters, he gives battle, June 14, at Marengo ; after a hard contest Fortune, aided by General Désaix,[2] and General Kellerman,[3]

his return to Russia, Markoff was often entrusted with important diplomatic missions. He died at a very advanced age.

[1] It would need a volume, and perhaps I shall make it, to give a full account of this important question. The Marquis de Lucchesini (*) has tried it, but in his work he has only occupied himself with personal justifications—a strange way of writing the history of one's times, for it rarely modifies the opinions of one's contemporaries. When one is called to settle political questions of great importance, one must leave to those whose private interests have been sacrificed to the general interest the consolation of blaming the negotiators and of calumniating them without scruple. Up to this time, that which appears to be most exact on that period is the work of Baron von Gagern (†), a man of sense, attached to the house of Nassau.—(*Talleyrand.*)
   * The Marquis Jerome de Lucchesini (1752-1825). a Prussian diplomatist, was ambassador at Paris in 1802. The work mentioned above : *Sulle cause e gli effetti della confederazione rhenana* (‡) was published anonymously in Italian (Florence, 1829).
   † The Baron Johan von Gagern (1766-1852) was minister of the Prince of Nassau at Paris, under the Consulate. He has left numerous works on history and political economy.
   ‡ Causes and Consequences of the Confederation of the Rhine.
[2] Louis-Antoine Désaix, issue of a noble family originally of Ayat, near Riom, and known before the Revolution under the name of Des Aix de Veygous. Born in 1768, Désaix was in 1789, sub-lieutenant in the Brittany regiment. He became Commissary of War in 1791, and general of division in 1794. He was intimately associated with Bonaparte, followed him into Egypt, returned to Europe after the treaty of El Arisch, and was killed at Marengo, June 14, 1800.
[3] François-Etienne Kellermann (1770-1835) was the son of the old Marshal

declares for him when even he himself no longer hoped for it.
The armistice which followed, made him again master of
Italy. Warned by the fears that he had had of a defeat, he
knew now better how to profit by his victory without abusing it.
He felt the need of strengthening his power before increasing
it, and knowing well that military glory would be his principal
title to power, he feared those victories for which France would
not be indebted to him. almost as much as the reverses he
endured himself. So he hastened to set up, by his armistice, the
basis of a new peace, in which the empire of Germany should be
comprised, which rendered almost useless the victory of Hohenlinden,[1] which had opened the road to Vienna to General Moreau.
The treaty between France and Austria stipulating for herself
and for the empire, was to be negotiated at Lunéville, and
Count Louis von Cobenzl[2] had been designated as plenipotentiary by the emperor, who had authorized him to go to Paris
before the opening of the negotiations. The court of Vienna
had chosen him because he had treated at Campo-Formio with
Bonaparte, who was then only General of the Army of Italy,
and because intimate relations had then sprung up between them
which Count von Cobenzl believed it would be easy to renew,
but which the First Consul soon caused him to forget. There
happened on this occasion a rather curious scene.

Bonaparte gave Cobenzl a first audience at nine o'clock in the
evening, at the Tuileries. He had attended personally to the
arrangement of the room in which he wished to receive the
Austrian plenipotentiary ; it was in the parlour which precedes
the king's study. He had caused to be put in the corner a
small, table in front of which he was seated ; all other seats had
been removed, there only remained sofas, which, however, were
rather far from the table. On this were papers and an inkstand

Kellerman, Duc de Valmy. He was general of brigade at Marengo, where he decided
the victory at the head of his cavalry. He became peer of France during the Hundred
Days,* was excluded from the Upper House by Louis XVIII., and did not re-enter it
until 1830.
    [1] A village of Bavaria thirty kilometres east of Munich. The victory of Moreau
over the Archduke Johan was obtained December 3, 1800.
    [2] Louis, Count von Cobenzl (1758-1808), ambassador from Austria at Copenhagen,
at Berlin and at St. Petersburg, plenipotentiary at Campo-Formio, at Rastadt and at
Lunéville. Chancellor of State and Minister of Foreign Affairs in 1802.
    * The period extending from March 20, 1815 (return from Elba), to June 28, 1815 (abdication of
Napoleon at Fontainebleau).—(Translator.)

with writing materials ; there was but one lamp ; the chandelier was not lighted. Count von Cobenzl entered : I led the way. The gloom of the room, the distance which separated the visitor from the table at which Bonaparte was sitting and whom the former barely perceived ; the kind of embarrassment resulting from these circumstances ; the attitude of Bonaparte, who rose and seated himself again ; the impossibility in which the Count was not to remain standing, set each at once in the right place, or, at least, in the place the First Consul intended each to occupy.

After the conferences held at Lunéville between Joseph Bonaparte and Count von Cobenzl, they soon signed the treaty,[1] and general peace was thus very nearly restored on the Continent.

A short time before, a convention made with the United States, signed at Mortefontaine also by Joseph Bonaparte, had terminated all the differences which existed between the French Republic and that power.[2]

England, without allies abroad, and experiencing some embarrassment within, felt herself the need of peace. The preliminaries, after some debates rather curious for all the wit displayed for and against a maritime armistice, were concluded at London between Mr. Addington[3] and M. Otto.[4] It was at Amiens, that Lord Cornwallis[5] and Joseph Bonaparte signed the definitive treaty. France, who had lost all her colonies,

[1] February 9, 1801.

[2] American commerce had greatly suffered from the measures taken by the Convention against neutrals. The United States having signed a treaty with England which gave to that power the right of confiscating all ships carrying enemies' goods (November 1794), the Convention retaliated by an identical measure, and broke off all relations with the American Cabinet. On its side, Congress annulled all past treaties with France. They were advancing towards an open rupture when Bonaparte, coming into power, abolished the decrees of the Convention. A treaty signed on September 30, 1800, smoothed all difficulties, and the relations between the two countries resumed their normal course.

[3] Henry Addington, Viscount Sidmouth, born in 1755. Member of the House of Commons in 1782. Chancellor of the Exchequer in 1801, he contributed actively to the Peace of Amiens. He retired in 1804, but re-entered office again for a short time in 1806. In 1812, he was appointed Home Minister, a post which he occupied until 1822. He died in 1844.

[4] Guillaume Otto, Comte de Mosloy (1754-1817), was minister at London in 1800. He became minister at Munich, Councillor of State, ambassador at Vienna (1809), Minister of State in 1813.

[5] Charles Cornwallis, statesman and English general, born in 1738, Member of the Chamber of Lords, 1762, Governor of India, 1786, Governor of Ireland, 1793. In 1801 he was one of the plenipotentiaries at Amiens. Again Governor of India in 1805, he died on reaching his post.

recovered them all, without having to restore anything. Perhaps her dignity may have suffered from her having left all
the burden of the compensations to the charge of Spain and
Holland, her allies, who had been engaged in the war only for
her sake and by her advice.[1] But that is a consideration made
by few people, and which never presents itself to the minds
of the multitude, accustomed to take the success of bad faith
for cleverness.

I must not omit to state that one of the articles of the treaty
of Amiens stipulated the abandonment of Malta by the English.
Bonaparte, who, by gaining possession of this island, had changed
the fate of the Mediterranean, put great stress upon having it
restored to its old masters, and could not bear to hear me say
that I would willingly have left Malta to the English, provided
the treaty had been signed by Mr. Pitt or by Mr. Fox, instead
of by Mr. Addington.

Previous to those treaties, a kind of compact or agreement
had put an end to the civil war which had broken out anew in
Vendée and the provinces of the west.

At the time of the battle of Marengo, a secret bond was
formed between Bonaparte and the Papal Court.[3] The victorious
general had held, at Milan, several conferences with an envoy
from Pius VII., elected at Venice as successor to Pius VI. : these
conferences eventually led to the *Concordat*[4] subsequently
signed at Paris by Cardinal Consalvi. This compact and its
immediate ratification reconciled France with the Holy See,
without any other opposition than that of a few military men,
very brave, be it said, but whose minds were not lofty enough
for a conception of that kind.

It was after this reconciliation with the Church, to which I
powerfully contributed, that Bonaparte obtained from the Pope

---

[1] Spain lost the island of Trinity, and Holland, Ceylon.
[2] A suspension of arms had been signed in December 1799. On January 18,
1800, M. d'Autichamp surrendered in the name of the provinces of the left bank of
the Loire. On the 20th, M. de Châtillon did the same in the name of the right
bank. In Brittany, M. de Bourmont gave himself up on January 24, and Georges
Cadoudal on the 27th, so that the whole country was soon pacified.
[3] As early as June 1800, Bonaparte had opened negotiations with the court of
Rome, through the medium of Cardinal Martiniane, Bishop of Verceil.
[4] The *Concordat* was signed on July 15, 1801. Cardinal Consalvi was the Secretary
of State to the Court of Rome.

a brief for my secularization. The brief is dated from Saint Peter's of Rome, June 29, 1802.[1] It seems to me that nothing expresses better the indulgence of Pius VII. towards myself, than what he said one day to Cardinal Consalvi, in speaking of me : " M. de Talleyrand ! ah ! ah ! may God have his soul ; as for me, I am very fond of him ! " Switzerland, whom the Directory, at the instigation of MM. La Harpe[2] and Ochs[3] wished to transform into a republic one and indivisible, had become again, as she desired, a confederation with the ancient leagues ; and this, by virtue of an act called the act of mediation, because France had served as mediator between all the old and new cantons.[4]

---

[1]   ACTE DU GOUVERNEMENT.
              ARRÊTÉ DU 2 FRUCTIDOR, AN X.

Les Consuls de la république ; vu le bref du Pape Pie VII. donné à Saint-Pierre de Rome le 29 Juin, 1802 ;
Sur le rapport du Conseiller d'Etat chargé de toutes les affaires concernant les cultes ;
Le Conseil d'Etat entendu ;
Arrêtent : Le bref du Pape Pie VII. donné à Saint-Pierre de Rome, le 29 Juin 1802, par lequel le citoyen Charles-Maurice de Talleyrand, ministre des relations extérieures de France, est rendu à la vie séculière et laïque, aura son plein et entier effet.

                         Le premier consul : BONAPARTE.
                         Le secrétaire d'Etat : H. B. MARET.*

[2] Frédéric-César de la Harpe (1754-1838), born in the Canton of Vaud, had taken an active part in the troubles which broke out in that country. Proscribed after the victory of the Canton of Bern, and obliged to take refuge in France, he brought about the intervention of the Directory ; he was named director at the time of the proclamation of the Helvetian Republic (1798).

[3] Pierre Ochs (1749-1824) was also a Swiss refugee compromised after the rising of the Canton of Vaud. He was a member of the Helvetian senate and director in 1798.

[4] The intervention of the Directory in Switzerland had only increased the disorder ; so, when in 1802, Bonaparte proposed his mediation, it was immediately accepted. All the cantons sent deputies to Paris who entered into conference with MM. Barthélémy, Fouché, and Roederer. The Act of Mediation was signed February 19, 1803. It fixed for each canton a special constitution, and organized a federal power. On October 19, following, a treaty of alliance was made between France and Switzerland.

              * ACT OF THE GOVERNMENT.
              ORDER OF FRUCTIDOR 2, YEAR X.

The Consuls of the Republic ; according to the brief of Pope Pius VII. given at Saint-Peter of Rome, on June 29, 1802 ;
In accordance with the report of the Councillor of State entrusted with all matters relative to public worship ;
After taking the advice of the Council of State ;
Order : The brief of Pope Pius VII., given at Saint-Peter of Rome on June 29, 1802, according to which citizen Charles Maurice de Talleyrand, Minister of Foreign Affairs of France, is authorized to resume secular and lay life, shall take full and entire effect.
                         The First Consul : BONAPARTE.
                         The Secretary of State : H. B. MARET.

Spain, in accordance with the clauses of the treaty of Basel, had restored Louisiana to France who, in consideration of the payment of a certain sum, ceded it to the United States (April 30, 1803). The latter kept a portion of the price as indemnity for the losses sustained by American citizens in consequence of the absurd decrees of the Convention.

The Ottoman Porte, Portugal, the Two Sicilies, had renewed their old ties of friendship and of commerce with France.[1]

The distribution of the secularized territories in Germany was being made under the double mediation of France and of Russia.[2]

It can be said without the least exaggeration, that at the time of the Peace of Amiens, France was without in possession of a power, a glory, an influence, than which the minds of the most ambitious could have desired no greater for their country ; and what rendered this situation more marvellous still was the rapidity with which it had been created. In less than two years and a half, that is to say from the 18th Brumaire (November 9, 1799), to March 25, 1802, date of the Peace of Amiens, France had passed from the humiliating depths into which the Directory had plunged it, to the first rank of Europe.

But while occupying himself with foreign affairs, Bonaparte had not neglected those at home. His incredible activity sufficed for all. He had given new regulations for the administration,

---

[1] Treaty with Turkey, June 25, 1802. With Portugal, September 20, 1801. With the Two Sicilies, March 28, 1801. These last two powers promised to close their ports to the English.

[2] Before the wars of the Revolution, the left bank of the Rhine was covered with secular and ecclesiastic principalities. The treaties of Campo-Formio and Lunéville in ceding to France all those territories had stipulated that the lay princes should be indemnified with the wealth of the secular clergy. It remained now to apply the principle. The emperor, who would have had to take this affair in hand, allowed himself to be forestalled by the First Consul, who, being solicited by several of the interested princes, was careful not to fail to profit by the occasion. He assured himself of the concurrence of Prussia, by promising that country considerable advantages (secret treaty, May 23, 1802). The Emperor Alexander, whom family alliances had united to the Houses of Bavaria, Baden, and Würtemberg, entered into his views, and declared himself the protector of the dispossessed princes (Convention of October 11, 1802). Immediately secret treaties were negotiated between France on the one side, and Würtemberg, Baden, Bavaria, Hesse-Cassel on the other, which assured their share to each of these States. Those treaties were submitted to the Diet, which adopted the whole of the plan of indemnities (decision of February 25, 1803) and the emperor, after much hesitation, ratified that decision on the 27th of the following April. (See Lefebvre, *History of the Cabinets of Europe*, vol. i. ch. vi.)

which he had made as much as possible monarchical. He had skilfully re-established order in the finances. The ministers of religion were honoured. Not satisfied with crushing the various political parties, he had sought to attach them to himself, and he had succeeded to a certain extent. To have been an *émigré*, or a Jacobin, was no longer considered a reason for exclusion. In order to further isolate Louis XVIII. and to take away from him the kingly air that a large emigration had given him, Napoleon permitted many *émigrés* to re-enter France. He bestowed appointments on many of them, and attached some to his own person. The Jacobins forgot their aversion for personal rule, and the *émigrés* were led to regret less that authority had passed into other hands.[1]

In spite of the prolonged troubles of the Revolution, industrial arts had reached a very prosperous state in France. Much capital had been attracted by them. To attain high internal prosperity, all that was now necessary was security, and the general opinion of France was that Bonaparte had given it.

Thus those who had helped in raising him to power, had reason to congratulate themselves. He had used his authority in a manner to render it useful, even to make himself loved. One could believe that he had put an end to the Revolution. In restoring power, he had become the auxiliary of all the thrones. The salutary influence it had acquired, gave the Consulate, in the eyes of Europe, the stability of an old government. Conspiracies, from one of which Bonaparte had miraculously escaped, had strengthened the sentiment felt towards him by the friends of order. Thus, when his two colleagues proposed the primary assemblies of France to name him First Consul for life, this proposition received an almost unanimous vote.[2]

The deputies of the Cisalpine Republic repaired to Lyons, in

---

[1] I remember, that one' day, as I seemed astonished at seeing some of the most shameless Jacobins of the Revolution leave the study of the First Consul, he said to me : " You do not know the Jacobins. There are two classes of them : the *sweet* and the *salt.** The one you just saw come out was a salt Jacobin ; with these, I do what I wish : no one better fit to defend all the daring acts of a new power. Sometimes it is necessary to stop them, but with a little money it is soon done. But the sweet Jacobins ! ah ! they are ungovernable. With their metaphysics they would ruin any government."—(*Talleyrand.*)

[2] August 2, 1802.

* *Les sucrés et les salés*, that is, the mild and the violent.

order to obtain from the First Consul a definitive organization
for their country.[1] Although the business which was to be
negotiated at Lyons was foreign to my duties, Bonaparte made
use of me considerably to conduct it. I was obliged to proceed
to that city in order to see the members of the deputation. In
such delicate matters he did not much rely on what was done or
said by M. Chaptal,[2] his Minister of the Interior, whom he deemed
heavy, vain, without tact, and whom he abstained from dismissing
in order not to grieve Cambacères[3] who protected him. On
arriving at Lyons, I saw M. de Melzi,[4] with whom I had been
acquainted a long time, and I unbosomed myself to him, not as to
what the First Consul desired, but as to what should be the demands of the Cisalpine Republic. In a few days, I achieved my purpose. At the moment Bonaparte entered Lyons all was prepared.
From the second day, the principal Milanese pressed him to
accept the presidency for life, and from *gratitude*, he consented
to substitute for the name of *Cisalpine Republic* that of *Kingdom
of Italy*,[5] and to name vice-president M. de Melzi, who, having

[1] The Cisalpine Republic, proclaimed in 1791, destroyed in 1799, re-established
after Marengo, had not seen its government reorganized in 1800. Bonaparte, in
conjunction with the leading men of the country, gave it a definite organization.
There were three electoral colleges, named for life : that of the great landlords, that
of the merchants, that of the men of letters and ecclesiastics—in all, 700 electors. These
elected a *Commission de Censure*, charged to name to all the bodies of the State,
namely, a *Senate* of eight members, a *Council of State*, and a *Legislative Body*, which
had the same privileges as in France. At the head of the republic were a president
and a vice-president. In January, 1802, Bonaparte summoned at Lyons a large
meeting of nearly 500 members to approve the constitution. The presidency of that
meeting was awarded to him.
[2] Antoine Chaptal, born in 1756, was already an illustrious *savant* when he
entered upon a public career. He became Councillor of State and Minister of the
Interior after the 18th Brumaire, then senator and Comte de Chanteloup, in 1804 ;
minister and peer of France during the Hundred Days. Louis XVIII. recalled him
to the Chamber of Peers in 1819. He died in 1832.
[3] Jean Jacques-Regis de Cambacères, born at Montpellier in 1753 of an old family
of magistrates. Counsellor at the Court of Accounts of Montpellier. Deputy from
Hérault to the Convention, he voted the death of the king, with this restriction, that
the decree was only to be put into execution if France should be invaded by the
enemy. He was president of the Convention after the 9th Thermidor, then member
and president of the Council of Five Hundred ; Minister of Justice in 1798. He was
elected Second Consul after the 18th Brumaire. In 1804, Cambacères became prince
arch-chancellor of the Empire and Duc de Parma. Exiled in 1815, he died in 1824.
[4] François Melzi d'Eril (1753-1816) had been, from its foundation, one of the most
ardent defenders of the Cisalpine Republic. He became afterwards Duc de Lodi,
Grand-Chancellor and Keeper of the Seals of the Viceroy Eugène.
[5] There is here an error in the text. The *kingdom* of Italy dates only from 1805
(the consecration at Milan was on May 26). M. de Talleyrand has evidently meant
to say that in 1802, the official denomination of *Italian Republic* was substituted for
that of *Cisalpine Republic*.

presented to him the keys of Milan on his first invasion, was sufficiently compromised towards Austria for Bonaparte to place in him every confidence.

Until the time of the Peace of Amiens, Bonaparte may have committed many faults, for what man is free from them ? But none of the plans he had conceived were such that any true and patriotic Frenchman could have felt any reluctance to contribute to their execution. One may not always have agreed as to the excellence of the means resorted to by Bonaparte, but the utility of the aim could not be contested, being simply, on the one hand to bring foreign wars to an end, and, on the other hand, to close the revolutionary era by re-establishing monarchy, which, in my candid opinion, it was then impossible to do in favour of the legitimate heirs of the last king.

The Peace of Amiens was scarcely concluded, when Bonaparte began to give up *moderation ;* the provisions of that peace had not yet been carried out, when he already sowed the seeds of new wars which, after overwhelming Europe and France, were to lead him to his ruin.

Piedmont ought to have been given back to the King of Sardinia immediately after the Peace of Lunéville ; it was merely in trust in the hands of France. To give it up would have been both an act of strict justice and a very wise policy. Bonaparte, on the contrary, annexed it to France. I made vain efforts to dissuade him from such a measure. He believed his personal interest required him to do so, his pride seemed to him to claim that arbitrary step, and all the counsels of prudence failed to alter his mind in that respect.[1]

Although he had by his victories contributed to the aggrandizement of France, none of the territories with which it had been aggrandized had been conquered by the armies which he had commanded. It was under the Convention that the county

---

[1] On December 9, 1798, King Charles-Emmanuel, being vanquished and dispossessed, had renounced the throne for himself and heirs, and given his subjects orders to obey in future the French authorities. Thereupon, Piedmont was subjected to the direct rule of French generals. In 1800, before Marengo and Hohenlinden, Bonaparte, in his preliminaries of peace, offered to return Piedmont to the King of Sardinia. His subsequent victories made him more exacting, and on the occasion of the treaty of Lunéville, he refused to bind himself at all in that respect. On April 19, 1801, Piedmont was divided into six departments and became a military division ; on September 4, 1802, it was annexed to France.

of Avignon, Savoy, Belgium, the left bank of the Rhine had
been added to France ; and Bonaparte could not claim any of
those conquests as coming from him personally. To rule, and
to rule hereditarily, as he aspired to do over a country aggrandized by generals formerly his equals, and whom he wished to
become his subjects, seemed to him almost humiliating, and
moreover, might arouse an opposition which he was anxious to
avoid. It was thus that, in order to justify his pretensions to
the title of sovereign, he deemed it necessary to annex to France
countries which he alone had conquered. He had crushed
Piedmont in 1796; and his victories in that quarter seemed to
him to justify the arbitrary views he entertained towards that
country. He accordingly caused the senate to assent to and
proclaim the annexation of Piedmont to France, never thinking that any one might call him to account for so monstrous a
violation of what the law of nations consider as most sacred.
His illusion was not destined to last long.

The English government had made peace only out of
necessity ; as soon as the home difficulties which had caused the
making of peace almost unavoidable, were overcome, the English
cabinet who had not yet restored Malta, and wished to keep it,
seized the occasion offered by the annexation of Piedmont to
France, and took up arms again.[1]

But events quickened Bonaparte's resolution to transform
the consulate for life into an hereditary monarchy. The English
had landed on the coasts of Brittany a few devoted and most
enterprising *émigrés*. Bonaparte took advantage of this new
royalist plot, in which he flattered himself to implicate, at the
same time, Dumouriez,[2] Pichegru and Moreau, his three rivals in
glory, to wrench from the senate the title of Emperor. But

---

[1] May 16, 1803.

[2] Charles-Francois Duperrier-Dumouriez, born at Cambrai in 1739, entered the
army at sixteen. In 1763, he changed the sword for diplomacy, and became one
of the most active secret agents of the king. Under Louis XVI., he was appointed
Governor of Cherbourg, and brigadier-general. In 1792, he joined the Girondist
Cabinet as Minister of Foreign Affairs (March 15), and three months later, was
appointed general-in-chief of the army of the north. Victorious at Valmy and at
Jemmapes, but defeated at Nerwinden, and on the point of being tried, he entered
into negotiations with Prince von Coburg, delivered into the hands of the Austrians
the Commissioners sent by the Convention to arrest him, and himself went over to
the enemy. He lived abroad until his death (1823), often engaged in royalist
intrigues and plots.

that title, which, with moderation and wisdom, he would just as well have obtained, though perhaps not quite so soon, became the meed of violence and crime. He ascended the throne, but a throne besmeared with innocent blood—blood which former and glorious recollections made dear to France.

The violent and unexplained death of Pichegru, the means used to obtain the conviction of Moreau, might be put to the account of policy ; but the assassination of the Duc d'Enghien,[1] committed solely in order, by placing himself in their ranks, to make sure of those whom the death of Louis XVI. caused to fear all manner of power not coming from them, this assassination, I say, could be neither excused nor forgiven, nor has it ever been so ; Bonaparte has therefore been reduced to boast of it.[2]

The new war in which Bonaparte found himself engaged with England necessitating the employment of all his resources, it only needed the most common prudence to abstain from undertaking anything that might induce the powers on the Continent to make common cause with his enemy. But vanity still prevailed in him. It was not sufficient for him to have himself proclaimed under the name of Napoleon, Emperor of the French ; it was not sufficient for him to have been consecrated by the Sovereign Pontiff ; he wished besides to be King of Italy, in order to be emperor and king as well as the head of the House of Austria. Consequently he had himself crowned at Milan, and instead of taking simply the title of King of Lombardy, he chose the more ambitious, and, therefore, more alarming title of King of Italy, as if his design were to submit Italy entirely to his sceptre ; and that there might be less doubt as to his intentions, Genoa and Lucca,[3] where his agents had skilfully aroused fear, sent him deputations by the agency of whom the one gave herself to him, the other asked as a sovereign a member of his family ; and both under different names, since then, form

---

[1] March 21, 1804.

[2] Prince Talleyrand has devoted to the affair of the Duc d'Enghien a special chapter, which will be published in one of the subsequent volumes of these *Memoirs*.

[3] After the conventions of October 10, 1796, and June 6, 1797, the Republic of Genoa, transformed into Ligurian Republic, was the ally of France. It was on June 3, 1805, that the senate and the doge solicited the annexing of their city to France, which was immediately enforced. As to Lucca, it was assigned to Élisa Bonaparte, Princess of Piombino (June 24, 1805).

a part of that which for the first time began to be called the great empire.

The consequences of that conduct were such as could be naturally foreseen. Austria took up arms, and a continental war became imminent. Then Napoleon tried negotiations on all sides. He attempted to draw Prussia into his alliance,[1] by offering her Hanover, and when on the point of succeeding, he caused everything to fail by sending to Berlin General Duroc,[2] who by his awkward bluntness, destroyed the good effect of the advances previously made according to my instructions by M. de la Forest,[3] who was there as Minister of France.

The emperor was more fortunate with the Electors of Bavaria, Würtemberg and Baden, whom he maintained this time in his alliance.

The camp of Boulogne, which he formed at this period for the purpose of menacing the coasts of England, had for first result to make the war popular in that country, and of creating there an as yet unheard-of thing, a numerous permanent army. And it was while Napoleon seemed absorbed by the organization of that camp, that the Austrians crossed the Inn, traversed Bavaria, occupied the centre of Suabia, and were already arriving on the banks of the Rhine. It was nevertheless this precipita-tion of the Austrians which preserved Napoleon from the more than critical position in which he would have been placed, if they had awaited the arrival of the Emperor Alexander and his hundred thousand Russians, who were on the march to join themselves to them, for Prussia would have been infallibly drawn into the coalition, but the Austrians wished to show that, alone, they were able to engage the struggle and win the day.

Napoleon, with the military genius and the celerity which make his glory, at once availed himself of this blunder.   In a

---

[1] From 1803 to 1805, Napoleon on the one side, and Austria and Russia on the other, disputed for the alliance of Prussia.   King Frederick William dared not take any decision.   However, in 1805, he signed with France a simple compact of neutrality.

[2] Duroc was from 1796 the favourite aide-de-camp of Napoleon.   Born in 1772, he became under the Empire general of division, Grand-Marshal of the Palace, and Duc de Frioul.   He was killed at Wurtschen, May 22, 1813.

[3] Antoine, Comte de la Forest (1756–1847), minister at Munich, 1801 ; at the Diet at Ratisbon, 1802 ; at Berlin, 1803 ; ambassador at Madrid in 1807.   Minister and peer of France under the Restoration.

few weeks, one might say in a few days, he transported the large army of the camp of Boulogne to the banks of the Rhine, whence he led it to new victories.

I received instructions to accompany him to Strasburg, there to be ready to follow his headquarters according to circumstances (September, 1805). A fit which happened to the emperor at the beginning of this campaign frightened me very much. The very day of his departure from Strasburg, I had dinner with him ; on leaving the table, he went to see the Empress Josephine. He had only been with her a few minutes, when suddenly he came out of her apartment ; I was in the drawing-room, he took me by the arm and led me into his room. M. de Rémusat,[1] the first chamberlain, who came for instructions, entered at the same time. We were hardly there, when the emperor fell on the floor ; he had barely time to tell me to close the door. I tore away his cravat, because it seemed to choke him ; he did not vomit, he groaned and foamed at the mouth. M. de Rémusat gave him some water, and I bathed him with Cologne water. He had a kind of convulsions that ceased after a quarter of an hour ; we placed him on an arm-chair ; he commenced to speak, dressed himself again, and enjoined secrecy on us ; half an hour later, he was on his way to Carlsruhe. On reaching Stuttgart, he wrote me to give me news of his health ; his letter ended with these words, " I am well. The Duke of Würtemberg came to meet me as far as outside the first gate of his palace ; he is a man of sense." A second letter from Stuttgart, bearing the same date, ran as follows : " I am acquainted with Mack's movements ; these are all I could desire. He will be caught in Ulm, like a fool ![2] "

Some people have since endeavoured to spread the rumour

---

[1] Auguste, Comte de Rémusat, born in 1762, was in 1789, an advocate to the *Cour des Comptes* at Aix. He stayed in France during the whole of the Revolution. In 1802, he became prefect of the palace ; chief chamberlain in 1804, and superintendent of theatres. In 1815, he was appointed prefect of the Nord, and subsequently of the Haute-Garonne department. He was dismissed in 1821, and died in 1823.

[2] Charles, Baron von Mack von Lieberich, born in 1752. He was several times in command of Austrian armies, but was always beaten. He signed the capitulation of Ulm on October 19. Having been, shortly after, tried by court-martial, he was sentenced to death, but the Emperor Francis commuted the sentence into an imprisonment which only lasted a few years. He died in oblivion in 1828.

that Mack had been bribed ; this is false ; it was only their presumption that caused the defeat of the Austrians.   It is known
how their army, partially beaten on several points and driven
back into Ulm, was obliged to capitulate ; it remained there
prisoner of war, after having passed under the yoke.

In announcing to me his victory, Napoleon wrote me what
were, in his idea, the conditions he wished to impose upon
Austria, and what territories he wished to take from her.
I replied to him that his real interest was not to enfeeble
Austria, that in taking from her on one side, he must return
to her on the other, in order to make of her an ally.   The
memorandum in which I set forth my reasons, struck him so that
he placed the matter for deliberation before the council he held
at Munich whither I had gone to meet him, and induced him
to follow the plan I had proposed to him, and which can still
be found in the archives of the government.[1]   But new advantages brought about by one of the divisions of his advance
guard, firing his imagination, made him desire to march upon
Vienna, to hasten to new successes, and to date decrees from
the Imperial Palace of Schoenbrunn.

Master in less than three weeks of all Upper Austria and
of all that part of the Lower which is at the south of the Danube,
he crosses this river and enters in Moravia.   If then sixty
thousand Prussians had invaded Bohemia, and sixty thousand
others come by Franconia had occupied the road to Lintz, it
is doubtful if he could have succeeded in escaping with his
person.   If the Austro-Russian army that he had in front of him,
and which was about one hundred and twenty thousand men
strong, had only avoided all general action and given to the
Archduke Charles time to arrive with the seventy-five thousand

---

[1] This memorandum has recently been published in the *Lettres inédites de Talleyrand à Napoléon, par Pierre Bertrand* (Paris, 1889, 1 vol. 8vo. pp. 156).   Foreseeing
that the design of the emperor was already to crush Austria in order to make sooner
or later his junction with Russia, Talleyrand seeks to turn him aside from his purpose,
and warmly recommends the Austrian alliance.   He wishes to make Austria the bulwark
of Europe against Russia, and for this end to put her in contact with this empire by
ceding to her Moldavia, Walachia, Bessarabia, and a part of Bulgaria.   In exchange,
they could then take away all her possessions in Italy and Suabia.   This system
would have besides another advantage ; it would remove all contact between the
empire of Napoleon and that of the Hapsburgs, and suppress thereby all pretext for
war.   Hence the Franco-Austrian alliance being made solid and durable, would be
the safeguard of all western Europe.

men who were under his orders, instead of dictating laws, Napoleon would have been under the necessity of submitting to them. But, far from coming with her army, Prussia sent a negotiator, who, out of folly or crime, did nothing of what he was charged to do, and dug the precipice where his country itself was shortly to be engulfed.[1]

The Emperor Alexander, who was wearily waiting at Olmütz, and who had not yet seen any battle, desired to have the amusement of it ; and, in spite of the representations of the Austrians, in spite of the advice the King of Prussia had sent him to abstain, he fought the battle known under the name of Battle of Austerlitz, and lost it completely, deeming himself fortunate to be permitted to withdraw by daily stages, as the armistice, subsequently signed, imposed on him the humiliating obligation of doing.

Never has a military feat been more glorious. I still see Napoleon re-entering Austerlitz on the evening of the battle. He lodged at a house belonging to *Prince von Kaunitz* ; and there, in his chamber, yes, *in the very chamber of Prince von Kaunitz*, were brought at every moment Austrian flags, Russian flags, messages from the archdukes, and from the Emperor of Austria, and prisoners bearing the names of all the great houses of the Austrian monarchy.

As all these trophies came in, I remember that a messenger entered the yard bringing letters from Paris, together with the mysterious portfolio in which M. de La Valette[2] inclosed the secret or private letters which were of any importance, and the reports of all the French police. In war, the arrival of letters is a most pleasant event. Napoleon, by having the letters immediately distributed, relaxed and recompensed his army.

---

[1] The King of Prussia had ended by yielding to the entreaties of the Emperor of Russia, and had signed with him a convention (November 3, 1805), according to which he bound himself to propose his armed mediation, and if it were not accepted by Napoleon on December 15, to declare war against him. Count von Haugwitz, who was entrusted with the negotiation, was only received by Napoleon on December 13, at Schoenbrunn, and there, frightened by the menaces of the emperor, instead of acting according to his instructions, he allowed to be imposed upon him a treaty of alliance, of which Hanover was the price (December 15).

[2] Marie Chamans, Comte de la Valette (1769–1830), was then director-general of the post-offices of France. He had, at first, entered the army, and had become a captain and confidential aide-de-camp of Napoleon. Sentenced to death in 1815, he was

I must not omit to mention here a peculiar incident which
fully depicts the character of Napoleon and his opinions. The
emperor, who at this time had great confidence in me, asked
me to read to him his correspondence. We began with the
deciphered letters of the foreign ambassadors in Paris; they
interested him but little, because all the great news of the world
took place about him. We then went on to the police reports;
several spoke of the difficulties of the Bank of France, brought
on by some bad measures of the Minister of Finances, M. de
Marbois.[1] However, the report to which he paid most attention
was that of Madame de Genlis; it was long and written entirely
in her own hand. She spoke of the spirit of Paris, and quoted
a few offensive conversations held, she said, in those houses
which were then called the Faubourg Saint-Germain; she
named five or six families, which, never, she added, would rally
to the government of the emperor. Some rather biting expressions which Madame de Genlis reported set Napoleon in
an inconceivable state of fury; he swore and stormed against the
Faubourg Saint-Germain. " Ah ! they think themselves stronger
than I," said he. " Gentlemen of the Faubourg Saint-Germain,
we shall see, we shall see." And that *we shall see !* came when ?
. . . . But a few hours after a decisive victory obtained over the
Russians and the Austrians. So much strength and power did
he recognize in public opinion, and especially in that of a few
nobles, whose only action was limited to keeping aloof from
him. So, on returning to Paris later on, he regarded as a great
achievement the fact that Mesdames de Montmorency,[2] de

saved, thanks to the devotion of his wife, Mademoiselle Emilie de Beauharnais, niece
of the Empress Josephine.
    [1] François, Comte, afterwards Marquis, de Barbé-Marbois (1745-1837), former
deputy to the *Conseil des Anciens,* Director, Minister of the Public Treasury in 1802;
he was later (from 1808 to 1837) first president of the *Cour des Comptes.* In connection with a financial crisis for which he was held responsible, he was dismissed
from the cabinet in 1806. He had consented that certain State-contractors, forming
a company known under the name of *Negociants réunis,* should be paid in such a way
as to exclude almost entirely the control of the Treasury. That company had betrayed
the confidence of the minister, and compromised the finances of the State in risky
speculations, the result of which was that in October, 1805, the Bank of France only
possessed £60,000 in cash, whereas the amount of payments it had to make was
£3,680,000. The panic that ensued much disturbed the market for several months.
On his return to Paris, the emperor appointed M. Mollien to M. de Barbé-Marbois'
post. (See Thiers's *Le Consulat et l'Empire* [vol. vi. p. 30 and fol., 187 and fol.,
375], and M. Mollien's *Memoirs.*)
    [2] Valentine de Harchies, married to Anne, Comte de Montmorency (1787-1858).

Mortemart,[1] and de Chevreuse,[2] accepted the post of ladies in waiting to the empress, thus ennobling Madame de Bassano[3] who had been appointed with them.

At the end of twenty-four hours, I left Austerlitz. I had spent two hours on this terrible battle-field; Marshal Lannes had taken me there, and I owe it to his honour, and perhaps to military honour in general, to say that this same man who, on the evening before, had performed such prodigious feats of valour, who had displayed unprecedented courage as long as he had enemies to fight, was about to faint when his eyes gazed on the dead and maimed soldiers of all nations; he was so moved that, when showing me the different points where the principal attacks had been made, he said to me : " I cannot stay longer, unless you wish to come with me to knock down these villanous Jews who are robbing the dead and the dying."

The negotiations, of which, before this great battle, there had only been a pretence, then became serious. They commenced at Brunn in Moravia, and ended at Presburg,[4] where General Giulay[5] and the loyal Prince Johan von Lichtenstein[6] had repaired with me.

While I was in the first of these cities, the Emperor Napoleon dictated to Duroc, and Count von Haugwitz, Minister of Prussia, signed, a treaty (Dec. 15, 1805), in which were mentioned the cessions exacted from Austria, and by which Prussia

---

[1] Eléonore de Montmorency, born in 1777, married to Victor de Rochechouart, Marquis de Mortemart. She was lady in waiting to the empress in 1806.
[2] Françoise de Narbonne-Pelet, married in 1802 to Charles-André d'Albert, Duc de Luynes and de Chevreuse. She was lady of the household of the empress in 1807, and died in 1813.
[3] Madame Maret, the wife of the emperor's minister.
[4] December 26, 1805. Austria lost all her Italian possessions, which were united with the new kingdom of Italy. The Tyrol and Vorarlberg, the principality of Eichstedt, the city of Augsbourg, and several other manors were assigned to Bavaria. The Count de Hohenberg, the Landgrave of Nellenburg, a part of Brisgau, and seven other important cities were given to Würtemberg. The Elector of Baden received Ortenau, the rest of Brisgau, and Constance. Finally, the title of King was acknowledged for the Electors of Bavaria and of Würtemberg, and that of Grand Duke for the Elector of Baden.
[5] Count Ignatius Giulay (1763–1831) became general in 1800. He took part in all the wars of his time, became field-marshal in 1813, chief commander of Bohemia in 1823, and president of the Aulic Council, 1830.
[6] Johan von Lichtenstein, Prince Sovereign of Germany, born in Vienna in 1766 : general in the Austrian army in 1794. In 1814, he retired to his principality, over which he reigned until his death. (Principality of Lichtenstein, between the Tyrol and Switzerland ; 8,000 inhabitants ; chief town, Vaduz.)

herself ceded Anspach and Neufchâtel, in exchange for Hanover which she received. Napoleon had successes of all kinds ; and he abused them beyond measure, above all by dating from Vienna, a short time after, the insolent decree in which he declared that Ferdinand IV., King of the Two Sicilies, had ceased to reign, and gave to Joseph Bonaparte, his eldest brother, the kingdom of Naples, which he conquered easily, and that of Sicily, over which his imagination only has ever reigned.

The system that Napoleon then adopted, the secret of which I have mentioned, was the first act that must be reckoned among the causes of his fall. I will make known later, with special reference to each of the new kings he made, all that there was impolitic and destructive in this method of overthrowing governments in order to create others which he was not slow to pull down again, and that in all parts of Europe.

Austria, in the state of distress to which she now was reduced, could not do otherwise than accept the conditions imposed by her victor. Those conditions were harsh indeed, and the treaty made with Count von Haugwitz made it impossible for me to mitigate them in any other clauses than those relative to the indemnity to be paid to France. I, at least, managed that the conditions imposed on Austria should not be rendered worse by any fallacious interpretation. Being master of the wording, on which Napoleon's influence was minimised by the distance I was from him, I applied myself to make it free from any ambiguity ; so that, although he had obtained everything that it was possible for him to obtain, the treaty did not please him. He wrote to me some time after : " You have made me, at Presburg, a treaty that annoys me a *great* deal ; " which did not, however, prevent him giving me, a short time after, a marked proof of satisfaction by creating me Prince of Benevento, the territory of which was occupied by his troops. I say with pleasure that, thereby, this duchy, which remained my property until the Restoration, was saved all sorts of vexations, and even conscription.

Count von Haugwitz surely deserved to pay with his head for the treaty he had dared to make without authority and against what he knew perfectly well to be the wish of his sovereign ; but to punish him would have been to attack Napoleon himself.

The King of Prussia dared not disclaim it ; he had even the weakness to resist the noble solicitations of the queen; and yet, ashamed to give his approbation to such an act, he at first only ratified the treaty conditionally. But, for the conditional ratification which Napoleon rejected, he was obliged, under pain of having him for an enemy, to substitute one pure and simple, which constituted Prussia at war with England.[1]

Napoleon, since he was emperor, wished for no more republics, above all in his vicinity. Consequently he changed the government of Holland, and eventually demanded that one of his brothers should be king of that country.[2] He did not suspect then that his brother Louis, whom he had chosen, was too honest a man to accept the title of King of Holland, without becoming a thorough Hollander.

The dissolution of the German Empire was already implicitly operated by the treaty of Presburg, since it had recognized as kings the Electors of Bavaria and Würtemberg, and the Elector of Baden as Grand-Duke. This dissolution was consummated by the act which instituted the Confederation of the Rhine,[3] an act which cost the existence of a host of small states preserved by the rescript of 1803, and that I tried once more to save. But I succeeded only for a small number of them, the principal confederates not wishing to accept this act unless they obtained territorial compensations.

Murat, one of Napoleon's brothers-in-law, to whom the countries of Clèves and Berg had been given in sovereignty, was included in that confederation, with the title of Grand-Duke ; he exchanged it later for that of King, which it would have been much better for him never to have obtained.

[1] Definitive treaty of alliance of February 15, 1806, ratified by the King of Prussia, March 9.

[2] Louis Bonaparte was proclaimed King of Holland, June 5, 1806.

[3] The old German Empire existed no longer, except in name, in 1806. Napoleon gave it the last blow, July 12, 1806, by the compact he signed with thirteen German princes, the principal of whom were Baron von Dalberg, Archbishop of Mayence, Prince Primate of Germany, the Kings of Bavaria and Würtemberg, the Grand Duke of Baden, the Landgrave of Hesse-Darmstadt, &c. By the terms of this compact, the contracting princes separated themselves from the Empire, and constituted a *Confederation of the Rhine*, acknowledging as *Protector* the Emperor Napoleon, and signed with him a treaty of alliance, offensive and defensive. The Emperor Francis could but recognize the accomplished facts. On August 6 following, he declared the German Empire dissolved, abdicated the title of Emperor of Germany, and took that of Emperor of Austria.

While the King of Prussia was embroiling himself with England by occupying Hanover, the latter was thinking of treating with France. Mr. Pitt being dead,[1] Mr. Fox, who was not destined to survive him long, had become, by dint of talent and in spite of the repugnance of the king, chief Secretary of State for Foreign Affairs in the cabinet of which Lord Grenville[2] was the nominal head. No one detested more than Mr. Fox the oppression of the government of Napoleon; but whether not to put his conduct in contradiction with the language he had used during some years as chief of the opposition, or from a real desire for peace, he believed he ought to make pacific demonstrations. He wrote to me[3] to inform me of an intended attempt on the life of the emperor (or of the *leader of the French*, as he named him in the letter), which had been revealed to him by one of the wretched authors of the plot.

I eagerly seized this occasion, and in thanking him in the name of the emperor, I expressed dispositions which were soon followed by overtures made by the channel of Lord Yarmouth. After two or three conferences, Mr. Fox, to be agreeable to Lord Grenville, adjoined Lord Lauderdale[4] with Lord Yarmouth.

On his side, the Emperor Alexander sent to Paris M. d'Oubri to arrange a reconciliation. I induced him to make a treaty, which he negotiated with Mr. Clarke.[5] The Emperor of Russia, who did not wish to go so far, refused to ratify it, and disgraced him who had signed it.

As to the negotiation which had been well begun by Lord Yarmouth, and spoiled by Lord Lauderdale, it ended in avenging England on Prussia much more than England herself would have wished.

---

[1] January 23, 1806.

[2] William Wyndham, Lord Grenville (1759–1834), Secretary of State for Home Affairs, and afterwards for Foreign Affairs (1791). He retired in 1801.

[3] February 20, 1806.

[4] James Maitland, Earl of Lauderdale, born in 1759, peer of Scotland in 1789. He came to France at this period, and associated himself with the leading Girondists. Always a friend of France, he combated the policy of Pitt, became, in 1806, Privy Councillor, Keeper of the Scotch Seal, ambassador extraordinary at Paris. In 1816, he protested loudly against the detention of Napoleon. He died in retirement in 1839.

[5] October 14, 1806. General Comte Clarke (1765-1818), became in the following year (1807), Secretary of War, and was created Duc de Feltre. He was appointed Marshal of France under the Restoration.

Peace between England and France was morally impossible without the restitution of Hanover ; and Napoleon having disposed of that country for equivalents, which he had also disposed of, the restitution was likewise morally impossible. But the emperor, who held as real only the difficulties which could not be overcome by sheer force, did not hesitate to admit this restitution as one of the bases of the agreement to be made. He said to himself : " Prussia, who has received Hanover through fear, will return it through fear ; and, as for the equivalents which she has given, I shall compensate them by promises which will meet the pride of the cabinet, and with which the country shall be obliged to be satisfied."

Prussia could not long be ignorant of this treacherous proceeding ; the English were interested in making Prussia know it, and, in addition, Prussia was soon to be the victim of another perfidy.

In the conversations which Count von Haugwitz had had at Vienna as well as at Paris, with the Emperor Napoleon, the latter had spoken to him of his project of dissolving the German Empire, and of substituting for it two confederations, one of the south, the other of the north. He did not wish, he said, to have any influence except over the first ; Prussia would be at the head of the second. The Prussian cabinet allowed itself to be allured by this project, but when they wished to proceed with the demarcation of the two confederations, Napoleon declared that Prussia could not include in her part either the Hanseatic cities or Saxony, that is to say, the only countries which were not already under the influence and protection of Prussia. The latter, seeing herself cheated, took counsel only of the irritation which reigned in all classes of the nation, and rushed to arms.

It was not without secret uneasiness that the emperor went, for the first time, to measure his strength with hers. The ancient glory of the Prussian army imposed upon him ; but after an action of only four hours, the phantom vanished, and the battle of Jena[1] put the Prussian monarchy completely at the mercy of a conqueror, all the more pitiless that the wrongs

[1] October 14, 1806.

were on his side, and that, besides, he had had some fear, and
that they knew it.

Napoleon was already at Berlin, when he received an imprudent proclamation from the Prince of the Peace, which seemed
to announce the approaching defection of Spain.[1] He then made
up his mind to destroy at any price, the Spanish branch of the
House of Bourbon ; and I, I took inwardly the oath to cease, at
whatever price, to be his minister, as soon as we should have
returned to France. He confirmed me in this resolution by the
barbarity with which, at Tilsit, he treated Prussia, although he
made me the instrument of it. This time he did not apply to me
to treat for contributions of war and for the evacuation of the
territories by his troops. He charged Marshal Berthier[2] with this
duty. He thought that, at Presburg, I had acted in a manner too
much opposed to what he believed to be his real interests ; but
I am anticipating events.

We remained but a few days at Berlin. Herr von Zastrow,
confidential aide-de-camp of the king, and Herr von Lucchesini
had had permission to repair to that place. Herr von Lucchesini
passed in Prussia for being very capable and above all very subtle.
His subtilty has often recalled to me the *mot* of Dufresne, " *Too
much sense, that is to say not enough.*" These two plenipotentiaries
came to negotiate an armistice which perhaps they might have
obtained if they had not been informed too late of the capitulation of Magdeburg. The Russian army, it is true, was still
intact, but it was too small, and besides the Prussians were
completely discouraged, all their strong places had opened their
gates, and finally Polish deputations hastened from all sides to

[1] In 1806, the Spanish government had for a moment the thought of breaking off
with France. The unsuccess of her struggle with England, the uneasiness caused her
by the dispossession of King Ferdinand, all contributed to force her that way. The
Prince of the Peace, who then directed the politics of the cabinet, seized the moment
when Napoleon was engaged with Prussia, and issued, not in the name of the king,
but in his personal name, a rather ambiguous proclamation, in which, without
designating any one, he excited the Spanish people to prepare for war. After the
victory of Jena, the Prince of the Peace, frightened, capitulated immediately, and spread
abroad the report that the only enemy of Spain was England, but no one was deceived
by this change of tactics—Napoleon least of all.

[2] Marshal Alexandre Berthier, born in 1753, was major-general of the Grand Army,
and grand master of the hunt. In 1807, he became vice-constable, Prince de Neufchâtel and Prince de Wagram. In 1814, he supported Louis XVIII., who named him
peer of France and captain of the guards. During the Hundred Days, he retired to
Bamberg (Bavaria), where he died June 1, under very mysterious circumstances.

meet Napoleon. It did not need all this to decide him to leave Berlin, and to march on rapidly by way of Posen to Warsaw.

What a singular sight it was to see Napoleon go out of the cabinet of the great Frederick, where he had just written a bulletin for his army, pass into the dining-room where Mollendorff,[1] who was a prisoner, and Müller,[2] who was the historiographer of the Prussian monarchy dined with him ; to offer to one and the other appointments which they accepted, then enter his carriage and depart for Posen !

He had sent on before him General Dombrowski[3] and Count Wybicki, who had both served under his orders in the campaigns of Italy. It was from Posen that they dated a kind of appeal to all Poland, announcing its re-establishment. This document which had been committed to them at Berlin, disclosed and at the same time concealed sufficiently the authorization of Napoleon, to enable him to own or disown it, according as circumstances favoured or arrested his undertaking. At Posen, they received him with enthusiasm. A deputation arranged by Murat, who was already at Warsaw, and composed of men of sufficient position to make it believed that they spoke in the name of the nation, was on the day after the arrival of Napoleon, at the gate of the palace he occupied.

This deputation was numerous; the names which have remained in my memory are those of Alexander Potocki, Malachowski, Gutakowski, Dzialinski. In the speech they addressed to the emperor, they offered him all the forces of the country. Napoleon seized upon this offer, and explaining himself little as to the rest of their demands, replied to them: " When you shall have an army of forty thousand men, you will be worthy of being a nation ; and then you will have a

---

[1] Field-Marshal Count von Mollendorff, former lieutenant of Frederick II., and one of the best generals of the Prussian army. He had been grievously wounded at Auerstadt (1725–1816).

[2] Johan von Müller, German historian, born at Schaffhausen in 1752, was Aulic councillor at Mayence, then at Vienna. He came to Berlin in 1795, and Frederic II. named him private counsellor and historiographer of his house. Napoleon saw him in 1806, attached him to himself, and employed him as minister of state of the new kingdom of Westphalia. He died in 1809.

[3] Jean Dombrowski, Polish general, one of the heroes of the insurrection of 1794. In 1795, he had offered his services to the Directory, which had authorized him to raise a Polish legion for the service of France. He commanded it up to 1814.

right to all my protection." The deputation returned promptly to Warsaw, full of hope.

It was at Posen that the emperor treated with the Elector of Saxony, until then an ally of Prussia. The elector joined the Confederation of the Rhine and took the title of king.[1] On this occasion, Napoleon received the list of pictures that M. Denon[2] induced him to take from the gallery of Dresden. He was reading it when I entered his study, and he showed it to me. "If your Majesty," said I to him, "carries away any of the pictures of Dresden, you will do more than the King of Saxony allowed himself to do, for he does not believe he has the power to put any of them in his palace. He respects the gallery as national property."

"Yes," said Napoleon, "he is a very good man ; we must not cause him any grief, I am going to give orders not to touch anything. We will see later."

The emperor, being certain of having a new army corps of at least forty thousand Poles, left a few days after for Warsaw.

Murat alone was informed of the exact moment of his arrival in that city, which he entered in the middle of the night. At six o'clock in the morning, the new authorities, all created by the influence of the French officers who belonged to the army corps of Murat, received the order to repair to the palace where they were to be presented to the emperor. He received with marked distinction the most ardent among the men who came there ; they belonged to that class of patriots always ready to welcome any change whatever in the organization of their country. He showed himself more severe towards the others, and particularly towards Prince Joseph Poniatowski,[3] whom he blamed very bitterly for not having consented to take his rank in the army again until positive orders had been given him by Murat in the name of the emperor. By deserving this reproach made to his fidelity, Prince Joseph secured a special place in the esteem

---

[1] December 11, 1806.

[2] The Baron Denon (1747-1825) was Director-General of Museums.

[3] Prince Joseph Poniatowski, nephew of the last King of Poland, Marshal of France in 1813. He was drowned in the Elster, the day after the battle of Leipzig. In 1806, he put himself at the head of the Polish army, after having exacted and obtained that this army should preserve its nationality and its autonomy, and should not be incorporated into the French troops.

of the emperor, who, at the moment he gave Poland a provisory government, appointed him Minister of War.

The first stay of Napoleon at Warsaw was very short. In
all the conversations he had had with the most influential
persons of the country, he had announced his intention to march
soon upon Grodno, adding that, the obstacles being insignificant,
he would in a short time have destroyed all what he already
called the remains of the Russian army, and driven back, as he
said, these *new* Europeans into their former frontiers. The quag-
mires of Pultusk[1] delayed for some time the execution of his
plans, without however modifying his language. On returning to
Warsaw, he announced that he had just had great successes, but
that he did not wish to avail himself of advantages which the
season rendered very painful to his troops, and that he was
going to take up his winter quarters.

He employed that period of rest which, after all, was not long,
in organizing Poland in such a manner that she became a great
help to him, at the opening of the campaign.

And as he knew that imagination only rules in that peculiar
country, he devoted his whole care during the three weeks which
he spent in Warsaw, to exalting the military spirit of the nation,
to giving fêtes, balls, concerts, to showing contempt for the
Russians, to displaying great luxury, and to speaking of John
Sobieski. He also laid his glory publicly at the feet of a beautiful Polish lady, Madame Anastase Walewska, who followed him
to Osterode and to Finkenstein, whither he betook himself, in
order to visit all his troops.

I was to remain at Warsaw, where there was a kind of diplomatic corps ; I was surrounded by German ministers, whose
masters, in these destructive times, had the face to think of obtaining enlargements of territory. Austria, from different
motives, had sent there Baron de Vincent.[2] His instructions

---

[1] Pultusk, a city of Russian Poland on the Narew (4,800 inhabitants). Victory of
Lannes over Benningsen in 1807.

[2] Baron Ch. de Vincent, born in Lorraine, entered the service of the Empire ; he
was employed in the negotiations with Pichegru ; was one of the signatories of the
treaty of Campo-Formio, became, in 1814, governor of the Low Countries in the
name of the allies, and was afterwards sent as ambassador to Paris. The provinces
whose interests were entrusted to his care in 1807, were the Palatinates of Cracow,
Sandomir, and Lublin, whose frontier follows the course of the river Boug.

were confined to seeing that order was not disturbed in the former Polish possessions which had fallen to the share of the Emperor of Austria since the last partition of Poland, and which were close to the seat of war. I entered into his views, and helped him by all the means in my power to fill his mission satisfactorily.

Napoleon had appointed as Governor of Poland a man so utterly incapable that he instructed me, during his absence, to watch over details which were naturally among the duties of the Governor. Thus, I clothed the troops, sent them off, bought the provisions, visited the hospitals, witnessed the dressing of wounds, distributed gratuities, and had even to go so far as to indicate to the Governor what he ought to put in the orders of the day. This kind of occupation, being entirely foreign to my usual pursuits, would have been very laborious, had I not found in the house of Prince Poniatowski, and in that of the Countess Vincent Tyszkiewicz, his sister, all sorts of help and assistance. The marks of interest at first, of affection afterwards, which I received in that excellent and noble family, are indelibly engraved on my grateful heart. I was grieved at leaving Warsaw. But the battle of Eylau had just been fought with a certain amount of success,[1] and Napoleon, being anxious to enter on negotiations, had instructed me to join him. However, all the attempts made in that direction failed ; it was still necessary for him to fight, and, after a few days, he understood it. The taking of Danzig,[2] had raised again what is called the *spirit* of the army, a little depressed by the difficulties it had experienced at Pultusk, by the battle of Eylau, by the climate, and, for Frenchmen, by too prolonged an absence from their country. The emperor, with all the troops he had collected, marched on Heilsberg, where he won a first victory[3] ; pursuing the Russians, he beat them again at Gutstadt and finally at Friedland.[4]

The terror that this last defeat spread among the Russians induced them to desire the quick termination of that great struggle. An interview, to take place in the middle of the Niemen, was proposed by Alexander ; it was so romantically conceived and might be so magnificently arranged, that Napoleon,

[1] February 8, 1807.   [2] May 26.   [3] June 11.   [4] June 14.

who saw in it a brilliant episode for the romance of his life,
accepted it. The bases of the peace were laid out there. We all
repaired immediately after, to Tilsit, where my instructions were,
not to negotiate with the Prussian plenipotentiaries, General
Kalkreuth[1] and Count von Goltz,[2] but to sign with them the treaty
which contained the territorial cessions of Prussia, as they had been
agreed upon between the Emperor Napoleon and the Emperor
Alexander.[3] The latter did not confine himself to making peace,
but he became, by a treaty that I negotiated and signed with Prince
Kourakin,[4] the ally of Napoleon, and, by that very reason, the
enemy of his own former allies.[5]

The Emperor Alexander, satisfied with losing nothing, and
with gaining even something (which, historians, however impartial
they may be, will not like to admit), and with having thus screened
the interests of his pride in regard to his subjects, thought he
had fulfilled all the duties of friendship towards the King of
Prussia, by helping him to retain nominally half of his kingdom ; after which he left, without even taking the precaution of
ascertaining whether the half which the king was to keep should
be promptly restored to him, whether that half should be entirely
restored, and whether His Prussian Majesty might not be obliged
to buy it again at the cost of fresh sacrifices. This was to be

---

[1] Frederick-Adolphus, Count von Kalkreuth (1737–1818). He enlisted in 1752,
became field-marshal in 1807, and Governor of Berlin.

[2] Augustus Frederick, Count von Goltz (1765–1832), entered in 1787 the diplomatic service of Prussia, was minister at Copenhagen, at Mayence, at Stockholm, at
St. Petersburg. He became, in 1814, marshal of the court, then deputy of Prussia
to the Diet and councillor of state.

[3] July 9, 1807. This treaty merely reproduced certain articles of the treaty with
Russia, for Napoleon, out of increased contempt for Prussia, wished to appear to have
consented to the existence of that state *solely out of consideration for the Emperor
Alexander;* thus he had insisted that the stipulations concerning Prussia should
appear to have been debated only between the Emperor of Russia and himself.
Prussia lost all she possessed between the Elbe and the Rhine, including Magdeburg,
and nearly all her Polish provinces. She was reduced from 9,000,000 of inhabitants
to 4,000,000.

[4] Field-Marshal Prince Kourakin had been minister and vice-chancellor of Russia.
After the Peace of Tilsit, he was ambassador at Paris.

[5] The treaty with Russia was signed on July 7, 1807. The Emperor Alexander
recognized the new state of things which had taken place in the west, as well as all
the kingdoms recently created by Napoleon. Besides, a secret treaty of alliance
was signed on the same day. Russia promised to declare war against England on
December 1 following. In return, France promised her mediation and, if need be,
her alliance against Turkey, and a plan of partition of the Ottoman Empire was
arranged. An expedition to India was likewise mentioned. Already, the winter before,
Napoleon had sent General Gardanne to Persia to prepare the way.

feared after the brutal question which Napoleon one day asked
the Queen of Prussia : " How did you dare to make war against
me, Madam, with such feeble means at your disposal ? " " Permit
me, Sire, to tell your Majesty that the glory of Frederick II. had
misled us as to the true state of our power." That word *glory*,
so happily placed, and at Tilsit, in the very study of the Emperor Napoleon, seemed to me superbly dignified. I repeated
this fine reply of the queen, often enough for the emperor to say
to me one day : " I cannot imagine what you think so fine in that
saying of the Queen of Prussia ; you might as well speak of
something else."

I was indignant at all I saw or heard, but was obliged to
conceal my indignation, and I shall ever be thankful that the
Queen of Prussia, who deserved to live in better days, was
graciously pleased to acknowledge it. If in the recollections
of my life, several are necessarily painful, I remember at
least with much sweetness the things which she then had the
goodness to say to me, and those which she almost entrusted to
me. " Prince de Benevent," she said to me the last time I had
the honour of seeing her to her carriage, "there are only two
persons who regret my having had to come here, I and yourself.
You are not angry, are you, at my thinking so ? " The tears
of compassion and pride that filled my eyes were my sole
reply.

The efforts made by this noble woman were without avail
with Napoleon ; he triumphed, and was therefore inflexible. The
promises he had caused to be broken, and those he had obtained,
had intoxicated him. He was pleased also to believe, that he
had made a dupe of the Emperor of Russia ; but time has proved
that the real dupe was himself.

By the treaty of Tilsit, the youngest of his brothers, Jérôme
Bonaparte, had been recognized as King of Westphalia. His
kingdom was composed of several of the provinces ceded
by Prussia, of the greater part of the electorate of Hesse,
and of the duchy of Brunswick-Wolfenbüttel, conquered but
not ceded. Napoleon desired greatly to add to them also the
principalities of Anhalt, Lippe and Waldeck. But, taking
advantage of the real embarrassment in which he found him-

self after the battle of Pultusk, which, however, he would not acknowledge, I had had these principalities admitted as well as those of Reuss and Schwarzburg into the Confederation of the Rhine, and he did not yet dare to attempt, as he did later, anything against the princes he had admitted to that body. The treaty of Tilsit having been signed and ratified, we could, at last, return to France.

The excitement which I had been subjected to for nearly a year, made me feel inexpressibly happy and comfortable, while passing through Dresden, where I spent several days. The noble and quiet manners of the Court of Saxony, the public and private virtues of King Frederick Augustus,[1] the benevolence and sincerity which appeared everywhere, made me preserve a special remembrance of this stay at Dresden.

Napoleon, on arriving in Paris, created for Marshal Berthier the post of vice-constable, and for myself that of vice-grand-elector. These posts were honourable and lucrative sinecures ; I then left the cabinet as I had intended to do.

During all the time I had charge of the management of foreign affairs, I served Napoleon with fidelity and zeal. As to the emperor, he adhered, for a long time, to the views which I considered it a duty to suggest to him. Those views were based upon these two considerations : To establish for France monarchical institutions which should secure the prerogatives of the crown and the authority of the sovereign, by keeping them within just limits ; to spare Europe in order that the Powers might pardon France her achievements and glory. In 1807, Napoleon had already for a long time past, it must be owned, kept away from the path on which I had done my best to keep him, but I had been unable, until the occasion which now presented itself, to give up the nominal direction of foreign affairs. It was not so easy as one might suppose to resign a post, the duties of which brought its occupant in daily contact with him.

---

[1] Frederick Augustus I., born in 1758, Elector of Saxony at the death of his brother in 1763. Married Amelia, Princess of Zwei-Brücken. He took the title of King in 1806, and remained faithful to Napoleon until 1813. The Congress of Vienna gave him back a portion of his possessions. He died in 1827, leaving the throne to his elder brother, Antoine.

Hardly returned from Tilsit, Napoleon devoted all his attention to the execution of his designs on Spain. The intrigue of
this undertaking is so involved that I have thought it necessary
to explain it separately.[1] I must only say here that the
emperor, clinging to the belief that I approved his projects,
chose precisely my estate of Valençay, to become the prison
of Ferdinand VII., his brother, and their uncle. But neither
these princes nor the public were deceived by this. He
succeeded no more in making people believe that, in this, I was
his accomplice, than he did in the conquest of Spain.

When the Emperor Alexander and he had separated at
Tilsit, they promised to see each other again soon. This was a
promise Napoleon had no desire to keep, at least unless the
state of his affairs made it necessary. But when General
Junot had been driven from Portugal by the English,[2] when
General Dupont was forced to capitulate at Baylen,[3] and when
a general insurrection in Spain, gave prospects of a resistance
which might be of long duration, he began to fear that Austria
might profit by these circumstances, and felt the need of
making more sure of Russia's intentions. He then grew
anxious to see the Emperor Alexander once more, and invited
him to an interview to take place at Erfurt.[4] Although
already very cold with me, he wished me to accompany him ;
he was persuaded that I might prove useful to him and that
sufficed him. The numerous and piquant incidents of this
interview form an episode by themselves : I have thought it
advisable to make a separate chapter of them.[5] The intention
of Napoleon, however, must find a place here. His purpose was

---

[1] See Part IV.
[2] General Andoche Junot, Duc d'Abrantès, had been placed at the head of the
army of Portugal. At first successful (1807), he was, on August 21, 1808, defeated
at Vimeiro by the Anglo-Portuguese army, and forced to sign at Cintra a capitulation,
by the terms of which he was to evacuate Portugal.
[3] General Pierre Dupont de l'Etang (1765–1839) had been, in 1808, placed at the
head of the Andalusian army. On July 22, being attacked by superior forces commanded by the Spanish general, Castanos, he capitulated in the open field near
Baylen. 8,000 French soldiers were disarmed and sent to the rocks of Cabrera
(Balearic Islands), where they died for the most part from sickness and misery.
General Dupont, having returned to France, was tried by a court-martial, and
sentenced to imprisonment for life. He came out of prison in 1814, and was Minister
of War under the first Restoration.
[4] A city of the kingdom of Saxony (to-day annexed to Prussia) on the Gera.
[5] See Part V.

to induce the Emperor Alexander to make a special alliance with him against Austria. That which he had concluded at Tilsit, although general, was particularly directed against England. If he had succeeded at Erfurt, he would, under some pretext easily invented, have sought a quarrel with Austria, and after a few military successes he would have tried to do with it as he had done with Prussia.

The complete co-operation of Russia would have thoroughly enabled him to reach his goal. Having a very small opinion of the genius and self-will of the Emperor Alexander, he hoped to succeed. His intention was to intimidate the Czar at first, and then to arouse both his vanity and his ambition ; and, indeed, it was to be feared that on these three points, the Emperor of Russia might prove only too accessible. But the star of Austria willed that M. de Caulaincourt,[1] who has always been persistently misjudged, should inspire the Emperor of Austria with confidence, and not cause the Emperor Alexander to lose that he placed in me. I had seen him several times in private at Tilsit. I saw him nearly every day at Erfurt. Our conversations were at first of a general turn concerning the common interests existing between the great powers of Europe ; the conditions on which the ties, which it was important to preserve between them, were to be broken ; the equilibrium of Europe in general ; the probable consequences of its destruction ; then, gradually our conversations turned more particularly to the States whose existence was necessary for this equilibrium, especially to Austria. These conversations put the emperor in such a state of mind that the coaxing, the persuasion, and the threats of Napoleon were a dead loss ; and that, before quitting Erfurt, the Emperor Alexander wrote in his own hand to the Emperor of Austria to reassure him with regard to the fears, which the Erfurt interview had caused him. It was the last service I was able to render Europe, as long as Napoleon continued to reign, and this service, in my opinion, I was also rendering to himself personally.

---

[1] Louis de Caulaincourt, born in 1773 at Caulaincourt (Aisne), of noble parentage. Under the Empire he became general of division, grand-equerry and Duc de Vicence (Vicenza). He went to Russia as ambassador in 1807, was appointed Minister of Foreign Affairs in 1813, and died in 1827.

R

After having given many fêtes and made a kind of treaty essentially different from that he had in view on coming to Erfurt, the emperor returned to Paris, and M. de Champagny,[1] thereafter had the sole direction of the department of Foreign Affairs. As for me, I resumed the insignificant life of a grand dignitary.

At all hazards, I did what was in my power to obtain the confidence of the Emperor Alexander, and I succeeded, sufficiently well for him to send to me, as soon as his first trouble broke out with France, Count de Nesselrode, councillor to the Russian Embassy in Paris, who, on entering my room, said to me, " I have just come from St. Petersburg ; I hold an official situation with Prince Kourakin, although it is really to you that I am accredited. I am keeping up a private correspondence with the emperor, and now bring you one of his letters."

---

[1] Jean-Baptiste Nompère de Champagny, Duc de Cadore (1756–1834), former deputy of the nobility to the States-General, became, in 1800, councillor of state, ambassador at Vienna (1801), and Minister of the Interior ; in 1807, he succeeded Talleyrand as Minister of Foreign Affairs.

.END OF THE THIRD PART.

PART IV.

SPANISH AFFAIRS.

1807

Napoleon at Finkenstein—His love of deceit—Situation of France at the close of the year 1807—Napoleon's designs on Spain—The pretext he chose to carry them out—Talleyrand endeavours to dissuade the emperor from wronging the old ally of France.—Treaty of Fontainebleau —Napoleon's shameful breach of faith towards Charles IV. of Spain— Don Juan de Escoïquiz, Canon of Toledo, and the Prince of the Asturias —The intrigues of Godoy, Prince of the Peace—Don Escoïquiz' plan to thwart them—The French ambassador and Don Escoïquiz—Napoleon's *ruse*—Letter of the Prince of the Asturias to Napoleon—Letter of the Prince of the Peace to the Emperor—Provisions of the treaty of Fontainebleau—Projected dismemberment of Portugal—Secret Convention aimed at Spain, though ostensibly, at Portugal—The French troops in Spain—Arrest of the Prince of the Asturias—He is put on his trial— Declared not guilty—Occupation of Navarra, Catalonia and Guipuzcoa by the French—Fears of the Prince of the Peace—Projected flight of the royal family—Indignation of the people—General discontent against Godoy, Prince of the Peace—The Aranjuez riots—Popular hatred against Godoy—Loyalty of the people towards the royal family—Arrest of Godoy—He is put on his trial—Abdication of King Charles IV. in favour of Ferdinand, Prince of the Asturias—Arrival of Ferdinand VII. at Madrid—The Grand Duc de Berg (Murat) and King Ferdinand—Change of the people's disposition towards the French—Negotiations between Don Escoïquiz and the Grand Duc de Berg—Murat insists on the suspension of Godoy's trial—Murat demands the release of the latter, in Napoleon's name—Ferdinand VII. sends his brother Don Carlos to meet Napoleon on his way to Spain—Charles IV.'s protest—Retracts his abdication—Don Antonio appointed Regent—Ferdinand VII. leaves Madrid, on his way to Bayonne—Free for eight hours—*Lasciate ogni speranza*—Arrival at Bayonne—Ferdinand and the Infante Antonio practically prisoners—Napoleon unmasks his designs—Offers to Ferdinand the kingdom of Etruria, in exchange for the cession of the rights of the latter to the Crown of Spain—Refusal of Ferdinand—Noble reply of the Marquis de Labrador to M. de Champagny—Napoleon and Don

R 2

Escoïquiz—It is too late !—Charles IV. at Bayonne—Ferdinand's renunciation of the crown—Murat appointed lieutenant-general of Spain
—The royal princes of Spain at the château of Valençay—Prince
Talleyrand welcomes them—Inaptitude of the princes for study—
Everyday life at Valençay—Talleyrand summoned to Nantes—Napoleon's bluster—Scathing retort of Talleyrand—Rupture between Napoleon and Talleyrand—Talleyrand summoned to Erfurt—Takes leave of
the Spanish princes—Their gratitude—*By the grace of God*—The
Emperor of Russia recognizes Joseph Bonaparte as King of Spain—
Treaty of Valençay—Failure of Napoleon's designs on Spain—The
result of Napoleon's threats against England—Want of dignity of
Ferdinand VII.—His return to Madrid—His cruel proceedings towards
his faithful supporters—England's fault in Spain.

NAPOLEON was at Finkenstein,[1] and said one day, in a cheerful
moment, " I know, when necessary, how to throw off the skin
of the lion, and put on that of the fox."

He was fond of deceiving, and would do so for the mere love
of it ; apart from his policy, his instinct would have made it a
necessity for him. For the carrying out of the projects which he
was always meditating, artifice was no less necessary than force.
It was especially in the accomplishment of his views on Spain
that he felt that force alone could not be sufficient.

Napoleon, seated on one of the thrones of the House of
Bourbon, considered the princes who occupied the other two, as
his natural enemies, whom it was his interest to overthrow.
But it was an undertaking in which he could not fail, without
ruining his own designs, and perhaps himself as well. It was
not then to be entered upon, without being fully certain of success.
The first condition to secure that success was that there
should be no occasion to fear a diversion on the Continent.

At the end of 1807, Napoleon was master of the whole of
Italy,[2] and of that portion of Germany that lies between the Rhine
and the Elbe.[3] He had, under the name of duchy of Warsaw,
restored a part of ancient Poland, extending from Silesia to the

---

[1] Head-quarters of the Emperor Napoleon during the campaign of 1807, in
Poland.
[2] The treaty of Presburg had given Venice to the kingdom of Italy. Joseph
reigned at Naples. Thus the Papal States alone were not directly dependent on the
emperor.
[3] Jerôme Bonaparte reigned in Westphalia ; Murat at Berg. The Kings of Bavaria
and Würtemberg, the Grand Duke of Baden, and the other princes of the Rhenish
Confederation, were at the time thoroughly devoted to France.

Niemen,[1] so that that country was devoted to him. Prussia was almost crushed. Austria, weakened by the losses of all kinds which she had suffered, was not in a position to undertake anything alone ; on the other hand, Napoleon had easily brought Russia to entertain ambitious plans, and in giving her two wars to carry on, had given her what would, for a long time, occupy all her forces.[2] Therefore, Spain appeared to him as completely isolated as he could wish. But in attacking her he had a two-fold danger to fear.

Since the Peace of Basel between France and Spain, that is to say for eleven years, Spain had been the faithful ally of France. Money, ships, soldiers, she had put everything at the disposal of the latter, she had lavished all on her. At this time, twenty thousand men, the flower of her troops, and the best of her generals were serving in the French army at the further extremity of Europe. How could he declare war against her ? What pretext could he allege ? Could he divulge the motives of his dynastic ambition ? In making them known, he exposed himself to the risk of turning against himself the feelings of his own subjects ; and all his contempt for the human race did not prevent him from understanding that the force of public opinion must count for something. In declaring war he would provoke Spain to resistance ; a thousand unforeseen circumstances might arise, and, however successful and short this war might be, it would none the less leave to the Spanish royal family both the means and the time to repair to its possessions on the other side of the ocean. Spain, in this case, would become for him a possession, dangerous and difficult to govern, for the nation, being attached to the royal family, would have formed wishes for the success of its legitimate rulers, and always sided with the American colonies ; this was leaving to the House of Bourbon, a hope, a favourable prospect of returning to Spain. Besides, the separation of the Spanish colonies from their metropolis would entail serious losses on French commerce, and Napoleon

---

[1] The Grand Duchy of Warsaw, formed of the Polish provinces taken from Prussia, had been given to the King of Saxony.
[2] The first against Sweden in order to annex Finland ; and the other against Turkey, in the hope of acquiring the Danubian principalities.

would consequently find that he had injured one of the dearest interests of his people.

He must then employ all his art to prevent this twofold danger. If it were possible for him to veil the odium of his undertaking, knowing the inclination of men to pardon successful crimes, he could flatter himself that the impression of the one he was meditating would be much weakened, if already accomplished when becoming known.

To conquer Spain, without striking a blow, there existed but one means: it was, to introduce under the shadow of friendship, sufficient forces to prevent, or to suppress everywhere, what resistance might be offered. He must have a pretext. The refusal of Portugal to break off relations with England furnished it. Napoleon had been careful to prepare that pretext at Tilsit, in his treaty of alliance with Russia, by stipulating that should Portugal remain at peace with England, it should be treated as an enemy. Instead then of declaring war against Spain, he concluded a new alliance with her against Portugal.[1] After being conquered, a portion of that kingdom was to be annexed by the Spanish monarchy, another portion was to be handed to the Infanta Maria Louisa, and to her son, as indemnity for the kingdom of Etruria which had been given to Napoleon,[2] and the remainder was to form a principality for the Prince of the Peace.[3] That was the bait, by means of which the emperor persuaded that traitor to obtain the signature of his sovereign to the treaty.

The emperor had spoken to me several times of his project of seizing Spain. I opposed this plan with all my might, showing the immorality and the dangers of such an undertaking. He always alleged, as an excuse, the danger which a diversion of the Spanish government would cause him, if he should meet with any reverse on the banks of the Rhine or in Italy, and he

[1] Treaty of Fontainebleau, October 27, 1807.

[2] The Treaty of Lunéville had given the Grand Duchy of Tuscany to Louis, Duke of Parma, son-in-law of Charles IV., King of Spain, in exchange for his States, which were annexed to the kingdom of Italy. Tuscany then took the name of Kingdom of Etruria. King Louis dying in 1803, his son, Louis II., was proclaimed under the regency of his mother, the Infanta Maria Louisa. The secret treaty of Fontainebleau, October, 1807, dispossessed the King of Etruria, whose States were incorporated with the French empire. In compensation he was promised the future kingdom of Lusitania, which was to be created at the expense of Portugal.

[3] Manuel Godoy, born 1767, died 1851. From simple body-guard, he rose to the post of Prime Minister. Was created Duke of Alcudia and Prince of the Peace after the signature of the Peace of Basel.—(Translator.)

quoted to me the unfortunate proclamation of the Prince of the Peace on the occasion of the battle of Jena. I had often refuted that objection, reminding him that it would be very unjust to hold the Spanish nation responsible for the fault of a man whom it detested and despised, and that it would be easier for him to overthrow the Prince of the Peace than to seize Spain. But he replied to me that the idea of the Prince of the Peace might be adopted by others, and that he would never be safe on the Pyrenean frontier. It was then that, driven into a corner by the artful arguments of his ambition, I proposed to him a plan which presented the guarantees of security which he was pretending to look for in Spain. I advised him to occupy Catalonia until he should obtain maritime peace with England. "You will declare," said I to him, "that you will keep that pledge until the peace, and by so doing you will hold the Spanish government in check. If peace should be deferred it is possible that Catalonia, which is the least Spanish of all the provinces of Spain, might become attached to France ; there are historical traditions for that; and perhaps it might become definitely united with France. But anything further that you may do will one day cause you bitter regrets." I did not convince him, and he mistrusted me on this matter.

As I have just said, he tempted the cupidity and ambition of the Prince of the Peace by a treaty relative to a dismemberment of Portugal.

That treaty was negotiated secretly and signed on the 27th of October, 1807, at Fontainebleau, by General Duroc, and Councillor Izquierdo,[1] (confidential agent of the Prince of the Peace),unknown to M. de Champagny, Foreign Minister, and also unknown to me, although at that time I was chief Councillor of State,[2] and was residing at Fontainebleau.

As a result of the treaty of Fontainebleau an army of 30,000 Frenchmen was to cross Spain to unite with a Spanish army in the conquest of Portugal. A second army of 40,000 men was to be assembled on the Pyrenean frontier in order to be ready in case

---

[1] Don Eugenio Izquierdo de Ribera y Lezaun, born at Saragossa, was a secret agent of Spanish diplomacy, when, in 1797, he obtained, thanks to the protection of Godoy, the position of Privy Councillor. He conducted several confidential missions, principally under the Directory, and later in 1807. He died in 1813.

[2] One of the prerogatives of the Chief Councillor of State was to sign all treaties.

of need to assist the first, which was commanded by Marshal Junot. This second army crossed the frontier under various pretexts, and occupied fortresses in the north of Spain, and in Catalonia. It was to take a solid footing in the country, which was moreover totally without an army, the only really good troops having been sent to serve with the French. These troops mustering 20,000 men, commanded by the Marquis de La Romana, had been sent to the borders of Denmark. Napoleon, as one may see, had taken every precaution.[1]

The only thing that Napoleon might still have to fear, was that the king and his family, taking alarm, should retire into a distant province, and give from there the signal for resistance, or that they should cross the sea.

I am now going to relate by what shameful *ruses* Napoleon compelled the whole of this unfortunate family to deliver itself into his hands.

In the month of March, 1807, the Prince of the Asturias, who was in secret correspondence with Don Juan de Escoïquiz,[2] Archdeacon and Canon of Toledo, his former tutor, sent to him at Toledo, where he lived, a private confidant of his, named Don José Maurrique. The prince had given him a letter which was to be handed to Don Escoïquiz. He spoke therein of his suspicions as to the ambitious intentions of the Prince of the Peace, who, obtaining every day from the king or the queen some favour or other, was becoming more powerful. He commanded, with the title of generalissimo and admiral, all the army, the militia, and the navy ; it was already announced that the King, Charles IV., tired of state affairs, and often ill, had left to him

---

[1] In 1807, Napoleon, wishing to punish the Madrid cabinet for the hostile demonstration which it had made at the time of the rupture with Prussia (proclamation of the Prince of the Peace), and to weaken the Spanish army, required the despatch of a body of 15,000 men, destined to serve in the north of Europe. The Marquis de la Romana, lieutenant-general, commanded it. He was quartered in Fionia when the news of the events of 1808 arrived. La Romana entered at once into negotiations with the English fleet, which was cruising in the offing, and had his troops embarked and transported to Spain. La Romana at their head fought energetically against the French. He was a member of the Supreme Junta when he died (1811).

[2] Don Juan de Escoïquiz, born in 1762, canon at Saragossa, was nominated by the Prince of the Peace tutor of the Prince of Asturias, over whom he exercised the greatest influence. He became Privy Councillor in 1808. He followed the prince to Valencay, was imprisoned at Bourges, returned to Madrid in 1814, was appointed minister, but did not exercise any further political influence.

the regency of the kingdom. Once regent, the death of the king would open a new career to his ambition, the bounds of which no one knew. The character of the Prince of the Peace, his marriage, which had placed him nearer the throne,[1] frightened all those who were attached to the royal family. Don Escoïquiz, alarmed by the letter of the Prince of the Asturias, believed, good man that he was, that he had only to enlighten the king and queen as to the designs of the Prince of the Peace. He believed in the influence, which a letter, handed by the Prince of the Asturias to the queen his mother would have, and in which he would show the danger which the royal family incurred on account of the blind confidence which the king had in the Prince of the Peace. This letter, too full of logic and truth, frightened the Prince of the Asturias, who did not dare to deliver it, he was satisfied with copying and preserving it. Ashamed of his want of resolution he wrote to Don Escoïquiz that he considered it impossible for the queen to be undeceived, and that it would be easier to make matters plain to the king, if he should chance one day to speak to him in *tête-à-tête.*

The good canon of Toledo wrote a note, which he adapted as well as possible to the foibles of the king, and he sent it to the Prince of the Asturias who waited in vain for the moment when he could hand it to his father. This document, like the first, was copied by the prince himself, and, also like the first, locked up in his desk, where it was found when his papers were seized.

The Prince of the Peace, who suspected that the conduct of the Prince of the Asturias hid some project scarcely favourable to his views, endeavoured to find means to pry into the privacy of the prince, and got the queen to propose to the latter to marry Dona Maria Theresa, his (Godoy's) sister-in-law, second daughter of the Infant Don Luis. This princess had a beautiful face, was ambitious, and had already shown little aversion for love affairs. The prince, who only knew her to be beautiful and pretty, had given his consent to this marriage. But for some months the ambition of the Prince of the Peace having become more asserted and bold, this match was no longer spoken of. Don Escoïquiz

---

[1] The Prince of the Peace had married a Spanish princess, daughter of the Infant Don Luis.

seeing that all means of getting the king and queen to know the truth were failing, and that the proposition of the marriage with Dona Maria Theresa had fallen through, fancied that a foreign and powerful interest would alone afford real support to the prince, in the critical position in which he found himself, and it occurred to him to marry the latter with one of the daughters of Napoleon's [1] family.

At this time a marriage with a niece of Napoleon seemed likely to ensure to the Prince of the Asturias the shaken throne of Spain, and to put this beautiful and noble country beyond the reach of divisions. This result was to be preferred to that which unexpected events soon brought about.

Don Escoïquiz thought more every day of the plan which he had adopted. Rumours disquieting to the royal family assumed every day more consistency, and were spread among all classes. Not being able now to bear the idea of being so far from his former pupil, he wished to be nearer the centre of affairs and went to Madrid. There he made the acquaintance of the Count d'Orgaz, a loyal Spaniard, particularly attached to the Prince of the Asturias. He spoke to him of his fears and his projects. In one of their conversations Count d'Orgaz told him that Don Diégo Godoy, brother of the Prince of the Peace, was distributing money to the Madrid garrison, and, by this means had secured the support of a large number of the subaltern officers ; a colonel of the dragoons, Don Thomas Jauregui, who was in the garrison kept him acquainted with all the attempts which were being made to corrupt the troops. There was not one officer of note to whom an agent of the Prince of the Peace had not said, " You see the wretched state of Spain, the Bourbon dynasty is absolutely on the decline ; the king is on the point of death ; the prince is an imbecile ; measures must be taken ; you are a good Spaniard, we count on you." A thousand propositions of this sort were openly made, and by men who inspired confidence on account of their reputation, and the positions they occupied. Don Luis Viguri, an

---

[1] This project had for a moment some consistency. Napoleon being sounded on the matter had appeared to reply favourably (letter of the Emperor to the Prince of the Asturias, April 16, 1808, *Correspondence*, vol. xvii.). A daughter of Lucien Bonaparte had been proposed, but this plan was not carried out. It is probable that the emperor never intended that it should be.

officer in the commissariat who had kept up relations with the chief officers, was one of the most active in that respect. In the schools, in the academies, in all public buildings, the same language was used. Abbé Stala, librarian of St. Isidro, had been so imprudent even as to show the documents of which the purport was to make clear to the Spanish nation, that, in the crisis which was being prepared, there could only be safety in placing entire confidence in the Prince of the Peace. Don Escoïquiz felt that there was not a moment to lose, and that all the friends of the throne must unite and form a league for its defence. With this aim, he asked the Prince of the Asturias for a credential in order that he could explain matters confidentially to the Duke of Infantado, a young man of noble birth, of a fine character, and pleasing and commanding appearance, and standing well in public opinion. With this letter, written by the prince, the canon sought the Duke of Infantado,[1] and spoke to him with the greatest frankness, but their principles not permitting them to adopt any measure which could be contrary to the fidelity they owed to the king, they confined themselves to taking measures of precaution for the time when the king, whose health was daily getting weaker and weaker, should die. The Prince of the Peace had it in his power to conceal for some moments the death of the king. The distrust, and the hatred which he had skilfully inspired in the queen for her son, enabled him to surround and fill the castle with devoted troops. Supported by etiquette, he could, and that was his intention, have brought the Prince of the Asturias to the bedside of the king, who would be supposed to be still alive; there to seize him, and all the royal family, and make them sign by force, all the necessary orders to place the authority in his hands, determining afterwards what should be done with the princes.

The Duke of Infantado and Don Escoïquiz considered that the only means of preventing this outrage would be to have

---

[1] The Infantado was an ancient manor of Castile, so named, because it had formerly been the appanage of the heirs presumptive of Spain. The duke, of whom mention is made here, belonged to the Silva family, who had acquired the duchy two centuries before. Born in 1771, he became the friend of the Prince of the Asturias ; in 1808, he recognized at first King Joseph, but soon separated from him and took command of a Spanish army corps. President of the Council of Castile in 1820, he retired in 1826, and died in 1836.

an act given beforehand by the new king, which would place
supreme military command in the hands of the Duke of
Infantado. This act would have also put all the authorities, even
the Prince of the Peace, under his absolute command, throughout New Castile, and especially at Madrid, and in all the royal
residences. With this order, the Duke of Infantado, at the
first news he should have of the coming death of the king, was
to prepare the notification of his powers, take the supreme command of all the military forces, appear in the town, and in the
royal houses in the uniform of generalissimo, and even have
the Prince of the Peace arrested should he give signs of the least
restlessness. Don Escoïquiz drew up the act in question, and
sent it to the prince, explaining to him the object of the measure ; he persuaded him to write it out with his own hand, to
sign it, and to place on it his seal. The prince carried out all
that was suggested. The act was handed to the Duke of
Infantado, who was to keep it carefully till the time when he
should be called upon to make use of it. This act read as
follows :—

"We, Ferdinand VII., by the grace of God, King of
Castile, &c. . . . .
"The Lord having deigned to take to Himself our dear and
well-beloved father, the King Charles IV., whom may God have
in His holy keeping, and consequently having ourselves ascended
the throne of Spain, as his natural and legitimate heir, knowing
that in the first moments of suspension of authority, which is
an inevitable consequence of the death of kings, it may happen
that there are persons who wish to take advantage of it, to
disturb the public peace, as the public voice seems to indicate ;
and considering that the best means of repressing malevolence
should it dare to take the form of any project of that sort, is to
put the entire military forces which surround us in the hands of
one whom we can trust, and who, besides talent, courage, and
noble birth, enjoys public esteem ; finding in you, Duke of
Infantado, my cousin, all these qualities united, we have
considered it our duty to confer on you, as we do by this
decree, the supreme command of the entire military forces in
New Castile, and in all the royal residences, infantry, cavalry,
artillery, militia, &c., without any exception, not even the
body-guard and the troops which compose our Royal Guard,
nor those which form the guard of the generalissimo, in order

that you may make use of them in the way in which you shall deem useful or necessary to put down any rising, to disperse any meeting, to dispel every seditious project against our person, or the Royal Family, or any which is capable of disturbing the public peace in any way whatever. Our wish being to suspend, as we do suspend, every authority, even all military power, which do not come under your orders, to that of the Prince of the Peace as generalissimo, as well as that of the Captain General of New Castile, we order, that all the military chiefs, of whatever class or rank they may be, obey strictly your orders as though they were our own, in everything which may concern the public peace, for which we hold you responsible. And we declare, subject to the punishment of traitors and enemies of the country all those who by ignorance, affected or intentional, shall oppose your orders, or shall not display the strict obedience they owe you. We decree also, that all the civil and military tribunals, and all magistrates of whatever class they may be, assist in the execution of your orders, and all that concerns them, under the same penalties for not so doing.

"We give you also all the necessary authority to imprison, if it be necessary, all persons of whatever class, condition, or rank they may be, without any exception, who shall be suspected of wishing to disturb the public peace, or who shall disturb it.

"This is our will, as also that this decree, although not bearing the ordinary sanction of one of the ministers, on account of the urgency of the circumstances in which we are placed, be observed and carried out as though it had the signature of one of our ministers, being written, signed and sealed as it is, by our own hand. The whole to be carried out under the penalties of high treason on those who oppose it.

"At . . . . . . the . . . . . . of the year . . . . .
                    " Signed   YO EL RÉ."

This decree had the date in blank, and it was to be filled in at the moment of the death of the king, by the Duke of Infantado.

Towards the middle of the month of June, 1807, Don Escoïquiz received another letter from the Prince of the Asturias, in which his Royal Highness told him that he had had it handed to him by Don Juan Manuel de Villena, his first equerry, who had received it from Don Pedro Giraldo, colonel of Engineers, and tutor of the Infante Don Francisco,[1] a letter which was

---

[1] The Infante Don Francisco was the third son of King Charles IV.

intended to be delivered into the hands of his Royal Highness, and was written by an individual, who said he belonged to the French Legation. The contents announced a very secret communication, which M. de Beauharnais,[1] the ambassador of France, desired to make to his Royal Highness. Don Escoïquiz, consulted by the prince, in order to know what he should answer, told him to say to the persons who had given him the letter, that he did not interfere in any matter, and did not make any private appointments. He offered the prince to find out exactly if this message was really from the ambassador of France or not. To be certain on this point might be very useful, because, if the message were false, the aim of it could only be to lay a trap for his Royal Highness, which it was important to find out; and that if it were true, it was of the greatest consequence for the interests of the prince not to lose the opportunity of becoming acquainted with the intentions of Napoleon, both as regards the position of the Prince of the Peace to the emperor, which was not sufficiently known, as well as the marriage of the Prince of the Asturias with one of the nieces of Napoleon, a subject on which vague rumours were already in circulation. The reply of Don Escoïquiz showed the utility as well as the security which the support of Napoleon would give to the prince, if this marriage should suit his ambition or his vanity.

To this letter, which, owing to subsequent circumstances, furnished documentary evidence at the Escurial trial, the Prince of the Asturias replied, giving his unreserved approval. Thereupon Don Escoïquiz saw the Duke of Infantado, and, after having told him of this new intrigue, asked him for an introduction, under some plausible pretext, to the ambassador of France, to whom he was not known. They chose as the pretext for the introduction to the ambassador, who was considered, in Spain, to be fond of literature, the presentation to him of a work entitled *The Conquest of Mexico*, an epic poem written by Don Escoïquiz. The ambassador, without showing any surprise

---

[1] François, Marquis de Beauharnais, brother-in-law of the Empress Josephine. Born in 1756, he was deputy from Sologne ; emigrated in 1792, and served in the army of Condé ; returning to France in 1800, he was nominated ambassador at the court of the King of Etruria in 1805 ; then at Madrid. He was recalled in 1808, and exiled to Sologne. Peer of France under the Restoration, he died in 1823.

at his supposed literary reputation replied to the Duke that he received the book and the author with pleasure. After a few words about the conquest of Mexico, and a few questions or remarks, which drew gradually nearer the object of his visit, Don Escoïquiz opened his mind to the ambassador on the subject of the message which was attributed to him, and of the wish of the Prince of the Asturias to know the truth.

M. de Beauharnais displayed some embarrassment, evaded the subject of the message, confining himself to saying that such a step on his part would not be becoming towards the heir to the throne, adding immediately, that his respect for the Prince of the Asturias was such that he would be delighted to have private opportunities of paying his court to his Royal Highness. Don Escoïquiz clearly saw that the ambassador admitted more than he denied. Emboldened by the indecision of M. de Beauharnais he explained in a manner more precise, and led the ambassador to say, that a letter from the prince in his hands would give him sufficient confidence to speak with him (Escoïquiz) of matters of the greatest interest to his Royal Highness. To which Don Escoïquiz replied laughing that it appeared to him that skilful diplomats liked to be able to deny messages, but that a sign agreed upon beforehand could produce the same effects, and give the same amount of confidence. It was then decided between them that as the court was coming to Madrid in two or three days, the ambassador should present himself, according to custom, at the head of the diplomatic corps, to his Royal Highness, and that there the prince should ask him if he had been to Naples ; that on leaving the ambassador, and passing to another foreign minister, he should draw his handkerchief from his pocket, and keep it in his hand for a moment.

On the 1st July, the ambassadors attended a presentation to the princes, and his Royal Highness made the sign agreed upon. Two days later, Don Escoïquiz, informed of what had taken place, went to the ambassador of France, from whom he received most positive assurances of the affection which Napoleon entertained for the Prince of the Asturias, of the inclination which he had to favour him in every way he could, and at the same time of the small esteem in which he held the Prince of the Peace. Vague as these assurances were, Don Escoïquiz, somewhat elated at the new part he was playing, and anxious on account of the position of the prince, exploded the question of marriage, and even went so far as to say that the prince left to Napoleon the choice of that niece of his whom he should think fit to give him. Secrecy was recommended on both sides. M. de Beauharnais wrote at once to Paris, and asked for the necessary authorizations to negotiate with the king, Charles IV., in order to prevent the Prince of the Asturias being compromised in the eyes of his father.

The vigilant watch kept by the Prince of the Peace over all that concerned the French Embassy, had determined M. de Beauharnais and Don Escoïquiz to select for their first interview a retired spot in the garden of the Retiro. Twenty days had elapsed when Don Escoïquiz received notice to be at the spot agreed upon at two o'clock in the afternoon, when the excessive heat would drive every one from the promenade. The reply which the ambassador had received was rather insignificant, and did not allude to the proposition of marriage. M. de Beauharnais attributed this silence to the fact that there was nothing officially written on the part of the prince, and he advised Don Escoïquiz to get His Royal Highness to write direct to Napoleon. Don Escoïquiz thought this step likely to cause too many difficulties for him to dare to propose it; and he persuaded, on his part, the ambassador to point out in his next despatch, that the position of the prince did not admit of such a delicate step being taken, until affairs were in a more advanced stage. It may be doubted, owing to the vague language of M. de Beauharnais, whether he had positive instructions; but either to serve the interests of the Beauharnais or that of the Bonapartes[1] he entered into an intrigue with the Prince of the Asturias, which intrigue could only serve the views of the emperor. However it may be, M. de Beauharnais promised to write again, and to send to Don Escoïquiz, who was obliged to return to Toledo, the answer of Napoleon.

---

[1] The Beauharnais wished the Prince of the Asturias to marry a niece of the Empress Josephine, while the Bonapartes wished him to marry a daughter of Lucien. The emperor only wished what would serve his purpose—(*Prince Talleyrand*).

Things remained in this state during the whole of the month
of August, and nearly the whole of September. It was only on
the 30th September, 1807, that Don Escoïquiz received at Toledo
a letter from the ambassador of France, in which were extracts
from Napoleon's letter, the following words being underlined :
. . . . . " *I do not buy, I do not sell, I do nothing without*
guarantee. Have you received any letter, any official note on this
matter ? " The terms of blunt frankness employed in this letter.
induced Don Escoïquiz to go to Madrid. He saw M. de Beauharnais at the Retiro. At this meeting, the ambassador complained that the prince had not had confidence in his first proposition, and he renewed it with greater insistence, saying, that
nothing was possible as long as his Royal Highness did not write
himself. Don Escoïquiz, who for a long time had been of opinion
that the support of Napoleon was the only means for the prince to
escape from the dangers he was incurring, allowed himself to be
persuaded. He drew up a draft of a letter, and M. de Beauharnais having agreed that the terms which were employed
would suit Napoleon, the canon sent it to the Prince of the
Asturias, who made a copy of it in his own hand, and forwarded
it to Don Escoïquiz to give to the ambassador. He inclosed
with it, a note in which he pointed out Don Escoïquiz as the
only man who had his entire confidence in this matter. The
letter of the Prince of the Asturias shows too clearly the
general feeling of the time, for it not to be here reproduced in
its entirety.

The Prince of the Asturias to the Emperor Napoleon.

" THE ESCURIAL, *Oct.* 11, 1807.

" SIRE,—I consider this day as the happiest of my life, seeing
that it affords me the opportunity of expressing to your Imperial
and Royal Majesty—to a hero, destined by Providence to
restore peace, order, and prosperity in Europe, threatened as
it is by a complete overthrow, and to strengthen tottering
thrones—the sentiments of regard, admiration and respect
with which your brilliant qualities inspire me. I should have
had, a long time since, this satisfaction, as well as that of assuring
your Imperial and Royal Majesty of the sincere desire which I
have to see increase happily the existing friendship between
our two houses, and to see this alliance, so advantageous to

both nations, become closer every day, by means of a marriage which would unite me to a Princess of your Majesty's family. But circumstances have obliged me to be silent, and it is only in consequence of the explanations of M. de Beauharnais and of the information which he has given me as to the wishes of your Imperial Majesty, that I have resolved to speak.

"I fear that this step, so innocent in the terms in which I make it, and in the position I·am in, might be considered as a crime should it be discovered.

"Your Imperial and Royal Majesty knows much better than I, that the best kings are the most exposed to become victims of the artifices of the ambitious and intriguing men who surround them. Our court is not free from such men, and the benevolence and uprightness of my dear parents expose them the more to be the victims of their unloyal plots. I fear then, that those men may have obtained their consent to some other projected marriage for me, more suitable to their own interests, and I take the liberty of asking your Majesty to open the eyes of my dear parents, and to get them to adopt the alliance which I beg to ask of you.

"The least intimation on the part of your Majesty will suffice to ruin all the prospects, and to destroy all the projects of those selfish and malicious men, regarding their Majesties, my august parents, who love your Majesty so sincerely.

"As for myself, full of respect and filial obedience towards their Majesties, I can only play a passive part in this matter, and this will be to refuse any alliance which shall not have the approval of your Majesty, and I shall expect from your kind offices, the happiness of my dear parents, that of my country, and my own, by the marriage with the princess whom I hope to receive from their hands, and from those of your Imperial and Royal Majesty.

"I am, &c.,

"(Signed) FERDINAND, PRINCE OF THE ASTURIAS."

The Prince of the Peace was informed by the spies whom he had in the house of M. de Beauharnais, of what was going on, and he immediately got the king to write a letter, which his ambassador, Prince Masserano,[1] had orders to carry immediately to Napoleon, wherever he might be. This letter reached

---

[1] Carlo Ferrero-Fieschi, Prince Masserano, captain of the body-guards of Charles III., ambassador at Paris in 1805, and grandmaster of ceremonies of King Joseph. He died in 1837.

the emperor three days before he received that of M. de Beauharnais at Fontainebleau.

The King of Spain complained very strongly to Napoleon
of his being in secret communication with his son, and he
spoke of the letter, which no doubt Napoleon had received from
the Prince of the Asturias.

For some weeks, affairs in Spain remained in suspense;
and suddenly they assumed a new aspect, owing to the unforeseen arrival of the French army in several provinces of the
kingdom. The apparent object of this singular arrangement
was, as one has seen above, to oblige the court of Portugal to
separate its cause from that of England. It was in consequence
of the communications made by the Prince of the Asturias, and of
the complaints made against him by his father to Napoleon,
that the latter, partly by threats, and partly by promises, induced
the Prince of the Peace to consent to the stipulations of the
two treaties of the 27th October, 1807, which we consider it our
duty to insert here, on account of their importance in the
question under consideration. We have already said that these
treaties had been negotiated at Fontainebleau with the utmost
secrecy, by Don Izquierdo, the secret agent of the Prince of the
Peace, and Marshal Duroc, that is to say, in reality, Napoleon
himself. The treaty ran thus :—

" His Majesty the Emperor of the French, King of Italy, &c. . .
and His Catholic Majesty the King of Spain, being spontaneously
desirous to regulate the interests of the two States, and to
determine the future condition of Portugal in a manner conformable to the policy of the two nations, have appointed for their
ministers plenipotentiary, namely: His Majesty the Emperor of
the French, General of Division Michael Duroc, Grand Marshal
of the Palace, &c., and His Catholic Majesty the King of Spain,
Don Eugene Izquierdo de Ribera y Lezaun, his honorary Councillor of State, &c. . ., who, after having exchanged their full
powers, have agreed upon what follows :

" Art. 1.—The provinces lying between the Minho and the
Duero, with the city of Oporto,[1] shall be given in all property and
sovereignty to His Majesty the King of Etruria, under the title
of King of Northern Lusitania.

[1] That is to say the northern part of Portugal, minus the province of Tras-os-
montes.

" Art. 2.—The kingdom of Alentejo and the kingdom of the Algarves,[1] shall be given in all property and sovereignty to the Prince of the Peace, to be henceforth known under the title of Prince of the Algarves.

" Art. 3.—The provinces of Beira, Tras-os-montes and Portuguese Estramadura,[2] shall remain in pledge until the general peace, when it will be disposed of according to circumstances, and in a manner which will then be determined by the high contracting parties.

" Art. 4.—The kingdom of Northern Lusitania shall be possessed by the hereditary descendants of His Majesty the King of Etruria, conformably to the laws of succession adopted, by the reigning family of His Majesty the King of Spain.

" Art. 5.—The principality of the Algarves shall be hereditary with the issue of the Prince of the Peace conformably to the laws of succession adopted by the reigning family of His Majesty the King of Spain.

" Art. 6.—In default of a descendant or legitimate heir of the King of Northern Lusitania, or of the Prince of the Algarves, these countries shall be given by form of investiture to His Majesty the King of Spain, on the condition that they shall never be re-united under one head, nor re-united to the crown of Spain.

" Art. 7.—The kingdom of Northern Lusitania and the principality of the Algarves recognize also as protector His Catholic Majesty the King of Spain, and the sovereigns of these countries shall not in any case, make war or peace without his consent.

" Art. 8.—In case the provinces of Beira, Tras-os-montes, and Portuguese Estramadura, held in pledge, should be, at the general peace, returned to the House of Braganza in exchange for Gibraltar, Trinity and other colonies that the English have acquired from the Spanish and their allies, the new sovereign of these provinces shall hold towards His Majesty the King of Spain the same obligations which are held towards him by the King of Northern Lusitania and the Prince of the Algarves.

" Art. 9.—His Majesty the King of Etruria cedes in all property and sovereignty the kingdom of Etruria to His Majesty the Emperor of the French, King of Italy.

" Art. 10.—When the definitive occupation of the provinces of Portugal shall have been effected, the respective princes who will be put in possession of them, shall name conjointly commissioners to fix the proper limits.

---

[1] All the southern part of Portugal, situated to the south of the Tagus, having about 600,000 inhabitants.

[2] All the central part of Portugal, situated between the Tagus and the Douro and, besides, the province of Tras-os-montes, that is, nearly half of the kingdom.

" Art. 11.—His Majesty the Emperor of the French, King of Italy, guarantees to His Catholic Majesty the King of Spain the possession of his states on the continent of Europe, south of the Pyrenees.

" Art. 12.—His Majesty the Emperor of the French, King of Italy, consents to recognize His Catholic Majesty the King of Spain, as Emperor of the two Americas, at the date which shall have been determined by His Catholic Majesty to take this title, which will take place at the general peace, or at the latest in three years hence.

" Art. 13.—It is understood between the two high contracting parties that they shall divide equally between themselves the islands, colonies and other maritime possessions of Portugal.

" Art. 14.—The present treaty shall be kept secret. It shall be ratified, and the ratifications shall be exchanged at Madrid twenty days at the latest after the date of the signing.

" Done at Fontainebleau, October 27, 1807.

" Duroc.
" E. Izquierdo."

Secret Convention of the Same Day.

" His Majesty the Emperor of the French, King of Italy, &c., and His Catholic Majesty the King of Spain, desiring to settle the bases of an arrangement relative to the conquest and occupation of Portugal, in consequence of the stipulations of the treaty signed to-day, have named, &c., who, after having exchanged their full powers, have agreed upon the following articles.

" Art. 1.—A corps of twenty-five thousand men of infantry, and of three thousand cavalry, of the troops of His Imperial Majesty will enter Spain to repair directly to Lisbon ; it will be joined by a corps of eight thousand men of the Spanish infantry and three thousand cavalry, with thirty pieces of artillery.

" Art. 2.—At the same time a division of ten thousand men of the Spanish troops shall take possession of the province of Entre-Minho-Duero and the city of Oporto, and another division of six thousand men of the Spanish troops shall take possession of Alentejo and of the kingdom of the Algarves.

" Art. 3.—The French troops shall be fed and supported by Spain, and their pay shall be furnished by France during the time of their march across Spain.

" Art. 4.—From the instant when the combined troops shall have effected their entrance into Portugal, the government

and administration of the provinces of Beira, Tras-os-montes
and of Portuguese Estramadura (which are to remain in pledge)
shall be handed to the general commanding the French troops,
and all contributions shall be raised to the profit of France. The
provinces which are to form the kingdom of Northern Lusitania
and the principality of the Algarves shall be administered and
governed by the Spanish divisions which shall take possession of
them, and the contributions there shall be levied to the profit of
Spain.

" Art. 5.—The central corps shall be under the orders of the
commander of the French troops, whom the Spanish troops
attached to this army shall be likewise bound to obey. Nevertheless in case the King of Spain or even the Prince of the Peace
should judge it proper to join this corps, the French troops as
well as the general who shall command them, shall submit to
their orders.

" Art. 6.—Another body of forty thousand men of French
troops shall be assembled at Bayonne on November 20 next, at
the latest, to be ready to enter Spain, for the purpose of going to
Portugal in case the English should send reinforcements or
threaten an attack. Nevertheless, this new corps shall not enter
Spain until the two high contracting parties shall have mutually
agreed on this point.

" Art. 7.—The present convention shall be ratified and the
ratifications shall be exchanged at the same time as those of
the treaty of this day.

" Done at Fontainebleau, October 27, 1807.

" DUROC.
" IZQUIERDO."

The entry of the French troops into Spain was considered in
various manners, according to the different interests which
then divided this unhappy country.

The Prince of the Peace regarded it as a means of putting
into execution his views on the sovereignty of a part of Portugal,
which had been assured to him by the treaty of Fontainebleau.

The persons attached to the Prince of the Asturias saw in
it a means employed by Napoleon to impose upon them the
Prince of the Peace, whom they supposed to be anxious to put
an obstacle in the way of the marriage of their prince and of the
abdication of King Charles which would result from it.

The mass of the Spanish people regarded Napoleon as a disinterested protector, who was going to relieve the nation from the oppression of the Prince of the Peace, and establish with the country relations which would be advantageous for France and for Spain.

A few months afterwards all these chimeras vanished. In the first place, the Prince of the Asturias was arrested at the end of the month of October, as guilty of high treason. Later, the Prince of the Peace barely escaped perishing in a riot, and only escaped death by being in his turn thrown into prison. As to the Spanish people, who had so desired the arrival of the French, and who looked upon them as liberators, they had to suffer on their part at Burgos, and above all at Madrid, a treatment which they had been far from anticipating.

It was on the same day that the treaty of Fontainebleau was signed, October 27, 1807, at ten o'clock in the evening, that the heir to the crown of Spain was arrested at the Escurial. They accused him—these are the terms of the writ :—*of having wished to dethrone his father and of having wished to assassinate him.* The same writ stated that *the king had received this intelligence from an unknown source,* and that the affair would be tried before a tribunal, composed of the Governor of Castile, Don Arias Mon, of Don Domingo Fernandez de Campomanès, and of Don Sebastian de Torrès. The duties of clerk to the court were to be performed by Don Benito Arias de Prada, the Court alcade. Out of regard for the person of the prince, they charged the Governor of Castile and the Minister of Justice, the Marquis de Cavallero[1] to receive his declarations. The persons accused as accomplices were : Don Escoïquiz, the Duke of Infantado, the Marquis d'Orgaz, Count de Bornos, Don Juan Emmanuel de Villena, Don Pedro Giraldo. Imprisoned in the cells of the Escurial, they were deprived of all communication between themselves and the outer world. To the three judges I have just named, and at their request, after two months and a half of examination, eight other judges drawn from the Council

---

[1] Joseph, Marquis de Cavallero, born at Saragossa in 1760, *Fiscal* of the Supreme Council of war in 1794, Minister of Justice, 1798. He was dismissed in 1808, but remained Councillor of State and head of the Council of Finances. President of the Section of Justice at the Council of State under King Joseph, he took refuge in France in 1814, returned to Spain in 1820, and died in 1821.

of Castile were added. The number of judges was thus increased to eleven.

They declared unanimously on January 11, 1808, that the prince and the others accused were not guilty. The verdict was sent to the king who did not publish it, and who, a few days after, exiled to various different parts all the persons against whom the accusation had been directed. The Prince of the Asturias was consigned to his palace.

During the course of the trial, the number of French troops entering the kingdom increased, and they took position at places near Madrid, such as Segovia, Avila[1] Olmedo and Aranda de Duero.

These positions, which were not on the route of an expedition coming from France to go to Portugal, and the manner in which they took possession of Pampeluna and Barcelona,[2] might lead one to believe in some menacing intentions towards Spain itself. Explanations between the two governments dissipated for a moment this uneasiness, but not enough however to prevent the Prince of the Peace believing he ought to give to the Spanish troops who were marching towards Portugal, under the command of Lieutenant-General Solano, orders to retrace their steps.[3]

The ambassador of France pretended to be ignorant of this, and a few days after received an order to say that the Spanish government, by the movement it had just had made by its troops, having failed in the plans agreed upon and necessary for the occupation of Portugal, the emperor found himself obliged, in order to ensure the success of the expedition, to introduce into Spain forces much greater than those of which the treaty authorized the introduction. For fear of a counter order from the Spanish government, which, in effect, arrived soon after, Napoleon had his troops make forced marches, and, in a few days, he occupied other places in Catalonia, Navarra and Guipuscoa such as Figuera, San-Sebastian, &c.

[1] Segovia and Avila are situated at only about sixty miles north-west of Madrid.
[2] These two cities were carried by force and by surprise by the French troops.
[3] Don Francisco Solano, Marquis del Socorro (1770-1808). A fervent admirer and partisan of France, he served as a common soldier in the army of Moreau. Named later Captain-General of Andalusia, he tried to prevent, and afterwards to quell, the insurrection, and was assassinated at Cadiz in a riot.

The Court of Spain wished to appear reassured ; the communications between the two governments followed the usual course, while the country was invaded, without at all comprehending such grave events. The Prince of the Peace began, nevertheless, to lose a little of the confidence he had in Napoleon, and thought of proceeding with the royal family towards the port of Cadiz. Without daring at first to disclose all his projects, he confined himself to proposing a journey to Andalusia. On March 13, 1808, he made the proposition to the king, who adopted the plan and gave that very night the necessary orders to the Marquis de Mos, Grand Master of the Palace, to the first Secretary of State, Don Pedro Cevallos,[1] and to the Marquis of Cavallero, Minister of Justice.

This departure, at first fixed for a near day, was put off to March 16, which gave time for the Marquis de Cavallero to oppose a project which he disapproved. His private opinion was that the king ought to wait at Madrid or at Aranjuez for the arrival of Napoleon to take with him a determination upon the political affairs of the two countries. The reasons given by the Marquis de Cavallero to the king, in the presence of the queen, produced a sufficient impression to cause him to revoke the order for the journey, which was beginning to be no longer a secret. The requisitions made in order to procure carriages and horses for conveyance, the departure of Madame Tudo,[1] who had crossed Aranjuez in a travelling carriage, accompanied by her children ; all these circumstances had caused agitation among the people.

A decree badly drawn up, whose object was to reassure, and which produced a contrary effect, increased the indignation already so strong against the Prince of the Peace. They accused him loudly of having counselled the king to abandon Madrid. This counsel, they said, could only come from a man who sought to fill the soul of the king with personal fears ; the moment has come, said they, for delivering the country from his oppressor.

[1] Don Pedro Cevallos, born in 1764, was Minister of Foreign Affairs. Deeply attached to the Prince of the Asturias, he was constantly the adversary of King Joseph, and became the leader of the National Junta. He was disgraced in 1820, and died in 1840. He had married a niece of the Prince of the Peace.

[2] Dona Josepha Tudo was the mistress of the Prince of the Peace. Some people have pretended that they were united by a secret marriage.

The body-guard, which, for several months, had not received their pay, showed themselves discontented at a journey burdensome to them ; the palace servants, whose wages were equally behindhand, and who found some aid at Madrid and at Aranjuez, were in great uneasiness. Their fears spread among the lower people ; the agitation had been manifesting itself for several days ; the hatred which the people bore towards the Prince of the Peace was still increased by the instigations of those who, fearing his return and his vengeance, would without grief have seen him perish in an insurrection. Popular risings are very convenient for intriguers ; the threads are broken there and researches become impossible. No measure of precaution had been taken ; there were at Aranjuez only the number of troops necessary for ordinary duty ; and besides they had not chosen those upon whom they might count the most. Two Swiss regiments, faithful and available, had been left and almost forgotten at Madrid.

In this state of affairs, the slightest event might have incalculable results. On the night of the 17th to the 18th of March, before midnight, a quarrel, in which were fired several pistol shots between a patrol of carabineers and some body-guards, became the signal for the insurrection. The people came out in crowds ; passion carried them towards the house of the Prince of the Peace ; they broke open the doors. The body-guard who were at Aranjuez, and the Spanish guards and Walloons, consulting only their duty, endeavoured to quell the disturbance. In spite of all their efforts the house was sacked ; the rioters, however, did not find the prince who had taken refuge on the roof, at a place which by foresight he had had prepared, and that each year of his administration had rendered more necessary. The people, in the midst of this tumult, were particular to testify by the cries of : " Down with Godoy ! Long live the king ! Long live the queen ! " who was the real object of their hatred ; they paid even some marks of regard to the Princess of the Peace whom they led to the palace with the Duchess of Alcudia, her daughter. The effervescence lasted through the night, and at daybreak, the people wishing to show the king their respect and attachment, repaired to the palace, demanding to see the king, who came out upon the balcony with all the royal family; and there, several times, they were applauded and greeted by the most lively demonstrations of love and fidelity. A few signs of kindness and of sensibility from the king, and the condescension shown in declaring himself that he would deprive the Prince of the Peace of the offices of general-in-chief and admiral, sufficed to cause the withdrawal of this multitude and to restore tranquillity for that day.

The troops, re-assured by the disposition of the people towards the king, saw with pleasure the humiliation of the Prince of the Peace. He was believed to have fled, and the crowd which at first seemed only to wish to be delivered from him retired and appeared satisfied. On the 19th, however, the rumour spread in the city that the prince was hidden in his house; he had been discovered by a sentinel who refused to give him the means of escape. The people ran in from all sides; the prince, perceiving some troops in the street, darted out; before he could reach the body-guards who surrounded him, he received several blows upon the head. The king, informed of what was taking place, and thinking that the Prince of the Asturias would have more influence over the people than himself, induced his son to go and announce to this immense crowd, that the Prince of the Peace would be put on his trial. The Prince of the Asturias executed promptly the orders of his father; he addressed himself to those who appeared the most excited and promised them, if they would retire, that the prince should be led to prison and tried according to the full rigour of the laws. These promises, the distance that was gradually covered, the watch of the body-guards brought the Prince of the Peace to the barracks of the guards. They closed the gates, and he was taken to a room, which by one of those chances destined to give men great lessons, happened to be the same that he occupied when he was a simple body-guard.

In the first moment, the king resolved to send the Prince of the Peace to Grenada, to the castle of the Alhambra; this project was soon renounced, because it was feared that the people might manifest displeasure at seeing him sent away and perhaps escape, for whom they demanded chastisement.

The irresolution in which the absence of the Prince of the

Peace left the king, the uneasiness which filled his mind, the little confidence he had in himself, the perfectly material life that he had led for many years, everything in fine made him think that his health was feeble enough so that in such difficult circumstances, he might, without dishonour, abdicate the throne.

Perhaps he was also influenced by the fear he had, as well as the queen, of seeing massacred under their own eyes the man who, for so long a time and with such sway, had enjoyed their confidence and all their favour ; but finally, this determination, whatever may have been the motive, was taken without having consulted any one. The king had Don Cevallos called and ordered him to draw up an act of abdication. Don Cevallos had already been informed of this resolution of the king by the members of the diplomatic corps whom His Majesty had seen in the morning, and before whom he had formally declared that circumstances impelled him to put into execution a project which his age and his infirmities had led him to conceive long before, and that he was going to entrust the crown to hands younger and more able to sustain the burden of it. The king, addressing himself afterwards directly to Count Strogonoff,[1] minister of Russia, said to him, with an air of satisfaction, that he had never taken a resolution that was more agreeable to him. His language was the same throughout the day with the persons whom he had occasion to see, and particularly with the ministers, the captain of the body-guard, and the colonel of the Walloons.

On the 19th, in the evening, the act of abdication being signed, and invested with all the necessary formalities, the king ordered the Prince of the Asturias to come into his presence, communicated it to him, and had it published. The prince, immediately after having kissed the hand of the king, his father, received by his order the felicitations and homage of the House of His Majesty and of all the court.

The new king, desiring to have the first act of his reign agreeable to his father, took on the instant, the measures he judged most proper to arrest the movements of the people which

---

[1] Gregory Alexandrowitch, Count Strogonoff, ambassador of Russia at Constantinople, then at Madrid and at London. He died in 1857.

at Madrid were directed against the relations and friends of the Prince of the Peace. The ministers of the King Charles IV. were retained in their offices, with the exception of Don Solar who, being a partisan of the Prince of the Peace, had been obliged in the first moments of the outbreak at Aranjuez to hold himself aloof. They replaced him by Don de Azanza,[1] former viceroy of Mexico ; the Duke of Infantado, to whom public opinion was favourable, became president of the Council of Castile and colonel of the Spanish Guards. The Prince of the Peace was transferred to Pinto under the guard of Lieutenant-General Marquis de Castellar.

The first arrangements made, the new king thought it proper for him to repair to Madrid and to pass some time there. This resolution, to which he was led at the instance of the people of the capital, and perhaps also by the secret desire that he had to see a general sanction given to the abrupt and important acts which had taken place at Aranjuez, may have had a very great influence over the destinies of Spain, since by this step Ferdinand closed for himself the road to Andalusia. This reflection was no doubt overlooked by the Grand Duc de Berg,[2] who, on being informed of the project of the king, instructed M. de Beauharnais to repair to Aranjuez, to dissuade His Majesty from coming to Madrid, while so many French troops were there. The king while refusing to accede to the proposition made to him by the ambassador, put forward the engagements he had taken with his capital.

The arrival of the king at Madrid was announced by a proclamation, and had the effect of re-establishing order in the city. The inhabitants of all classes hurried to meet him, and with the most lively and most affectionate expressions, testified to him their joy, and showed the hopes the new reign raised in them.

---

[1] Don Jose Miquel de Azanza, born in 1746, was at first *chargé d'affaires* in Russia, then in Prussia. He entered the army afterwards, was appointed Minister of War in 1795, then Viceroy of Mexico. Having returned to Spain in 1799, he became Minister of Finances on the accession of Ferdinand (1808). He was one of the first to attach himself to King Joseph, became Minister of Justice, then of Foreign Affairs. Exiled in 1814, he took refuge in France, where he died.

[2] Murat, Grand Duc de Berg, was then lieutenant of the Emperor in Spain, and resided at Madrid.

The object, which at this moment filled all minds and occupied them solely, did not allow them to perceive the situation in which the country was placed. Very few of the inhabitants of Madrid knew that the city was surrounded by 60,000 Frenchmen, and on March 23, when the Grand Duc de Berg, followed by his staff-officers, entered Madrid, he astonished the greater number of the inhabitants who were ignorant of his arrival in the kingdom, and he frightened no one. The species of revolutionary giddiness which agitated the minds, led the multitude to believe there were no dangers which could not be conquered by men who had defeated the power of the Prince of the Peace.

On the day after the arrival of King Ferdinand VII. in Madrid, the foreign ministers, with the exception of the ambassador of France, the minister of Holland and the *chargé d'affaires* of Saxony,[1] presented themselves at the palace to have the honour of paying their respects to the new king.

M. de Beauharnais, ambassador of France, saw him in private, and announced the approaching arrival of the emperor in Spain. The relations he had previously had with the king, authorized him in believing that he might counsel him to go and meet Napoleon. He tried to induce him even to pursue his journey as far as Bayonne, assuring him that the emperor, touched by this proof of confidence, would not delay a moment in recognizing him as King of Spain, and according him one of his nieces in marriage. The ambassador added that it would be suitable for the king to take the necessary precautions for putting the life of the Prince of the Peace out of all danger, and for giving his orders to have the procedure which had been commenced against him suspended. The Grand Duc de Berg, who saw King Ferdinand VII. at the house of the Queen of Etruria on two occasions, used the same language, with this difference, that in speaking of the Prince of the Peace, his expressions were less measured than those of M. de Beauharnais. Both, in addressing the king, used no title except that of Royal Highness, and even displayed some affectation in making use of this title. The king

---

[1] The minister of Holland was M. de Verhuell, and the *chargé d'affaires* of Saxony Baron von Forell. As is known, Louis Bonaparte was then King of Holland and the King of Saxony was entirely devoted to Napoleon, which explains the reserve of the two diplomatists.

made no agreement with them; his replies were polite, and a slight embarrassment enabled him to make them very laconic.

The difficult circumstances in which King Ferdinand found himself, induced him to form a private council immediately. He composed it of Dons Infantado, Escoïquiz, San Carlos,[1] Cevallos, Cavallero, Olaguer, and Gil de Lemos. The Duke of San Carlos had the position of grand master of the household of the king, the Marquis de Mos, who had filled it, having been dismissed. The king charged Don Escoïquiz to follow up particularly all the affairs that the cabinet might have to treat of with the ambassador of France and the Duc de Berg. The choice of Don Escoïquiz had been determined by the idea that the ambassador of France, whose position was believed to be uneasy, would feel more at home, or, what would amount to the same thing, more embarrassed with Don Escoïquiz than with any other member of the council.

The first conference of Don Escoïquiz with the ambassador of France took place a few days later, but it threw no light upon the state of affairs. The Grand Duc de Berg was present ; the language used was the same. In the menacing volubility of Murat, and the meek, vague and reserved words of M. de Beauharnais, Don Escoïquiz believed he could see that the real interest of the two principal personages that were supposed to act by direct order of Napoleon, bore especially upon the journey of Ferdinand VII. to Bayonne, where he was to find the emperor, and upon the interruption of the trial of the Prince of the Peace. M. de Beauharnais, restrained and directed in this conference by the language of the Grand Duc de Berg, perceived that he had not, up to that time, been thoroughly on the side of his government, and like people who change opinion, not from reflection but solely from interest, he threw himself without

---

[1] Don Jose Miquel de Carvajal, Duke of San Carlos, born in 1771, was brigadier-general, then chamberlain of the Prince of the Asturias and governor of his children : Viceroy of Navarra in 1807. He was compromised in the plot of the Escurial and disgraced in 1808. Ferdinand afterwards recalled him to his council. The duke followed his master to Valençay, but was afterwards confined at Lons-le-Saunier. He returned to Spain in 1814, was named minister of state, then ambassador at Vienna (1815) and at London (1817). After the Revolution of 1820, he retired to Lucca, where an Infanta of Spain (the Duchess Maria Louisa, former Queen of Etruria), was reigning, and was named by her minister to France. After the return of Ferdinand, he became ambassador of Spain at Paris. He died in 1828.

reserve into all the ideas of the Grand Duc de Berg, in whom he did not inspire so much confidence as that he had lost on the part of King Ferdinand. The Grand Duc de Berg terminated this conference by observing to Don Escoïquiz that it was important to take measures to put an end to the agitation raised among the people by the presence of so large a number of Frenchmen in Madrid.

This change of feeling towards the French came from the people's believing they no longer had need of them. They were delivered by their own efforts from the oppression of the Prince of the Peace, and were full of confidence in their new king ; thus no longer regarding the French as liberators, they found them very dear and inconvenient guests.

Don Escoïquiz reported to the council the result of his conference with the Grand Duc de Berg and the ambassador of France. Thereupon his colleagues associated with him for further conferences the Duke of Infantado ; and both were instructed by the king to go to Murat and say to him that it was the intention of King Ferdinand VII. to go to meet the emperor as soon as he should have certain news of his arrival on the frontier, but that the letters from France did not advise him yet of his departure from Paris ; that, as to the Prince of the Peace, his trial could not be suspended, because the prosecution and the publicity of this act of justice were one of his duties towards the nation, but he promised that the sentence, whatever it might be, should not be executed until after having been submitted to the approval of the emperor. Dons Infantado and Escoïquiz added that they had just taken the most efficacious measures to restore tranquillity in Madrid, and, in effect, it had been ordered that all house-owners should patrol night and day the quarters in which they lived. The garrison of Madrid, at the request of the Grand Duc de Berg, had been reduced to two battalions of Spanish guards and Walloons, and the body-guards. This small number of troops were employed in seeing the orders of the magistrates of police executed, and in putting a stop to the quarrels which might arise between the inhabitants of the city and the French.

These answers did not satisfy Murat, who, after having insisted most strenuously as to the suspension of the trial of the Prince of the Peace, complained bitterly of the delays experienced in the execution and even in the replies to all the demands he made for the support of his troops. These new complaints would furnish special motives for independent action, of which he could make use according to his views, and this remark received, a few days after, its application. A body of troops on horseback, under the pretext of seeking fodder, came with artillery to occupy the heights of Pinto. The Marquis de Castellar informed the king of this new movement of the French. After some altercation between the Grand Duc de Berg and the Spanish government on this subject, the latter decided that the Prince of the Peace should be transferred from Pinto to the Castle of Villa Viciosa situated three leagues from Madrid, and where there were no French troops.

The council of the king believed itself perfectly secure on this point, when the Grand Duc de Berg sent for the Duke of Infantado and Don Escoïquiz and declared to them that he had received new orders from the emperor demanding that the person of the Prince of the Peace should be delivered into his hands. He engaged to have him taken out of Spain, and gave his word of honour that he should never re-enter the country, adding that the will of the emperor was so precise that it was his duty to take possession of the Prince of the Peace by force, if he were not given up immediately. The king authorized Dons Infantado and Escoïquiz to reply that the arrival of the emperor was announced as being very near at hand, and that it would be so decisive for the internal affairs of Spain, of which he was going to be the arbiter, that he did not doubt that the Grand Duc would put off until that moment the mode of action which he had threatened to employ. They added that if he resorted to force to carry off the Prince of the Peace, his safety would certainly be compromised, in consequence of the inevitable popular rising which would be provoked by such a measure.

To the menacing instances of Murat were added those of

the ambassador and of General Savary.[1] The latter, in presenting the same demands in the name of the emperor, whom
he had left only a few days before, brought positive news of his
arrival at Bordeaux. He was pleased to speak of the disposition
of Napoleon for Ferdinand VII., employing all the terms calculated to inspire confidence. Thus, he assured the new king that
he would be recognized ; that his marriage would be concluded ;
that the integrity of Spain would be guaranteed at the first
interview that the prince would have with the emperor ; and
that, for so many advantages, the emperor wished only to hear
from the mouth of the prince, in whom he confided, that Spain,
under his authority, would be as faithful an ally of France as it
had been after the Family Compact.[2]

The same demands, the same replies repeated for several
days left matters in the same state, up to the 8th of April, when
the king, after having taken the advice of his council, decided to
send the Infante Don Carlos [3] to meet Napoleon. The prince
was to go even to Paris, if he did not find the emperor on the
road. He was the bearer of a letter from the king, his brother,
in which, after having spoken of the desire to form the closest
alliance with the emperor, and having renewed his demand for
one of his nieces in marriage, he announced that he would go
to meet His Majesty, as soon as he should be aware of his
approaching the frontiers of Spain. He concluded his letter by
leaving to the equitable decision of His Majesty the affair of
the Prince of the Peace.

The Infante departed with this letter April 9. He was
accompanied by the Duke of Hijar, Don Vallejo, Don Macañaz,[4]

---

[1] René Savary, born in 1774 at Marc, near Vouziers, entered the army at an early
age, and was colonel of gendarmes in 1800. Closely attached to the emperor, he
became general of division and Duc de Rovigo, and was named ambassador at St.
Petersburg in 1807. In 1808, he commanded for a short time the French troops in
Spain. He became Minister of Police in 1810. Having been sentenced to death
per contumaciam in 1815, he returned to France and had the sentence quashed. He
lived in retirement under the Restoration. In 1831, he was named Governor of
Algeria, and died in 1833.
[2] The treaty concluded in August, 1761, by which all the branches of the House
of Bourbon agreed mutually to assist one another.—(*Translator.*)
[3] The Infante Don Carlos, second son of King Charles, was born in 1788. In
1808, he accompanied Ferdinand to Valençay, and did not return to Spain until 1814.
At the death of his brother, his brother, he vainly claimed the throne in the name of
the Salic law. The Carlist party dates from that time.
[4] Don Pedro Macañaz, born in 1760, was Secretary of Embassy in Russia. He

and the Marquis of Feria. At Bayonne, he found the Duke of Frijas, the Duke of Medina-Cœli, and Count of Fernan-Nunèz,[1] already sent by King Ferdinand to pay his respects to Napoleon, who a few days after arrived at Bayonne.

The news of his departure from Paris, reached Madrid on April 11. King Ferdinand, harassed by all the claims of the Grand Duc de Berg, the entreaties of General Savary, and the suggestions of M. de Beauharnais, took the resolution of leaving on the 10th for Burgos. His ministers had advised this unanimously. Seeing that the king could neither negotiate nor defend himself, nor escape, they thought there was no other course for this unhappy prince to take, than to place himself with confidence in the hands of Napoleon.

They could not negotiate seeing that Ferdinand VII. had not been recognized : Napoleon had not replied to any of his letters, and there was reason to suspect that the frequent communications which took place between the king, the queen and the Grand Duc de Berg, through the medium of the Queen of Etruria, had for their object to induce King Charles to withdraw his abdication. These secret negotiations, which had adjutant-general de Monthion,[2] for messenger, and the Queen of Etruria for instrument, produced the antedated act of March 21, in which King Charles declares :

" I protest and declare that my decree of March 19, by which I abdicate the crown in favour of my son, is an act to which I was forced in order to prevent the greatest misfortunes, and the shedding of the blood of my beloved subjects. It must, in consequence, be regarded as of no value.

" I, the KING."

accompanied the princes of Spain into France, was shut up for some time at Vincennes, and kept afterward under supervision at Paris. In 1814, he became Minister of Justice, was arrested for malversations and suffered two years imprisonment. He died shortly after.

[1] Count of Fernan-Nunez, born in 1778, was one of the most ardent supporters of the Prince of the Asturias. He accepted, nevertheless, the office of *Grand Veneur** at the court of King Joseph ; but having been convicted of treason, he was forced to fly. In 1815, he was named by Ferdinand ambassador at London, and then at Paris in 1817. He died in 1821.

[2] General Monthion had been instructed by Murat to approach Charles IV. for the purpose of pressing him to protest against his first abdication in favour of Ferdinand. (See on this episode *Memoirs on the Affairs of Spain*, by Abbé de Pradt.)

* Grand-Master of the Hunt.

The natural result of this protest, which was as yet only suspected by the ministers of Ferdinand VII., must be an appeal of King Charles to Napoleon against his rebellious and usurping son.

It could not be prevented; the essential forces of the kingdom were enfeebled by the absence of a corps of nearly twenty thousand men, who, under the command of the Marquis de la Romana, were fighting in the north of Europe with the French armies. Ferdinand VII. had hardly three thousand men about him; the people were without arms, and when, under any pretext whatever, the government spoke of bringing a few battalions to Madrid, the Grand Duc de Berg opposed it with all the boldness inspired by the one hundred and fifty thousand men whom he commanded.

Flight was impossible; the least preparation would have betrayed the project; the suspicion aroused by the attempted escape of Charles IV., some days before, kept the people upon the alert. The king was surrounded by spies, perhaps even in the very council, although Don Cavallero and Don Olaguer were no longer members of it, and had been replaced by Don Peñuelas and Don O'Farril.[1] Besides, to retire without an army, without strongholds, and without money, even to Algesiras, was a desperate step. The council was lacking in energy.

Besides, it was known that, in a treaty drafted at Paris about March 20 by Don Izquierdo, Napoleon had inserted among the bases of an agreement, the obligation for Spain to cede to him a portion of her territory by fixing the Ebro as the boundary of the two countries. No one revolted at this idea; everybody, it is true, grieved at the necessity of making this sacrifice, but it was hoped that, at the moment of the marriage, Napoleon would forego his project, and restrict himself to securing the military route which was necessary for France in order to communicate with Portugal, and to obtain for French commerce, the

---

[1] Don Gonzalo O'Farril, born in 1753 of an Irish family in the service of Spain, was lieutenant-general and inspector of infantry. After the departure of the king, he was a member of the Junta of government presided over by the Infante Don Antonio. Nevertheless, he recognized King Joseph, and served him faithfully. Condemned to death in 1814, he took refuge in France, where he died.

free introduction into France of the products of the Spanish colonies.

Ferdinand VII., before leaving Madrid, entrusted the care of the government, during the time of his absence, to a Junta presided over by the Infante Don Antonio,[1] his uncle, and composed of Dons Penuelas, O'Farril and Azanza. He was accompanied by the Dukes of Infantado and of San Carlos, and by Dons Cevallos, Escoïquiz, Musquiz, Labrador,[2] and a very small number of attendants. He had with him only a single squadron of the body-guards. Two companies of Spanish guards and Walloons were ordered to await him at Burgos. He took three days to reach there. The determination that had been taken had been preceded by so much irresolution, that all motives for retarding his progress agreed with the disposition in which the king and his retinue were at the time. The king found the roads covered with French troops all armed, and did not meet with a single Spanish soldier on his route. At Burgos, Marshal Bessières was in command of a body of nearly ten thousand men ; he offered to the king to reach Vittoria by means of the relays prepared for Napoleon ; the king availed himself of them. General Savary, who had accompanied him so far, went on in advance to Bayonne, whence he returned on the 18th to Vittoria with new instructions. Vittoria was occupied by the first brigade of General Verdier's division, which was composed of nearly four thousand men. General Lefebvre had brought, on the evening before, from Burgos, two hundred dragoons of the guard, and Lieutenant-Colonel Henri was there with fifty chosen gendarmes. On the 20th, Marshal Bessières was to be there with four battalions of Napoleon's guard.

King Ferdinand VII. took up his quarters at the Vittoria town-hall, and remained there three days. General Savary brought him a letter from Napoleon. In spite of the ob-

[1] The Infante Don Antonio, brother of King Charles IV., was born in 1755. He had married his niece, the Infanta Maria-Amelia.
[2] Pedro Gomez Kavelo, Marquis de Labrador, born in 1775. He was in 1807 minister of Spain at Florence. He accompanied King Ferdinand to Valençay, was in 1814 named councillor of state, ambassador at Paris, and plenipotentiary at the Congress of Vienna. He became after this, ambassador at Naples, then at Rome, and died in 1850.

scurity of some of the expressions of this letter, the difficulties of the situation in which King Ferdinand found himself were such that he felt inclined to put a favourable interpretation upon all that came from Napoleon, and this disposition was shared by all the persons attached to the king, even by those who had preceded him to Bayonne. Count of Fernan-Nunèz, Dons Hijar, Vallejo, and Macañaz wrote that they anticipated the happiest results from the interview about to take place between the two sovereigns.

The king, decided though he was to go on to Bayonne, liked to have reasons given him for continuing his route. Several times in the day, he took the advice of his council, and although the opinion was always the same, he consulted them still. The slow progress occasioned by the inaction in which they remained during three days, gave uneasiness to General Savary, who had orders to bring the princes to Bayonne, willingly or by force. Plans were made to carry them off on the 19th, if, during the day of the 18th, a last attempt at persuasion did not succeed. The town-hall was to be surrounded on the 19th, in the morning, by the infantry of General Verdier ; three pieces of artillery, loaded with grape-shot, were to be placed at the three gates of the city ; General Savary, at the head of his gendarmes, and supported by a hundred men of light infantry, was to force his way into the palace. All these arrangements proved useless, the king having announced that he would leave the next day at nine o'clock in the morning. At the moment the king stepped into his carriage, popular instinct collected a great crowd around it ; they cut the traces of the mules ; cries of fury were heard on all sides. This tumult might have become very serious, if the king had not decided at once to make a proclamation the effect of which upon the people was remarkable ; their cries became tears, and shortly after they became prostrated. The mules were again put to the carriages ; the body-guards mounted their horses and all set out. At eleven o'clock in the evening, the king arrived at Irun with his retinue. He alighted at the house of Don Olazabal, which was outside that little city. It was guarded by a battalion of the king's regiment. General Savary did not arrive at Irun until the

20th at seven o'clock in the morning. An accident to his carriage had caused this delay.

Thus, the king and his attendants were eight hours alone, without a French escort in a Spanish house on the seashore, where several boats were fastened to stakes placed in the garden itself. General Savary, on alighting from his carriage, repaired in great haste and perplexity to the house where the king was staying, and found him asleep. At eight o'clock in the morning, they all left for Bayonne. At the moment when the king arrived on French territory, detachments of the Imperial Guards surrounded his carriage. Their number appeared to some of the Spaniards rather large for a simple escort of honour. This remark, vague at first, became a sinister foreboding, when, on passing Ogunna, they read on the arch of triumph, these words : " *He who makes and unmakes kings is more than a king himself.*" Such an inscription was a startling menace for the princes of Spain, and said to them, like that of Dante :

" *Lasciate ogni speranza, voi ch'entrate.*" [1]

Thus was achieved the most memorable, perhaps, of all the outrages of Napoleon. The princes of Spain were outside of Spanish territory, and the emperor held them in his power.

Their sojourn at Bayonne possesses no other interest than that proceeding from the different means the imagination of Napoleon employed to deceive himself, or that his character and malice furnished him for prolonging for some hours the error of his simple and unfortunate victims, and for exciting gigantic efforts on the part of France, which did not offer any other prospect than to place one of his brothers on the throne of Spain. All that passed then is found described in detail, with exactness and interest, in the work of M. de Pradt ;[2] and therefore my object

---

[1] " All hope abandon, ye who enter here."

[2] Dominique Dufour de Pradt, born in 1759 at Allanches (Auvergne), of a noble family. He was at first an officer, but left the military career to enter orders. Vicar-general at Rouen, he was afterwards deputy of the clergy to the States-General. He emigrated in 1791, returned to France under the Consulate, and became chaplain to the emperor, then Bishop of Poitiers (1805). Napoleon employed him in the affairs of Spain in 1808, and gave to him soon after the archbishopric of Malines. He was ambassador to Warsaw in 1812. In 1814, he was named Grand Chancellor of the Legion of Honour. He was, in 1817, elected deputy from Clermont-Ferrand. He died in 1837. M. de Pradt has written much. The work mentioned above, *Mémoires Historiques sur la Révolution d'Espagne*, was published in Paris in 1815.

is simply to follow, as a mere thread, the special events of each of the days that the young princes passed at Bayonne, before proceeding to Valençay, where I was to have the honour of receiving them, and where I was fortunate enough to be able to spare them, at least, some anxiety and cares.

Between Vidante and Bayonne, King Ferdinand met the Infante Don Carlos, who, accompanied by Dons Frias, Medina-Cœli, and Fernan-Nunèz, came to meet his unhappy brother. The king had them enter his carriage, and there he learned from them, with the greatest surprise, that Napoleon had declared to them the day before at ten o'clock in the morning, that they should never return to Madrid, and that one of his, Napoleon's, brothers was to occupy the throne of Spain. I mention the hour at which this declaration was made because it proves that it had taken eighteen hours to bring this news to Irun ; and at Irun, as has been seen, King Ferdinand could still have released himself from his despoilers. At one league from Bayonne, there no longer remained for the princes anything but sad resignation or confidence in reasons, on the force of which it would have required much simplicity to rely.

The carriages advanced towards Bayonne ; at half-past twelve the princes arrived there, and a few moments later, King Ferdinand received a visit from Napoleon. In this first inter-view, all was insignificant, except the alarming word *Elle* employed by Napoleon, and this word, an ordinary expression of regard, was as applicable to the title of Majesty as to that of Royal Highness. Ferdinand VII. hastened at once to repair to the palace to present his homage to Napoleon who had paid him the first visit. Napoleon invited him to dine at the Château of Marrac ;[1] he also invited the Dukes of San Carlos, of Medina-Cœli, and of Infantado ; the Prince de Neufchâtel was the only Frenchman present at the dinner. They did not speak of politics. On the morrow, Napoleon granted private audiences to the Dukes of San Carlos, and of Infantado and to Don Escoïquiz. He told them he was determined to change the dynasty that reigned

---

[1] The Château of Marrac, situated one kilometre south of Bayonne, was built in 1707 for the Queen-Dowager of Spain, widow of Charles II., refugee in France. Napoleon bought it in 1807. It was destroyed by fire in 1825.

on the throne of Spain, and, forgetting that he had repeated a
thousand times that his existence at the head of France was
incompatible with that of a prince of the House of Bourbon on
one of the thrones of Europe, he craftily gave for the date and
motives of his projects as to Spain, the proclamation made by the
Spanish government at the time of the battle of Jena. It had
been, he said, regarded in France, if not as a declaration, at least
as a menace of war : he then announced, in a firm voice, that
nothing could move him from his purpose. There he stopped, as
if to note the full effect of the terrible words he had just pronounced. After a moment of silence, which he broke by the softest
expressions, he spoke of the misfortunes of the young princes,
and said that his policy being in veritable contradiction to his
heart, he could not refuse any means of happiness for them,
which would be compatible with the system he had adopted.
He even went so far as to offer King Ferdinand, provided he
would cede his right to the crown of Spain, Etruria, with the
title of King, a year of this kingdom's revenue so that he might
form his establishment, one of his nieces in marriage, and, in
case he died without children, to establish the succession in the
male line of the princes, his brothers.

Struck by what they had just heard, the Dukes of Infantado,
and of San Carlos, and Don Escoïquiz, tried to combat the system
of Napoleon, who, entering into their feelings, but as a man whose
ideas are irrevocably settled, bade them to omit nothing which,
on returning to their master, they might reproach themselves for
having failed to mention. With one mind they said that the
object of the emperor being to secure the durable alliance of
Spain, the known character of the young king, and his marriage
with one of Napoleon's nieces, was for the time being a guarantee
preferable to all others, and that, if they wished to carry forward
their ideas to a distant future, they must own that besides the
track of human policy being lost in its mists, the descendants of a
prince of the House of Napoleon, in proportion to their removal
from their common origin, would become indifferent to family
sentiment, and, might even, on occasion, endure impatiently the
yoke imposed by an older and more powerful branch. And with
a noble and touching expression, they added that it would be

very difficult for history, to whose burin he had furnished such
beautiful illustrations, to set down the motives for the despoiling
of a powerful king, who had come in confidence to render homage
to a sovereign, who had been his ally for six years. Then entering
into the examination of the political consequences of the resolution of the emperor, they predicted that the Spanish colonies,
whose fidelity under the actual dynasty was nothing less than
assured, would under another dynasty become the prey of
England or constitute themselves an independent power ; that
England would then pour therein the products of her manufactures, and that this new and great outlet would secure for her a
commercial superiority absolutely crushing for the other powers
of the world. These reasonings, which seemed more like the
discharge of a conscientious duty than an argumentation from
which any advantage might be expected, were minutely gone
into. Napoleon listened to them without showing any impatience,
but said, that for a long time he had considered the question
under all its aspects, that Don Escoïquiz and the Dukes of San
Carlos and of Infantado had pointed out to him nothing new,
and that he persisted immovably in the system he had adopted.

Dons Infantado, Escoïquiz and San Carlos retired and reported
to the persons who had accompanied Ferdinand VII., and who
were in his confidence, the conversation they had had with
Napoleon, and added—believing that in this they were performing
an act of courage—that their opinion was that his offers must
not be declined.

Their grounds for this opinion were : the situation of the
king and of the Infante, now in the hands of Napoleon, the
number of French armies actually in Spain, the positions they
occupied, the inefficiency of the Spanish army, few in numbers
and scattered about the country, and finally, the feebleness of
King Charles IV., who was lending himself to all the wishes of
Napoleon. Don Cevallos, who was the only one of a contrary
opinion, based it upon very strong considerations, and proposed
as a sequel to the negotiation, to refuse all verbal communication and to resort to written notes, as if Napoleon were still in
Paris, King Ferdinand at Madrid, the French troops in Germany
and the Spanish troops occupying all the strong places on the

frontiers. He accused of weakness and even of cowardice, the members of the council who expressed an opinion different from his own ; he sustained that no arrangement must be made whose basis was to be the cession of the crown, and he demanded that all the members of the council having to answer for their opinion to the Spanish Court should express it in writing.

Their courage returned when there was no longer need for anything but resignation. Is it not remarkable that the same men who in Spain had not known how to resist either the Prince of the Peace, the Grand Duc de Berg, or General Savary, believed they could achieve anything by establishing at Bayonne, in writing, the right of principles, the law of abdication, the dangers they ran on the subject of the colonies, &c. ?

Dons Infantado and Escoïquiz were instructed to acquaint Napoleon with the decision taken by the princes to name a plenipotentiary, who should be authorized to treat in writing the points which were to be settled. Napoleon, while saying that the resolution of the princes did not appear to him calculated to advance affairs, complied with the request to name a plenipotentiary. He told Dons Infantado and Escoïquiz that he would give his powers to M. de Champagny, his Minister of Foreign Affairs. He asked who was the person to whom the princes would give their powers. The Duke of Infantado said that it would probably be among the Spaniards in the service of the department of Foreign Affairs that the princes would choose their plenipotentiary, and he named as attached to that career, Dons Cevallos, Labrador, Musquiz, Vallejo, and Macañaz. At the name of M. de Labrador, he made some unkind remarks, the very nature of which were honourable for the character and abilities of that minister.

Dons Infantado and Escoïquiz acquainted the king's council with the result of their new conference with Napoleon. They proposed there and then to name a plenipotentiary, and Don Cevallos saw in Napoleon's opinion of the Marquis of Labrador only another motive for proposing him to the council. The king acted upon this advice and appointed the marquis. The latter had a conference with M. de Champagny, who demanded, as a preliminary act, the cession of the crown of Spain. The Marquis of Labrador declared *that he had not, and that before God, he hoped he never would have, the power to cede it.* They broke up the conference, and while the council was discussing the question as to whether they should, or should not, give the necessary powers for continuing the negotiation, Napoleon sent for Don Escoïquiz, and told him that if before eleven o'clock in the evening, he did not bring to him the formal renunciation of King Ferdinand to the throne of Spain, and his request for that of Etruria, he would treat with Charles IV., who was to arrive on the morrow. Don Escoïquiz reported to the council the determination of Napoleon. Don Cevallos begged the king to refuse unreservedly the propositions made to him. On the following day, Don Escoïquiz ventured to speak again of Tuscany to Napoleon who, without entering into the matter, said to him, " My dear sir, it is too late."

On the 30th at four o'clock in the evening, Charles IV. and the queen arrived at Bayonne. Napoleon had sent one of his chamberlains to congratulate them at Irun. In the carriage following that of the king was the Duchess of Alcudia, daughter of the Prince of the Peace. Orders had been given that the entry of the king and queen into Bayonne should be brilliant. The princes, their children, went to meet them and re-entered the city with them. The Prince of the Peace, who at the repeated request of the Grand Duc de Berg had been released from Villa Viciosa, left the private house where he was lodging, and went to dwell with the king and queen.

The arrival of King Charles changed the aspect of affairs ; he consented to everything. Napoleon charged Don Escoïquiz to tell King Ferdinand that, King Charles having protested against his abdication, the duty of the Prince of the Asturias was to return him the crown by a renunciation pure and simple. The council induced Ferdinand VII. to announce his submission, but to propose to perform the act of renunciation only at Madrid.

A threatening letter from King Charles to his son, the severity with which he had treated him in the presence of Napoleon, the intention he had announced of having the counsellors of King Ferdinand tried as rebels ; all these means combined produced the effect Napoleon had hoped from them ; the prince sent his resignation pure and simple to King Charles, who immediately named the Grand Duc de Berg lieutenant-general of the kingdom.

This nomination put an end to the powers of the Infante Don Antonio, who had been left at Madrid by the young king as president of the Junta. He had been ordered to Bayonne by a command of King Charles IV., addressed to the Grand Duc de Berg, who intimated it to him and had it executed immediately. The Infante, at the commencement of his short administration, had been under the unpleasant necessity of being forced by the Grand Duc de Berg to give up the Prince of the Peace into his hands. Murat had declared to him that he would carry him off by force if he were not delivered up to him, and he had added that the lives of the princes who were at Bayonne should answer for that of the Prince of the Peace. Don Antonio had believed he ought to yield, and an aide-de-camp of the Grand Duc de Berg had been charged to escort the Prince of the Peace as far as Bayonne where he had arrived on the 25th. On the road, he had incurred some danger, particularly at Tolosa, where the people, greatly excited, had, in order to detain him, unharnessed and overturned the carriages on the bridge. The prince only owed his safety on this occasion, to the captain of the cuirassiers who commanded the escort.

King Charles IV. and the queen, during their journey from Madrid to Bayonne, 'had been received with marks of neither hatred nor esteem.

Murat, on the arrival of the powers which conferred upon him the rank of lieutenant-general of the kingdom, had, as has been seen, hastened the departure of the Infante Don Antonio for Bayonne. The Queen of Etruria arrived there at the same time with the Infante Don Francisco.

The renunciation pure and simple of Ferdinand VII. had been sent to King Charles. Napoleon believed that the moment had come to propose to the Prince of the Asturias, his brothers, and his uncle, to make a treaty of cession of all their rights to the crown of Spain. He agreed to give them the territory of Navarre, and to allow them to receive the revenues of their commanderies and of their lands in Spain. The bases of this treaty, the drafting of which was entrusted to Don Escoïquiz and

to General Duroc, having been settled, the princes started for
Valençay, where Napoleon sent them until the château of
Navarre should be made habitable. They stopped two days at
Bordeaux, and, on the 19th of May, they made their entry into
Valençay. I had been there several days when the princes
arrived. This moment has left on my mind an impression which
will never be effaced. The princes were young, and over them,
around them, in their clothing, in the liveries of their servants, was
seen the image of bygone centuries. The coach from which I saw
them alight might have been taken for a carriage of Philip V.
This air of antiquity, in recalling their grandeur, added to the
interest of their position. They were the first Bourbons that I
saw again after so many years of storms and disasters. It
was not they who felt embarrassed, it was I, and I am pleased
to say it.

Napoleon had had them accompanied by Colonel Henri,
a superior officer of the *gendarmerie d'élite*,[1] and one of those
police-agents who believe that military glory is acquired by
fulfilling with severity a mission of this kind. I soon perceived
that this man affected to show his suspicions and fears, which
might make the sojourn at Valençay insupportable for the
princes. I adopted with him the tone of a master, in order to
make him understand that Napoleon did not reign either in the
apartments or in the park of Valençay. This reassured the
princes, and was my first recompense. I surrounded them with
respect, attention and care ; I allowed no one to present
himself before them until after having obtained permission
from them. No one approached them except in full dress ; I
never failed myself in what I had prescribed in this respect. All
the hours of the day were distributed according to the habits of
the princes ; mass, hours of rest, promenades, prayers, &c., each
of these had its proper time. Will it be credited that at
Valençay, I made the princes of Spain acquainted with a kind
of liberty they had never known when near their father's throne ?
Never, at Madrid, had the two elder princes walked out together without a written permission from the king. To be alone,
to go out ten times a day in the garden, in the park, were

---

[1] A picked police force.

pleasures new to them. They had never before been able to be
so unconstrained towards each other.

I cannot understand why hunting, horse-riding, and dancing
had been forbidden them in Spain. I had them take their first
shot with a gun ; I confided them to the care of a former
keeper of *Monseigneur* the Prince de Condé, named Aubry,
who had taught the Duc de Bourbon how to shoot. This old
man, full of respect and affection, mentioned persons of their
family to them, on every occasion. I had them ride horses with
Foucault who had long been attached to me ; brought up in the
chief stables of the king, he had been special attendant of
Madame Elizabeth of France ; all the examples he cited, all his
recollections, were drawn from their House. Boucher put all his
skill and all his heart into making them bad Spanish stews.
The terrace which is in front of the château became our ball-
room, where the princes could witness, as by chance, some
of those dances the French call *rondes*, and in which they might
join without knowing how to dance. Guitars, and amongst
others, that of Castro, were heard in all corners of the garden.

I had endeavoured to have them spend some hours in the
library ; in this I did not meet with great success, although the
librarian, M. Fercoc, and I, tried all the means that we could
imagine to retain them there. Having failed by books alone to
arouse their interest, we called their attention to the beauty of
the editions, and to the works which contained engravings ; we
even resorted to common pictures ; yet, I dare not say how
useless all our efforts proved. Don Antonio, their uncle, who
feared for them the greater number of books which compose a
good library, soon imagined some reason for inducing them to
retire to their apartments ; and for this he met with less resistance
than when he wished them to leave the exercises and the amusements which form the charm of summer evenings in the country.
In addition to these distractions, which everybody about the
château helped me to organize, the princes had the consolations
of religion ; great misfortune always renders faith more lively
and the soul more sensitive. Each day closed with a public
prayer at which I had all visitors to the château, the officers
of the departmental guard and even the men of the *gendar-*

merie attend. Every one left these gatherings with softened hearts ; the prisoners and their guards praying on their knees, next each other, to the same God, appeared to regard one another less as enemies ; the guards were no longer so fierce, nor the prisoners so alarmed ; perhaps some displays of interest made them even conceive a little hope. The feeling hearts of the princes led them to ascribe to me the consolation they experienced. I cannot remember without emotion the grief they showed when, a letter from Napoleon, on his way from Bayonne, directed me to go to meet him at Nantes, and leave them for a few days.

The emperor had for some time been wounded at the opinion I had expressed as to his undertaking in Spain ; nay, more, he had thought that the plans I had made at the time of the arrival of the princes at Valençay, had too much their safety in view. Thus, as soon as we met at Nantes, we had some conversations—I might say rather some irritating discussions. On one occasion among others, taking a bantering tone with me, rubbing his hands, and walking up and down the room, while looking at me with a mocking air, he said to me, " Well, you see what all your predictions as to the difficulties I should encounter in regulating the affairs of Spain according to my views have amounted to ; I have, however, overcome these people here ; they have all been caught in the nets I spread for them, and I am master of the situation in Spain, as in the rest of Europe." Provoked by this boasting, so little justified in my eyes, and above all by the shameful means he had employed to arrive at his ends, I replied to him, calmly, that I did not see things under the same aspect as he, and that I believed he had lost more than he had gained by the events at Bayonne. " What do you mean by that ? " he replied. " *Mon Dieu*," I said, "it is very simple, and I will show you by an example. If a man in the world commits follies, has mistresses, conducts himself badly towards his wife, does even grave wrongs to his friends, he will doubtless be blamed ; but if he is rich, powerful, and clever, he may still expect to be treated with indulgence in society. If he cheats at gaming, he is immediately banished from good company, which will never pardon him."

The emperor turned pale, remained confused, and spoke to me no more on that day; but I can say that from this moment dated the rupture which, more or less marked, took place between him and me. Never after did he pronounce the name of Spain, of Valençay, or mine, without adding to it some injurious epithet which his temper furnished. The princes had not been three months at Valençay before he already believed that he saw all the vengeances of Europe proceeding therefrom. The persons who surrounded him have often said to me that he spoke of Valençay with uneasiness, whenever his conversation or questions bore upon that place.

My absence lasted only a few days; the princes saw me again and received me with extreme kindness. A letter from Napoleon which I found on my return merits being preserved; here it is literally :—

"Prince Ferdinand, in writing to me addresses me as his cousin. Try to have the Duke of San Carlos understand that this is ridiculous, and that he must simply call me *Sire.*"

After Ajaccio and Saint Helena, comment is useless.

I have not added to this recital any fragments but what are absolutely necessary to the subject, the others being found in the different writings which are already published, or in records which are not at my disposal.

Our uneventful life at the château continued some weeks longer, and only ended when the journey to Erfurt recalled me to Paris. On my departure all three princes came to take leave of me in my apartment, with tears in their eyes; they asked what they could do to give me some mark of their friendship and gratitude, for it is thus they expressed themselves. Each of them offered me the old prayer-book which he used at church; I received them with respect, and with an emotion I shall never have the temerity to express. I have dared to recall the word gratitude of which they deigned to make use on this occasion, because this expression is so rare with princes that it honours those who employ it. It is in order to avoid discharging this noble debt that ancient dynasties affect to trace their origin to Providence : "*By the grace of God*" is a formula of ingratitude.

On leaving Valençay, I returned to Paris; I spent only a few days there before leaving for Erfurt, where Napoleon and the Emperor of Russia were to meet. The details of this interview will form a separate chapter. The frequent conversations I then had with Napoleon, led me to apprehend that he meditated causing the princes of Spain to fall into a snare that his minister of general police had laid for them by his order. The results might be fatal to them ; I believed there was not a moment to lose to forewarn them of it, so I had M. Mornard, my secretary, leave immediately for Paris, and call, with the utmost speed, on the Duke of San Carlos, who was then in that city. His zeal and interest for the princes took him only four days to reach there.

My mind, my heart, my memories, were filled with interest for the princes of Spain. I have still present to my mind the effect produced upon me, at the first interview at Erfurt, when the Emperor of Russia, among the obliging things he said to Napoleon, announced to him that he had recognized his brother Joseph as King of Spain.

From this moment, the existence of the princes up to the time of their return to Spain was uneventful ; all that can be said of them during these five years is, that they lived.

M. de la Forest came to negotiate at Valençay the treaty[1] by virtue of which the return of the princes to Spain was consented to by the Emperor Napoleon, who signed on February 8, 1814, at Nogent-sur-Seine, the order for their departure. It was desired to give the appearance of a free consent to an order which was drawn out in the hope of preventing the army of the coalition from entering France by the frontier of the Pyrenees. The respectful forms employed by M. de la Forest in all his relations with the Spanish princes must have been so much the more appreciated by them, that for several years they had been obliged to preserve themselves from the bad conduct and heavy dealings of MM. de Darby, Henri, Kolli, and a host of other

---

[1] The treaty of Valençay was signed December 11, 1813. The integrity of Spain was promised. The French troops were to evacuate the country, the Spanish and English armies were not to cross the Pyrenees. Finally, Ferdinand had admitted in principle the idea of a marriage with the daughter of King Joseph. The treaty was brought by the Duke of San Carlos before the Cortès, and Ferdinand left Valençay March 3.

agents who had been placed near them to guard and spy upon them. Before leaving the French territory the princes had still to submit to an insult provoked by the Duc de Feltre, who, without having received the order from Napoleon, but in the hope of pleasing him, had one of them stopped on the frontier as hostage.

If ever the success of an enterprise should have appeared infallible, it was assuredly an enterprise in which treason had combined everything in such a manner as to leave nothing to be done by force of arms. It must have seemed impossible that Spain, invaded before she could possibly expect it, deprived of her government and of a portion of her strongholds, with a regular army mediocre in number, and more mediocre in quality, without harmony between her provinces, and almost without the means of establishing any, could think for a moment of offering resistance, or of attempting to do so except for her ruin. However, those who knew Spain and the Spaniards judged otherwise, and were not deceived. They predicted that Spanish pride would calculate neither ultimate result nor present dangers, but would find in indignation and despair, a vigour and resource continually renewed.

Napoleon, in menacing England with an invasion, had forced her to create an army of considerable strength, and thus, without foreseeing it, had prepared help for the Peninsula. Seventeen thousand English, and some thousand Portuguese, made the French evacuate Portugal ; the latter re-entered momentarily, but were unable to establish a firm footing there. The Portuguese soon had a numerous army, brave and well-disciplined, and, with the English, developed into the auxiliaries and the support of the resistance which had burst forth simultaneously over all parts of Spain, and which could be entirely suppressed only by immense armies, which it was impossible to maintain in that country, because it was impossible to nourish them. The title "invincible" that the continual victories over regular armies had attached to the name of Napoleon became contestable, and it was from Spain that Europe learned that he could be conquered, and how it could be done. The resistance of the Spaniards, in setting a precedent prepared that made later by the Russians, and led to the fall of the man who had promised himself the domination of the world. Thus was verified what Montesquieu had said of the projects of an universal monarchy : *that they could not fail in a single point without failing everywhere.*

At the first indications they had in France of the projects of Napoleon on Spain, a few persons said : "This man is undertaking a thing which, if it fail, will ruin him ; and if it succeed, will ruin Europe." It has failed enough to ruin him, and perhaps it has succeeded sufficiently to ruin Europe.

Ferdinand VII., at Valençay, humbled himself beyond measure, to the point of congratulating his oppressor on his victories over the Spaniards. Hardly had he remounted the throne, than without discriminating between his faithful subjects and those who, carrying into the Cortès the revolutionary spirit, wished to annihilate the royal power to substitute their own to it, Ferdinand VII. sentenced to exile, to irons, to death even, those who had inflamed their countrymen for his defence, those whose constancy had broken his irons for him, those by whose aid he was now reigning. All the weakness he had shown in misfortune, changed into a furious craving for absolute power. The English, who boast of being the liberators of Spain, who ought to have made stipulations in her favour, and who could have done it, did not do it. They confined themselves to making representations, the inutility of which could easily be foreseen, and the success of which, there is reason to believe, was most indifferent to them, for they hate tyranny abroad, only when, as under Napoleon, it menaces their existence, and they delight, (we need not furnish any instance of it) in turning the subjection of peoples to the profit of their pride or of their prosperity. A more far-sighted policy would have inspired the Cabinet which governed England at that time with very different views.

---

[1] Qu'ils ne pouvaient échouer sur un seul point qu'ils n'échouassent partout.

END OF THE FOURTH PART.

PART V.

THE ERFURT INTERVIEW.

1808.

Napoleon holds out a bait to Russia—The prospective partition of Turkey
—Silesia to France as compensation for Wallachia and Moldavia to
Russia—Alexander incensed—Napoleon's letter to the Czar, desisting from
all pretensions to Silesia and proposing to meet him in order to arrange
the best means of carrying war into India—Reply of Alexander accept-
ing to meet Napoleon—Count Romanzoff and Turkey—Russia wants
Constantinople—The Turks must be driven back to Asia—France and
the Porte—Russia and Sweden—Conquest of Finland—Talleyrand
receives orders to accompany Napoleon to Erfurt, the emperors' meet-
ing-place—Confidence displayed by Napoleon towards Talleyrand—
A brilliant journey—Napoleon wishes to dazzle the Germans—Invites
Talleyrand to induce the kings and princes to come to Erfurt—
Napoleon and Dazincourt—Choice of plays—Cinna—The actors of the
Comédie Française ordered to repair to Erfurt—The military retinue of
Napoleon—Napoleon discloses to Talleyrand his projects for Erfurt—
Orders Talleyrand to draw up a convention aimed against England—
Text of that convention—Napoleon objects to certain expressions—
Austria, Napoleon's enemy—Napoleon insists on inserting in the
convention a clause directed against Austria—Rebukes Talleyrand—
Vous êtes toujours Autrichien!—Final instructions of Napoleon to
Talleyrand—Talleyrand's arrival at Erfurt—M. de Caulaincourt and
Talleyrand—List of the crowned heads and eminent personages present
at Erfurt—Arrival of the Emperor Napoleon at Erfurt—General
enthusiasm—The attendant kings and princes humble themselves in the
presence of their victor—Arrival of the Czar Alexander—His friendly
meeting with Napoleon—The latter introduces changes into the projected
convention—Austria's fears—M. de Vincent and Talleyrand—Interview
between Napoleon and Goethe—Napoleon's judgment on Schiller's
Thirty Years' War.—The play at Erfurt—The impressions of the kings
and princes—Delight of the Czar—Private interview between Napoleon
and the latter—Uneasiness of the Austrian envoy—The Princess of
Tour and Taxis—Napoleon invites Goethe and Wieland to lunch—
Napoleon's judgment as to the influence of Christianity on the development

IN the course of the conferences preceding the treaty of Tilsit, the Emperor Napoleon often spoke to the Czar Alexander of Moldavia and Wallachia as provinces destined some day to become Russian. Affecting to be carried away by some irresistible impulse, and to obey the decrees of Providence, he spoke of the division of European Turkey as inevitable. He then indicated, as if inspired, the general bases of the sharing of that empire, a portion of which was to fall to Austria, in order to gratify her pride rather than her ambition. A shrewd mind could easily notice the effect produced upon the mind of Alexander by all those fanciful dreams. Napoleon watched him attentively and, as soon as he noticed that the prospects held out allured the Czar's imagination, he informed Alexander that letters from Paris necessitated his immediate return, and gave orders for the treaty to be drafted at once. My instructions on the subject of that treaty were, that no allusion to a partition of the Ottoman Empire should appear in it, nor even to the future fate of the two provinces of Wallachia and Moldavia. These instructions were strictly carried out. Napoleon thus left Tilsit, having made prospective arrangements which could serve him as he pleased for the accomplishment of his other designs. He had not bound himself at all, whereas, by the prospects he had held out, he had allured the Czar Alexander and placed him, in relation to Turkey in a doubtful position which might enable the cabinet of the Tuileries to bring forth other pretensions untouched in the treaty.

In the month of January 1808, at one of the receptions of the court, Napoleon tried, for the first time, to take advantage of that situation. He went up to M. de Tolstoï,[1] then Russian ambassador, took him aside, and, in the course of a conversation, in which he called attention to the great advantages Russia was likely to derive from the possession of Wallachia and Moldavia, ventured to speak incidentally of the compensations France was to obtain, and mentioned Silesia as the province which would suit her best. On this occasion, as on all those when he meditated some fresh aggrandisement, he emphasised his fears of England's ambition: that country, he said, refused to listen to any proposal of peace, and obliged him to resort to all the means dictated by prudence, in order to reduce the power of all the countries with which there was some reason to believe she was in league. For the present, he added, all prospects of a partition of the Ottoman Empire must be abandoned, because, to make an attempt upon Turkey, without possessing greater naval facilities, would be to place one's most valuable possessions at the mercy of Great Britain. M. de Tolstoï whose duty it was to listen, and who, besides, was hardly fit for any other, reported to his sovereign the hints thus given him. These were received most unfavourably by the Emperor Alexander who, rather sharply, said to the French ambassador :[2] "I can hardly believe the intelligence contained in Tolstoï's despatches ; is it intended to tear up the treaty of Tilsit ? I do not understand the emperor ! It cannot be that he wishes to cause me personal trouble. On the contrary, it is indispensable that he should clear me from responsibility in the eyes of Europe, by at once placing Prussia in the situation agreed to in the treaty. This is really an affair of honour with me."

This incident gave rise to certain explanations, culminating in a letter from the Emperor Napoleon, which reached St. Petersburg about the end of February 1808.[3] That letter contained :

---

[1] Pierre, Count Tolstoï, born in 1769, served in the army under the command of Souvaroff, and became general in 1805. After Friedland, he was employed in negotiations, and in 1807, he was chosen as ambassador at Paris. Napoleon asked and obtained, a short time after, his recall, which was granted. In 1812, he commanded the militia in Moscow, and served in the campaigns of 1813 and 1814. Later, he became the director of the military colonies, made the campaigns of Poland in 1834, became president of the department of Military Affairs in the Council of the Empire ; he died in 1844. He was a brother of the grand-marshal Count Tolstoï.

[2] General Caulaincourt, Duc de Vicence.

[3] A letter of February 2, 1808, *Correspondance de Napoléon I*^{er}., t. xvi., p. 498.

1st. The implicit renunciation of all pretensions to Silesia ; 2nd. Fresh suggestions concerning the eventual division of the agreed portion of Turkish territory ; 3rd. A plan for carrying war into India ; 4th. A proposal, either to send a responsible person to Paris to settle these important questions, if the Czar could not come himself, or to appoint a suitable place where the two sovereigns could meet.

It may be noticed that, in his letter, the Emperor Napoleon, whilst proposing a partition of the Ottoman Empire, made no mention of the manner in which the territories wrenched from Turkey were to be divided. Thus, with the exception of the difficulty relative to Silesia, which was now removed, things remained in the same uncertain state. Nevertheless, the Emperor Alexander experienced so much relief at being no longer obliged to stand up in defence of the private interests of the King of Prussia, that he received the letter with the utmost satisfaction, and decided there and then to have an interview with the Emperor Napoleon to whom he wrote to that effect in reply.

This interview was sought by the Emperor of Russia only with the idea and upon the condition, that the partition of Turkey should be settled previously, and that the only object of the interview should be simply to come to a thorough understanding respecting the means to be adopted in carrying out the said partition, and to make their ratification still more solemn and binding, by mutually pledging their word as man to man, that each should conform to the clauses of that arrangement. M. de Romanzoff[1] was instructed to open negotiations on those bases with the French ambassador, M. de Caulaincourt.

It is most important to indicate here, in all their essentials, the various arrangements and the special intentions of the Emperor Napoleon, and of the Czar Alexander, as also those of Count Romanzoff as the representative of public opinion in Russia.

---

[1] Count Nicholas Romanzoff, born in 1750, was the son of the field-marshal of that name. He at first entered the diplomatic service. Later, he became Minister of Commerce, and afterwards Minister of Foreign Affairs at the accession of Alexander. He was a warm advocate of the French alliance, which led to his being obliged to resign in 1812. He afterwards lived in retirement and died in 1826.

Count Romanzoff considered the destruction of the Ottoman Empire as a victory for his family. He was anxious to complete the great work begun by his father. Thus, if the point to be debated in the conferences consisted of a mere dismemberment, it seemed to him full of difficulties; if, on the contrary, he foresaw the possibility of a partition, nothing hindered him ; he became exceedingly generous, and, first of all, boldly claimed Constantinople and the Dardanelles for Russia. " Any division," he said, in one of the conferences, "that did not give Constantinople and the Dardanelles to Russia would not obtain the approval of the nation, nay, would even dissatisfy it more than the present state of affairs, bad as it was in everybody's opinion." At any rate, he offered everything in exchange for that advantage : fleets, armies, and the co-operation of Russia in an expedition against India, but he refused that co-operation in an attack against Syria and Egypt, in case of a simple dismemberment that would leave Constantinople to the Turks. When the French ambassador proposed, as a compromise, to found a civilized and independent government at Constantinople, alluding, in support of that suggestion, to the intention previously expressed on the subject by the Emperor Alexander ; the chancellor dismissed the proposal by saying that his sovereign no longer entertained that idea. Count Romanzoff wanted Constantinople ; that acquisition was to give everlasting glory to his name. With the exception of Constantinople, he gave up the rest of the world to France. He put forth no pretensions to India, and was quite willing that the Emperor Napoleon should place the crown of Spain on the head of one of his brothers, and annex, either to France, or to the kingdom of Italy, whatever country he thought fit.

The Emperor Alexander affected scarcely to care about possessing the two provinces of Wallachia and Moldavia ; his ambition was confined to acquiring the banks of the Danube. "And yet," he said, " it is merely because I see, in that arrangement, the means of strengthening our alliance. Anything that suits the Emperor Napoleon will suit me ; if I wish for new territories, it is merely in order to promote the attachment of my people to French policy, and justify our undertakings." When, in the course of discussion, he brought forth higher pretensions, he merely seemed to uphold the plans of his minister, and to yield to some old Russian ideas ; he seemed to be more influenced by philosophical maxims than by political views. " It is more than ever the case," he remarked one day, " of giving to the projects we formed at Tilsit, the liberal appearance which should always mark the acts of enlightened sovereigns. The times we live in, more than political necessity, doom the Turks to be driven back to Asia. It is a noble action that of ridding those beautiful countries from Turkish ignorance and tyranny. Humanity requires that those barbarians should no longer remain in Europe. Civilization demands it ;" and so on. I repeat word for word what he said.

The French ambassador, a faithful agent of Napoleon, made use of all his influence and dexterity in getting the Russian cabinet to indicate how far they carried their views, and at each imperial meeting, he exerted himself to increase the infatuation for Napoleon which possessed the Czar Alexander, so as to induce the latter to ask for an interview with Napoleon, as being the only means by which they could arrive at a mutual understanding. When discussing with M. de Romanzoff, he skilfully came to the point ; with the Czar he criticized the plans of M. de Romanzoff, but never intimated those of Napoleon ; he refused all, but did not ask anything. Like the Emperor Alexander, he was of opinion that the requirements of the times were indeed rather imperative, but affected to be fearful of so vast an undertaking as that proposed by M. de Romanzoff, and was ever calling attention to difficulties that could be solved only by the sovereigns themselves. The vagueness of Alexander's ideas led him to confess the truth of these statements, and the interview was fixed for September 27, 1808.

The cabinet of the Tuileries had done all in their power to raise as many incidents as possible. Unknown to Russia, they gave their word to the Ottoman Porte that the armistice with Russia should be prolonged. The report of General Sebastiani,[1]

---

[1] Horace Sebastiani, born in 1772 near Bastia, was a lieutenant in 1789, general of division in 1805, ambassador at Constantinople in 1806, where he distinguished

made just after his voyage in the Levant, was communicated to the Russian cabinet ; and the consequence of this communication was to render problematical all that had been said and written relative to the division of Turkey, of whom the French cabinet still spoke as the old ally of France, and for whom, on every occasion, they displayed some sort of interest. Silesia was no longer alluded to, but the right to delay the evacuation of Russia was claimed as a compensation for the cession of the two provinces.

From this it is easily seen that the Emperor Napoleon, fully appreciating the strength of his position after the treaty of Tilsit, was anxious to remove all pretexts for hostilities in Europe until such time as his designs on Spain were accomplished. Until then, the project of a war in India, and that of a division of the Ottoman Empire, seemed like mere phantoms intended to occupy Russia's attention. Thus, during the time that elapsed between the two interviews of Tilsit and Erfurt, all the points that were discussed in Paris or in St. Petersburg made no apparent progress. Nothing had been done. What the Czar Alexander said to the ambassador of France five days before his departure for Erfurt, he might have said five days after the departure from Tilsit. "We must come to terms, and act in concert in order to obtain mutual advantages ; I shall ever remain true to my word, for I have always done so ; what I have said to the emperor and what he said to me, is as sacred and binding to me as treaties, and so on . . . ."

The words were the same. With the exception of the conquest of Finland [1] on the one hand, and of the invasion of Spain on the other, the situation was unaltered on the 27th of September, 1808. This did not however lead to any remonstrance worth mentioning between the respective cabinets. Thus, at

himself by his energy at the appearance of the English squadron in the Bosphorus. He was elected a deputy under the Restoration ; was appointed Minister of Foreign Affairs and ambassador under Louis Philippe, and Marshal of France in 1840. He died in 1851.

[1] In accordance with the treaty of Tilsit, the Czar Alexander was to declare war against Sweden if that power did not break off with England. Sweden having by a convention dated February 8, 1808, renewed her relations with the cabinet of London, Alexander began the campaign by invading Finland. The treaty of Friedrichshaum, September 5/17, 1809, put an end to the war. According to the treaty, Sweden joined the continental system and gave up Finland to Russia.

Erfurt, the two sovereigns could be looked upon as coming direct from Tilsit.

The part I had taken in the treaty of Tilsit ; the marks of special kindness which the Czar Alexander had shown me ; the annoyance caused to the Emperor Napoleon by M. de Champagny, who, as His Majesty himself said, displayed his zeal every morning in order to be forgiven his blunders of the day before ; my intimacy with M. de Caulaincourt, whose great abilities must, in justice, be acknowledged some day ; were the reasons that induced the emperor to apologize for having reproached me so violently for the disapproval I had dared to express of his designs on Spain. He then proposed that I should follow him to Erfurt, and personally conduct the negotiations to be carried on there, with the exception that the treaty, likely to result from those negotiations, should be signed by his Minister of Foreign Affairs. I consented to this. The confidence which he displayed in our first interview I looked upon as a sort of apology for his treatment of me. He had all the despatches of M. de Caulaincourt delivered to me ; I found them everything that could be desired. In a few hours, he acquainted me with all the negotiations that had taken place at St. Petersburg ; and my sole object was so to check the spirit of enterprise that it should not get the upper hand at this singular interview. Napoleon wished the latter to be very brilliant. It was his custom to speak continually to those about him of the one idea which possessed him. I was still grand chamberlain. At every moment, he summoned me to his presence, as well as General Duroc, grand marshal of the palace, and M. de Rémusat, who had the management of the plays. " I wish my journey to be brilliant," he repeated to us every day. At one of his lunches, where we were all three present, he asked me who were the chamberlains on duty. " It seems to me," he said, " that we have not any very aristocratic names ; I must have some. The fact is, that the members of the aristocracy are the only men who know how to be dignified at court. We must do justice to the French nobility. They are admirable in that respect."

" Sire, you have M. de Montesquiou." [1]

[1] The Comte Pierre de Montesquiou-Fezensac was born in 1764. He was an

" Good."—

" Prince Sapieha." [1]

" Not bad."

" It seems to me that two will be sufficient. The journey being short, your Majesty could always have them with you."

" Very soon, Rémusat, I must have a play. Send for Dazincourt [2]—is he not the director ? "

" Yes, your Majesty."

" I wish to astonish Germany by my splendour."

Dazincourt was out. The arrangements for the play were put off until the next day.

" Your Majesty's intention," said Duroc, " is to engage certain important personages to come to Erfurt, and time is limited."

" There is one of Eugène's [3] aides-de-camp," replied the emperor, " who leaves to-day. You might hint to Eugène what he must say to his father-in-law, the King of Bavaria ; and if one of the kings come, they must all come. But no," he added, " we must not employ him. As for that, he is not quick enough. He knows how to do just what I wish, but he is worth nothing for acting a part. Talleyrand would do better. Moreover," he said, laughing, " that, to criticize me, he will tell them that they will please me in coming. It will then be for me to show that I am perfectly indifferent, and that, if anything, their coming has annoyed me."

officer in the cavalry in 1789. He remained in retirement during the Revolution. In 1804, he was elected deputy of the legislature. He replaced M. de Talleyrand as High Chamberlain in 1808. He became president of the legislative body, 1810 ; peer of France under the first Restoration, again High Chamberlain during the Hundred Days. In 1819, he re-entered the House of Peers. He died in 1834.

[1] Prince Alexander Sapieha, descended from an old and illustrious Polish family which was forced to exile itself after the reverses of its country, was born in Strasburg in 1773. Prince Alexander applied himself exclusively to study. He became chamberlain to the Emperor and died in 1812.

[2] Joseph Albouis Dazincourt, born in 1747 at Marseilles, was first librarian to Marshal Richelieu. He afterwards joined the *Théâtre Français*, of which he became associate in 1778. In 1808, he was elected professor of elocution at the Conservatoire, and director of the Court plays. He died in 1809.

[3] Eugène de Beauharnais, son of General Vicomte de Beauharnais and of the Empress Josephine, was born in 1781. He enlisted in 1796, followed Bonaparte in Italy and Egypt, and became brigadier-general in 1804 ; then French prince and arch-chancellor (Lord High Chancellor), February 1, 1805. In June, he was chosen as Viceroy of Italy. In 1814, he retired to Bavaria where he died in 1824, under the title of Duke of Leuchtemberg. The Prince Eugène married Amélie, daughter of the King of Bavaria. His eldest daughter married the prince royal of Sweden, son of Bernadotte.

At lunch the next day the emperor had Dazincourt sent for. The latter awaited his Majesty's orders. Napoleon had told M. de Rémusat, General Duroc, and myself to meet Dazincourt there.

" You have heard that I am going to Erfurt ? "

" Yes, your Majesty."

" I should like the Comédie Française to come."

" Would it be to play comedies and tragedies ? "

" I only want tragedies. Our comedies would be of no use. They would not understand them across the Rhine."

" Your Majesty would undoubtedly wish for a brilliant play."

" Yes, our most beautiful piece."

" Sire, we could have *Athalie* represented."

"*Athalie !* fie on it ! Here is a man who does not understand me. Am I going to Erfurt to put some Joash in those Germans' heads? *Athalie !* How silly of you ! My dear Dazincourt, enough of this ! Tell your best tragedians that they must prepare to go to Erfurt, and I shall give you instructions as to the day of our departure and the pieces that shall be played. How stupid those old people are ! *Athalie*, indeed !— but then it is my fault ; why consult them ? I should not consult any one. Still, if he had mentioned *Cinna*. That is a very interesting play, especially the scene of mercy, which is always good. Though I knew nearly all *Cinna* by heart, yet I never could declaim well. Rémusat, are not the following lines in *Cinna* ?—

> " ' Tous ces crimes d'Etat qu'on fait pour la couronne
> Le ciel nous en absout *lorsqu'il* nous la donne.' [1]
> *Cinna*, Act V., Scene II.

I am not sure if I repeat the verse correctly."

" Sire, it is in *Cinna*, but I believe that it is—*Alors qu'il nous la donne.*"

" What are the following lines ? Take a Corneille."

---

[1] " All those foul deeds to secure a crown,
Heaven condones them, when this it gives us."

" Sire, it is not necessary ; I remember them—

" '*Le ciel nous en absout, alors qu'il nous la donne ;*
Et dans le sacré rang où sa faveur l'a mis,
Le passé devient juste et l'avenir permis.
Qui peut y parvenir ne peut être coupable ;
Quoi qu'il ait fait ou fasse, il est inviolable.' " [1]

" That is capital, and especially for those Germans who always stick to the same ideas, and who still speak of the death of the Duc d'Enghien. Their minds must be enlarged. I do not say that for the Czar Alexander. Such things have no effect upon a Russian ; but it is a good thing for men with melancholy ideas like the Germans, and Germany is full of such. We shall, then, have *Cinna* represented : that will do for the first day. Rémusat, you will look up the tragedies that can be given the following days, and you will report to me before making any final arrangements."

" Sire, does not your Majesty desire that a few good actors be left in Paris ? "

" Yes—substitutes. We must take all the good ones. It will do no harm to have too many."

The order to be present at Erfurt for September 22, was sent immediately to Saint Prix, Talma, Lafont, Damas, Desprès, Lacave, Varennes, Dazincourt, Mademoiselle Raucourt, Mme. Talma, Mdlle. Bourgoin, Mdlle. Duchesnois, Mdlle. Gros, Mdlle. Rose Dupuis, and Mdlle. Patrat.[2]

---

[1] " Heaven condones them, when this it gives us ;
And in the sacred rank obtained from its favour,
All past deeds become legitimate and future ones permitted.
He who can reach it, cannot be held guilty ;
Whatever those deeds may be or have been, he is inviolable."

[2] They were given before their departure the list of the pieces that were to be played. The first, as we have already mentioned, was *Cinna*, then *Andromaque, Britannicus, Zaïre, Mithridate, Œdipe, Iphigénie en Aulide, Phèdre, La Mort de César, Les Horaces, Rodogune, Mahomet, Kadamiste, Le Cid, Manlius, Bajazet.*— (*Prince Talleyrand.*)
Some of these artists have become famous. The first among them was, without doubt, Talma (1766-1826), the most celebrated of our tragic actors. It is well known that Napoleon was very fond of him, and honoured him with his protection during his reign. Pierre Lafon, born in 1775, entered the Théâtre Français in 1800, and contested with Talma for the first place. He excelled equally in tragedy and comedy. Afterwards came St. Prix, whose real name was Foucault. He made his *début* in 1782, and played successively at the Feydeau theatre, at the Odéon, and finally at the Théâtre Français in 1803. Amongst the actresses, the best known of them are Mesdemoiselles Raucourt and Duchesnois. The former made her first appearance

The journey having been announced in the *Moniteur*,[1] every one tried to be of the party. The emperor's two aides-de-camp, Savary and Lauriston,[2] were chosen first. The military retinue was to be very brilliant. The emperor wished to be accompanied by those lieutenants whose names had caused *most* excitement in Germany. First, Marshal Soult, Marshal Davoust, Marshal Lannes, the Prince de Neufchâtel, Marshal Mortier, Marshal Oudinot, General Suchet, General Boyer, General Nansouty,[3] General Claparède,[4] General St. Laurent,[5] M. Fain[6] and M. de Méneval.[7] These two last, private secretaries of the emperor, received, as did M. Daru,[8] M. de Champagny, and

on the stage in 1772, and met with the most brilliant success: she was long imprisoned under the Terror. She died in 1815, and her funeral gave rise to riotous scenes in Saint-Roch's church. Mademoiselle Duchesnois entered the Théâtre Français in 1802, and soon rose to the foremost rank as a tragedian.

[1] The official gazette.

[2] Jacques Bernard Law, Marquis de Lauriston, was born at Pondichery, in 1758. He was the grandson of the famous financier of the Regency. He enlisted in the artillery in 1793, became colonel in 1795, and aide-de-camp to Bonaparte, brigadier-general in 1800. He was, at different times, charged with diplomatic missions. In 1811, he was named ambassador at St. Petersburg. He remained in retirement during the Hundred Days, was peer under the Restoration, then minister of the king's household, marshal in 1823, grand master of the hunt, and minister of state. He died in 1828.

[3] Etiene Champion, comte de Nansouty, born in 1768 of a humble family of Burgundy, was in 1789 captain in the Lauzun Hussars. He served in all the campaigns of the Revolution and of the Empire, became general of division in 1803, and had (on several occasions) important commands in the cavalry. In 1804, he was appointed first chamberlain to the empress; then first equerry to the emperor (1808). He died in 1815. He had married Vergennes' niece.

[4] The comte Claparède, born in 1774, served in the army of the Republic, and was chief of battalion in 1798. Brigadier-general in 1804, he took part in all the wars of his time; he distinguished himself in 1809. He was appointed, under the Restoration, general-inspector of infantry and peer of France. He died in 1841.

[5] Louis St. Laurent, born in 1763, was officer of artillery in 1789, became general of division in 1807, baron of the Empire in 1810. He left the army in that same year and died in 1832.

[6] François Fain, born in 1778, entered the administration in 1794, and for twelve years was engaged in sundry employments in the offices of the conventional committees, then in those of the Directory and of the State Secretary. In 1805, he became private secretary of the emperor. He became baron of the Empire and *maître des requêtes* in 1809. He followed Napoleon in all his campaigns. He lived in retirement under the Restoration. In 1830, he was appointed private secretary of the king, administrator of the civil list and councillor of State. In 1834, he was elected to the Chamber of Deputies. He died in 1837.

[7] François de Méneval, born in 1778, was at first secretary to Joseph Bonaparte in 1802. He entered Napoleon's service as secretary, an office which he retained until 1815. In 1812, he became baron of the Empire and *maître des requêtes*. He has left historical memoirs on Napoleon and Marie Louise (three octavo volumes).

[8] The Comte Daru, born in 1767, was lieutenant in the artillery; afterwards commissariat-officer. Arrested in 1793 he remained in prison until Thermidor 9. In 1796, he became *commissaire-ordonnateur*, then after, Brumaire 18, inspector of

M. Maret, orders to repair to Erfurt. General Duroc appointed M. de Canouville to make arrangements for the lodgings. "Bring Beausset,[1] also," said the emperor. "We really must have some one to introduce our actresses to the Grand Duke Constantin.[2] He can also, at dinner, discharge his duties of *préfet* of the palace, besides he bears a great name." Each day some one left for Erfurt. The route was covered with waggons and saddle- and coach-horses, and some of the emperor's livery servants.

The month of September was drawing to a close. I had read over all the correspondence, but the emperor had not yet had with me the principal conversation on those affairs that were to be treated. A few days before that fixed for my departure, the grand marshal informed me that the emperor desired him to tell me to present myself at the grand reception that evening. I was scarcely in the drawing-room than he led me to his study. "Well," he said, "so you have read all the Russian correspondence? What do you think of my move with the Czar Alexander?" and then he recalled in an amusing retrospect all he had done and written for the past year. He concluded by pointing to me the influence he had gained over the Czar, whereas, as far as he was concerned, he had executed only what suited him of the treaty of Tilsit. "Now," said he, "I shall go to Erfurt. I wish, in returning, to be free to do what I wish in Spain. I wish to be assured that Austria will be afraid and hold back, and I do not desire to be engaged in too precise a manner with Russia concerning the affairs in the East. Prepare me a convention which will satisfy the Czar Alexander, and be directed especially against England, and in which I shall

reviews. In 1800 he was chosen as general secretary to the minister of war, and entered the Tribunate in 1802. In 1805, he became intendant-general of the emperor's household and councillor of state; intendant-general of the grand army, 1806; minister at Berlin in 1807; minister and Secretary of State in 1811. He lived in retirement under the Restoration, and died in 1829.

[1] Louis de Beausset, nephew of the cardinal of that name and born in 1770, became in 1805, *Préfet* of the Imperial palace, and retained that appointment until 1815. He followed then the Empress Marie Louise to Vienna, and was for a time grand master of her household. He has left memoirs on the Empire.

[2] The Grand Duke Constantin (1779–1834), was the youngest brother of the Czar Alexander. He devoted all his life to military affairs, but never obtained any important command. In 1845, he was appointed generalissimo in the army of the new kingdom of Poland and retained that post until his death.

be perfectly free for the rest.   I shall help you, and the *prestige* shall not be lacking."   I was two days without seeing him.   In his impatience he had written what he wished the articles to contain and sent the note to me, requesting that I should bring them to him drawn up, as soon as possible.   I did not make him wait, and a few hours later I went to him with the projected treaty drawn up as he had indicated.

It ran as follows :—

"His Majesty the Emperor of the French, &c., and his Majesty the Czar of all the Russias, &c., wishing to render more and more binding and durable, the alliance which unites them, and reserving to themselves to endeavour to come to an agreement, as soon as possible, on the new means and methods of directing an attack upon England, the common enemy of themselves and of the Continent, have resolved to set down in a special convention the *principles* they have determined to follow—[Here the Emperor interrupted me and said, "*Principles* is good, it is not binding"] and which will direct them in all their steps towards the restoration of peace. They have therefore, to that effect, named for their pleni-potentiaries, &c. . . . . who have agreed to the following articles :—

"Art. I.—His Majesty the Emperor of the French and his Majesty the Czar of Russia confirm, and in case of need, will renew the alliance agreed upon between them at Tilsit, not only binding themselves. to make no treaties of peace with the common enemy, but also not to enter into any negotiations with her—nor to listen to any propositions but by common consent.

"Art. II.—Resolved to remain closely united in peace and in war, the high contracting parties agree to appoint pleni-potentiaries to treat for peace with England, and to send them into such continental town as England may indicate.

"Art III.—In the course of the negotiation, if it should take place, the respective plenipotentiaries of the two high con-tracting parties will act invariably in the most perfect accord, and it will not be permitted to either of them to accept, or approve, against the advice of the other, any proposition or demand of the English plenipotentiary.

"Art. IV.—The two high contracting parties agree not to receive on the part of the enemy, during the whole of the negotiations, any proposition, offer or communication whatever

without letting it at once be known to the respective plenipotentiaries.

"Art. V.—It will be proposed to England to treat all questions pending, on the basis of the *uti possidetis*, including Spain ;
and the condition *sine qua non* which the high contracting parties
agree never to depart from, will be that England recognize on
the one hand, the union of Wallachia and Moldavia, and of
Finland with the Russian Empire, and, on the other, Joseph
Napoleon Bonaparte as King of Spain and the Indies.

"Art. VI.—The Ottoman Porte having experienced since the
treaty of Tilsit many changes and revolutions which seem not to
leave to it any possibility to give, and does not, consequently, leave
any hope of obtaining from it, sufficient guarantees for the
respect of the lives and properties of the inhabitants of Wallachia
and Moldavia, his Majesty the Czar of Russia, who, since the
said treaty, has contracted towards them special engagements,
and who, as a consequence of the said revolutions, has been
involved in enormous expenses to protect those provinces, being
for those motives resolved not to relinquish them, the more so
as their possession can alone give his empire its natural and
necessary boundary, his Majesty the Emperor Napoleon *will
not oppose*, as far as he is concerned, their being annexed to the
Russian Empire. And His said Majesty foregoes the mediation
offered by him, and accepted by Russia in the treaty of Tilsit."

("I will not have this article, it is too positive."   "Nevertheless, Sire, *ne s'opposera point*, is certainly one of the expressions
which bind the least ; besides, the following article is a great
corrective.")

"Art. VII.—Nevertheless his Majesty the Emperor of all the
Russias will limit himself, for the present, to continue, as in the
past, to occupy Wallachia and Moldavia, leaving everything on
the same footing as it is to-day, and will propose to open
either in Constantinople, or in an island of the Danube, and
under the mediation of France, negotiations, in view of obtaining peacefully the cession of those two provinces. Those
negotiations, however, will be opened only when the negotiations
with England shall have had an issue, in order not to give rise to
new discussions which may delay the peace."

("That article is good ; with my mediation, I remain the
master, and the preceding article will perplex Austria, my true
enemy."   "Your enemy, Sire, at present, perhaps, but at heart

her policy is not in opposition to that of France; she is not aggressive, but conservative." " My dear Talleyrand, I know that this is your opinion ; we will speak of that when the Spanish business is over.")

" Art. VIII.—His Majesty the Emperor Napoleon will act conjointly with his Majesty the Czar of Russia, in order to obtain from the Ottoman Porte an amicable cession. All the notes of, and all the steps taken by, the two allied courts, in order to reach this end, will be made in conjunction and in the same spirit.

"Art. IX.—In case a refusal from the Ottoman Porte led to a renewal of the hostilities and to the continuation of the war, the Emperor Napoleon would take no part in it, and will confine himself to help Russia by his good offices. But if it should happen that Austria or any other power made common cause with the Ottoman Porte in the said war, his Majesty the Emperor Napoleon will at once make common cause with Russia, being obliged to regard this case as being that of the general alliance which binds the two empires."

("That article is insufficient ; it does not quite convey my idea. Nevertheless, proceed, I will tell you what you must add to it.")

" Art. X.—The high contracting parties agree besides, to maintain the integrity of the other possessions of the Ottoman Empire, not wishing to decide, or to undertake of themselves, anything with regard to them, nor to suffer that anything be undertaken by whomsoever without their having previously agreed upon it.

" Art. XI.—In the negotiations with England, his Majesty the Emperor Napoleon will support Russia's claim to obtain the recognition of Wallachia and Moldavia as provinces of the Russian Empire, whether the Ottoman Porte has consented to it or not.

"Art. XII.—In return for the relinquishment made by the Emperor Napoleon in the above article, his Majesty the Czar Alexander desists from the eventual engagement taken towards him by the fifth of the secret articles of the treaty of Tilsit, and the said article remains null and void—

" That is about all I have said to you ; leave me this draft, I will arrange it. We must add to one of the last articles, to that one where I stopped you, that, in case Austria gave any

uneasiness to France, the Czar of Russia, on the first demand
which would be made to him, pledges himself to declare against
Austria, and to make common cause with France, this case
being equally one of those to which the alliance which binds
the two powers applies.—This is the essential article. How
could you have left it out? You are still an Austrian!"—
"Somewhat, Sire. Yet I think it would be more exact to say
that I am never a Russian, but always a Frenchman."

"Make your arrangements to leave : you must be at Erfurt
a day or two before me. During the time of our stay there,
you try to see the Czar as often as possible. You know him
well, you will speak to him in that language that suits him. You
will tell him that in the benefit our alliance may prove to
mankind, one recognizes one of the great purposes of Providence.
Together we are destined to restore general order in Europe.
We are both young, we need not hurry. You will insist greatly
upon that—for Count Romanzoff is sanguine about the Eastern
question. You will say that nothing can be done without public
opinion, and that it is necessary that, without being scared
by our combined power, Europe should see with pleasure the
achievement of the great undertaking we contemplate. The
security of the neighbouring powers, the respect of the legitimate interest of the Continent, seven millions of Greeks restored
to independence. All this constitutes a fine field for philanthropy. I will give you *carte blanche* for that. I wish only that it
be distant philanthropy. Good-bye."

I returned home, I put my papers in order, I carried
away all that I thought I should require and I got into my
carriage. I arrived at Erfurt, Saturday, September 24th, at ten
o'clock in the morning. M. de Canouville lodged me in a
house very near that which the emperor was to occupy. A few
minutes after my arrival, M. de Caulaincourt came to see me.
The first day I spent with him proved very useful to me. We
spoke of St. Petersburg, and of the disposition in which the two
sovereigns had come to the interview. We told each other
what we knew, and soon agreed upon all points.

I found all Erfurt in excitement, there was not a respectable house that did not provide accommodation for a sovereign

and his retinue. The Emperor of Russia arrived there with the Grand Duke Constantin, Count Romanzoff, Count Tolstoï, grand marshal, General Tolstoï, ambassador to France, Prince Wolkonski, Count Oszarowski,[1] Prince Troubetzkoï, Count Ouwaroff,[2] Count Schouwaloff,[3] Prince Gagarin, M. Speranski, M. Labenski, Herr Bethmann, General Hitroff, State Councillors Gervais and Creidemann, Herr von Schröder, Prince Léopold of Saxe-Coburg.[4] I think that I have mentioned there almost all those who had the honour to accompany the Czar Alexander. He was expected a day later than the Emperor Napoleon, having to stop twenty-four hours at Weimar.

A chamberlain of the King of Saxony has just told me that his master would sleep at Erfurt on the 25th, and that he was followed by Count von Bose,[5] cabinet minister, Count Marcolini,[6] master of the horse, Baron von Funck,[7] Baron von Gutschmidt, Major Thielemann, Chamberlain von Gablenz, Herr von Marxhansky and by Herr von Schönberg. M. de Bourgoing,[8] minister of France at Dresden, also had permission to follow the king.

---

[1] Count Adam of Alkcantara Oszarowski, descended from an old Polish family allied to Russia. He was the Czar Alexander's aide-de-camp.

[2] Count Theodore Ouwaroff, commander-in-chief of the imperial guard and first aide de-camp general to the Czar. He had been one of the conspirators who assassinated the Czar Paul.

[3] General Count Schouwaloff (1775-1823), aide-de-camp to the emperor. He held important commands in all the wars of that time. In 1814, he was one of the commissioners charged to accompany Napoleon to Fréjus.

[4] Prince Leopold of Saxe-Coburg Saafeld, born in 1790, son of Francis, Duke of Saxe-Coburg, and of Caroline, Countess of Reuss, entered the Russian army quite young with the grade of general. In 1810, he was obliged to leave the Russian service to obey the injunctions of Napoleon, re-entered the ranks in 1813, served in the campaigns of Germany and France, and entered Paris with the allied sovereigns in 1814 and in 1815. In the following year, he married the Princess Charlotte, the grand-daughter of King George III. and heiress to the Crown. Leopold was naturalized English, but the princess died in the following year. In 1830, he was elected King of the Belgians. Two years later, he married the Princess Louise d'Orléans, the eldest daughter of King Louis-Philippe. He died in 1865.

[5] Frederick William, Count von Bose (1753-1809) was minister of Saxony at Stockholm, then marshal of the court at Dresden, and grand chamberlain. In 1806, he signed peace with Napoleon and became Minister of Foreign Affairs.

[6] Count Marcolini (1739-1814) was grand chamberlain and master of the horse to the King of Saxony. He became minister of state in 1809. He was devoted to the French alliance, to which he remained faithful until his death.

[7] Baron von Funck, a Saxon general (1761-1828), took an active part in the war of 1806. In 1812, he served in our ranks in the campaign of Russia, at the head of the Saxon cavalry. In 1813, he was employed on various diplomatic missions, and was minister at London in 1818.

[8] Jean-Francois, Baron de Bourgoing, born in 1748 at Nevers, was at first an officer

It may be interesting to know now the names of the important personages who, from time to time, arrived at Erfurt.[1] The Duke of Saxe-Gotha,[2] accompanied by Baron von Thümmel, Herr von Studnitz, Herr von Zigesar, Barons Herda and Wangenheim, and by Herr von Hoff;[3] the Duke of Saxe-Weimar with the hereditary prince,[4] Baron von Egloffstein,[5] Baron Einsiedel, Herr Goethe, and Herr Wieland,[6] both of whom were intimate counsellors of Weimar; the Duke of Oldenburg,[7] with Baron von Hammerstein,[8] and Baron von Gall; the Duke of Mecklenburg-Schwerin,[9] the hereditary prince of Mecklenburg-Strelitz,[10] the Prince of Dessau,[11] the princes von Waldeck, Hesse-Homburg, Reuss-Greitz, Reuss-Ebersdorff, Reuss-Lobenstein,[12]

and then secretary of embassy. In 1787, he became minister of France at Hamburg, then at Madrid (1791), and was, in 1795, charged to negotiate the peace at Basel. Minister at Copenhagen, then at Stockholm under the Consulate, he became, later on, minister to Saxony, and died in 1811.

[1] In the long enumeration that is about to follow, a great number of personages who have left no trace in history, and on whom we have not been able to procure any information, are mentioned. We have furnished particulars only of the most important among them. As for the sovereign princes, we noticed only those who, by their fame or by their family alliances, deserved special mention.

[2] Augustus, Duke of Saxe-Gotha and Altenburg (1772-1822), member of the Confederation of the Rhine (December 15, 1806).

[3] Karl von Hoff (1771-1831). Secretary of embassy in the service of the Duke of Saxe-Gotha, and afterwards Aulic Councillor and state minister. He has left numerous books on politics and history.

[4] Karl Augustus of Saxe-Weimar (1757-1828), member of the Confederation of the Rhine (December 15, 1806). His son, Prince Charles-Frederick, married the Princess Marie, daughter of the Czar Paul.

[5] Augustus, Baron von Egloffstein (1771-1834). Officer in the service of Prussia, then of the Duke of Saxe-Weimar. In 1807, he became general of brigade and commander of the Saxon troops in the service of France, in Austria, Spain, and Russia, and during the siege of Danzig (1814).

[6] Christopher-Martin Wieland, born in 1733, became in 1792 the preceptor of the Princes of Weimar, then intimate counsellor. He was a member of the academy of that town, which then included the most distinguished men and the most illustrious *savants* in Germany. He has left many works, including poems, novels, comedies, &c. He died in 1813.

[7] Peter Frederick, Prince of Lubeck, regent of the duchy of Oldenburg, in the name of his cousin. His son, heir presumptive to the duchy, married the Grand-duchess Catherine, daughter of the Czar Paul.

[8] Hans Detlef, baron of Hammerstein (1768-1826), minister of the Duke of Oldenburg. Later he went to Hanover, and became member of the private council of war, and plenipotentiary to the Diet of Frankfort.

[9] Frederick Francois, Duke of Mecklenburg-Schwerin, born in 1756. His son married the Grand-duchess Helena, daughter of the Czar Paul. By a subsequent marriage he had a daughter, the Princess Helena, who married the Duc d'Orleans.

[10] George Frederick, born in 1779, succeeded his father 1816. He was brother to Louise, Queen of Prussia.

[11] Leopold, Prince von Anhalt-Dessau (1740-1817) one of the most faithful allies of France, member of the Confederation of the Rhine.

[12] The house of Reuss was divided into four reigning branches, the Greitz, Ebers-

the Duchess of Saxe-Hildburghausen,[1] the Prince of Schwarz-
burg-Rudolstadt,[2] with Herr von Kettelhutt, Herr von Weisse
and Herr von Gleichen ; the Prince and Princess of Tour and
Taxis[3] with Herr von Leikam ; the Prince of Hesse-Rothenburg,
the Prince of Hohenzollern-Sigmaringen,[4] with the Prince of
Reuss-Schleiz and Major von Falkenstein ; the Duke William
of Bavaria, the prince-primate[5] (Furst von Dalberg), to whom
each inhabitant of the town readily offered lodging accommodation ; he had been governor of that town and was beloved
by all: the Prince of Hohenzollern-Hechingen,[6] with the
hereditary prince ; Herr von Hövel, Herr von Bauer ; the hereditary Prince of Baden, with the Princess Stéphanie Napoléon ;[7]
Frau von Venningen and Mlle. de Bourjolly ; Baron von Dalberg,
minister of Baden at Paris,[8] the Prince of Reuss XLI., the
hereditary Prince of Darmstadt,[9] Count von Keller,[10] Prince

dorff, Lobenstein, and Schleiz. All these princes had joined the Confederation of the
Rhine (April 1807).
[1] Member of the Confederation of the Rhine (December 15, 1806).
[2] Member of the Confederation of the Rhine (April 1807).
[3] Charles Alexander, Prince of Tour and Taxis, born in 1770, Privy Councillor of
the Austrian Empire.   He was grand-master of the Imperial post offices, a post
which was held in his family since 1695. He married in 1773, the Princess Theresa,
daughter of the Grand Duke of Mecklenburg-Strelitz.
[4] Antoine, Prince of Hohenzollern-Sigmaringen, born in 1762, member of the Confederation of the Rhine (July 12, 1806).   The princes of the different branches of
the house of Hohenzollern, having abdicated in favour of the branch of the house of
Hohenzollern-Brandenburg, which occupied the throne of Prussia, the King of
Prussia assumed the sovereignty of these principalities.
[5] Charles, Prince of Dalberg, born in 1744, took holy orders and became, in 1772,
intimate counsellor of the Elector of Mayence, then governor of Erfurt, coadjutor
of the Archbishop of Mayence, to whom he succeeded in 1802. He was afterwards
named Archchancellor of the empire.   In 1806, he had to resign this dignity ; was in
compensation named by Napoleon, prince-primate of the Confederation of the Rhine,
prince-sovereign of Ratisbonne, Grand Duke of Fulde and of Hanau. He died in 1817.
[6] Member of the Confederation of the Rhine (July 12, 1806).
[7] Charles Louis Frederick, hereditary prince of Baden, married Stephanie Tascher
de la Pagerie, cousin of the Empress Josephine, an adopted daughter of Napoleon.
He became Grand Duke in 1811 and died 1818. He was member of the Confederation of the Rhine.
[8] Emeric-Joseph, Baron von Dalberg, born in 1773, entered the diplomacy in
the service of the prince primate, his uncle. In 1803 he became minister of Baden
at Paris. From that time dates his connection with M. de Talleyrand. In 1809, he
became Minister of Foreign Affairs of Baden, but did not relinquish his situation in
Paris.   The same year, he was naturalized French, was created Duke by Napoleon
and councillor of state with an endowment of four millions. In 1814, he became
member of the provisory government, afterwards peer of France and state minister
in 1815. He died in the year 1817.
[9] He was the son of Prince Louis, who took the title of grand duke on joining
the Confederation of the Rhine (July 12, 1806). He succeeded his father in 1830,
and abdicated in 1840.
[10] Louis Christopher, Count von Keller (1757-1827), was first chamberlain and

Dolgorouki,[1] Count von Lerchenfeld, Prince von Leyen,[2] Prince William of Prussia,[3] Count von Goltz, Minister of Foreign Affairs ; M. Le Cocq, M. de Déchen, Jérôme Napoleon, King of Westphalia, with the queen, who was born Princess of Wurtemberg ; Prince of Hesse-Philippsthal,[4] Count and Countess von Bucholz, Counts von Truchsess and Wintzingerode, the King of Bavaria,[5] Baron von Montgelas,[6] Counts von Wurtemberg and von Reuss, the King of Wurtemberg[7] the Prince of Hohenlohe, the Duchess of Wurtemberg, Count von Taube, Baron von Gorlitz, Baron von Moltke, Count von Salm Dyck.[8] I surely must forget some people, and apologize for so doing.

Already the emperor's pages had arrived and were walking about the town in full dress. The military duties were performed by a battalion of grenadiers of the imperial guard ; a detachment of picked gendarmes ; the 6th regiment of cuirassiers ; the 1st regiment of hussars ; and the 17th regiment of light infantry.

counsellor of the Embassy of Frederick II., minister of Prussia at Stockholm (1779) at St. Petersburg, and at Vienna. In 1811, he became minister of the Grand Duchy of Frankfort at Paris.

[1] There were then several princes of the Dolgorouki family. He who attended the meeting at Erfurt is doubtless Prince George, Prussian general and diplomat, who commanded in Finland (1795), and at Corfou (1804), was ambassador at Vienna and to Holland ; or his cousin, Prince Michel, aide-de-camp of the emperor, and Major-general, who was killed a short time later in Finland.

[2] Member of the Confederation of the Rhine.

[3] Prince William of Prussia was the fourth son of Frederick II. He was general in the Prussian Army, and took an active part in the wars of 1806, 1813 and 1814. In 1831, he was governor of the Rhine provinces.

[4] Francis of Hesse-Philippsthal, died in 1810. He was the brother of Louis of Hesse-Philippsthal, general in the service of the King of the two Sicilies, who sustained the memorable siege of Gaeta, in 1806.

[5] Maximilian-Joseph (1756-1825) Duke of Bavaria in 1799, king December 26, 1805. He was a member of the Confederation of the Rhine. His daughter married Prince Eugène de Beauharnais, Napoleon's adopted son.

[6] Maximilian-Garnerin, Baron von Montgelas (1759-1838), Aulic Counsellor of Bavaria, Minister of Foreign Affairs (1799). He was a sincere ally to France ; he knew how to profit by it in obtaining great advantages for his country. He retired in 1814.

[7] Frederick (1754-1816), Duke of Würtemberg in 1797, elector in 1803, king 1805, member of the Confederation of the Rhine in 1806. He married an English princess. One of his daughters, Princess Frédérique Sophie Dorothée, married the King Jérôme Napoleon.

[8] Joseph Count von Salm-Reiferscheid-Dyck, younger branch of the house of Salm. His estates, which were situated near Cologne, were united with France in 1801, then with Prussia in 1814. He received in exchange a pension of 28,000 florins and the title of prince (1816). At first, he married Maria-Theresa, Countess von Hatzfeld, and afterwards, Constance Marie de Theis, daughter of a forests-superintendent of Nantes. The latter is renowned on account of her literary works.

The emperor entered Erfurt, September 27, 1808, at ten
A.M. An immense crowd surrounded the avenues leading to the
palace. Every one wished to see and would approach him who
dispensed all : thrones, misery, fears, and hopes. Augustus,
Louis XIV. and Napoleon are the men on whom most praises
have been bestowed. Times and talent gave different forms
to these praises ; but they were, in reality, the same thing. My
duties as grand chamberlain enabled me to see the forced, simu-
lated, or even sincere homage which was rendered to Napoleon,
more than I could have done otherwise, and gave it proportions
which appeared to me monstrous. Never did baseness display
so much genius : it suggested the idea of having a hunt on the
very ground where the emperor had gained the famous battle
of Jena. A slaughter of wild boars and beasts was there to
remind the victor of the success of this battle. I have often
remarked that the more resentment people were justified in
feeling against the emperor the more they smiled at his good
fortune, which, they said, was Heaven's will.

I am inclined to believe that flattery possesses secrets with
which princes alone,—not those who have lost their thrones, but
those who subjected their crowns to some ever-threatening
protectorate,—are acquainted ; they know skilfully how to make
use of them, when placed in the presence of the power which
rules over and could overthrow them. I have heard the following
line, of I know not what wretched tragic play, quoted :

> " *Tu n'as su qu'obéir, tu serais un tyran.*" [1]

I have not met with a single prince at Erfurt, to whom I
should not have been more justified in saying :

> " *Tu n'as su que régner ; tu serais un esclave.*" [2]

It is easy to understand this. Mighty sovereigns wish their
courts to convey the idea of the importance of their power. On
the contrary, petty princes wish theirs to disguise the narrow
limits of their rule. Everything magnifies, or rather swells,
about a petty sovereign : etiquette, regard, and flattery ; the
latter is the standard of his greatness ; he never thinks it

---

[1] " You would be a tyrant, seeing that you have only known how to obey."
[2] " You would be a slave, seeing that you have only known how to reign."

exaggerated. This way of judging things becomes quite natural to him, and is not altered by the vicissitudes of fortune. Thus, if victory brings into his dominions, into his very palace, a man before whom he can himself be but a courtier, he will stoop, in the presence of his victor, as low as he wished his own subjects to do before himself. He cannot conceive any other form of flattery. At powerful courts, they know another means of raising themselves : it is to bow ; petty princes only know how to crawl, and remain crawling until fortune comes to raise them. I did not see at Erfurt a single hand nobly stroking the lion's mane.

After these scathing remarks, illustrations of which I refrain from giving, I am happy to resume my subject. On September 28, news came of the arrival of the Emperor Alexander, who had been spending the night at Weimar. Napoleon, followed by his aide-de-camp and by his generals in full dress, rode up to meet him. When within sight of each other, the two sovereigns rushed to each other's arms in the most friendly fashion, after which Napoleon led the Emperor Alexander to the residence prepared for him, and having carefully ascertained that the Czar was provided with everything he needed, took leave of him.

I was in the Emperor Napoleon's palace, awaiting his return. He seemed very pleased with the first impressions of his journey, and he told me that he augured well of it, but that nothing should be hurried. "We are so glad to see each other again," he said, laughing ; "that we must be allowed to enjoy that feeling a little." He had scarcely finished dressing when the Czar arrived, and I was introduced to him. "He is an old acquaintance," said the Emperor of Russia ; " I am delighted to see him again. I hoped he would be of our party." I wanted to retire ; but, as Napoleon wished to avoid conversing on any serious subject, and was only too glad that I should be there, he desired me to stay. The two sovereigns conversed with the most lively interest on insignificant family matters. The Empress Elizabeth was the first topic of conversation.[1] Then it turned on the Empress Josephine, and then on the Grand

---

[1] Louise Elizabeth, daughter of Charles-Louis, hereditary prince of Baden and of Amelia of Hesse-Darmstadt, born in 1779. Married in 1793, to Alexander, future Czar of Russia.

Duchess Anne,[1] and the Princess Borghese,[2] &c. Had the time of a first visit permitted, there probably would have been a word about the health of Cardinal Fesch. The two sovereigns, feeling quite comfortable as to the state in which they had left their respective families, separated. Napoleon showed the Czar to the stairs, and I the Emperor of Russia to his carriage. While walking together, the latter said to me several times : "*Nous nous verrons,*"[3] and that, with an expression that proved that M. de Caulaincourt, who had met him on his arrival, had told him that I knew what was going to happen. I then went up to the emperor, who said to me : " I have modified the draft of the treaty ; I am taking more precautions against Austria ; I will show it you."—He did not enter into any more particulars.— " The Czar seems to me disposed to do anything I wish. If he speaks to you on the subject, tell him that I at first intended the negotiation to be made between Count Romanzoff and yourself, but that I have changed my mind, and that my confidence in him is such that I think it better for everything to pass between ourselves. When the convention is settled, the ministers will sign it. Remember, though, in everything you say, that any delay will be useful to me. The language of all the kings about to meet here will be submissive ; they fear me. Before discussing the real object of this meeting, I wish the Emperor of Russia to be dazzled by the sight of my power. For there is no negotiation that it could fail to render easier."

On returning home, I found a note from the Princess of Tour and Taxis, informing me of her arrival. I immediately went to her. It afforded me much pleasure to see her again, she was such an excellent lady. She told me she had come to Erfurt to ask the Czar to use, in her favour, his influence over

---

[1] Anne, daughter of the Czar Paul and of Sophia Dorothy, Princess of Wurtemberg, born in 1795, married, in 1816, to William Prince of Orange, who in 1840 became King of the Netherlands.

[2] Marie-Pauline Bonaparte, second sister of the emperor, born at Ajaccio in 1780 ; she married in 1801, General Leclerc, who died at San-Domingo in 1802. In 1803, she married the Prince Borghese, the head of one of the most illustrious families of the Roman nobility. The Princess Pauline's brother had created her Duchess of Guastalla in 1806, but this country was shortly after incorporated with the kingdom of Italy. In 1814, she accompanied the emperor to the Island of Elba, and, in the following year, went to Rome, where she died in 1825.

[3] " We will see each other."

the German Princes, with whom her husband, grand master of the German Posts and relays, vainly tried to make arrangements for some years. I was not with her a quarter of an hour, when the Czar was announced ; he was most amiable and communicative, and asked the princess to give him some tea, telling her that she ought to give us some every evening after the play ; for it would be the best way to chat at one's ease and finish the day pleasantly. It was agreed upon, and nothing of interest was discussed that evening.

This interview at Erfurt, without Austria being invited or even officially informed, had alarmed the Emperor Francis, who, of his own accord, had sent Baron de Vincent straight to Erfurt with a letter to Napoleon, and I also think one to the Czar. M. de Vincent, a gentleman from Lorraine, had entered the Austrian service long before the French Revolution, on account of the relationship of his family with the House of Lorraine. I knew him well ; for ten years, I had had frequent intercourse with him, and I can add that he had cause to congratulate himself that he knew me, for, eighteen months before, it pleased me to render his mission in Warsaw a brilliant one, by assuring him that the influence I could dispose of—it was then considerable— would be applied to thwarting all the outbreaks ready to take place in Galicia. M. de Vincent showed me a copy of the letter of which he was the bearer : the style of this letter was noble, rendering any uneasiness on the part of his sovereign imperceptible. M. de Vincent had been ordered to confide in me. I told him that his mission gave me much pleasure, for I was not without fear concerning the opinions of the two sovereigns. At the beginning, it was easy to see from Napoleon's own words that he recognized me to be, and he was right, a partisan of the alliance of France with Austria. I then thought, and I still believe that such alliance was to the interest of France. I assured M. de Vincent that I had done, and was still doing, all in my power to prevent any of the resolutions arranged at Erfurt causing prejudice to the interests of his government.

Napoleon, faithful to his present dilatory system, had disposed of the first days so as never to be able to find a moment to speak of business matters. He spent a good deal of time over his lunch. He received visitors with whom he willingly chatted ; then followed some visits to the public establishments of the country, from whence he went to manœuvres outside the town, at which the Czar and the Grand Duke never failed to meet him. Then, only sufficient time remained to dress for dinner, which was succeeded by the play, which took up the rest of the day.

I have known many of those *déjeûners* to last more than two hours. To them, Napoleon generally bid the eminent and remarkable men who had come to Erfurt to see him. Every morning, he perused, with much interest, the list of new arrivals. One day, having noticed the name of Herr Goethe among the number of newly-arrived visitors, he sent for him.

"Monsieur Goethe," he said to him on seeing him, "I am delighted to see you."

"Sire, I see that when your Majesty travels, you do not neglect to notice even the most insignificant persons."

" I know you are Germany's first dramatic poet."

" Sire, you wrong our country ; we are under the impression we have our great men. Schiller, Lessing, and Wieland are surely known to your Majesty."

"I confess I hardly know them. However, I have read *La Guerre de Trente Ans*,[1] and that, I beg your pardon, seemed to me to furnish dramatic subjects only worthy of our boulevards."

" Sire, I do not know your boulevards, but I suppose that popular plays are given there. I am sorry to hear you judge so severely one of the greatest geniuses of modern times."

"You generally live in Weimar ; it is the place where the most celebrated men of German literature meet ? "

" Sire, they enjoy great protection there ; but, for the present, there is only one man in Weimar who is known throughout Europe ; it is Wieland."

" I should be delighted to see Monsieur Wieland ! "

"If your Majesty will allow me to ask him, I feel certain that he will come here immediately."

---

[1] *Geschichte des dreissigjährigen Krieges*, Schiller's chief and last historical work. It was published in 1792.—(*Translator.*)

" Does he speak French ? "

" He knows it, and has corrected several French translations of his works."

" While you are here, you must go every night to our plays. It will not do you any harm to see good French tragedies."

" I'll go willingly. I must confess to your Majesty that it was my intention, for I have translated, or rather imitated, some French pieces."

" Which ones ? "

" *Mahomet* and *Tancrède.*"

" I shall ask Rémusat if he has any actors here to play them. I should be very glad for you to see them represented in our language. You are not as strict as we are in theatrical rules."

" Sire, unity with us is not so essential."

" How do you find our sojourn here ? "

" Very brilliant, sire, and I hope it will be useful to our country."

" Are your people happy ? "

" They hope to be so soon."

" Monsieur Goethe, you ought to remain with us during the whole of our stay and write your impressions of the grand sight we are offering."

" Ah ! sire, it would require the pen of some great writer of antiquity to undertake such a task."

" Are you an admirer of Tacitus ? "

" Yes, sire, I admire him much."

" Well, I don't; but we shall talk of that another time. Write and tell Monsieur Wieland to come here. I shall return his visit at Weimar, where the duke has invited me. I'll be very glad to see the duchess ; she is a lady worthy of much esteem. The duke was troublesome enough, for some time. But he has been punished." [1]

" Sire, troublesome though he may have been, the punishment was a little severe. But I am not a judge of such things ; he

---

[1] The Grand Duke of Saxe-Weimar had taken Prussia's part in 1806. His troops were literally crushed, at Jena, and his capital, which was on the line of retreat of the Prussian army, was devastated by the pursuers.

protects literature and sciences, and we have nothing to say
against him, but rather everything in his favour."

"Monsieur Goethe, come to-night to *Iphigénie;* it is a good
piece. It is not, however, one of my favourites, but the French
think a good deal of it. You will see in my pit a great number
of sovereigns. Do you know the Prince Primate?"

"Yes, sire; almost intimately. He is very clever, very well
informed, and very generous."

"Well, you will see him, to-night, fast asleep on the
shoulder of the King of Wurtemberg. Have you already seen
the Czar?"

"No, sire, never; but I hope to be introduced to him."

"He speaks your language; should you write anything on
the Erfurt interview, you must dedicate it to him."

"Sire, it is not my habit to do so. When I first commenced
to write, I made it a principle never to dedicate anything to any
one, in order that I should never repent it."

"The great writers of Louis the Fourteenth's time were not
of your opinion."

"But your Majesty cannot be sure they never repented doing
what they did."

"What has become of that scoundrel, Kotzebue?"[1]

"Sire, they say he is in Siberia and that your Majesty
will solicit his pardon from the Czar."

"But he is not the man for me."

"Sire, he has been very unfortunate, and is a man of great
talent."

"Good-bye, Monsieur Goethe."

I followed Herr Goethe to invite him to dine with me. On
coming home, I wrote this first conversation, and, while at
dinner, I ascertained, by different questions I put to him, that

---

[1] Augustus von Kotzebue, born in 1761, at Weimar, entered the Russian service,
and became secretary to the government of St. Petersburg, and President of Justice
in Esthonia. He was arrested and transported to Siberia in 1800, as the author of
libels against the Czar Paul; he returned in the following year, and was appointed
Aulic councillor. He came afterwards to Paris, where he remained from 1802 to
1806. After the battle of Jena, he fled to Russia, where he circulated pamphlets of a
violent nature against France and Napoleon. In 1813, he was one of the promoters
of the national insurrection of Germany, but he changed his colours in 1815, and
became one of the most ardent political defenders of the Holy Alliance. He was
assassinated in 1819.

what I had written was correct. On rising from table, Herr Goethe went to the theatre ; I was anxious that he should be near the stage, but that was difficult enough, for the seats in front were occupied by the crowned heads, and the chairs placed behind them were taken up by the hereditary princes, while the seats still farther off were filled by ministers and princes. I, therefore, recommended Herr Goethe to Dazincourt who, without wounding propriety, found the means of placing him advantageously.

The choice of the pieces for those plays at Erfurt had been made with great care and art, the subjects having been taken from heroic times or great historical events. Napoleon's idea in causing heroic times to appear on the stage, was to mislead all that old German nobility in the midst of which he was, and to carry them away by imagination into other regions where men great by themselves, fabulous by their actions, creators of their race, and pretending to draw their origin from the gods, passed before its eyes. In the pieces drawn from history, the representation of which he ordered, the policy of some chief character always recalled some circumstances analogous with those which occurred daily since he himself had appeared on the stage of the world ; and all that became the subject of flattering allusions. The hatred of Mithridates against the Romans called to mind Napoleon's hatred against England, and after hearing the following verses :

> " Ne vous figurez pas que de cette contrée,
> Par d'éternels remparts, Rome soit séparée,
> Je sais tous les chemins par où je dois passer,
> Et si la mort bientôt ne vient me traverser," [1]

everybody whispered : " Yes, he knows all the roads to success ; yes, it must be borne in mind, he knows them all."

The ideas of immortality, glory, undaunted bravery, and fatality, which, in *Iphigénie*, recur constantly, either as the chief idea, or as accessory, served the purpose of his main thought,

---

[1]   " Do not fancy that from this country
    Rome be protected by everlasting obstacles,
    I know all the paths which lead to that city,
    And if death does not soon thwart my purpose," . . .
    —(*Mithridates*, Act III., Scene I.)

which was to arouse unceasing amazement in all who approached him.   Talma had received orders to deliver slowly the following fine passage :

> " L'honneur parle, il suffit, ce sont là nos oracles.
> Les dieux sont de nos jours les maîtres souverains,
> Mais, seigneur, notre gloire est dans nos propres mains,
> Pourquoi nous tourmenter de leurs ordres suprêmes ?
> Ne songeons qu'à nous rendre immortels comme eux-mêmes,
> Et laissant faire au sort, courons où la valeur
> Nous promet un destin aussi grand que le leur," . . .[1]

But the play of Napoleon's choice, that which indicated best the causes and the source of his power, was *Mahomet*, because, during the whole performance, it seemed to him that he was the chief character.   From the beginning of the first act :

> " Les mortels sont égaux, ce n'est point la naissance,
> C'est la seule vertu qui fait la différence.
> Il est de ces esprits favorisés des cieux
> Qui sont tout par eux-mêmes et rien par leurs aïeux.
> Tel est l'homme, en un mot, que j'ai choisi pour maître ;
> Lui seul dans l'univers a mérité de l'être ;
> Tout mortel à ses lois doit un jour obéir," . . .[2]

the eyes of all present were riveted on him ; they listened to the actors but could not help looking at him.   And, in another passage, every German prince must naturally have applied to himself the following verses uttered by Lafont in a dismal tone :

> "Vois l'empire romain tombant de toutes parts,
> Ce grand corps déchiré dont les membres épars

---

[1]   " The dictates of honour suffice, they constitute our oracle.
The gods are the sovereign masters of our life,
But, my Lord, our glory depends on ourselves,
Why trouble about their supreme orders ?
Let us only think of becoming immortal like themselves,
And letting fate take its course, let us hasten where valour
Holds out for us the prospect of a fate as great as their own," . . .
—*(Iphigénie*, Act I., Scene II.)

[2]   " All men are equal, it is not to birth,
But to virtue alone that difference between them is due.
There are some men, favoured by Heaven,
Who are everything by themselves and owe nothing to their ancestors.
Such, in short, is the man I chose for master ;
He alone in the world deserved to be mine ;
All nations will some day submit to his sway," . . .
—*(Mahomet* (Voltaire), Act I., Scene IV.)

Languissent dispersés, sans honneur et sans vie ;
Sur ces débris du monde élevons l'Arabie.
Il faut un nouveau culte, il faut de nouveaux fers,
Il faut un nouveau Dieu pour l'aveugle univers." [1]

At this point, respect only prevented the audience from demonstrating their approval ; and the applause almost broke forth at the following verse :

" Qui l'a fait roi ?   Qui l'a couronné ?   La Victoire." [2]
Mahomet, Acte I., Scene IV.

Perhaps they only affected to be touched when Omar added :
" Au nom de conquérant et de triomphateur,
Il veut joindre le nom de pacificateur." [3]
Mahomet, Acte I., Scene IV.

At this last verse, Napoleon cleverly evinced an emotion which showed that it was there, he wished them to find the explanation of all his life.

They even plainly displayed their approbation when Saint-Prix, in *La Mort de César*, said, with admirable expression, in speaking of Sylla :

" Il en était l'effroi, *J'en serai les délices*, etc." [4]
La Mort de César (Voltaire), Acte I., Scene IV.

I do not wish to quote any more applications, or inductions of the same kind which I heard people make every day.   I only cite those that are indispensable in order to enable my readers to grasp more fully the spirit of this great assembly.

After each play, I saw the Emperor Alexander at the house of the Princess of Tour and Taxis, and sometimes M. de Vincent

[1]   "Behold the Roman empire breaking up everywhere,
Great tattered body whose scattered limbs
Linger disconnected in inglorious death ;
We must raise Arabia on this wreck of the world.
A new worship is needed, men require fresh fetters,
A new God must rule over blind mankind."
—*(Mahomet*, Act II. Scene V.)
[2]   " Who made him king ?   Who crowned him ?   Victory."
[3]   " To the name of victor and of conqueror,
He wishes to add that of pacifier."
[4]   " He was the dread of Rome, I shall be her delight " . . .

called on me. Their impressions on the entertainment were very different. The emperor was always delighted with the performance, and M. de Vincent always despondent. He had the greatest difficulty in persuading himself that the emperors were not making some arrangement ; and yet he was positive that during the first days no business had been touched upon. However, when they did speak, the conversation was a long one. The emperors discussed thoroughly everything that had been treated of between the two cabinets for the last year, and the Emperor Napoleon finished by communicating a project of convention which, he said, he had drawn up for their mutual advantage. He gave it to the Emperor Alexander, after having made him promise not to show it to anybody ; not even to one of his ministers. It was an affair, he added, which must be treated of between themselves, and to prove the importance which he attached to its being kept a secret, he himself had written out some of the articles, not wishing any one to know them.

The words, " not any one," which he repeated, were evidently meant for Count Romanzoff and me. The Emperor Alexander had the goodness not to understand them so ; and, after having begged the Princess of Tour and Taxis to admit nobody, he took the treaty out of his pocket. Napoleon had taken the trouble to copy, as well as he could, nearly all the project I had given him. He had, however, changed one or two articles, and added that a corps of the Russian army, under pretext of the position of the cabinet of St. Petersburg with regard to the Ottoman Porte, should be placed near the Austrian frontiers. The Emperor Alexander, after having remarked to the Emperor Napoleon that the bases of the treaty differed from those which had been almost decided on at St. Petersburg, reserved to himself to make in writing any observations he should think proper. Russian secrets seem to be badly kept, for the next morning, M. de Vincent came to me and told me that he knew the negotiations had commenced, and that there was already a project of convention drawn up. I advised him to keep quiet, and take only the necessary steps, and above all not to show any uneasiness. I also told him that I was placed so as to have some influence on the resolutions which would be taken, and he knew how strongly I was opposed to any measures which would be detrimental to the security or dignity of Austria.

Two or three days elapsed without the two emperors seeing each other, except at parade, at dinner time, or at the play. I continued to go every evening to the Princess of Tour's; the Emperor Alexander also came there regularly; he seemed preoccupied, so I did my best to make the conversation as frivolous as possible. One day, however, as I was looking over *Mithridate*, which had just been given me, I remarked on the number of passages in the piece which might serve as allusions. Addressing myself to the Princess of Tour, I quoted several verses, but my little plan did not succeed. The emperor said he had a headache and withdrew, but his last words were "*à demain.*" Every morning, I saw M. de Caulaincourt. I asked him if he did not think that the Emperor Alexander was growing cooler. He said, No; that he thought he was only perplexed, but that his enthusiasm for Napoleon was still the same, and that his perplexity would soon cease.

During these days of political reserve, the Emperor Napoleon continued to see, every morning after his breakfast, the Germans he prized and whose suffrage he wished to have. The errand he had given to Herr Goethe had been faithfully executed, and Herr Wieland had arrived. He had them both invited to lunch. I remember that the prince-primate and many other people were present that day. The emperor was always anxious to shine in conversation, and so, carefully prepared some subject, which he broached unexpectedly to the person with whom he was speaking. He was never embarrassed by a direct contradiction, for he easily found a reason for interrupting the person who spoke. I have several times had opportunities for remarking that, when out of France, he was fond of speaking on elevated subjects, which are generally unknown to military men; this fact gave him at once a character apart. His self-confidence in this respect, whether it was owing to the brilliancy of his life, or to the illusions of his pride, would not have been shaken by the presence of either Montesquieu or Voltaire.

There were three or four subjects on which he spoke willingly. At Berlin, the preceding year, addressing himself to Johan von Müller, he had tried to fix the different epochs of the great efforts of the human mind. I fancy I still see the astonishment on Müller's face when he heard him assert that the propagation and the rapid development of Christianity had worked an admirable reaction of the spirit of Greece against that of Rome, and lay stress on or applaud the skill which Greece, vanquished by physical force, displayed in dealing with the conquest of the empire of intellect, a conquest, he added, which had been effected by taking advantage of the beneficial seeds of Christianity, whose influence on mankind had been so great. He must have known this sentence by heart, for I have heard him repeat it in the same way to M. de Fontanes [1] and to M. Suard.[2] Müller did not reply. He was quite taken aback ; the emperor took advantage of this opportunity to ask him to write his history.

I do not know what he wished to obtain from Wieland, but he was particularly affable with him.

" M. Wieland, we like your works much in France : it is you who are the author of *Agathon* and *Oberon*. We call you the Voltaire of Germany."

" Sire, the comparison would be a flattering one, if it were justified. It is very great praise from very kind people."

" Tell me, *Monsieur* Wieland, why your *Diogenes*, your *Agathon*, and your *Peregrinus* are written in the equivocal style which mixes romance with history and history with romance. A superior man like yourself ought to keep each style distinctly separate. What is mixed is generally confused. That is the reason we like the drama so little in France. But I am afraid to say too much on this subject, because I am dealing with some one so much more conversant with the matter than I am ; especially as what I say has as much reference to Monsieur Goethe as to you."

[1] M. de Fontanes, born in 1787, occupied himself, before the Revolution, with literature and poetry. He entered the *Institut* under the Consulate, became a member of the legislative body in 1804, and president of that assembly (1805). Grandmaster of the University in 1808, and senator in 1810. He died in 1821.

[2] Jean Baptiste Suard, *littérateur* and distinguished writer, member of the French Academy. He became Censor under the Restoration. (1733-1817.)

"Sire, your Majesty will permit us to point out to you that, in the French theatre, there are very few tragedies which are not a mixture of history and romance ; but I am now on Herr Goethe's land. He will reply himself, and certainly he will reply well. As to myself, I wished to give man some useful lesson. The authority of history was necessary. I intended that the examples I borrowed should be easy and agreeable to imitate, and to do that, it was necessary to mix the ideal and the romantic. Men's ideas, sometimes, are worth more than their actions, and good novels are more valuable than mankind. Compare, sire, the century of Louis XIV. with *Télémaque*, where are found the best lessons for sovereigns and for the people. My *Diogenes* is virtuous, though living in a cask."

"But do you know," said the emperor, "what happens to those who always display virtue in their stories ? They cause the impression that virtue is but a dream. History has often been calumniated by historians themselves."

This conversation, in which Tacitus could not fail to be introduced, was interrupted by M. de Nansouty, who just came to tell the emperor that a messenger from Paris had brought him some letters. The prince-primate left with Wieland and Goethe, and begged me to go with them to dine at his house. Wieland, who in his simplicity did not know whether he had replied well or badly to the emperor, had gone into his room to write the conversation he had just had. He brought that recital to the prince-primate, such as has just been read. All the great minds of Weimar and suburbs attended that dinner. I observed a lady from Eisenach who was seated opposite the primate. No one spoke to her without giving her the name of a muse, and that without affectation. " Clio, will you have so and so ? " was the primate's manner of addressing her, to which she would reply simply " Yes " or " No." She was called Baroness Bechtolsheim. After dinner, every one went to the play, and, when it was over, following my custom, I saw the emperor home, and went, afterwards, to the Princess of Tour's.

The Czar Alexander was already there. His face did not wear its ordinary expression. It was plain that his uncertainties still existed, and that his observations on the project of the treaty were not made.

" Has the emperor been talking to you lately ? " was his first question.

" No, sire ; " and I ventured to add that if I had not seen M. de Vincent, I could have believed that the Erfurt interview was only a pleasure party.

" What does M. de Vincent say ? "

" Sire, only very reasonable things. He hopes that your Majesty will not allow yourself to be led by the Emperor Napoleon to take *threatening*, or at least, *offensive* measures against Austria ; and if your Majesty will permit me to tell you so, I have formed the same opinion."

" I should also like to refrain from them, but it seems very difficult to do so, for the Emperor Napoleon seems to me much incensed."

" But, sire, you have certain observations to make. Can your Majesty not consider as useless those provisions relative to Austria and say that they are included in the treaty of Tilsit ? It seems to me that one could add that the proofs of confidence ought to be reciprocal ; and that your Majesty, while allowing the Emperor Napoleon to be, in a measure, the judge of the circumstances where certain articles of the draft submitted to you could be executed, has, on the other hand, the right to exact that he leave you to judge the cases where Austria might become a real obstacle to the projects adopted by the two sovereigns. This being understood between you, everything concerning Austria should be erased from the draft of the treaty. And if your Majesty thinks of the fright that the Erfurt interview, arranged without the knowledge of the Emperor Francis, must have caused at Vienna, perhaps you would like to re-assure him in a letter, on everything which interests him personally." I saw that the Czar Alexander was pleased. He took notes with his pencil on all that I had said ; but it was necessary to decide, and that he had not yet done. It was M. de Caulaincourt who, by his personal influence over him carried his determination.

The next day the Czar Alexander showed me his observations on the project of the treaty, and said to me blandly :

" You will recognize yourself there, perhaps, in several places. I have added many things taken from the past conversations the Emperor Napoleon and I have had together." Those observations were sufficiently good. I found him decided to propose them the next morning. It gave me pleasure, for his expression was not yet so free from anxiety that it did not cause me to wish the first step had been taken. My fears were not without foundation, for at a conference which lasted three hours, he yielded nothing to the Emperor Napoleon, who sent for me at the time of their separating.

" I have done nothing with the Emperor Alexander," he said.

" Sire, I believe your Majesty has done a great deal since he has been here, for the Czar Alexander is completely under the spell."

" He is simply acting a part. If he cares so much for me, why does he not sign ? "

" Sire, there is something so chivalric in his nature that so many precautions quite shock him. He believes that by his word and his affection for you, he is more bound than by treaties. His letters, which your Majesty gave me to read, are full of passages which prove it."

" That is all nonsense ! "

He walked up and down in his room, interrupting the silence now and then by saying :

" I shall not return to that subject again with him—that would show him that I placed too much interest in it. Our only interview, by the mystery in which it was enveloped, will impose on Austria. She will believe in the existence of secret articles, and I shall not undeceive her. If, at least, Russia, by her example, induce the Emperor Francis to recognize Joseph as King of Spain, that would be something, but I don't expect it. What I have done in eight days with the Czar Alexander would require years to do at Vienna. I do not understand your leaning towards Austria. It is the ancient policy of France."

" Sire, I believe that such ought to be the policy of the new France, and if I dared add it, your own, for you, sire, are the one sovereign on whom the world depends most to preserve civilization. The presence of Russia at the peace of

Teschen[1] has been a serious misfortune for Europe, and a grave error on the part of France, who did nothing to prevent it."
"That is no longer the question, my dear. We must take things as they are. You must charge M. de Vergennes with the responsibility of the past. Few people now take an interest in civilization."
"We think of our business."
"You do not understand ; you know why it is that no one deals openly with me? It is that having no children, they believe I only have a life-interest in France. That is the secret of all that you see here. They are afraid of me, and each one gets out of trouble as well as he can. It is a bad state of things for everybody. And," he added gravely, "it must needs some day be remedied. Continue seeing the Czar Alexander. I have been perhaps a little brusque in our conferences, but I desire that we part on friendly terms. I have still a few days before me. To-morrow we shall go to Weimar and it will not be difficult to be gracious on the grounds of Jena where they are having a fête for me. You will be at Weimar, before myself ; tell the duchess who is too grand a lady to come to Jena, that I should like to see all the *savants* who live in her midst, and that I beg her to acquaint them with my wish. It would be a pity that all the plans for this journey should fail."
The emperor had sent all the Comédie Française to Weimar. The day began by a hunt on the grounds of Jena, afterwards there was a grand dinner served on a table in the shape of a horse-shoe, at which were placed only *reigning princes*. I lay stress on that expression, for that title enabled them to render a fresh homage to Napoleon by calling on the prince of Neufchâtel and myself to sit at that table. On leaving the table they went to the play, where *La Mort de César* was to be represented before all the sovereigns and princes who had come from Erfurt to Weimar. After the play, we passed into the ball-room. It was

[1] The peace of Teschen (Silesia), signed on May 10, 1779, between Austria and France, put an end to the war of the succession of Bavaria that the Emperor Joseph II. had instigated in the preceding year, in endeavouring to take possession of that state, after the death of the Duke Maximilian-Joseph. King Frederick II. being opposed to that claim, a short war was the result. The Empress Catherine II., had been clever enough to place herself as mediator between the two powers, in concert with France.

a very beautiful hall, large, lofty and square, illuminated from above, and adorned with many columns. The impression that *La Mort de César* had left was soon driven away by the sight of a quantity of young and pretty girls, who had come to the ball. Napoleon loved to touch upon serious questions in the drawing-room, at the hunt, at a ball, sometimes opposite the gaming table. He intended to prove, by it, that he was not susceptible to the impression that such displays give to men in general. Having made the rounds of the room and pausing near some young ladies, the names of whom he inquired of Herr Friedrich von Müller, the duke's chamberlain, who had received the order to accompany him, he retired at a distance from the vast throng, and requested Herr von Müller to fetch Herr Goethe and Herr Wieland. Herr von Müller is not of the same family as the renowned Johan von Müller, the historian, but he is a member of the literary society of Weimar, and I believe that he is the secretary of it. He went to fetch those gentlemen, who, with a few other members of that academy, looked upon that beautiful and extraordinary sight. Herr Goethe, on approaching the emperor, asked his permission to introduce them. I do not give their names, because they are not found in the notes, albeit quite complete in other respects, which Herr von Müller gave me the next day. I had asked him to write all he saw on this journey, so that I might compare them with what I had written myself.

"You are pleased with our plays I hope," said the emperor to Herr Goethe. "Have these gentlemen come to them?"

"To the one of to-day, sire, but not to those at Erfurt."

"I am sorry for it. A good tragedy should be looked upon as the most worthy school for superior men. From a certain point of view, it is above history. In the best history, very little effect is produced. Man when alone is but little affected, men assembled receive the stronger and more lasting impressions. I assure you that Tacitus, the historian, that you are always quoting, never taught me anything. Could you find a greater and, at times, more unjust detractor of the human race? In the most simple actions he finds criminal motives, he makes emperors out as the most profound villains, in order to awake admiration for the

genius that has penetrated them.   People are right in saying that
his *Annals* are not a history of the empire, but an abstract of the
prison-records of Rome.   They are always dealing with accusations, with convicts, and with people who open their veins in their
baths.   He who speaks incessantly of accusations, he is the most
notorious informer.   What an involved style!   How obscure!   I
am not a great Latin scholar, but Tacitus' obscurity displays
itself in ten or twelve Italian and French translations that I have
read.   I, therefore, conclude that his chief *quality* is obscurity,
that it springs from that which one calls his genius, as well as
from his style, and that it is so connected with his manner of
expressing himself only because it is in his conception.   I have
heard people praise him for the fear he awakes in tyrants ; he
makes them afraid of the people.   That is a great mistake, and
does the people harm.   Am I not right, *Monsieur* Wieland ?   But
I am interrupting you.   We are not here to speak of Tacitus.
Look! how well the Czar Alexander dances.

" I do not know why we are here, sire," replied Herr Wieland,
"but I know that, at this moment, your Majesty makes me very
happy."

"Ah! Really ?   In what way ? "

" Sire, the manner in which your Majesty has spoken to me,
makes me forget that he has two thrones. I see in him only a man
of letters, and I know that your Majesty will not disdain that title,
for I remember that, on leaving for Egypt he signed his letters,
' *Bonaparte, membre de l'institut et général en chef.*'   It is, then,
to a man of letters, sire, that I shall try to reply.   I felt, at
Erfurt, that I defended myself but feebly when I was the object
of your criticism ; but I believe I am able to defend Tacitus better.
I understand that his principal aim is to punish tyrants—but if
he denounces them it is not to their slaves, whose revolt would
only bring a change of tyranny ; he denounces them to the justice
of ages and to mankind.   And the latter ought to have had
enough trouble and experience, that its reason should henceforth
acquire the rule heretofore solely enjoyed by its passions."

" That is what all our philosophers say ; but that supremacy
of reason I look all about for and find it nowhere."

" Sire, it is not long since Tacitus began to have so many

readers. That hankering for him is a clear progress of the human mind, for, for centuries, he was shut out of academies as well as from courts. The slaves of taste were quite as much afraid of it as the servants of despotism. It is only since Racine named him *Le plus grand peintre de l'antiquité*,[1] that your universities and our own have thought this judgment might be true. Your Majesty says that in reading Tacitus, you see nothing but assassins, informers, and scoundrels; but, sire, that is exactly what the Roman Empire was, governed by those monsters fallen under Tacitus' pen. The genius of Tacitus travelled the world with the legions of the Republic. The genius of Tacitus must almost always have been applied to the study of the prison-records of Rome, for there only could he find all the history of the Empire. It is even only in prison-records," said he, in an animated voice, "that historians can become acquainted with those unhappy times, amongst all nations, when princes and their people, opposed in views and principles, live trembling before each other. Then, the slightest pretext gives rise to criminal trials, and death appears to be inflicted by centurions and executioners oftener than by time and nature. Sire, Suetonius, Dion, and Cassius relate a much greater number of crimes than Tacitus, in a style void of energy, while nothing is more terrible than Tacitus' pen. However, his genius is as impartial as it is inexorable. Whenever he can see any good, even in the monstrous reign of Tiberius, he looks it out, takes hold of it, and shows it off in the bold relief he gives to everything. He can find even praise for that imbecile Claudius, who was really so only by nature and by his dissipation. That impartiality—the most important quality of justice—Tacitus exercises on the most opposite subjects, on the republic as well as the Empire; on citizens as well as on princes. By the stamp of his genius one would believe he could love only the republic. One could confirm that opinion by his words on Brutus, Cassius and Codrus, so deeply engraven in the memory of our youth; but when he speaks of the emperors who had so happily reconciled what was thought could not be reconciled, the Empire and liberty, one feels that the art of governing appears to him the most beautiful discovery on earth."

[1] The greatest painter of antiquity.

The prince-primate who had approached, and all the little academy of Weimar which surrounded Wieland, could not contain their joy.

" Sire," he continued, "if it be true to say of Tacitus, that tyrants are punished when he paints them, it is still more true to say that good princes are rewarded when he traces their images and presents them to future glory."

" I have too strong a party to cope with, *Monsieur* Wieland, and you neglect none of your advantages. I think you knew that I did not like Tacitus; do you correspond with Herr von Müller,[1] whom I saw at Berlin ?"

" Yes, sire."

" Confess that he has written to you on the subject of our conversation ?"

" It is true, sire. It is by him that I knew your Majesty liked to speak of Tacitus, but did not, however, like him."

" I do not like to say I am beaten, *Monsieur* Wieland : to that I would consent with difficulty. To-morrow I return to Erfurt, and we shall continue our discussion. I have a good store of weapons in my arsenal for sustaining that Tacitus has not entered far enough into the development of the causes of events; that he has not sufficiently shown the mystery of the actions that he relates, and their mutual linking together in order to prepare the judgment of posterity, which must judge men and governments such as they were in their time and in the midst of the circumstances which surrounded them."

The emperor concluded that conversation by saying to Herr Wieland, with a mild expression, that the pleasure of being with him caused him to be for some time, an object of *scandal* for the dancers, and he went away with the prince-primate. After having paused for some moments to witness the beautiful *contre-dance*, and having spoken to the Duchess of Saxe-Weimar about the elegance and beauty of that brilliant fête, he left the ball and went back to the magnificent apartment prepared for him. All the young academicians, fearing to trust to their memory, had already gone away to write down among themselves all that they had just heard. And the next day, the day of our

---
[1] Johan von Müller, the historian.

departure, Herr von Müller was with me at seven o'clock, to ask me if the onslaught of the emperor against Tacitus was truthfully recorded. I had altered some words in it, and that gave me the right to have a complete copy of these gentlemen's works, destined for the archives of Weimar. We left this beautiful place in the morning. The Kings of Saxony, Wurtemberg, and Bavaria set off in order to return to their dominions.

When Napoleon returned to Erfurt, he was more friendly, more confidential with the Czar Alexander than he had been yet. The convention that had become so insignificant, was settled almost without discussion ; the emperor did not appear to take a real interest in anything except in what pleased his august ally. A life of excitement fatigued him, he said to the Czar Alexander. He needed rest, and he only longed at present, after the time when he could give himself up to domestic life, to which all his tastes led him. "But that happiness," he added with a deeply concerned expression, "is not for me. Is there any home without children; and can I have any ? My wife is ten years older than myself—I beg your pardon, this must all appear ridiculous to you, but I obey the dictates of my heart, which it soothes me to unbosom to you." And then he talked about the long separation, the great distance, the difficulty in seeing each other again. "But there is only a short time before dinner," he said, "and I must again assume all my composure in order to give M. de Vincent his audience of leave." That evening the Czar Alexander was still fascinated by the charm of that intimate conversation. I was only able to see Napoleon at a very late hour. He was very much pleased with the day, and bade me stay with him a long time after he had retired. His agitation was singular. He asked me questions without waiting for my answer. He tried to speak to me, he wanted to say something else than what he did say ; and, at last, he pronounced the one word *divorce*. " My destiny exacts it," he said, "and the tranquillity of France demands it. I have no successor ; Joseph is nothing, and he has only daughters. It is I who must found a dynasty. I can only do so by getting married to a princess from one of the reigning houses of Europe. The Emperor Alexander has sisters. There is one whose age suits me. Speak of that to Romanzoff. Tell him that once my affairs in Spain are settled, I will enter into all his views for the partition of Turkey; besides, other arguments will not fail you, for I know you are an advocate of divorce. The Empress Josephine believes in it also, I can tell you."

" Sire, if your Majesty permits I will say nothing to Count Romanzoff, although he be the hero of the *Chevaliers du Cygne* of Mme. de Genlis.[1] I do not think he has sense enough. Besides, after I have told him what you have suggested he will have to repeat it all to the Czar Alexander. Will he repeat it correctly, or will he choose to repeat it incorrectly? I cannot tell. It is much more natural, and I may say, much more simple, to have a conversation with the Czar Alexander himself about so important a question ; and if your Majesty adopts this opinion, I shall undertake to prepare the way for him."

" Well and good," said the emperor, " but remember that it is not as coming from me you must speak. It is as a Frenchman that you must address him, in order that he may obtain from me a decision ensuring the stability of France whose fate would be uncertain at my death. As a Frenchman you could say everything you liked. Joseph, Lucien and all my family offer you a free field. Say about them all you like, they are nothing for France. My son even, but that is useless to say, would need to be my son over again, in order to succeed peacefully to the throne of France."

It was late, I ventured however to go to the Princess of Tour, whose door was not yet closed. The Czar Alexander had remained there longer than usual. He related with admirable good faith to the princess the sad scene of that morning.

"Nobody," said he, "has a true idea of that man's character. What alarming measures he sometimes resorts to,

---

[1] *Les Chevaliers du Cygne, ou la Cour de Charlemagne,* is a historical romance of Madame de Genlis in the style of the romances of chivalry of the eleventh century. The authoress endeavoured to write, in the guise of fiction, numerous allusions to the scenes of the Revolution, and in several of her personages, she wished to depict certain celebrities of her time. Count Romanzoff had, it appears, been one of her models.

for other countries, he is by his position forced to take. We do not know how good he is. You think so, do you not, you that know him well?"

"Sire, I have many personal reasons for, and I always state them with great pleasure. Dare I ask your Majesty if to-morrow morning you can grant me an audience?"

"To-morrow? yes, willingly, before or after I have seen M. de Vincent. I have a letter to write to the Emperor Francis."

"After, sire, if you permit it. I should be very sorry to retard that good work. The Emperor Francis is in great need of comfort, and I have no doubt that your Majesty's letter will procure that for him."

"That is at least my intention." The Czar remarked with astonishment that it was nearly two o'clock.

The next day, before going to the appointed audience, M. de Vincent called on me, and I told him how much reason he had to be satisfied with every one in general, and with the Czar Alexander in particular. His face beamed with satisfaction. In bidding me good bye, he gave me an affectionate and grateful grasp of the hand. He set off for Vienna immediately, having obtained his audience, during which I weighed in my mind the means I should employ to discharge the errand I had accepted, in such a way as to please every one as well as myself. I confess I was frightened for Europe at the idea of another alliance between France and Russia. As for me, it was necessary that the idea of that alliance should be sufficiently admitted by Europe to satisfy Napoleon, and that, on the other hand, it contained reservations hindering its application. All the art I thought I wanted was useless to me with the Czar Alexander.

At the first word, he understood me, and he understood me precisely as I wished him to.

"If it were only a question of myself I would willingly give my consent; but my consent is not the only one we must have. My mother has retained a power over her daughters, that I must never question. I can try to give her certain advice which it is probable she may follow, but I do not dare to take it upon myself to say she will. All that, inspired by a real friendship, ought to satisfy the Emperor Napoleon. Tell him that I shall be with him in a moment."

"Sire, your Majesty will not forget that that conversation ought to be solemn and affectionate. Your Majesty will speak of the interests of Europe and of France. Europe requires that the throne of France be protected from every storm, and it is the manner of reaching that great end which your Majesty is about to propose."

"That will be my text. It is a fertile field. I will see you this evening at the Princess of Tour's."

I informed the Emperor Napoleon of the result of my interview ; he was delighted with the idea that he would have to reply instead of asking. I had scarcely time to add several words. Already the Czar Alexander dismounted from his horse in the yard. The two sovereigns remained several hours together, and all the court was from that moment, struck with the familiar expression of friendship that existed between them ; even etiquette seemed to be relaxed between them during those last days. An air of harmony displayed itself everywhere, and it was also true that they were perfectly happy The great divorce question was mooted ; and it was so in a way to furnish Napoleon with replies to all those who, attached to the Empress Josephine, found in her accession a guarantee of their personal situation.

Napoleon was already dreaming of founding a lasting empire ; the Czar of Russia believed he had bound Napoleon to himself, and flattered himself that, by his personal influence he had given to Russian policy the support of him to whom the entire world rendered homage, and before the genius of whom all difficulties vanished. Thus, at the play, in the presence of all Erfurt, he arose and took the hand of Napoleon, at this line of *Œdipe* :

> " *L'amitié d' un grand homme est un present des dieux.*" [1]
> —(*Œdipe* (Voltaire), Act I., Scene I.)

They then both looked upon each other as essential to their

---

[1] " The friendship of a great man is a gift from the gods."

common future. When the number of days that should occupy the interview had passed, they separated in testifying the most sincere regrets, and the most complete confidence. The last morning that Napoleon spent at Erfurt, was employed in seeing people. The scene that his palace presented that last day will never vanish from my memory. He was surrounded by princes, of whom he had either destroyed the armies, or reduced the dominions, or humbled the pride. There was no one who dared ask for anything. They simply wished to be seen, and to be seen the last to be remembered by him. All such humility was without recompense. He noticed only the academicians of Weimar. It was to them alone that he spoke, and he desired at the last moment to leave with them a new variety of impression. He asked them if there were many ideologists in Germany.

"Yes, sire," replied one of them, "a sufficiently large number."

"I pity you. I have some at Paris. They are dreamers, and dangerous dreamers. They are all plain or disguised materialists.

"Gentlemen," he said, in raising his voice, "philosophers labour hard to create systems; they will search in vain for a better one than that of Christianity, which, in reconciling man with himself assures at the same time public order and the tranquillity of the state. Your ideologists destroy all illusions, and the age of illusions is, for nations, as for individuals, the age of happiness. I take away with me on leaving you a thought that is very precious to me, it is that you will preserve a pleasant remembrance of me." A few minutes after, he was in his carriage, on his way, as he thought, to the conquest of Spain.

I subjoin here, the treaty, such as it was signed at Erfurt. A few differences will be found in the order of the articles, between the project which the emperor had requested of me to draw up, and that treaty. The article concerning Wallachia and Moldavia has the appearance of being modified, and, nevertheless the Emperor Napoleon, though he had formally recognized the union of those two provinces with Russia, exacted so profound a secret on the consent that he gave to that union, that in his thoughts the two articles had very nearly the same sense. It will be noticed, especially in this last drafting of the treaty, that there is no longer any question of the two articles that the Emperor Napoleon had introduced in the second, the one by which he established himself as judge of the motives that should determine Russia to declare war upon Austria, the other rela- tive to the march of a body of Russian troops near the Austrian frontiers, under the pretext of the position of the cabinet of Saint Petersburg with the Ottoman Porte.

THE ERFURT CONVENTION, OCTOBER 12TH, 1808, RATIFIED ON THE 13TH.

" H.M. the Emperor of the French, King of Italy, protector of the Confederation of the Rhine, &c., and H.M. the Emperor of Russia, &c., wishing to render more binding and for ever durable the alliance which unites them, and taking it upon themselves to come to an ulterior understanding, if there should be any need of it, on the new decisions to take, and on the new methods of attack to be directed against England, their common enemy and the enemy of the Continent, have resolved to establish in a special convention the principles that they have determined to invariably follow, in all their undertakings, to secure the restoration of peace.

" They have, to that effect appointed, namely, H.M. the Emperor of the French, &c., H. Exc. M. Jean Baptiste Nom- père de Champagny, Count of the Empire, &c., his Minister of Foreign Affairs.

" And H.M. the Czar of all the Russias, &c., H.Exc. the Count Nicolas de Romanzoff, his private counsellor, actually a member of the Council, Minister of Foreign Affairs, &c.

" Who agree to that which follows :

" Art. I.—H.M. the Emperor of the French, &c. and H.M. the Czar of all the Russias, &c., confirm, and inasmuch as there is need, renew the alliance concluded between them at Tilsit, engaging themselves not only to abstain from making with the common enemy any separate peace, but also not to enter with her on any negotiation and not to listen to any of her pro- positions except by mutual consent.

" Art. II.—Thus resolved to remain inseparably united in peace as in war, the high contracting parties agree to name plenipotentiaries to treat for peace with England, and to send them to that effect in that town of the Continent that England shall designate.

"Art. III.—In all the course of the negotiation, if there should be one, the respective plenipotentiaries of the two high contracting parties will ever act with the most perfect harmony, and it will not be permissible to any one of them, not only to support, but even to accept or to approve of, against the interests of the other contracting party, any proposition or request from the English plenipotentiaries which, taken in itself, and being favourable to the interests of England, might also offer some advantages to one of the contracting parties.

"Art. IV.—The basis of the treaty with England will be the *uti possidetis.*

"Art. V.—The high contracting parties bind themselves to regard as the absolute condition of peace with England that she recognize Finland, Wallachia, and Moldavia, as forming a part of the Russian Empire.

"Art. VI.—They likewise bind themselves to regard as an absolute condition of peace that England recognize the new order of things established by France in Spain.

"Art. VII.—The two high contracting parties bind themselves not to receive from the enemy during the continuation of the negotiations any proposition, offer, or communication whatever, without immediately reporting the same to their respective courts, and if the said propositions are made at the congress assembled for the discussion of peace, the plenipotentiaries will communicate the same to each other respectively.

"Art. VIII.—H.M. the Czar of all the Russias on account of the revolutions and changes which agitate the Ottoman Empire, and leave no possibility of giving, and, consequently, no hope of obtaining sufficient guarantees for the persons and property of the inhabitants of Wallachia and Moldavia, having already extended the limits of her empire to the Danube, on that side, and annexed Wallachia and Moldavia to her empire, can only, on that condition, recognize the integrity of the Ottoman Empire. H.M. the Emperor Napoleon therefore, recognizes the said annexation and that the limits of the Russian Empire, on that side, are carried to the Danube.

"Art. IX.—H.M. the Czar of all the Russias binds himself to keep in utmost secrecy the preceding article, and to open, be it at Constantinople or elsewhere, negotiations in view of obtaining, in a friendly manner, if possible, the cession of those two provinces. France renounces her mediation. The plenipotentiaries or agents of the two nations will agree on the language to use in order not to compromise the friendly relations exist-

ing between the French nation and the Porte, as well as the
security of the French subjects resident in Levantine ports, and
to prevent the Porte from throwing itself upon the protection
of England.

" Art. X.—In case the Ottoman Porte refuse the cession of
the two provinces, war shall then be declared. The Emperor
Napoleon will take no part in it, and will limit himself to employing his good offices to decide the Ottoman Porte; but, if it
should come to pass that Austria, or any other power make
common cause with the Ottoman Empire in the said war,
H.M. the Emperor Napoleon will make common cause immediately with Russia, such case being one of those foreseen by
the General Alliance that unites the two empires.

" In case Austria declared war against France, the Czar of
Russia binds himself to declare war against Austria, and to
make common cause with France.

" Art. XI.—The high contracting parties bind themselves
to maintain moreover the integrity of the other possessions of
the Ottoman Empire, not willing to make themselves, or to
suffer that there should be made, any attempt against any
portion of that empire, without their having previously agreed
to it.

" Art. XII.—If the attempts made by the two high contracting parties to bring about peace should fail, be it that England
decline the propositions that shall be made her, or that the
negotiations be broken, Their Imperial Majesties shall meet
again within the delay of one year, to agree upon the mutual
operations of the war and upon the methods or means to
continue it with all the resources of the two empires.

" Art. XIII.—The two high contracting parties, willing to
recognize the loyalty and the perseverance with which the King
of Denmark has sustained their common cause, bind themselves to procure him compensation for his sacrifices and to
recognize the acquisitions he might make in the course of the
war above alluded to.

" Art. XIV.—The present convention shall be held secret
during the space of at least ten years.

" ERFURT, *October* 12, 1808."

END OF THE FIFTH PART.

RICHARD CLAY AND SONS, LIMITED,
LONDON AND BUNGAY.

www.ingramcontent.com/pod-product-compliance
Lightning Source LLC
Chambersburg PA
CBHW051512100726
47898CB00005B/1428